James Burks

BIRD & SQUIRREL

ALL or NOTHING

An Imprint of

SCHOLASTIC

For all those living in a dream world,
keep on dreaming. The world is a
better place because of you.

Library of Congress Control Number: 2019950165

ISBN 978-1-338-25219-4 (hardcover)
ISBN 978-1-338-25207-1 (paperback)

10 9 8 7 6 5 4 3 2 1   20 21 22 23 24

Printed in China   62
First edition, April 2020
Edited by Adam Rau
Book design by Phil Falco
Publisher: David Saylor

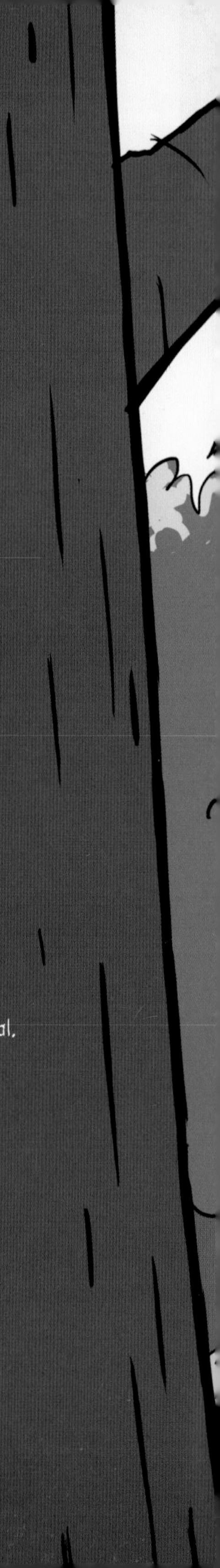

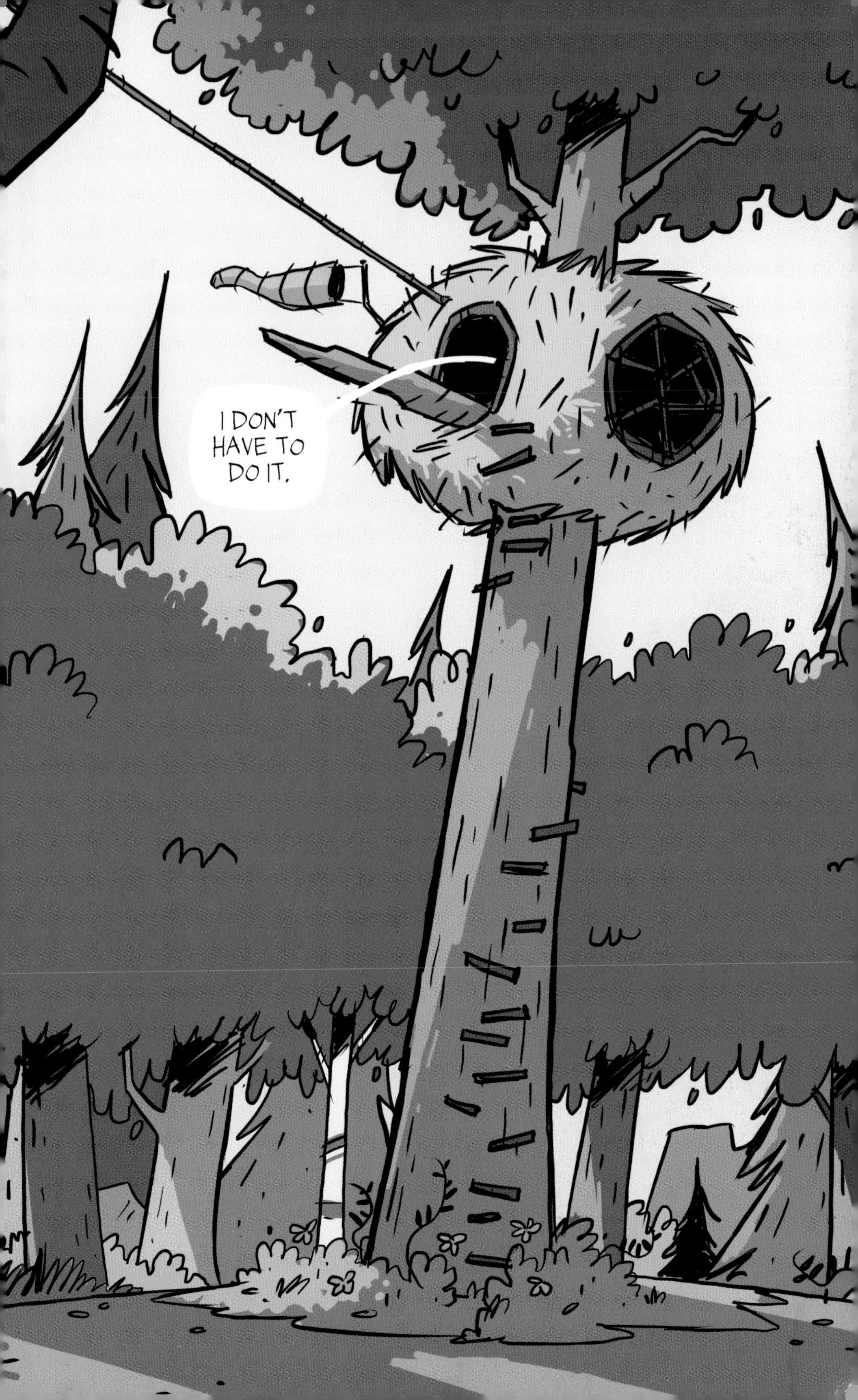
I DON'T HAVE TO DO IT.

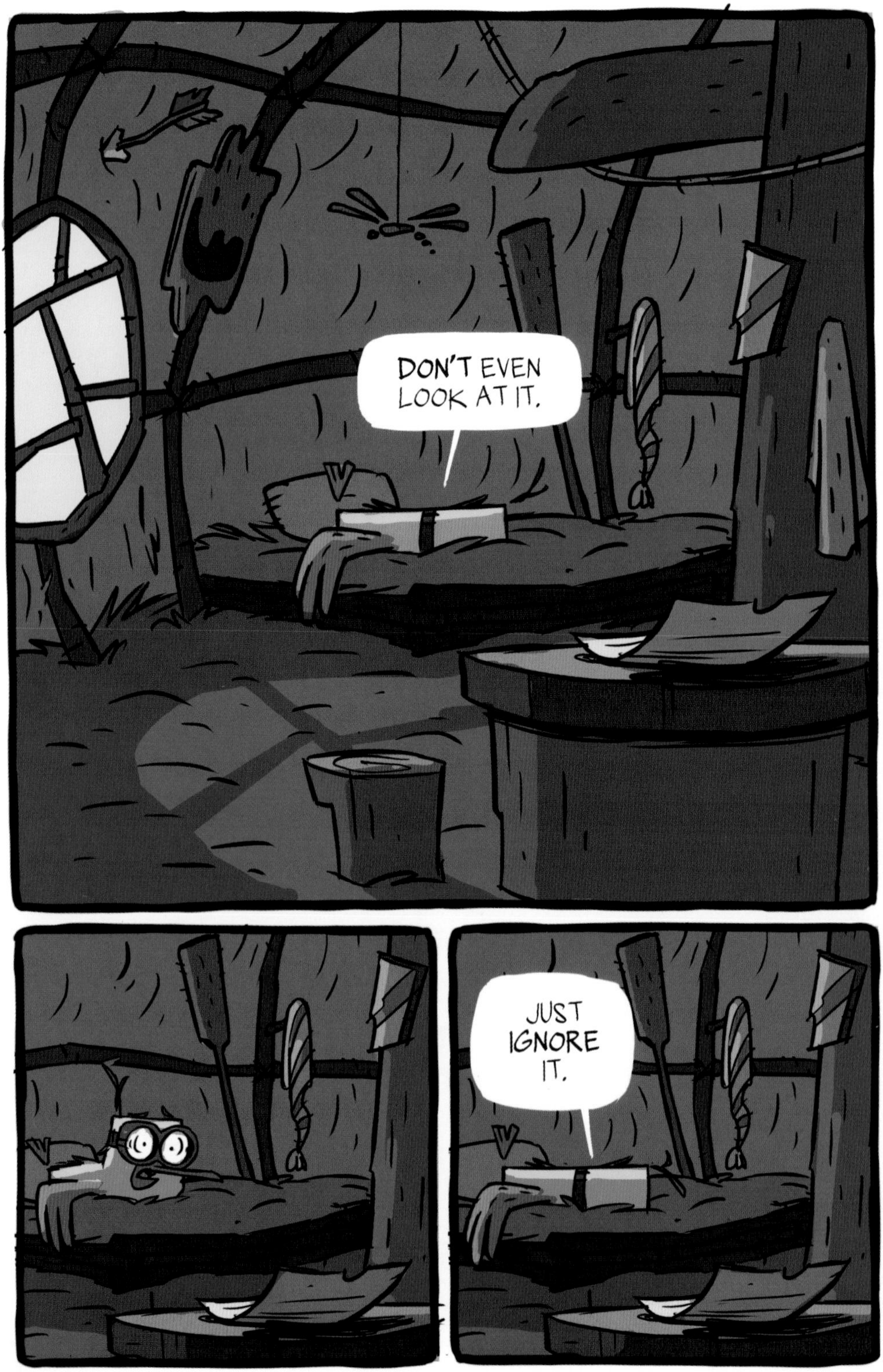
DON'T EVEN LOOK AT IT.
JUST IGNORE IT.

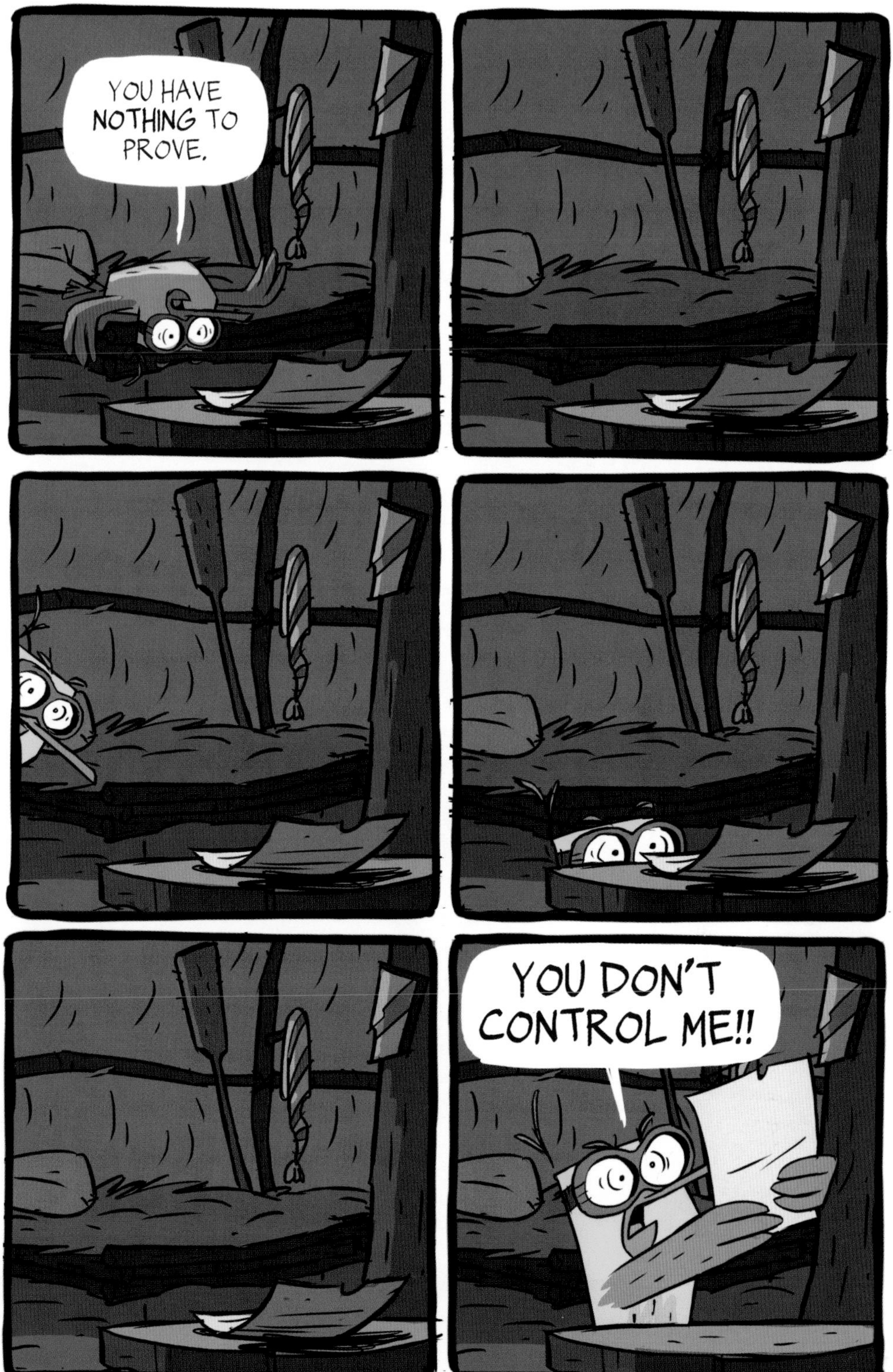
YOU HAVE NOTHING TO PROVE.
YOU DON'T CONTROL ME!!

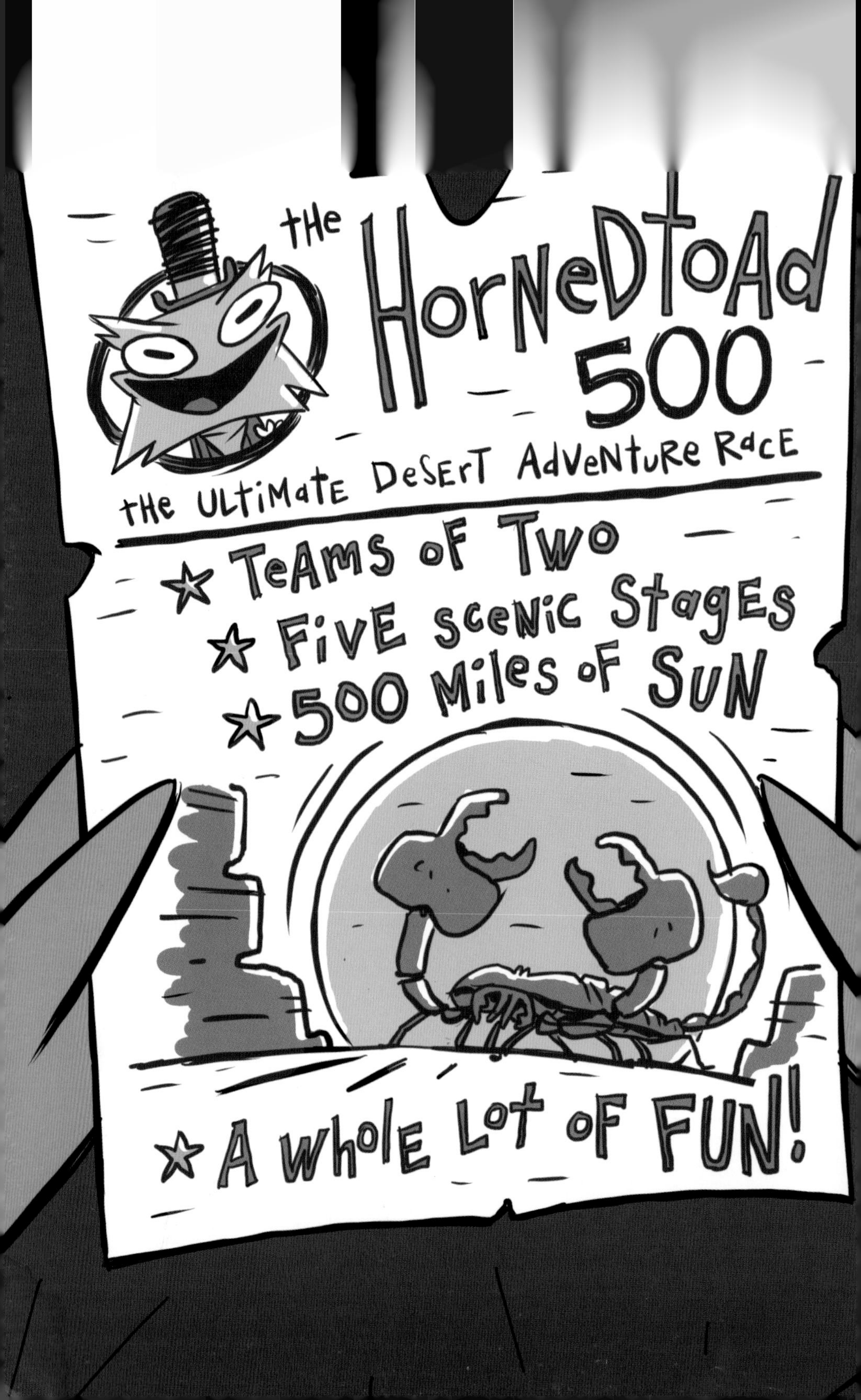
the HornedToad 500
the Ultimate Desert Adventure Race
★ Teams of Two
★ Five scenic Stages
★ 500 Miles of Sun
★ A whole Lot of FUN!

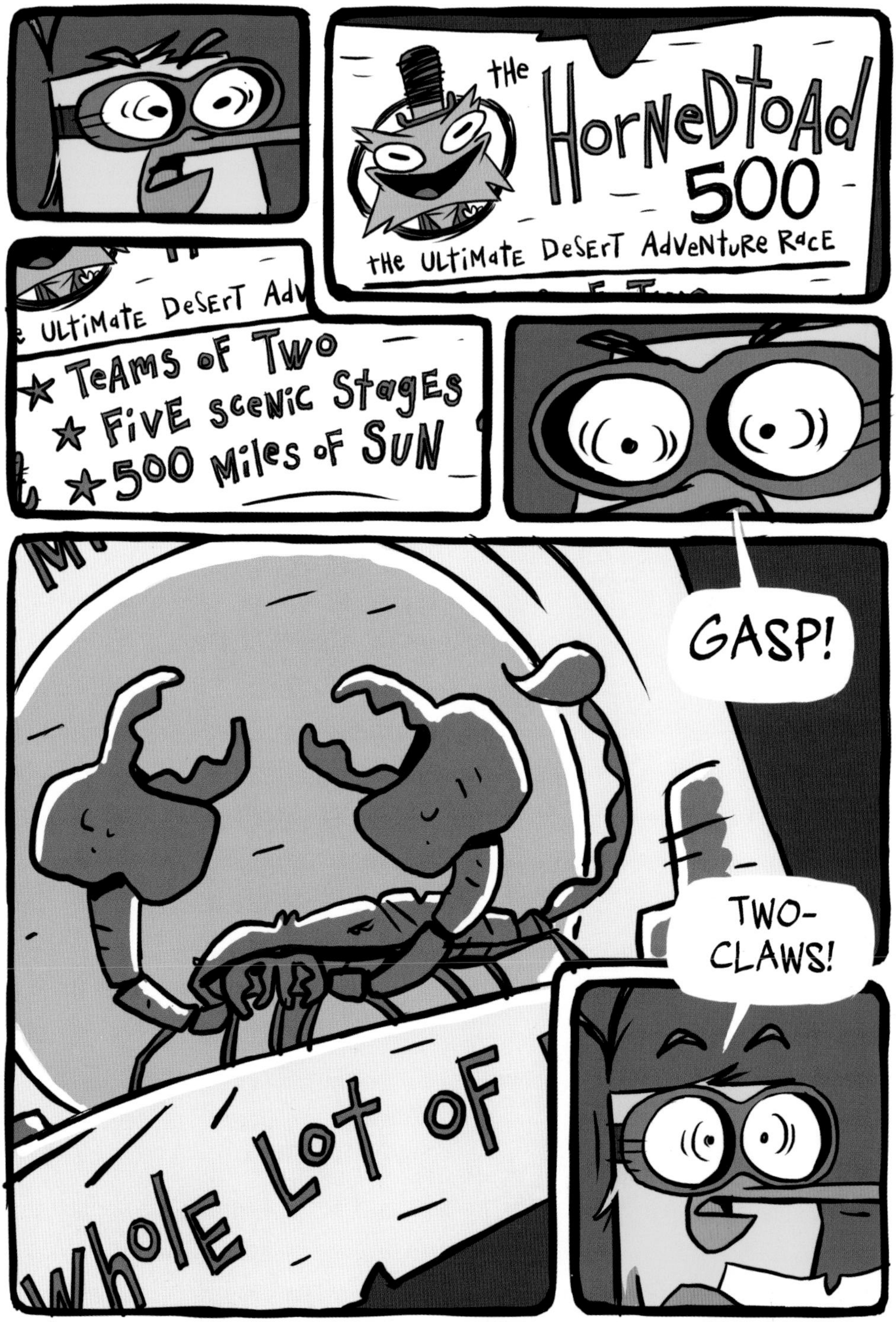
the HorNeDtoAd 500
the ULtiMate DeSErT AdVeNtuRe RacE
ULtiMatE DeSErT Adv
★ TeAms of Two
★ FivE sceNic StagEs
★ 500 Miles oF SUN
GASP!
Whole Lot of
TWO-CLAWS!

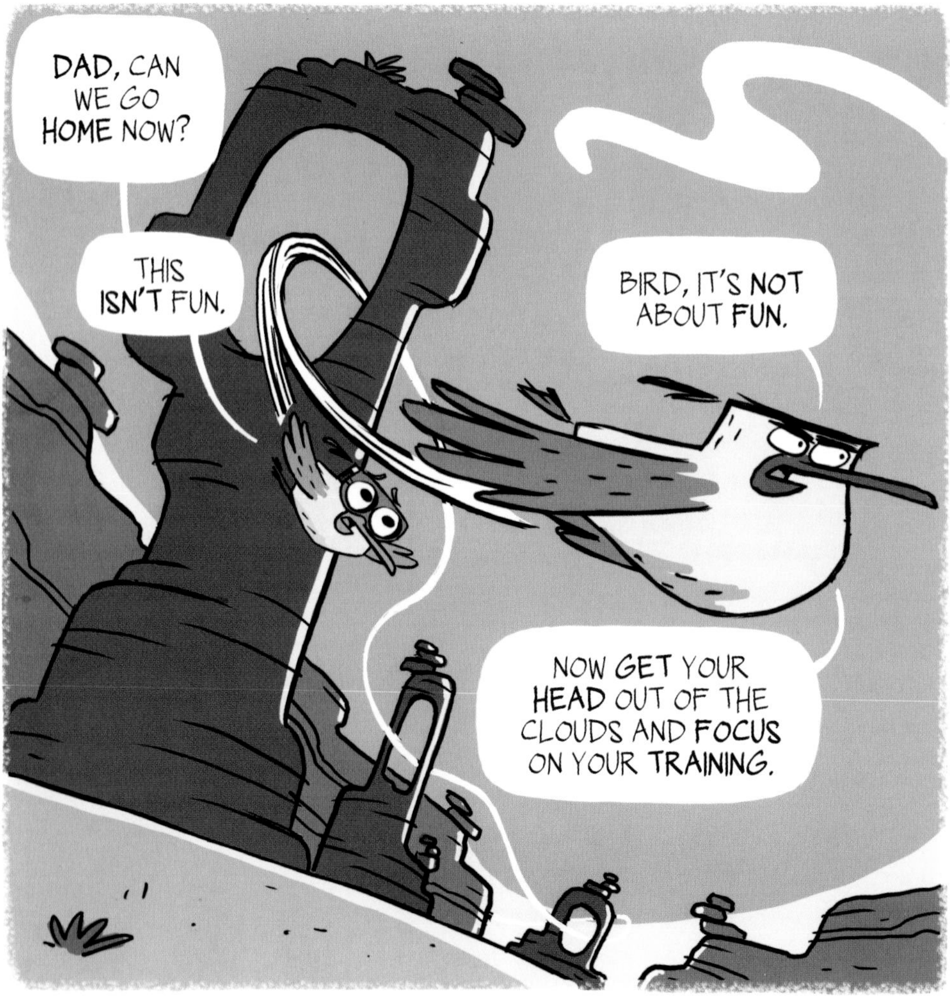
DAD, CAN WE GO HOME NOW?
THIS ISN'T FUN.
BIRD, IT'S NOT ABOUT FUN.
NOW GET YOUR HEAD OUT OF THE CLOUDS AND FOCUS ON YOUR TRAINING.

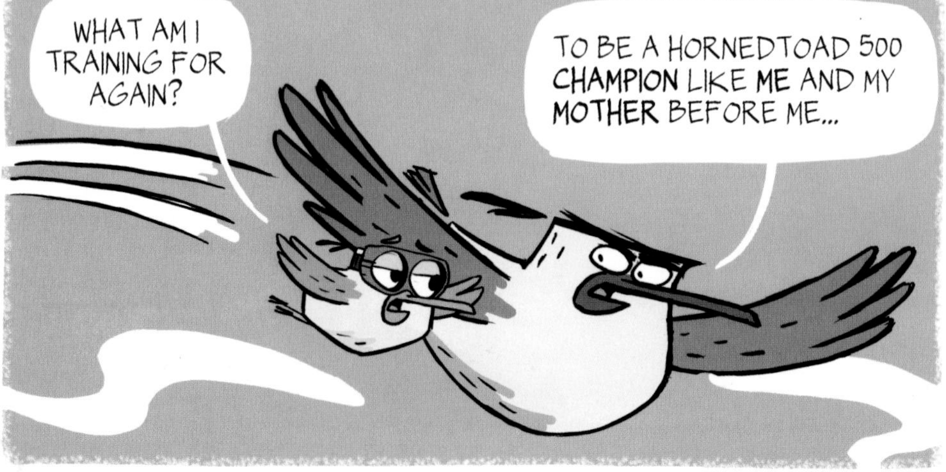
WHAT AM I TRAINING FOR AGAIN?
TO BE A HORNEDTOAD 500 CHAMPION LIKE ME AND MY MOTHER BEFORE ME...

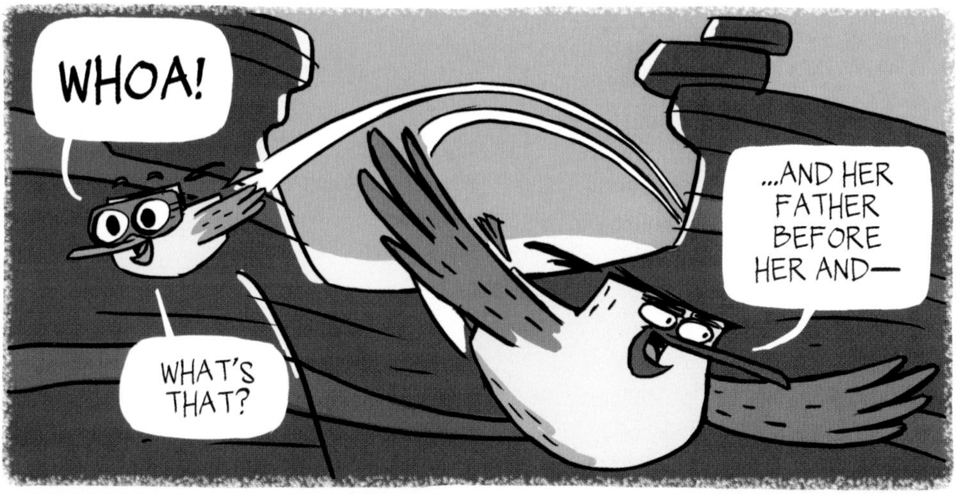
WHOA!
WHAT'S THAT?
...AND HER FATHER BEFORE HER AND—

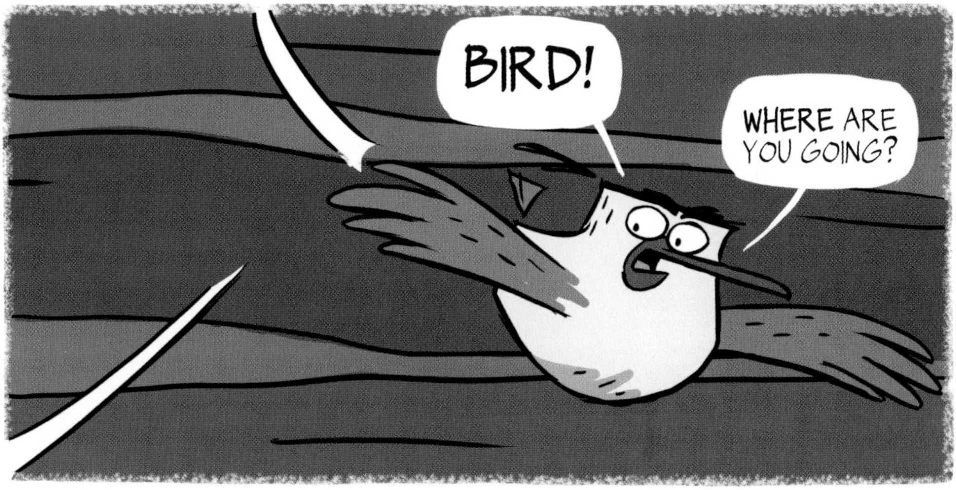
BIRD!
WHERE ARE YOU GOING?

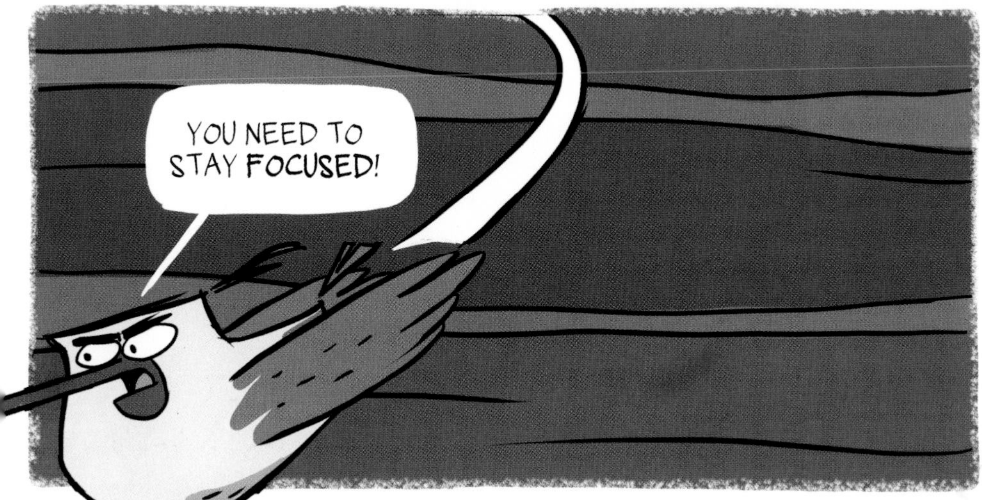
YOU NEED TO STAY FOCUSED!

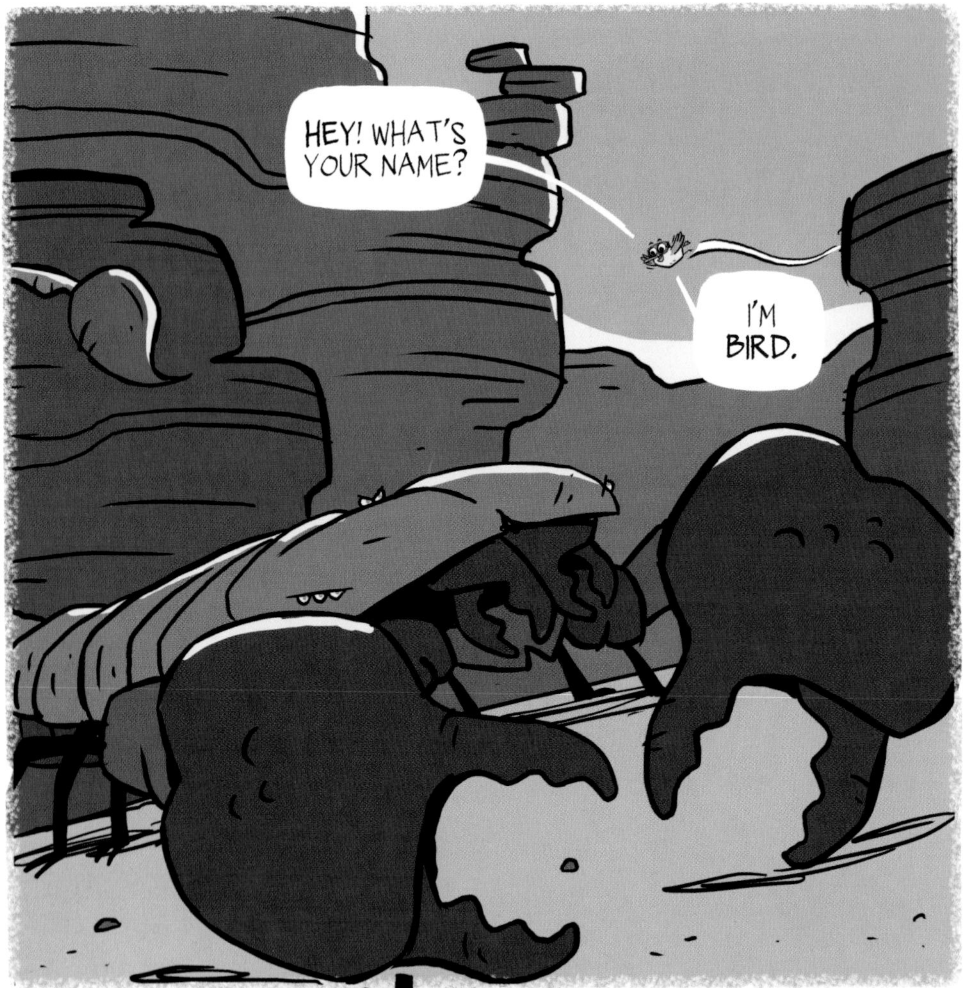
HEY! WHAT'S YOUR NAME?
I'M BIRD.

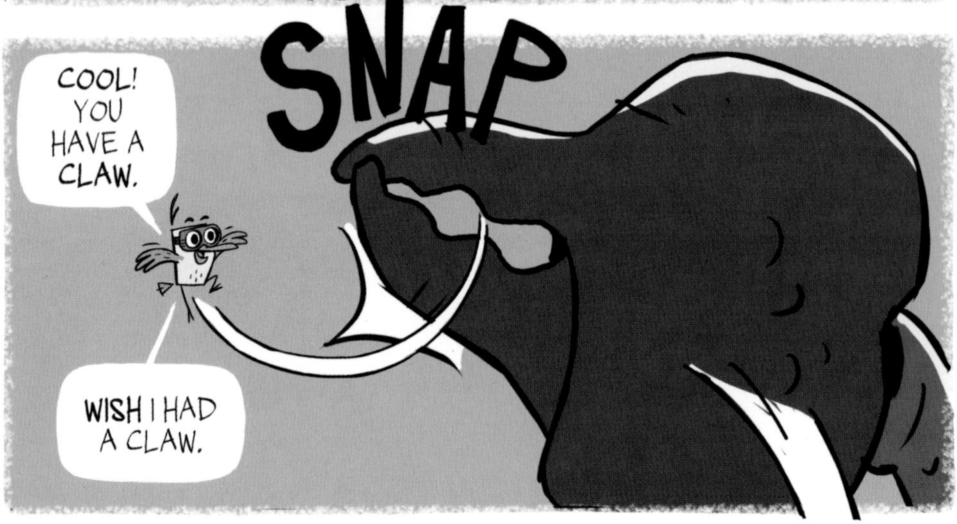
SNAP
COOL! YOU HAVE A CLAW.
WISH I HAD A CLAW.

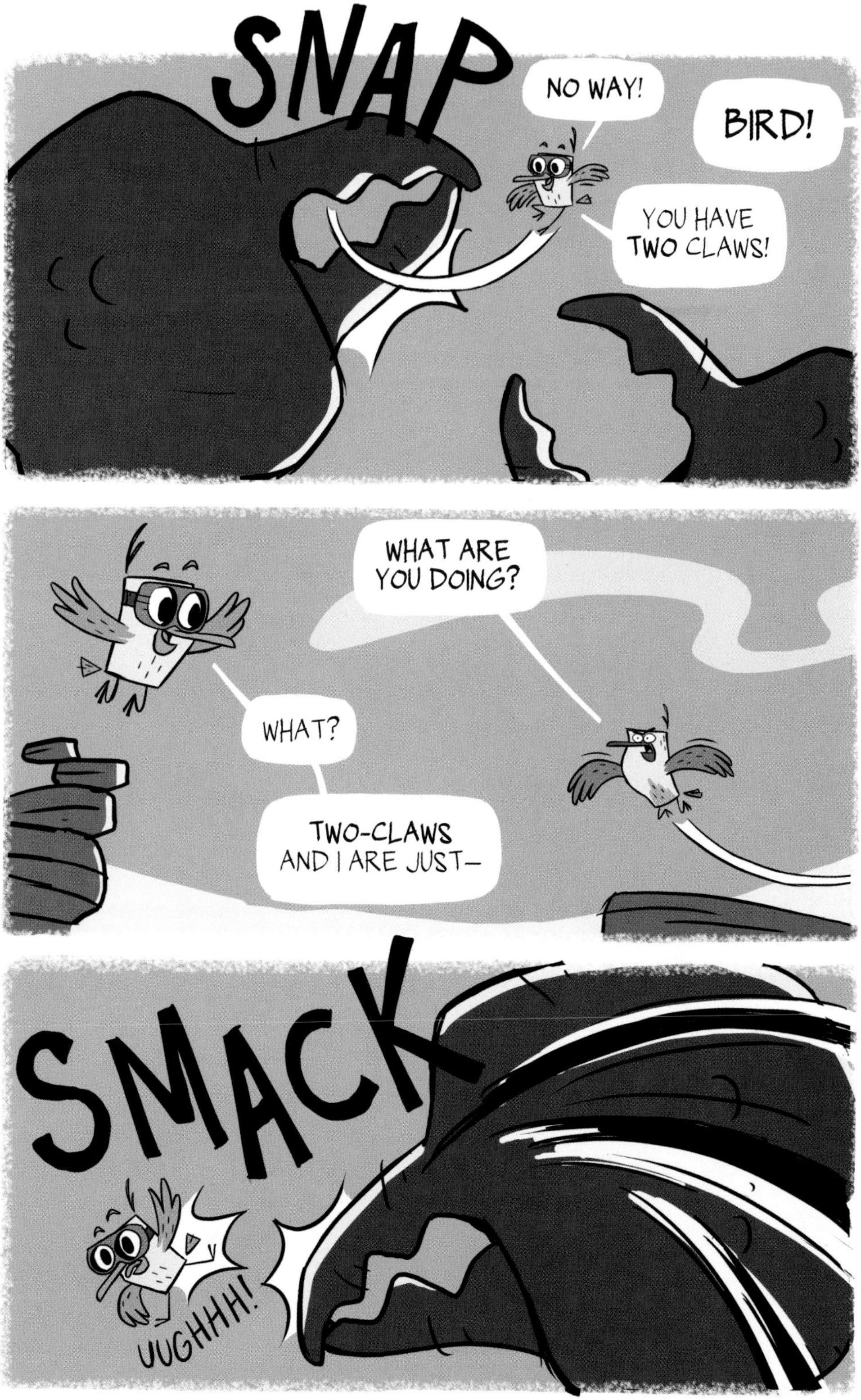
SNAP
NO WAY!
BIRD!
YOU HAVE TWO CLAWS!
WHAT ARE YOU DOING?
WHAT?
TWO-CLAWS AND I ARE JUST—
SMACK
UUGHHH!

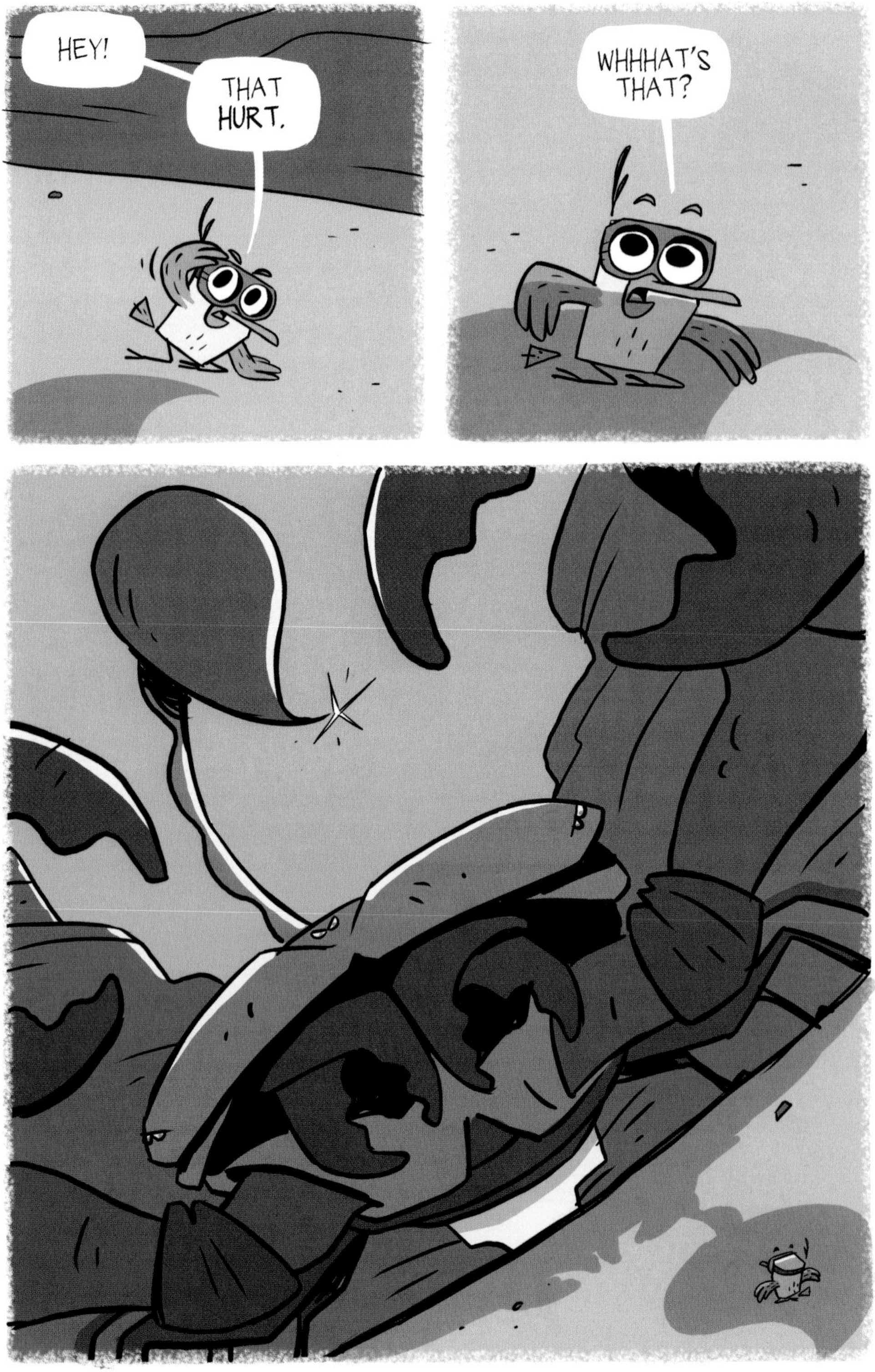
HEY!
THAT HURT.
WHHHAT'S THAT?

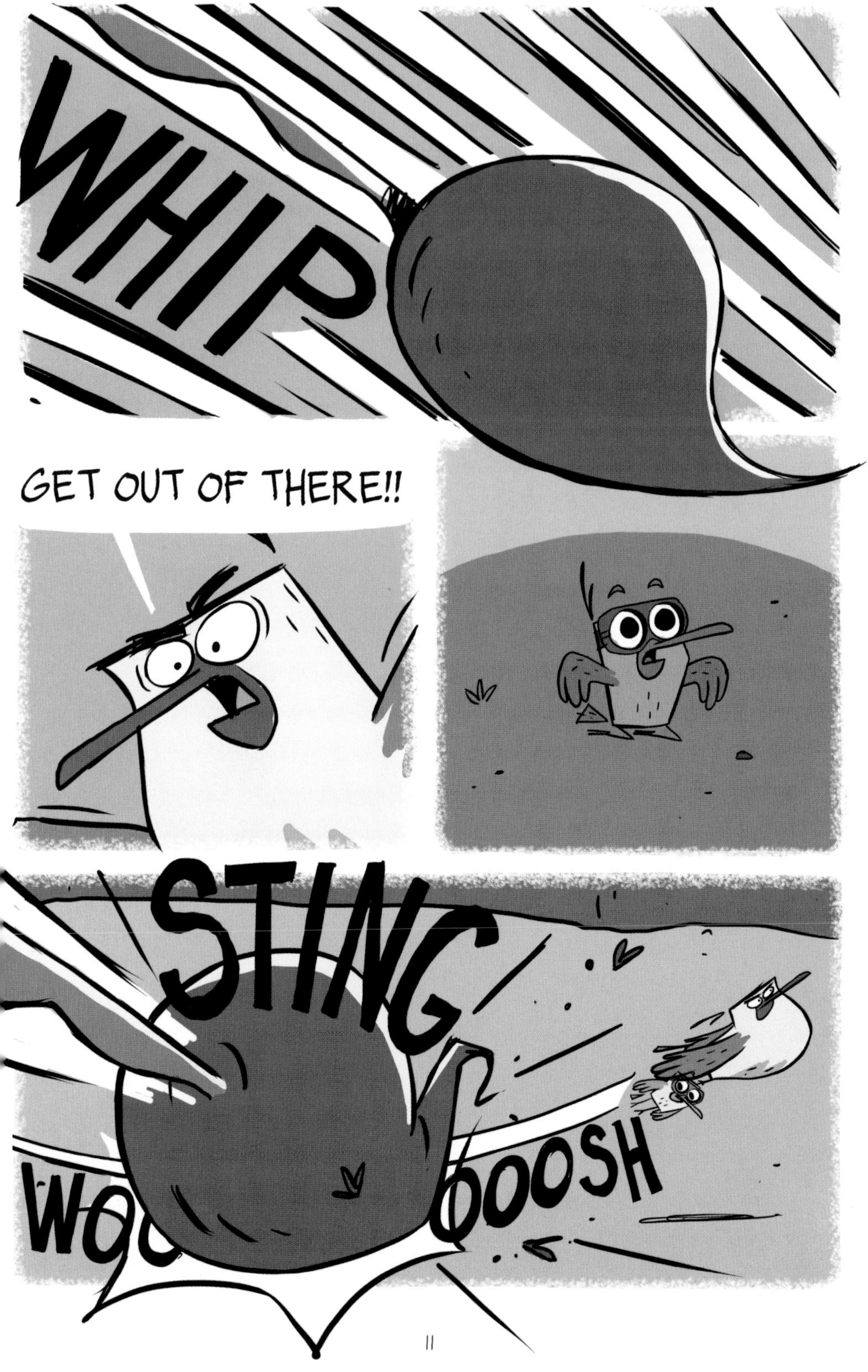
WHIP
GET OUT OF THERE!!
STING
WOO
OOOSH

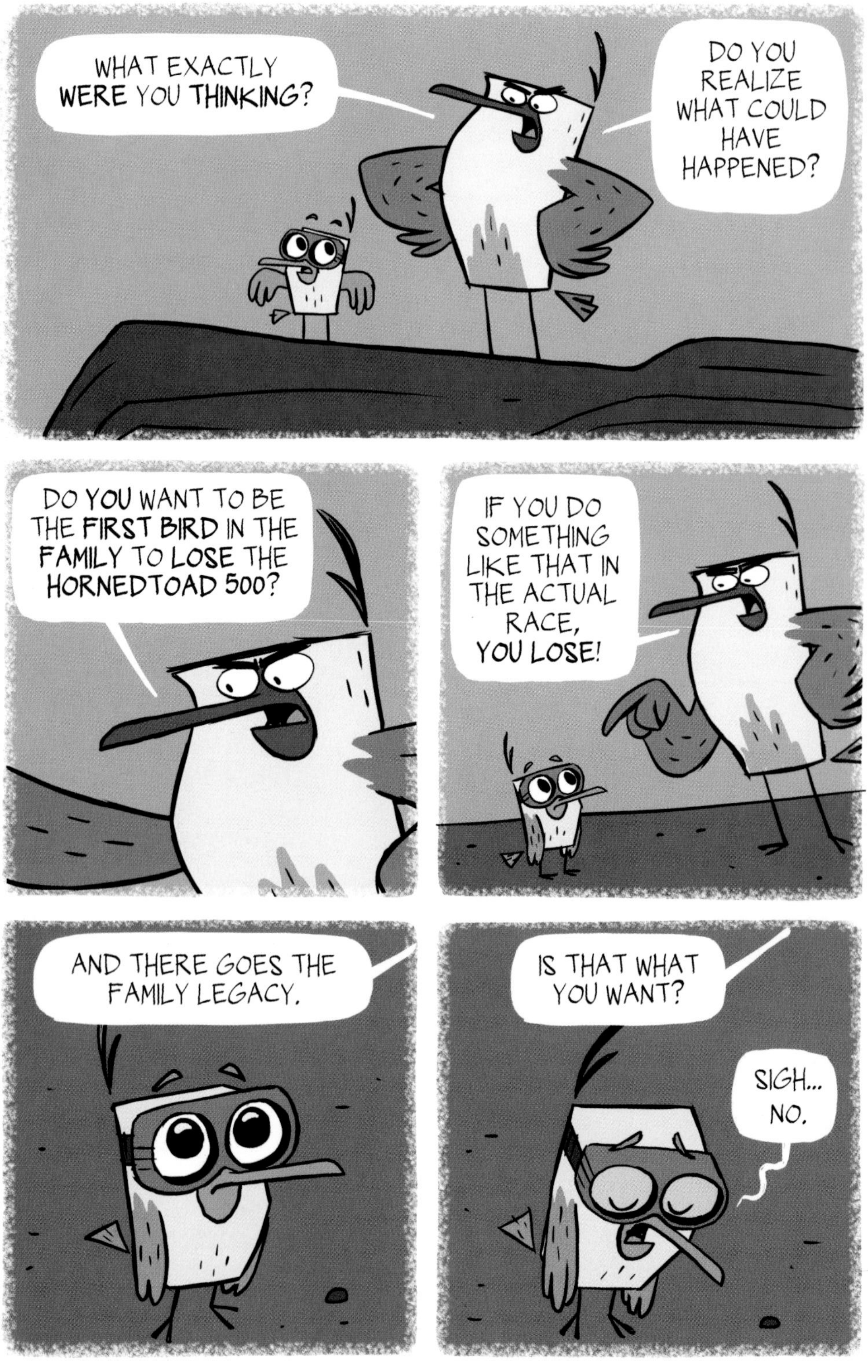
WHAT EXACTLY WERE YOU THINKING?
DO YOU REALIZE WHAT COULD HAVE HAPPENED?
DO YOU WANT TO BE THE FIRST BIRD IN THE FAMILY TO LOSE THE HORNEDTOAD 500?
IF YOU DO SOMETHING LIKE THAT IN THE ACTUAL RACE, YOU LOSE!
AND THERE GOES THE FAMILY LEGACY.
IS THAT WHAT YOU WANT?
SIGH... NO.

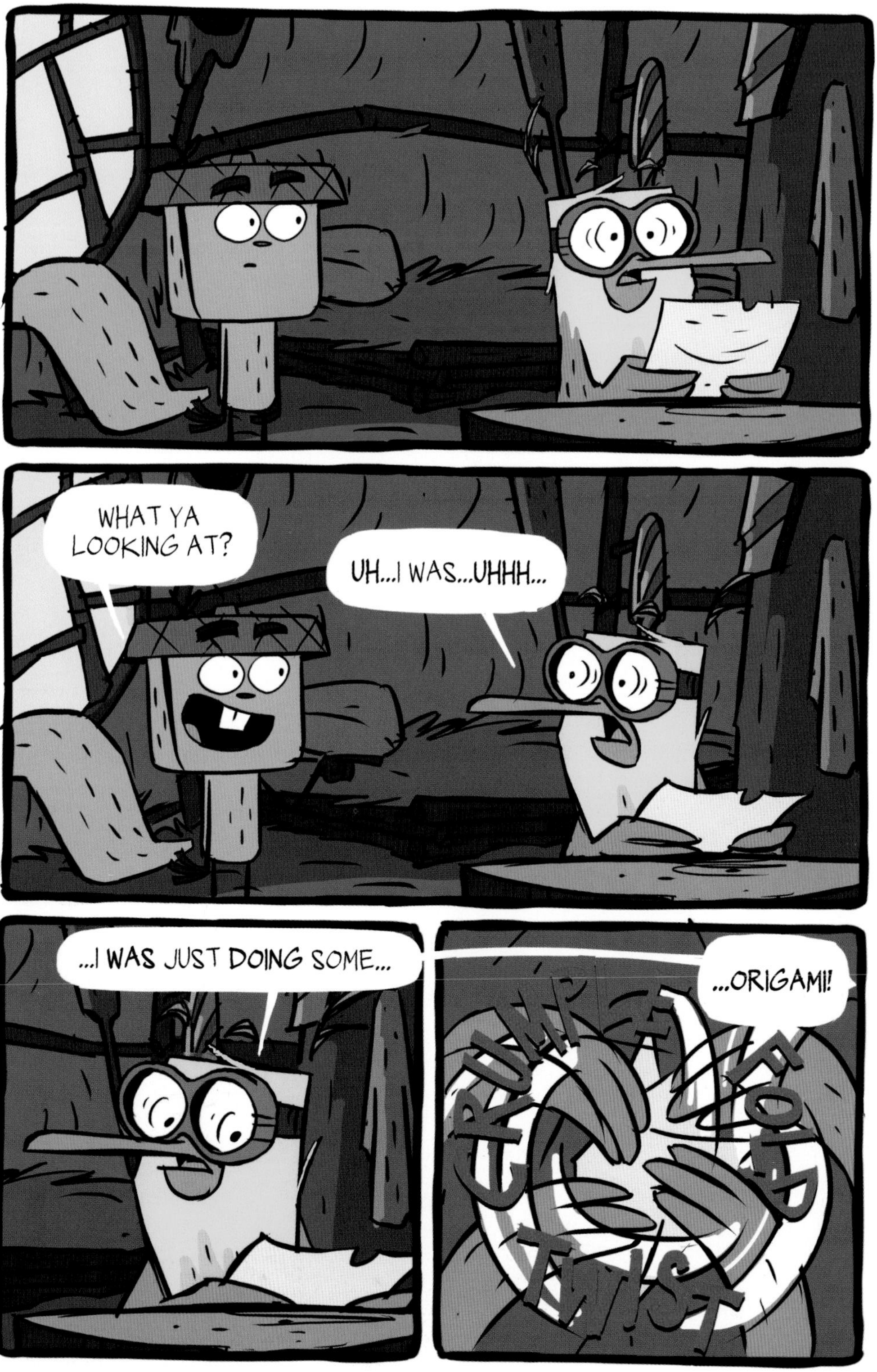
WHAT YA LOOKING AT?
UH...I WAS...UHHH...
...I WAS JUST DOING SOME...
...ORIGAMI!
CRUMPLE
FOLD
TWIST

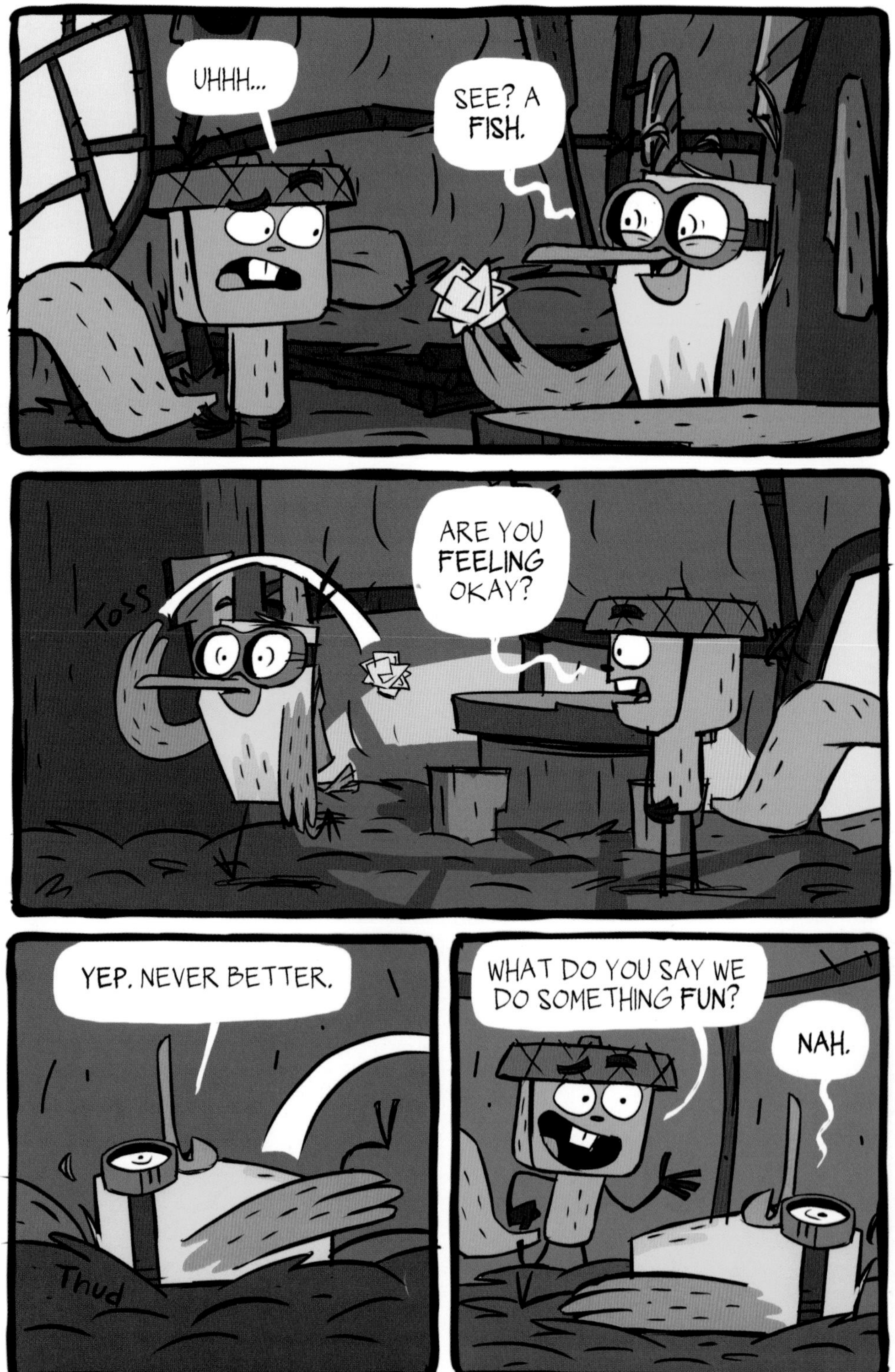
UHHH...
SEE? A FISH.
TOSS
ARE YOU FEELING OKAY?
YEP. NEVER BETTER.
Thud
WHAT DO YOU SAY WE DO SOMETHING FUN?
NAH.

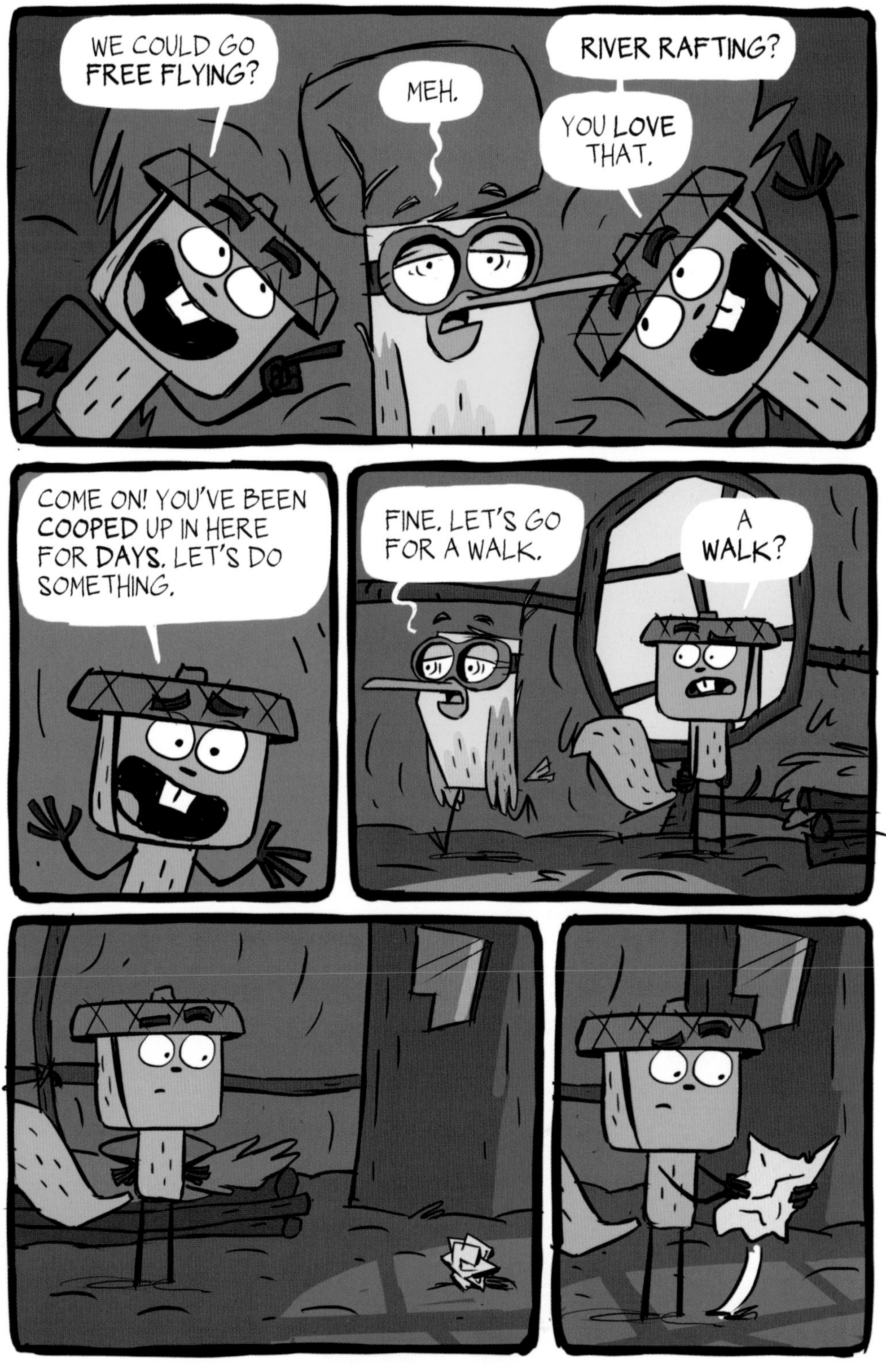
WE COULD GO FREE FLYING?
MEH.
RIVER RAFTING?
YOU LOVE THAT.
COME ON! YOU'VE BEEN COOPED UP IN HERE FOR DAYS. LET'S DO SOMETHING.
FINE. LET'S GO FOR A WALK.
A WALK?

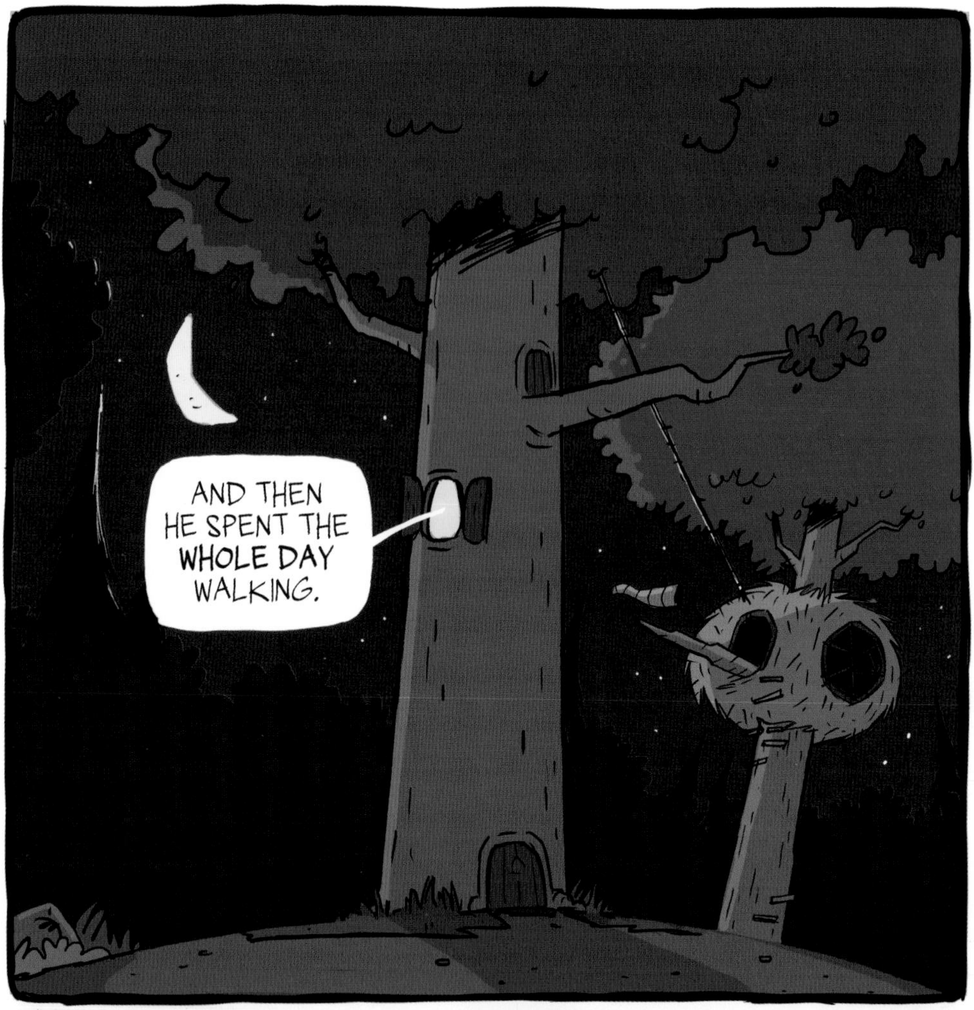
AND THEN HE SPENT THE WHOLE DAY WALKING.

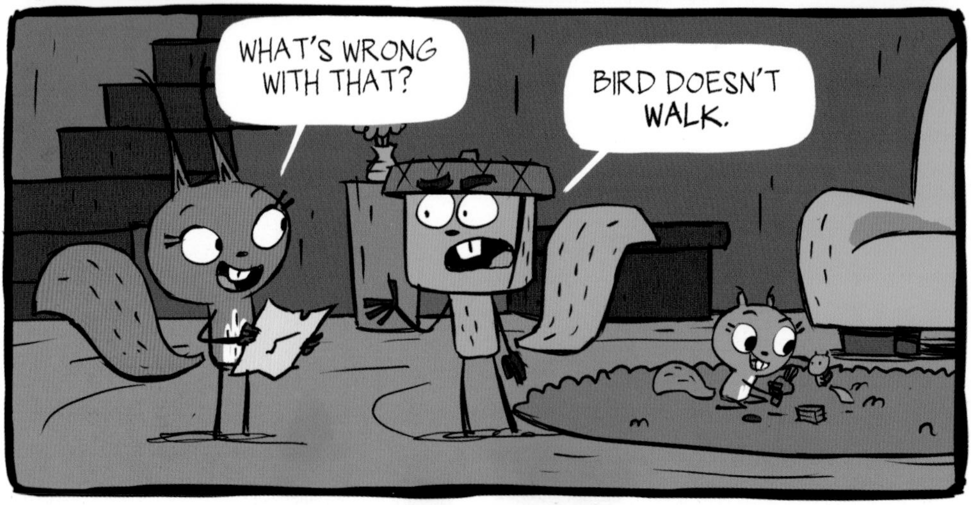
WHAT'S WRONG WITH THAT?
BIRD DOESN'T WALK.

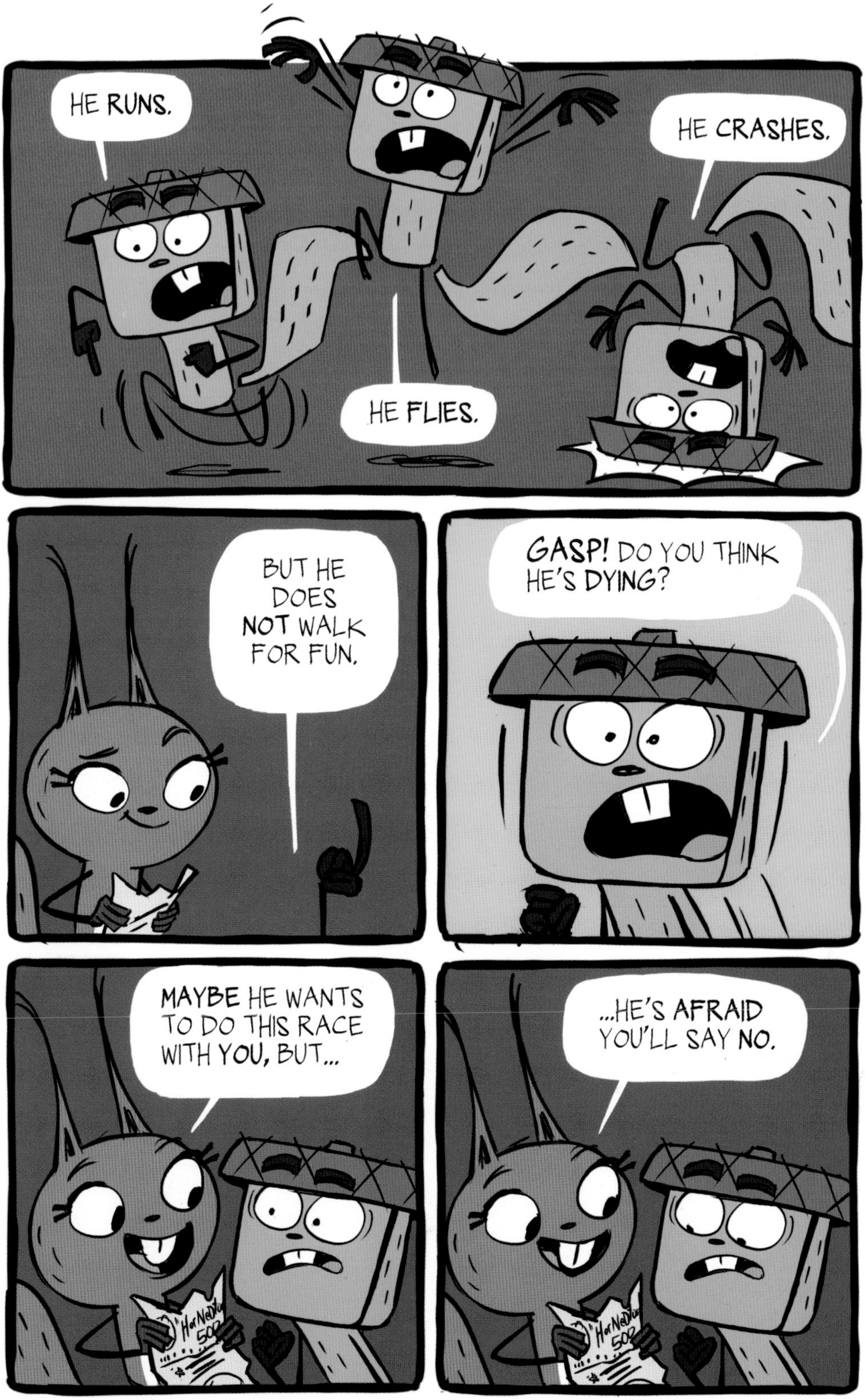
HE **RUNS.**
HE **FLIES.**
HE **CRASHES.**
BUT HE DOES **NOT** WALK FOR FUN.
GASP! DO YOU THINK HE'S **DYING?**
MAYBE HE WANTS TO DO THIS RACE WITH **YOU,** BUT...
...HE'S **AFRAID** YOU'LL SAY **NO.**

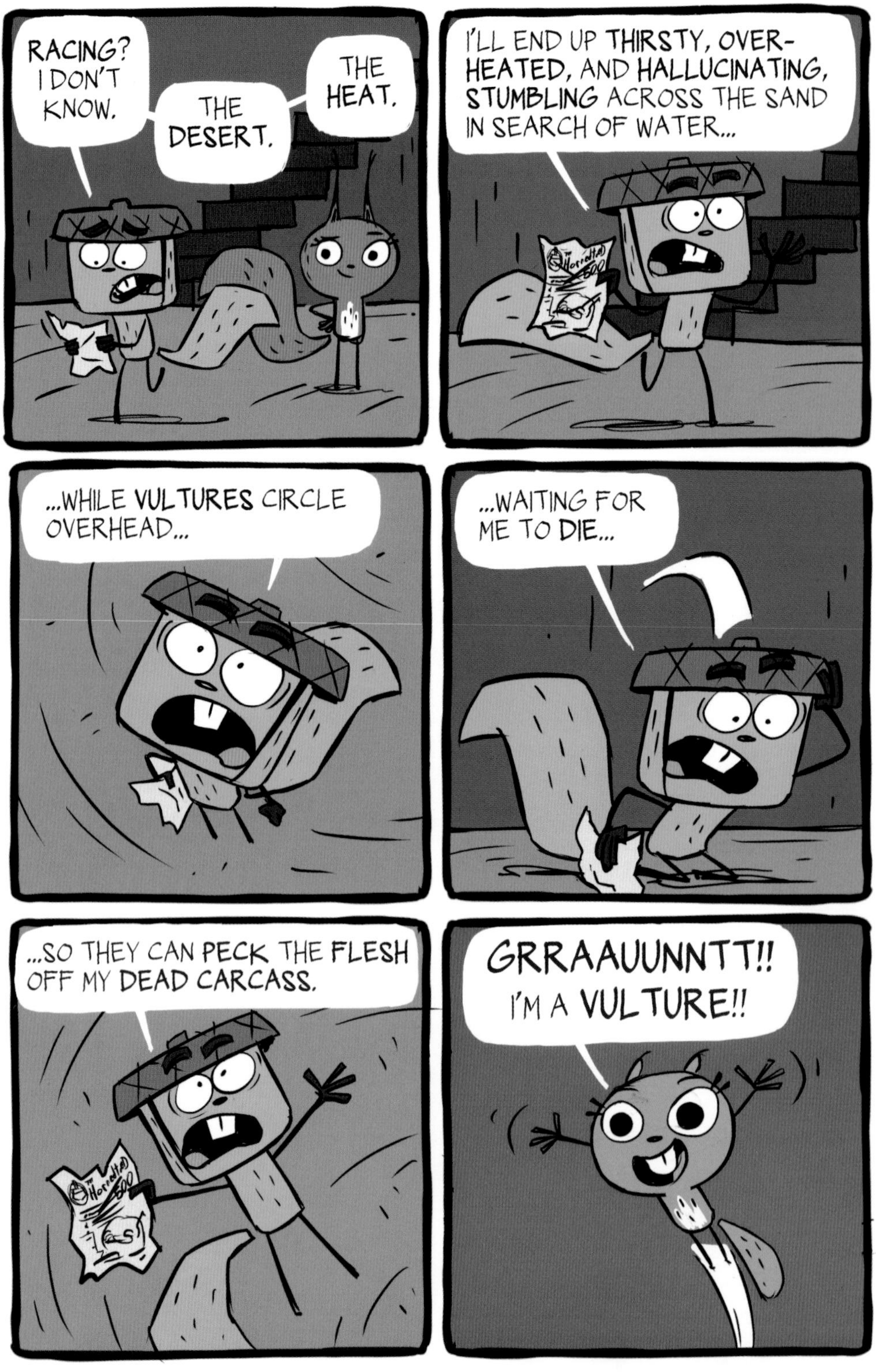
RACING? I DON'T KNOW.
THE DESERT.
THE HEAT.
I'LL END UP THIRSTY, OVER-HEATED, AND HALLUCINATING, STUMBLING ACROSS THE SAND IN SEARCH OF WATER...
...WHILE VULTURES CIRCLE OVERHEAD...
...WAITING FOR ME TO DIE...
...SO THEY CAN PECK THE FLESH OFF MY DEAD CARCASS.
GRRAAUUNNTT!! I'M A VULTURE!!

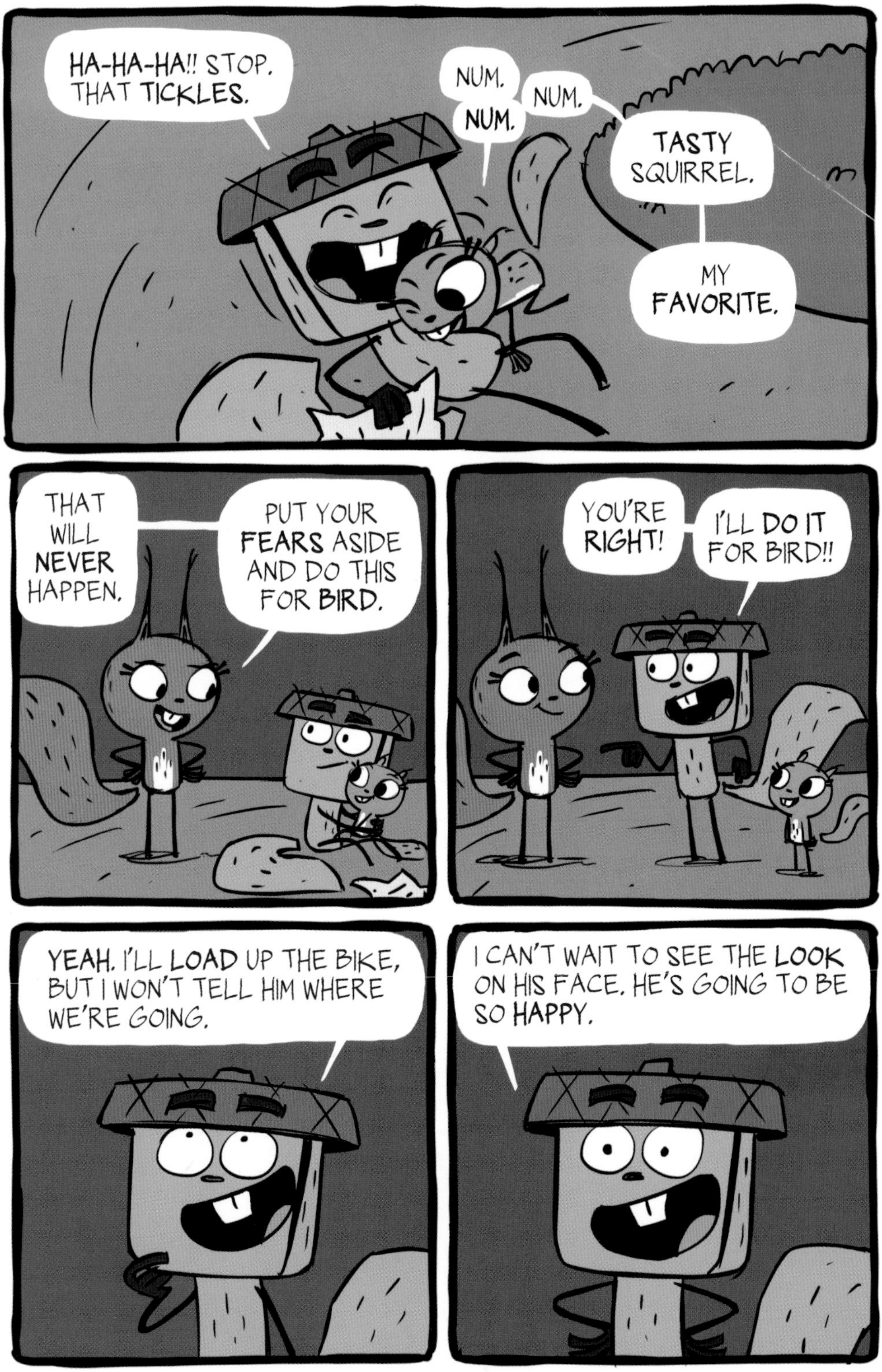
HA-HA-HA!! STOP. THAT TICKLES.
NUM.
NUM.
NUM.
TASTY SQUIRREL.
MY FAVORITE.
THAT WILL NEVER HAPPEN.
PUT YOUR FEARS ASIDE AND DO THIS FOR BIRD.
YOU'RE RIGHT!
I'LL DO IT FOR BIRD!!
YEAH. I'LL LOAD UP THE BIKE, BUT I WON'T TELL HIM WHERE WE'RE GOING.
I CAN'T WAIT TO SEE THE LOOK ON HIS FACE. HE'S GOING TO BE SO HAPPY.

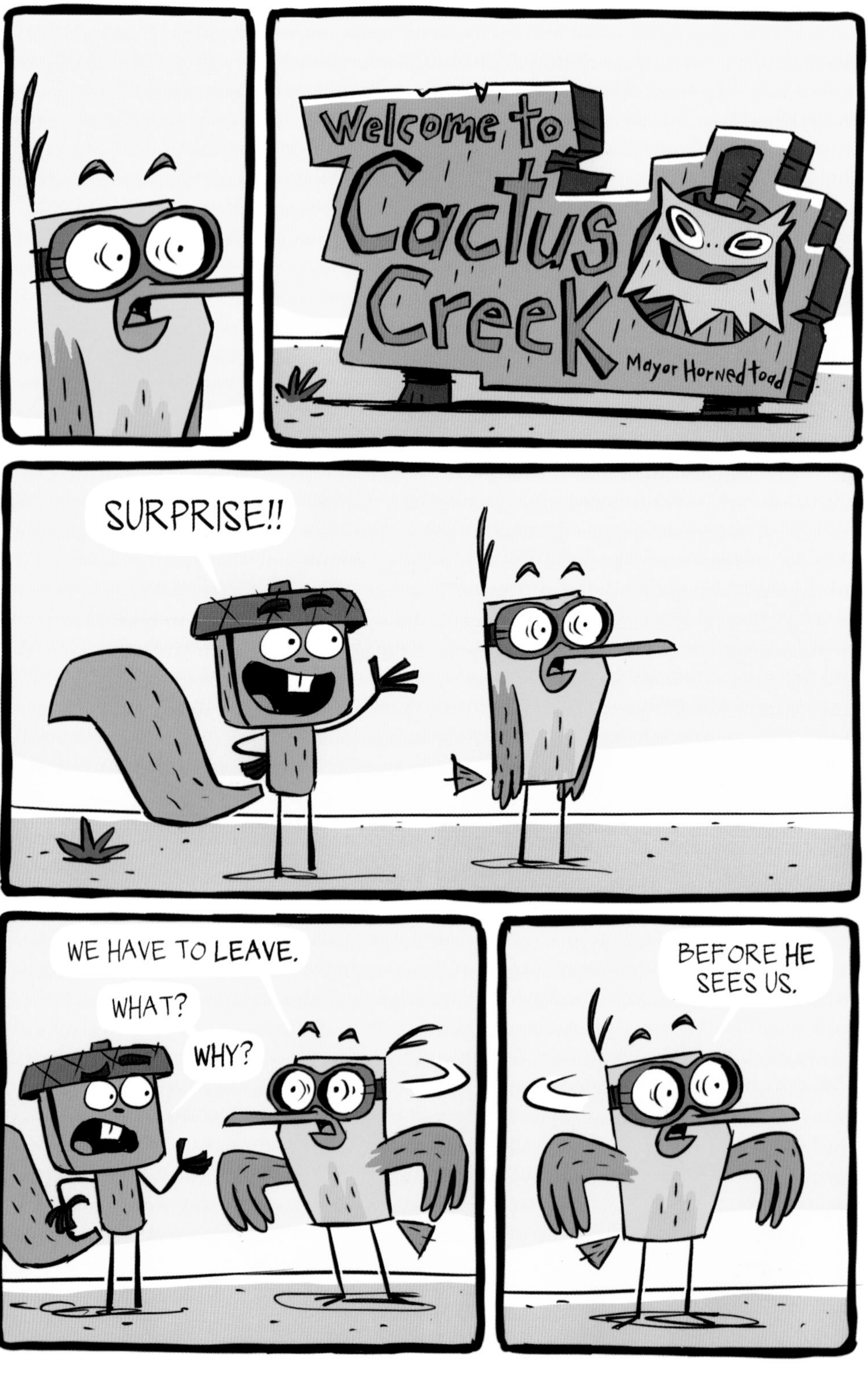
Welcome to
Cactus Creek
Mayor Horned toad
SURPRISE!!
WE HAVE TO LEAVE.
WHAT?
WHY?
BEFORE HE SEES US.

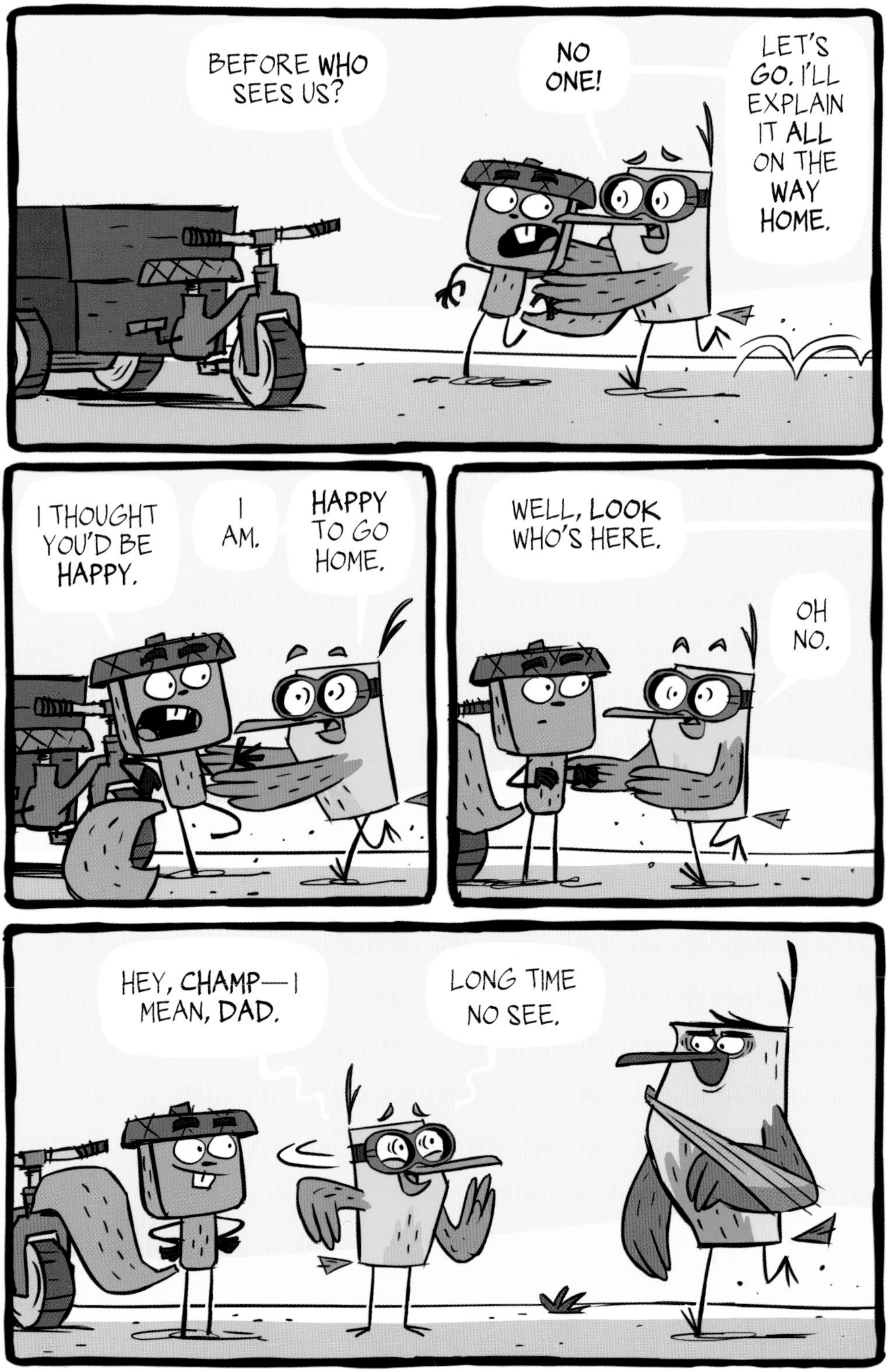
BEFORE WHO SEES US?
NO ONE!
LET'S GO. I'LL EXPLAIN IT ALL ON THE WAY HOME.
I THOUGHT YOU'D BE HAPPY.
I AM.
HAPPY TO GO HOME.
WELL, LOOK WHO'S HERE.
OH NO.
HEY, CHAMP—I MEAN, DAD.
LONG TIME NO SEE.

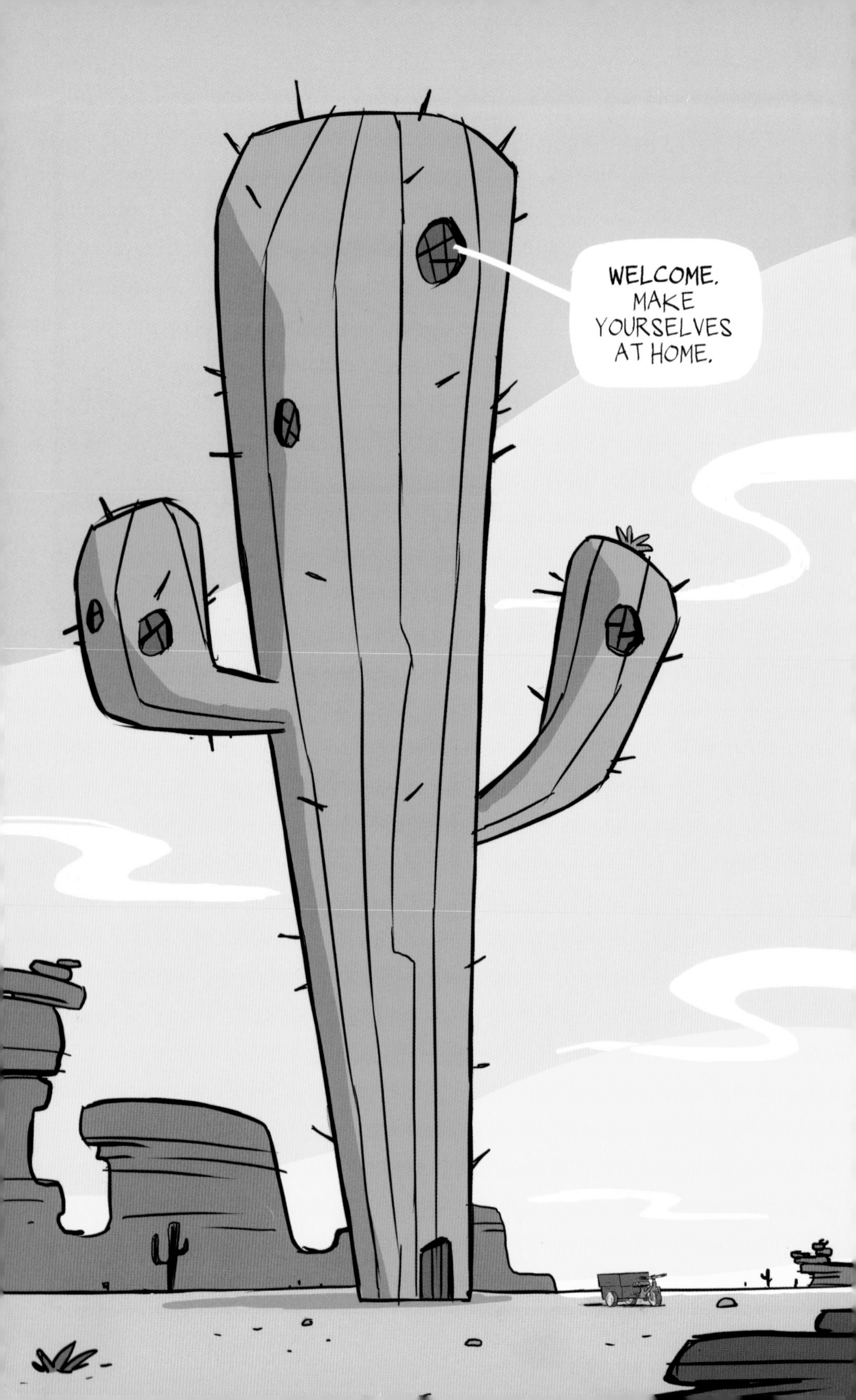
WELCOME. MAKE YOURSELVES AT HOME.

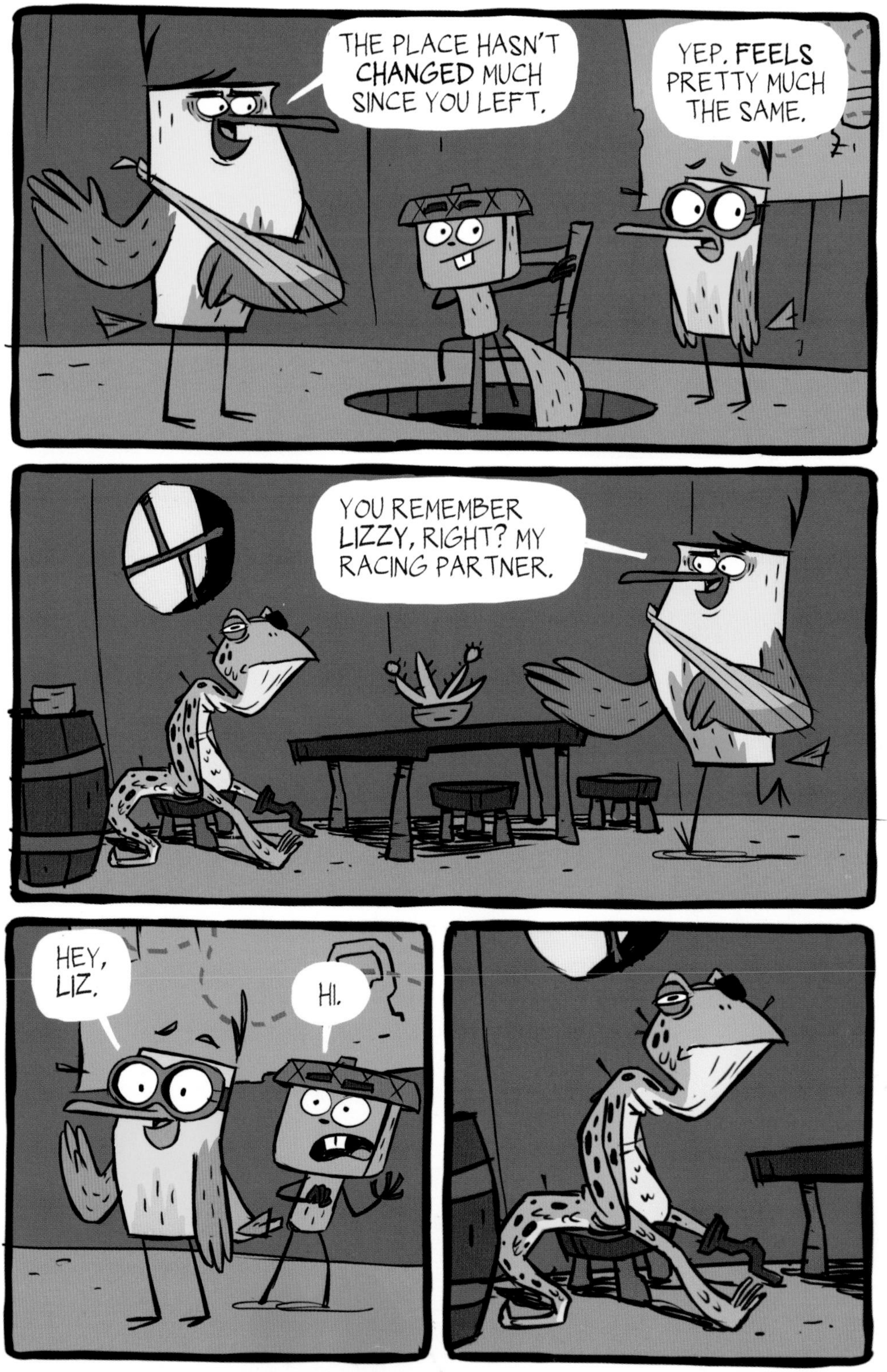
THE PLACE HASN'T CHANGED MUCH SINCE YOU LEFT.
YEP. FEELS PRETTY MUCH THE SAME.
YOU REMEMBER LIZZY, RIGHT? MY RACING PARTNER.
HEY, LIZ.
HI.

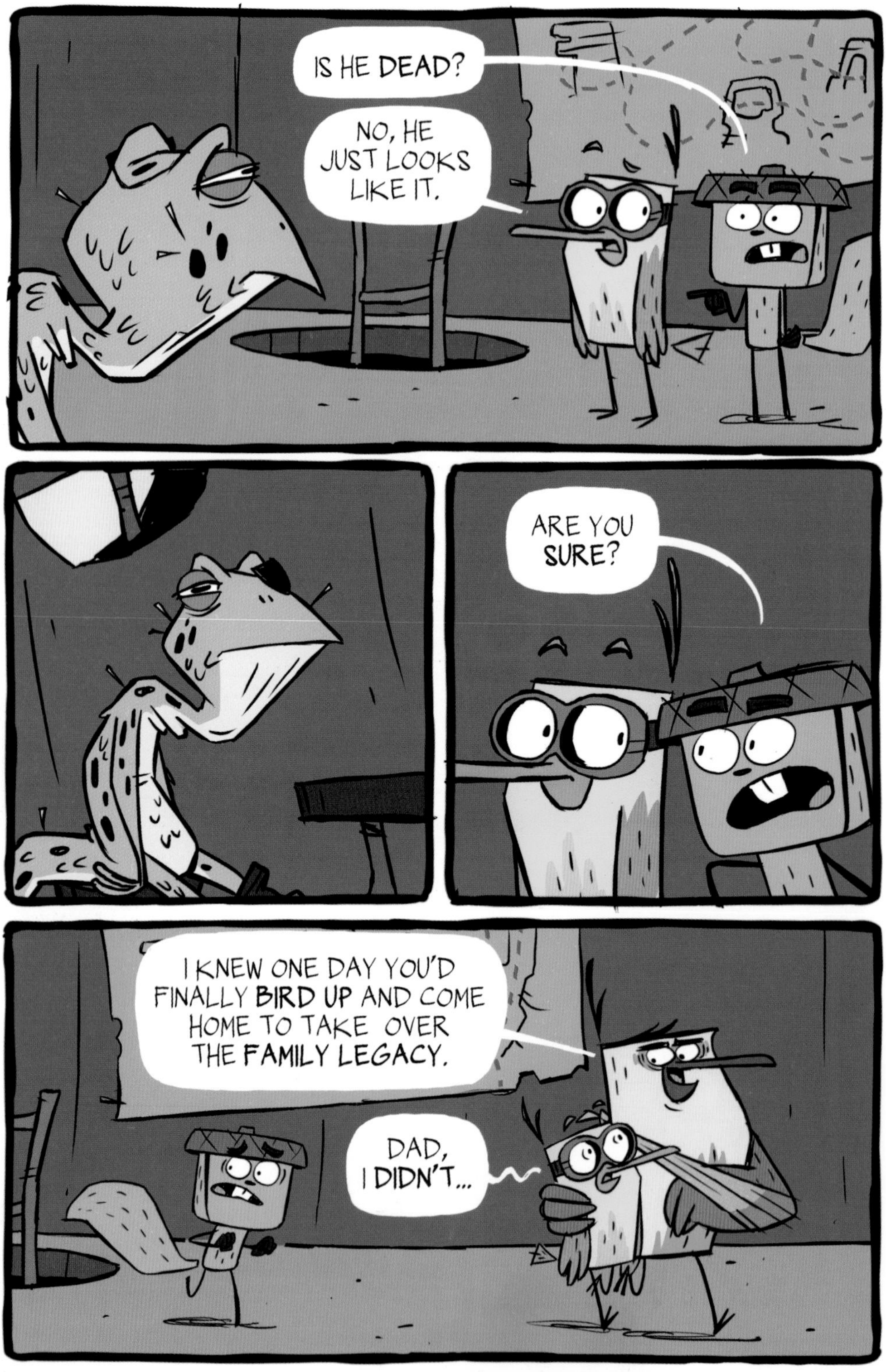
IS HE DEAD?
NO, HE JUST LOOKS LIKE IT.
ARE YOU SURE?
I KNEW ONE DAY YOU'D FINALLY BIRD UP AND COME HOME TO TAKE OVER THE FAMILY LEGACY.
DAD, I DIDN'T...

BIRD FAMILY
WALL OF CHAMPIONS
WE'LL FINALLY BE ABLE TO ADD YOU TO THE BIRD FAMILY **WALL OF CHAMPIONS.**
I'VE BEEN **SAVING** YOU A SPOT **RIGHT HERE.**

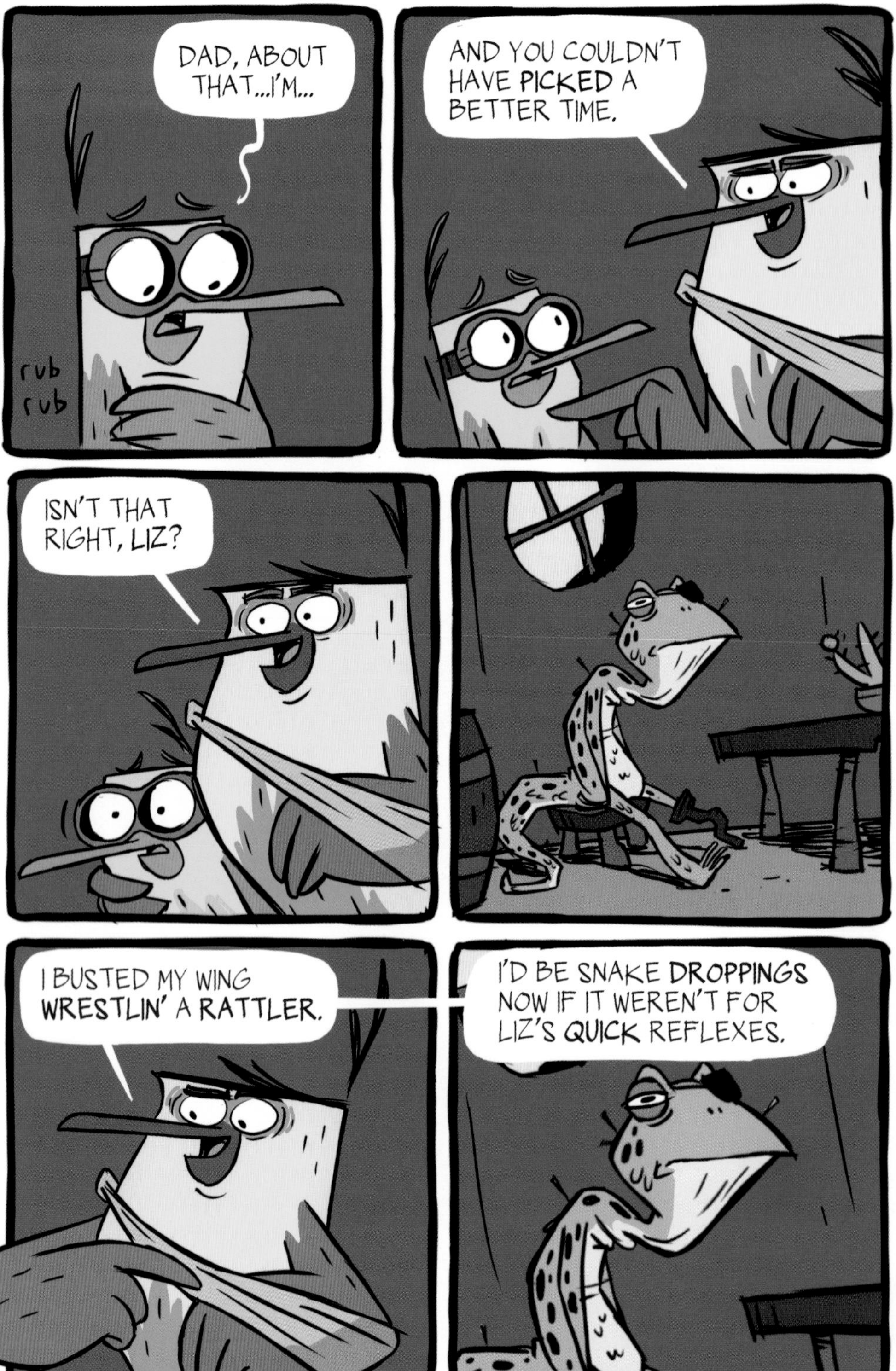
DAD, ABOUT THAT...I'M...
rub rub
AND YOU COULDN'T HAVE PICKED A BETTER TIME.
ISN'T THAT RIGHT, LIZ?
I BUSTED MY WING WRESTLIN' A RATTLER.
I'D BE SNAKE DROPPINGS NOW IF IT WEREN'T FOR LIZ'S QUICK REFLEXES.

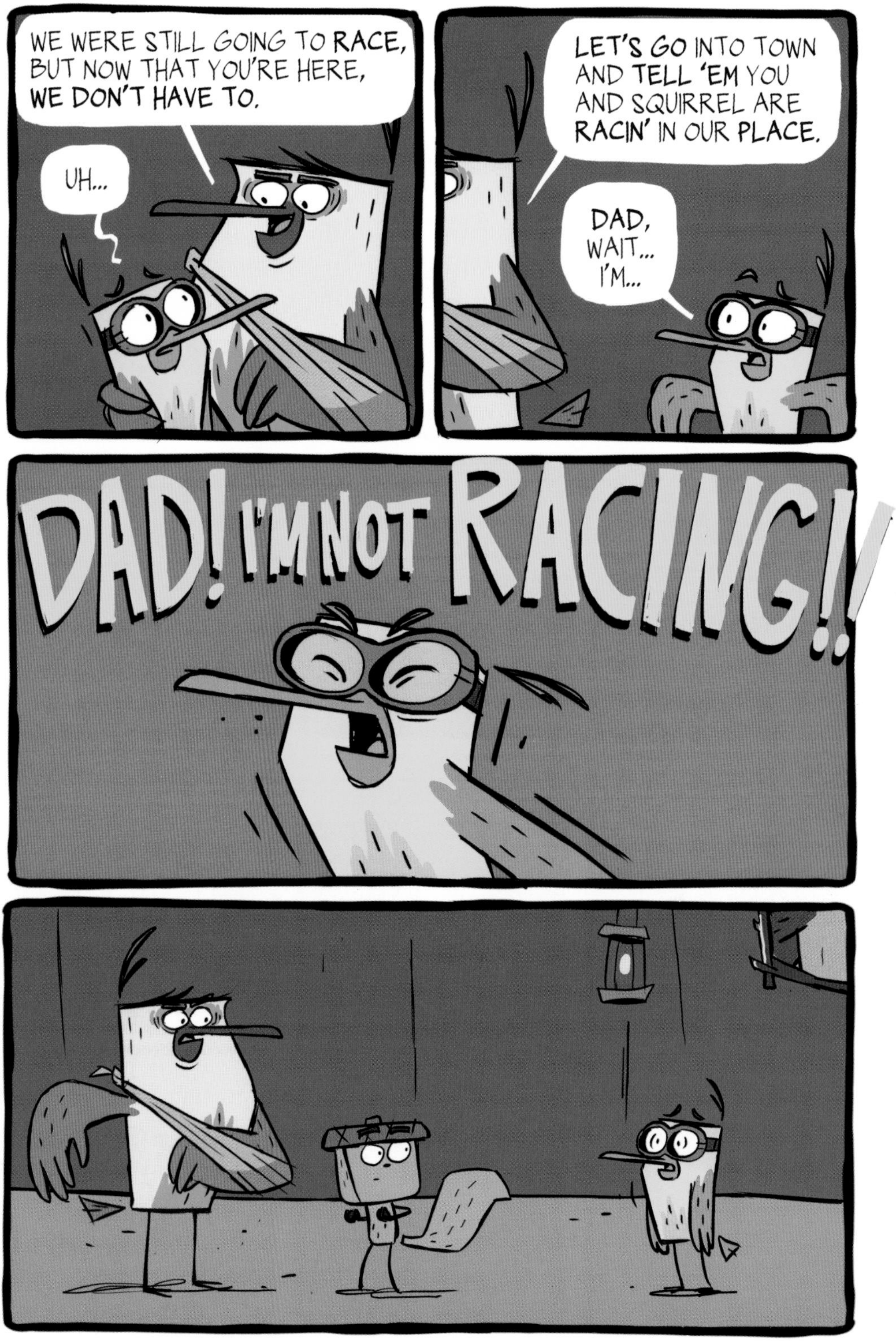
WE WERE STILL GOING TO RACE, BUT NOW THAT YOU'RE HERE, WE DON'T HAVE TO.
UH...
LET'S GO INTO TOWN AND TELL 'EM YOU AND SQUIRREL ARE RACIN' IN OUR PLACE.
DAD, WAIT... I'M...
DAD! I'M NOT RACING!!

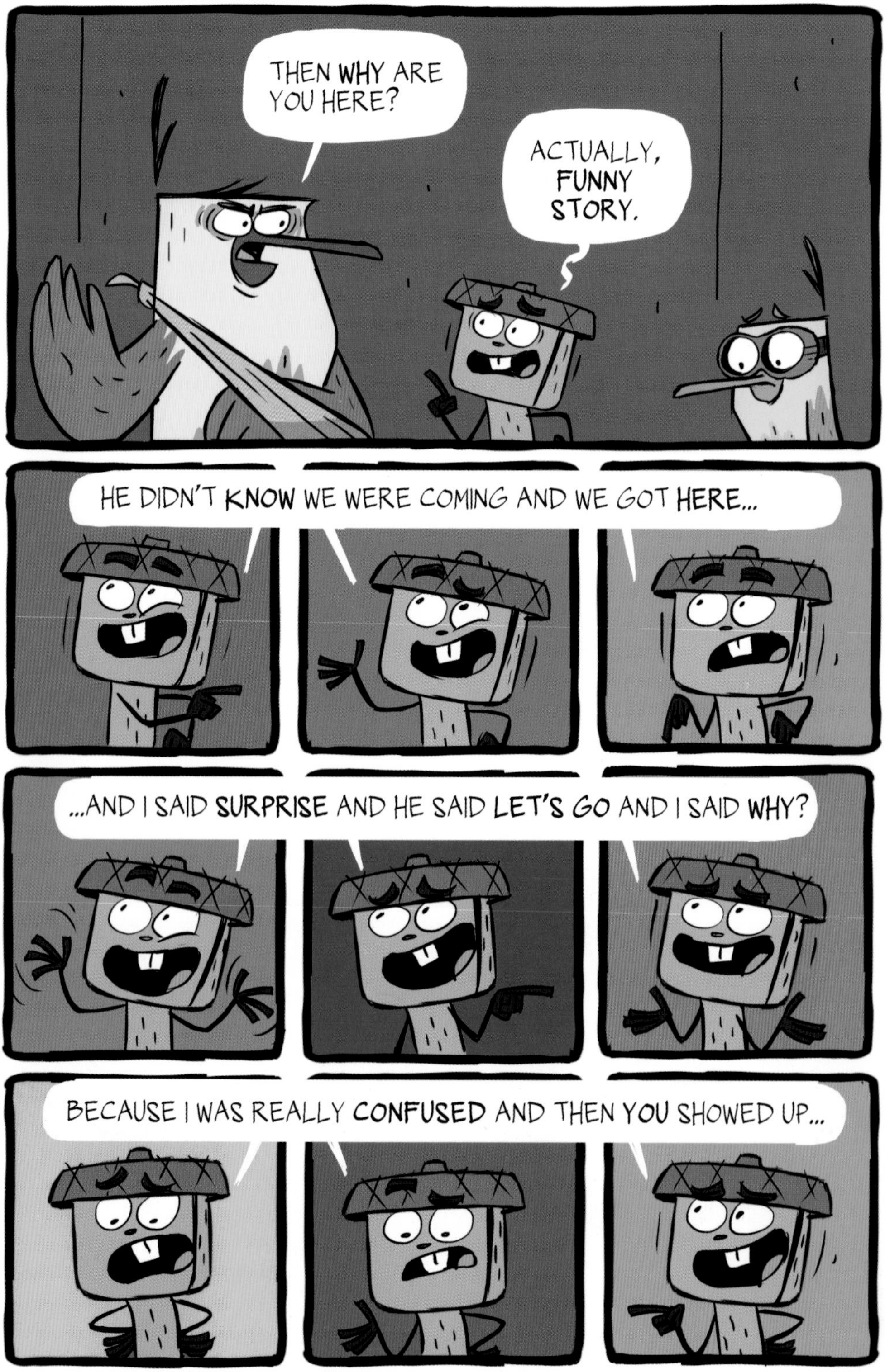
THEN WHY ARE YOU HERE?
ACTUALLY, FUNNY STORY.
HE DIDN'T KNOW WE WERE COMING AND WE GOT HERE...
...AND I SAID SURPRISE AND HE SAID LET'S GO AND I SAID WHY?
BECAUSE I WAS REALLY CONFUSED AND THEN YOU SHOWED UP...

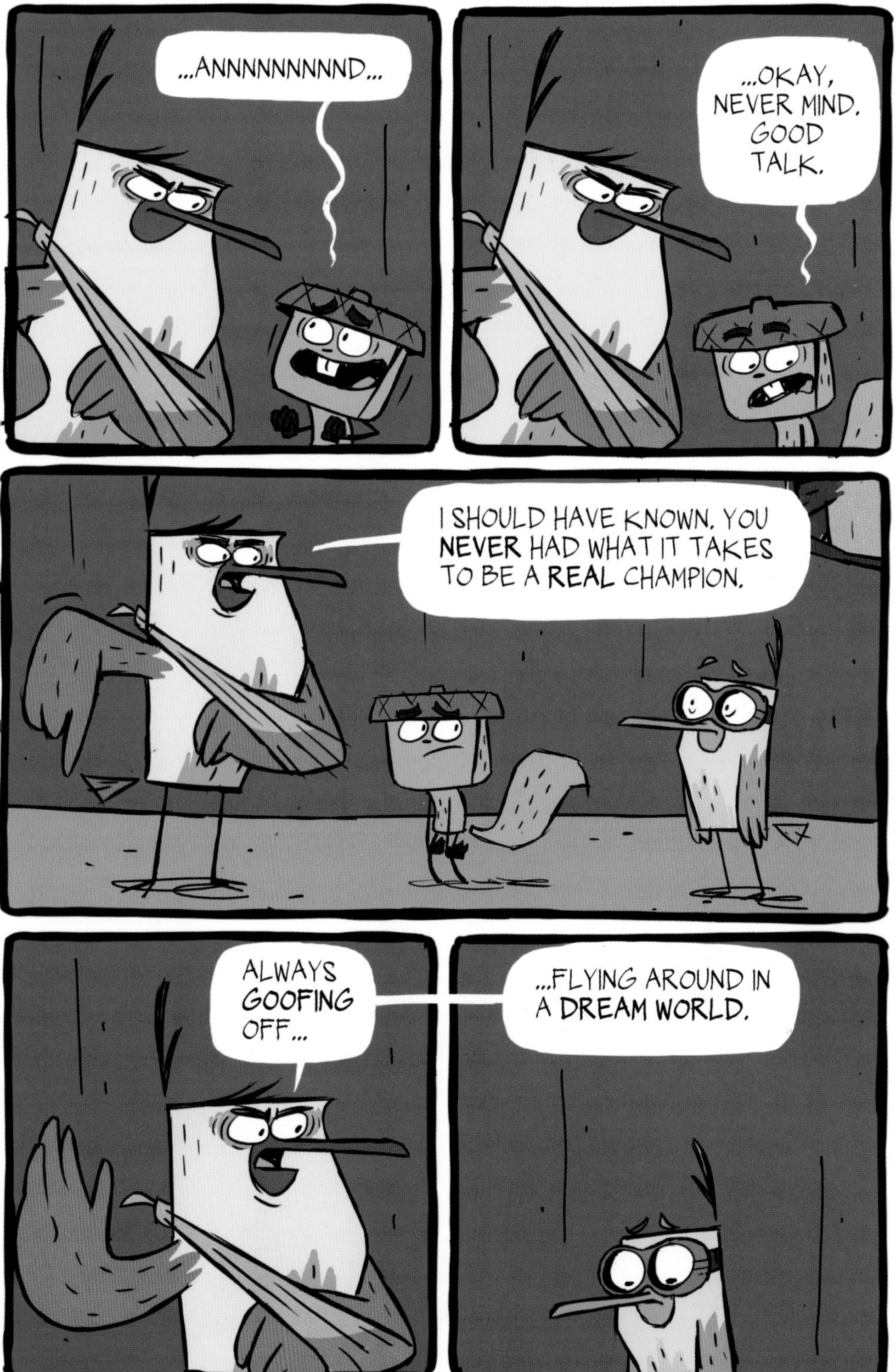
...ANNNNNNNNND...
...OKAY, NEVER MIND. GOOD TALK.
I SHOULD HAVE KNOWN. YOU NEVER HAD WHAT IT TAKES TO BE A REAL CHAMPION.
ALWAYS GOOFING OFF...
...FLYING AROUND IN A DREAM WORLD.

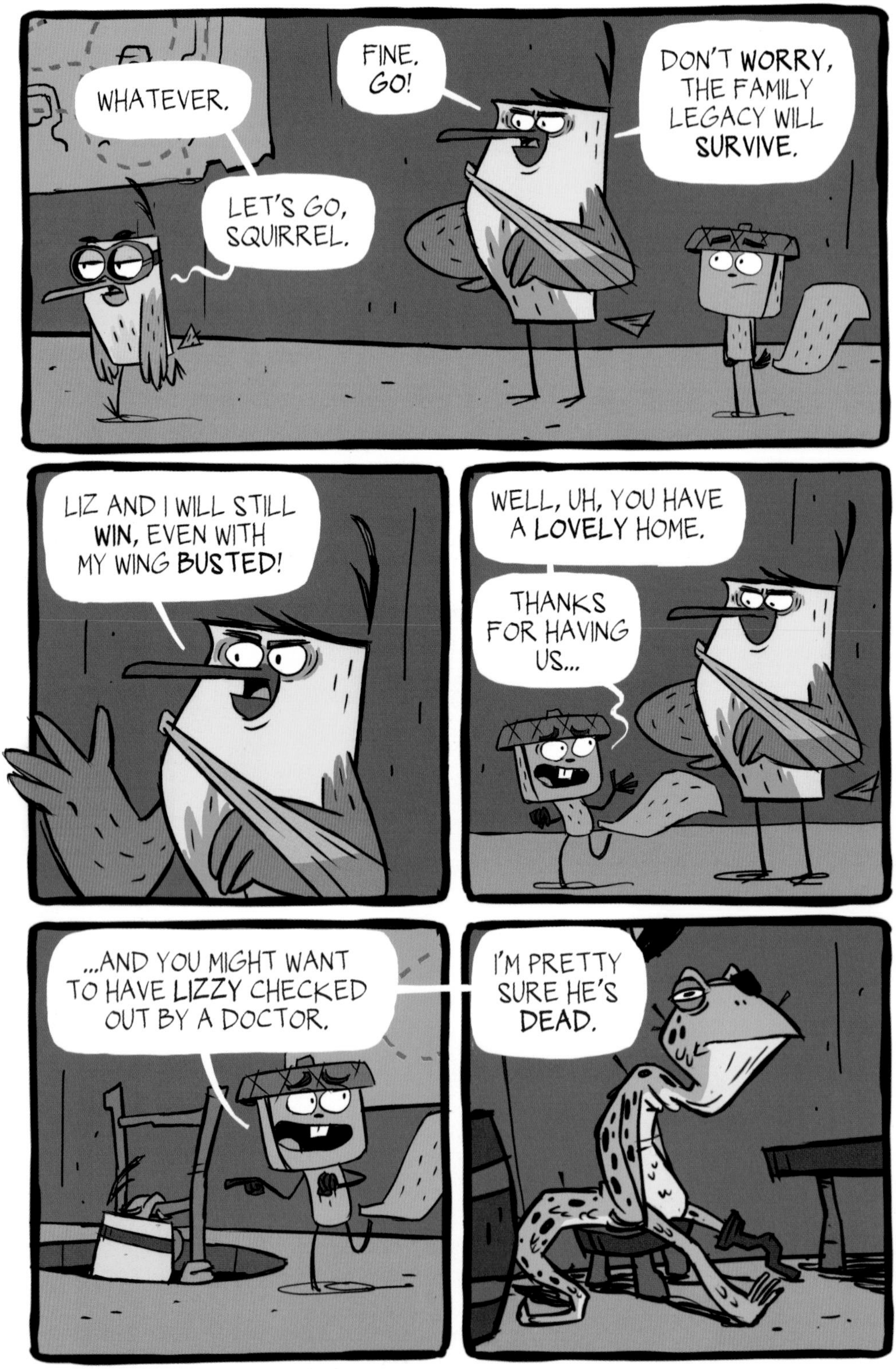
WHATEVER.
LET'S GO, SQUIRREL.
FINE. GO!
DON'T WORRY, THE FAMILY LEGACY WILL SURVIVE.
LIZ AND I WILL STILL WIN, EVEN WITH MY WING BUSTED!
WELL, UH, YOU HAVE A LOVELY HOME.
THANKS FOR HAVING US...
...AND YOU MIGHT WANT TO HAVE LIZZY CHECKED OUT BY A DOCTOR.
I'M PRETTY SURE HE'S DEAD.

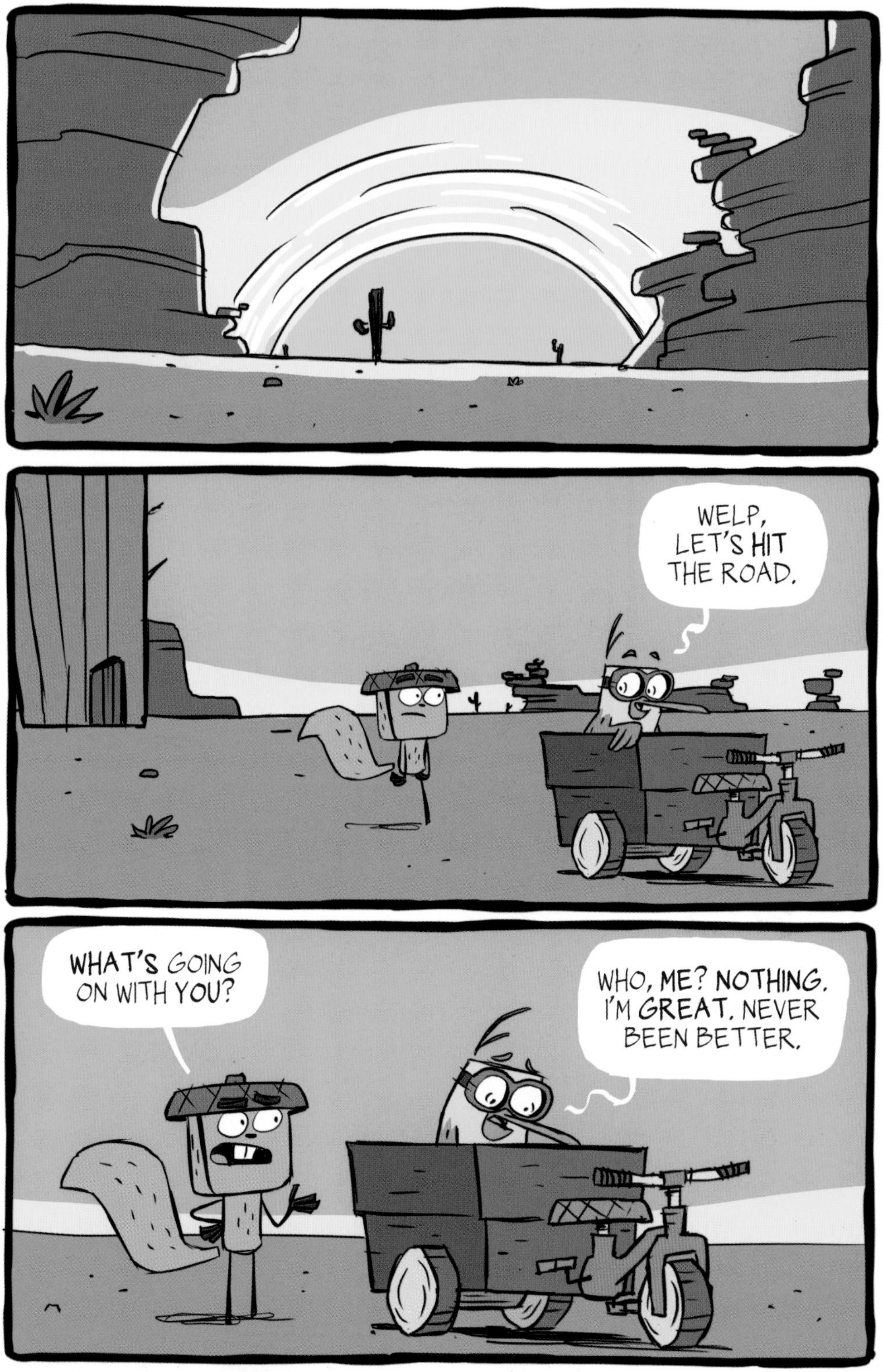
WELP, LET'S HIT THE ROAD.
WHAT'S GOING ON WITH YOU?
WHO, ME? NOTHING. I'M GREAT. NEVER BEEN BETTER.

TELL ME THE TRUTH. IT'S NOT LIKE YOU TO RUN AWAY FROM AN ADVENTURE.

SIGH...ALL MY DAD CARES ABOUT IS CARRYING ON THE STUPID FAMILY LEGACY.

IT'S ALWAYS BEEN ABOUT WINNING THAT RACE.

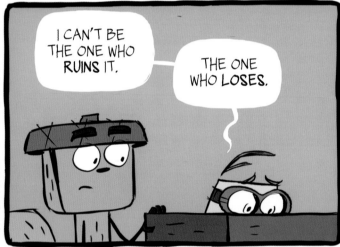

I CAN'T BE THE ONE WHO RUINS IT.

THE ONE WHO LOSES.

IT DOESN'T HAVE TO BE ALL OR NOTHING. JUST GIVE IT YOUR BEST SHOT.

I'M SORRY. I CAN'T.

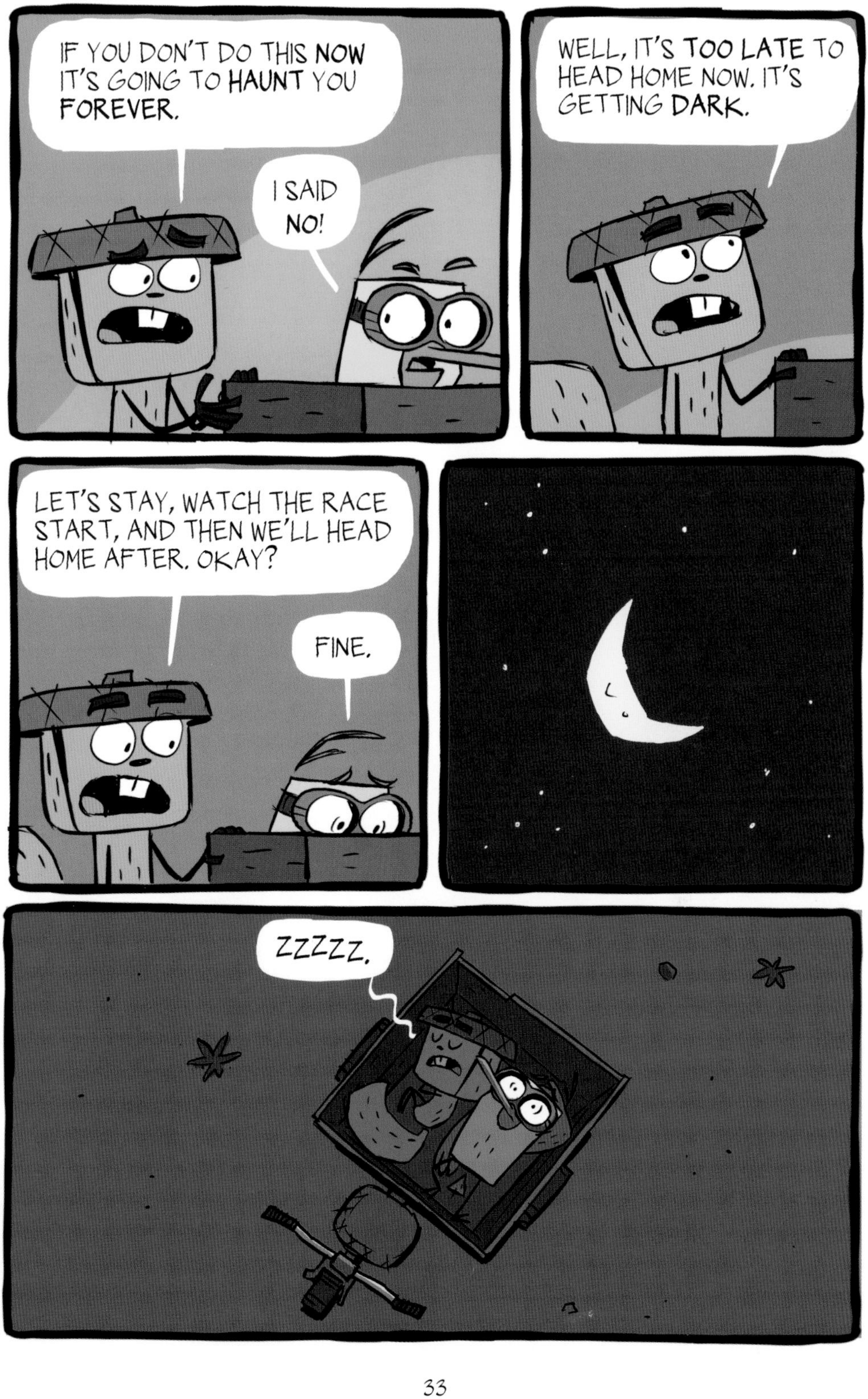
IF YOU DON'T DO THIS NOW IT'S GOING TO HAUNT YOU FOREVER.
I SAID NO!
WELL, IT'S TOO LATE TO HEAD HOME NOW. IT'S GETTING DARK.
LET'S STAY, WATCH THE RACE START, AND THEN WE'LL HEAD HOME AFTER. OKAY?
FINE.
ZZZZZ.

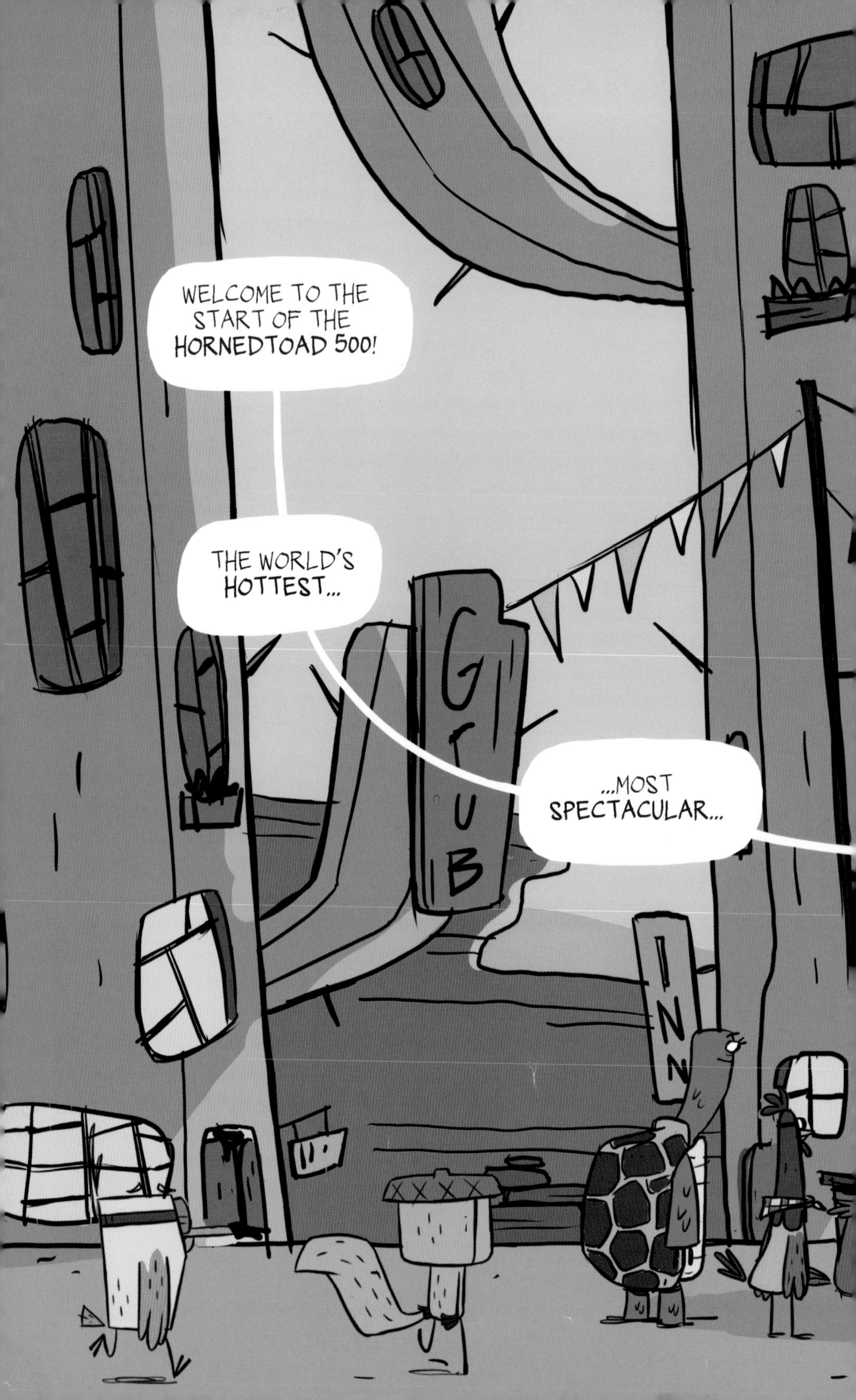
WELCOME TO THE START OF THE HORNEDTOAD 500!
THE WORLD'S HOTTEST...
...MOST SPECTACULAR...
GRUB
INN

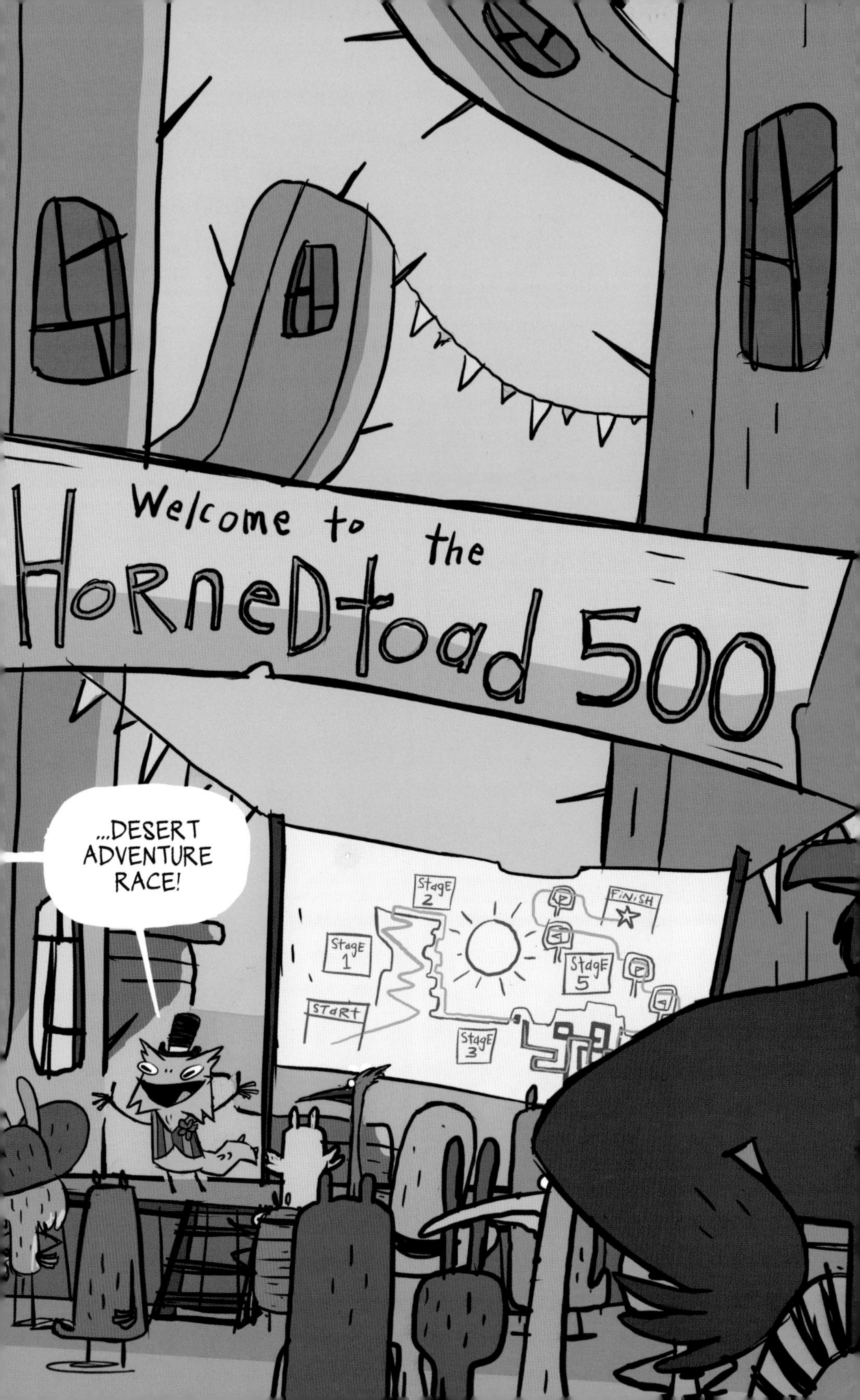
Welcome to the
HorneDtoad 500
...DESERT ADVENTURE RACE!
START
Stage 1
Stage 2
Stage 3
Stage 5
FINISH

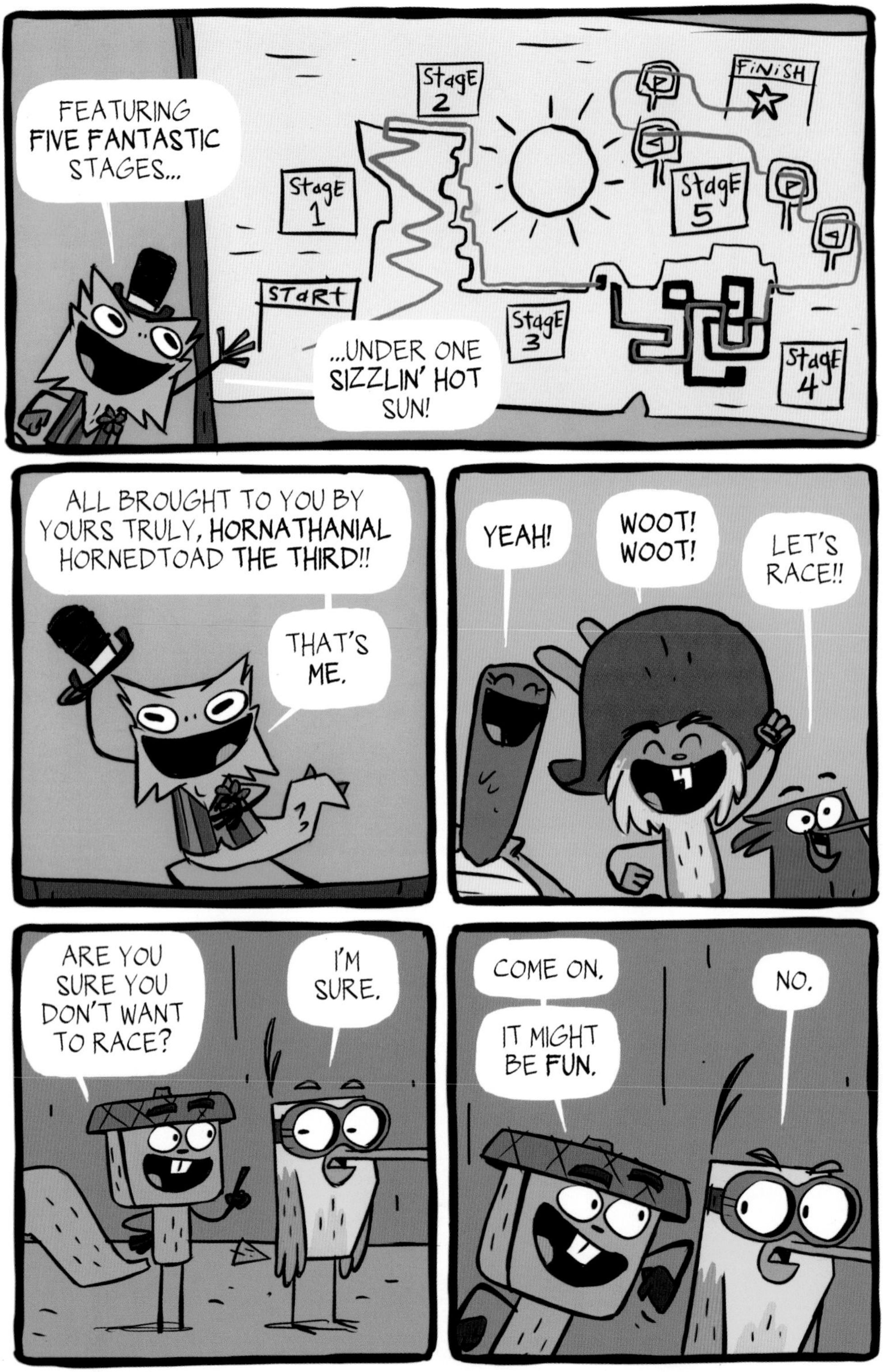
FEATURING FIVE FANTASTIC STAGES...
Stage 2
FINISH
P
Stage 1
Stage 5
START
Stage 3
...UNDER ONE SIZZLIN' HOT SUN!
Stage 4
ALL BROUGHT TO YOU BY YOURS TRULY, HORNATHANIAL HORNEDTOAD THE THIRD!!
THAT'S ME.
YEAH!
WOOT! WOOT!
LET'S RACE!!
ARE YOU SURE YOU DON'T WANT TO RACE?
I'M SURE.
COME ON.
IT MIGHT BE FUN.
NO.

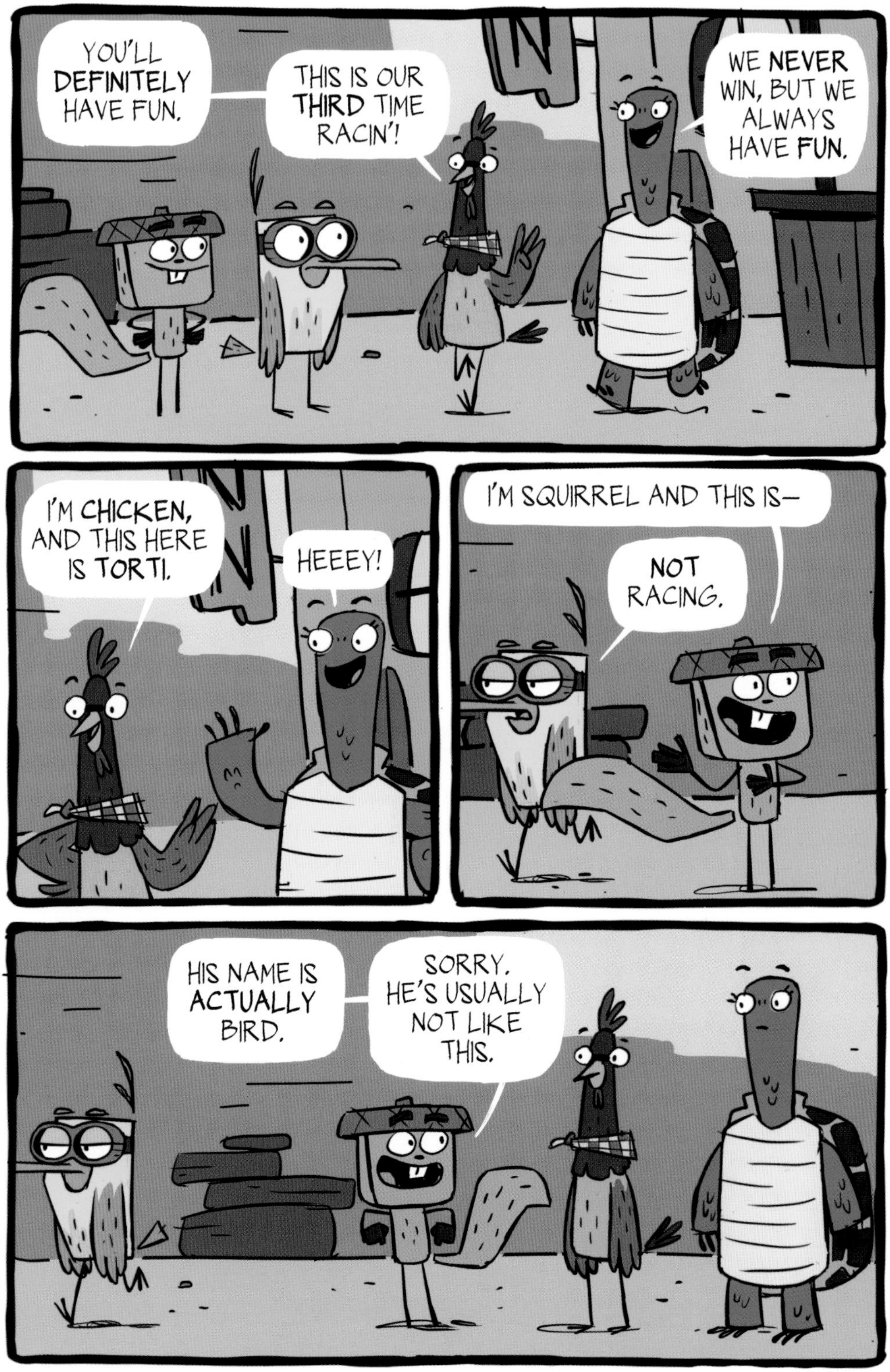
YOU'LL DEFINITELY HAVE FUN.
THIS IS OUR THIRD TIME RACIN'!
WE NEVER WIN, BUT WE ALWAYS HAVE FUN.
I'M CHICKEN, AND THIS HERE IS TORTI.
HEEEY!
I'M SQUIRREL AND THIS IS—
NOT RACING.
HIS NAME IS ACTUALLY BIRD.
SORRY. HE'S USUALLY NOT LIKE THIS.

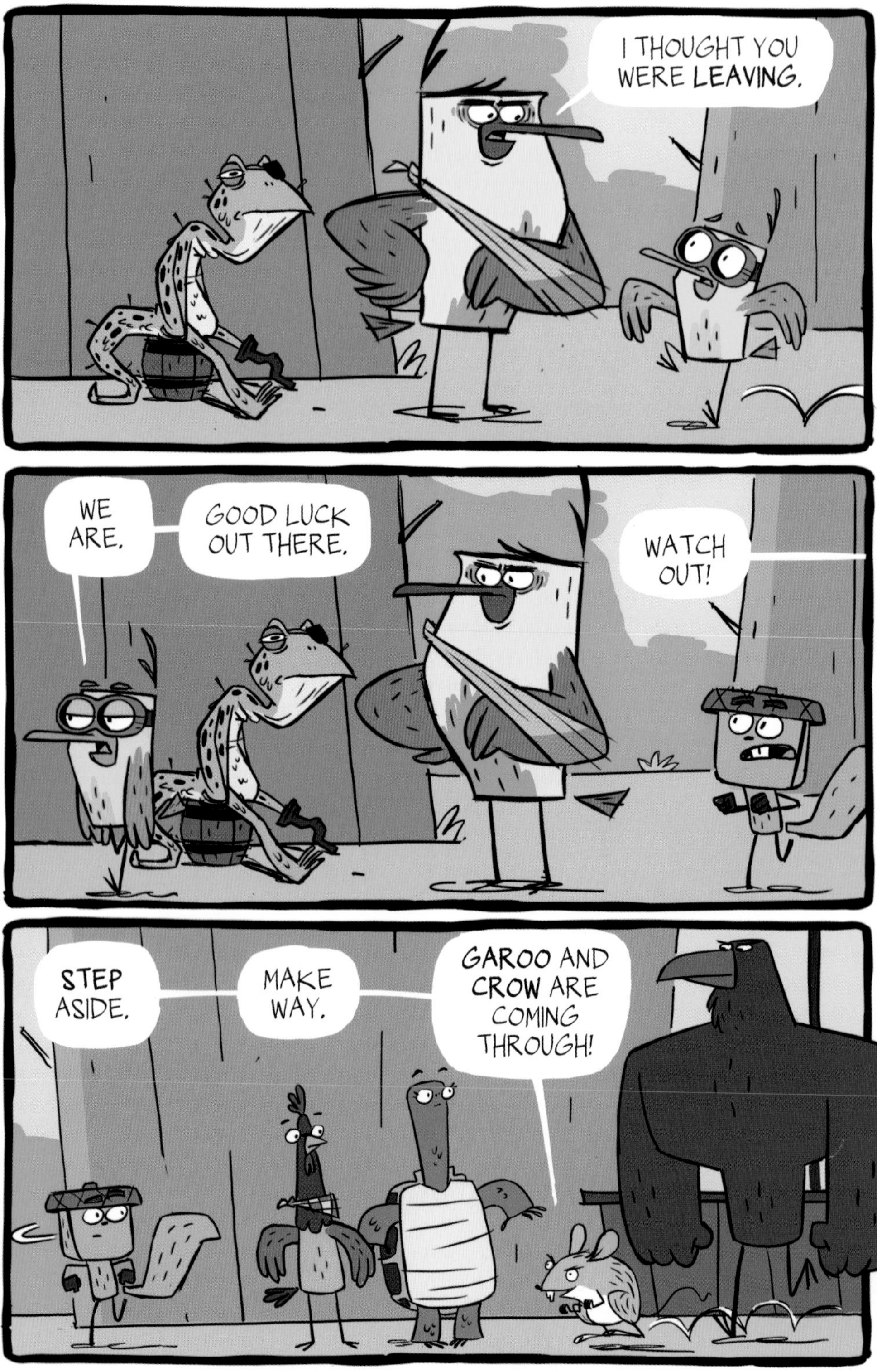
I THOUGHT YOU WERE **LEAVING.**
WE ARE.
GOOD LUCK OUT THERE.
WATCH OUT!
STEP ASIDE.
MAKE WAY.
GAROO AND **CROW** ARE COMING THROUGH!

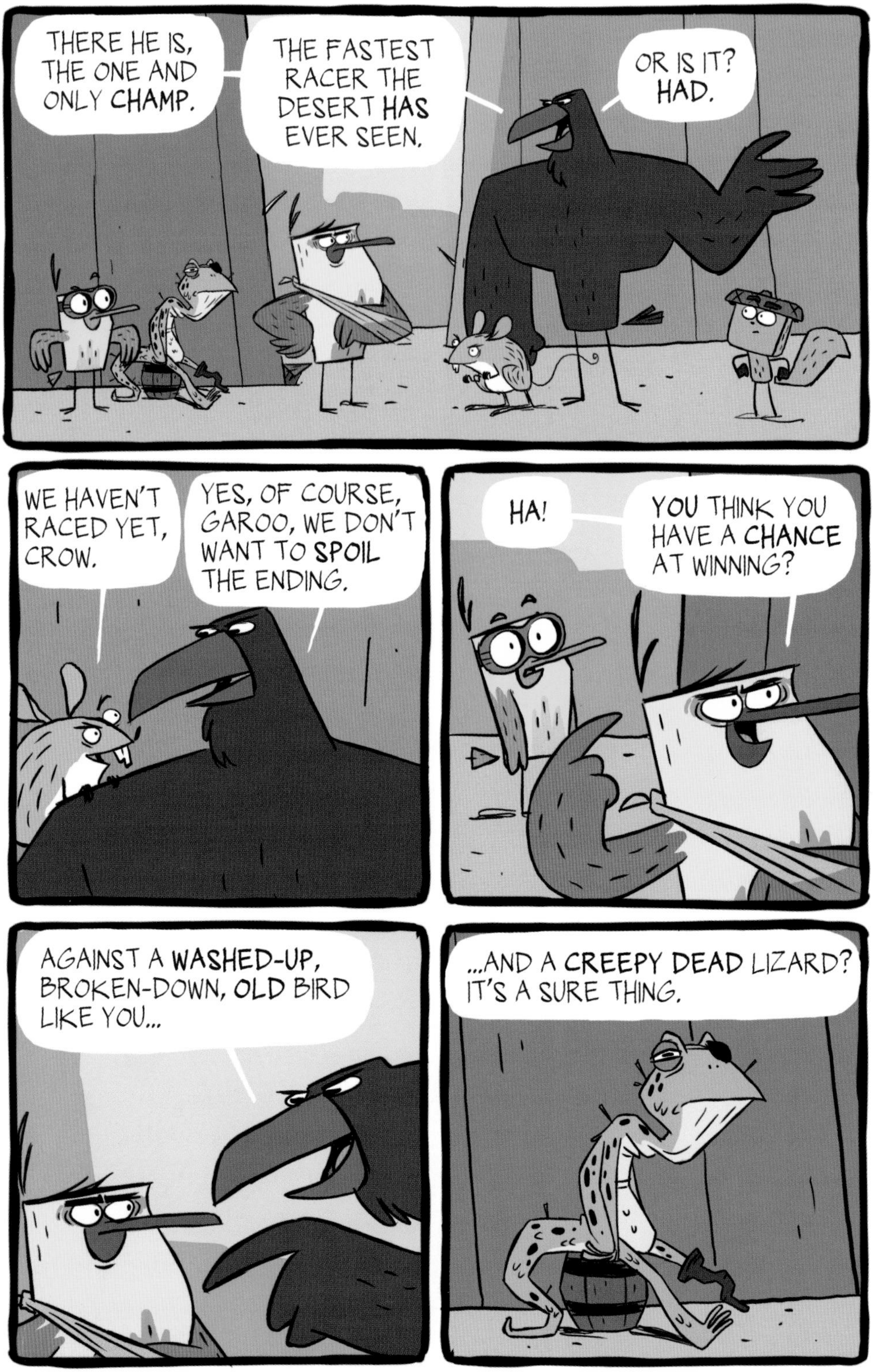
THERE HE IS, THE ONE AND ONLY CHAMP.
THE FASTEST RACER THE DESERT HAS EVER SEEN.
OR IS IT? HAD.
WE HAVEN'T RACED YET, CROW.
YES, OF COURSE, GAROO, WE DON'T WANT TO SPOIL THE ENDING.
HA!
YOU THINK YOU HAVE A CHANCE AT WINNING?
AGAINST A WASHED-UP, BROKEN-DOWN, OLD BIRD LIKE YOU...
...AND A CREEPY DEAD LIZARD? IT'S A SURE THING.

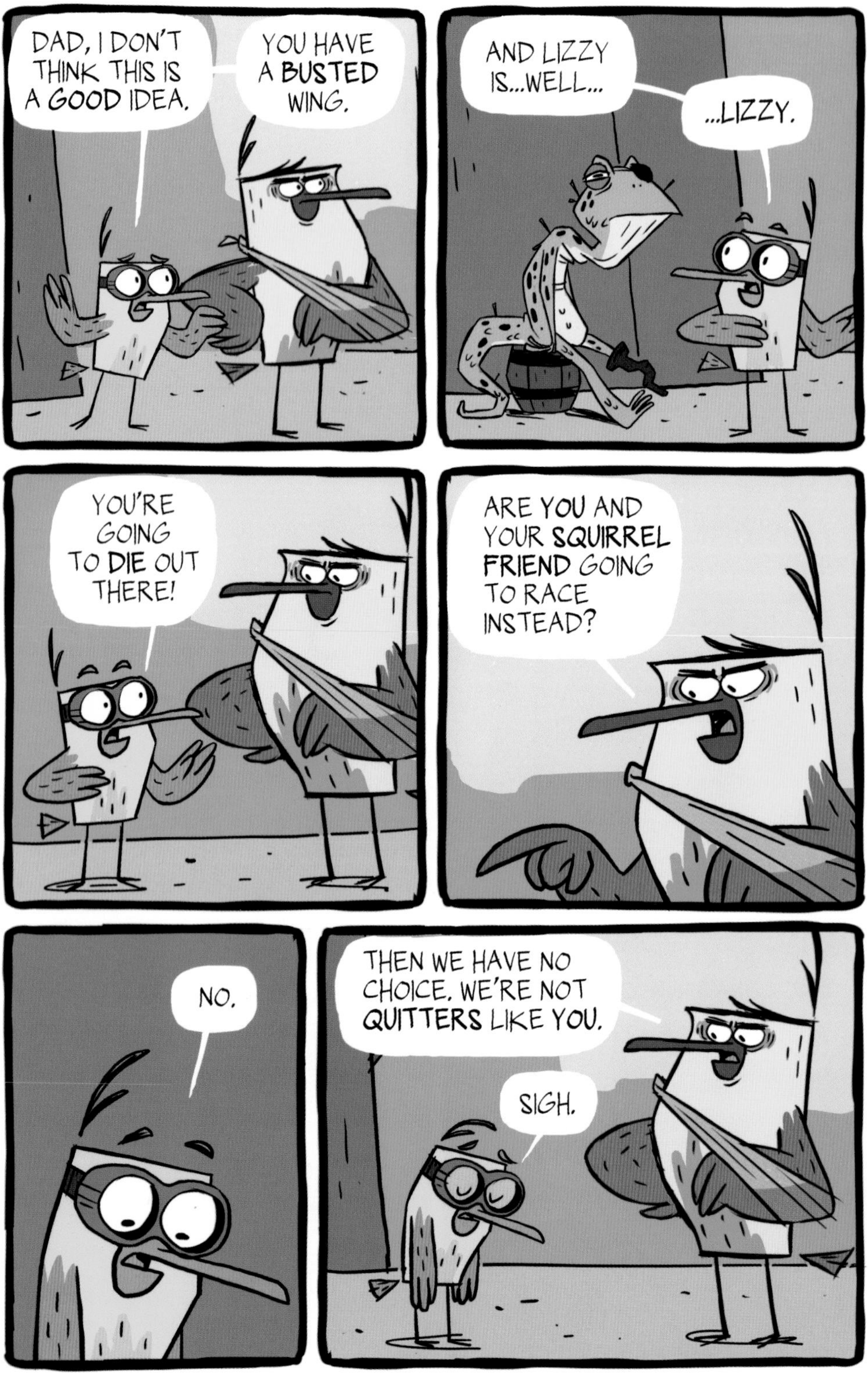
DAD, I DON'T THINK THIS IS A GOOD IDEA.
YOU HAVE A BUSTED WING.
AND LIZZY IS...WELL...
...LIZZY.
YOU'RE GOING TO DIE OUT THERE!
ARE YOU AND YOUR SQUIRREL FRIEND GOING TO RACE INSTEAD?
NO.
THEN WE HAVE NO CHOICE. WE'RE NOT QUITTERS LIKE YOU.
SIGH.

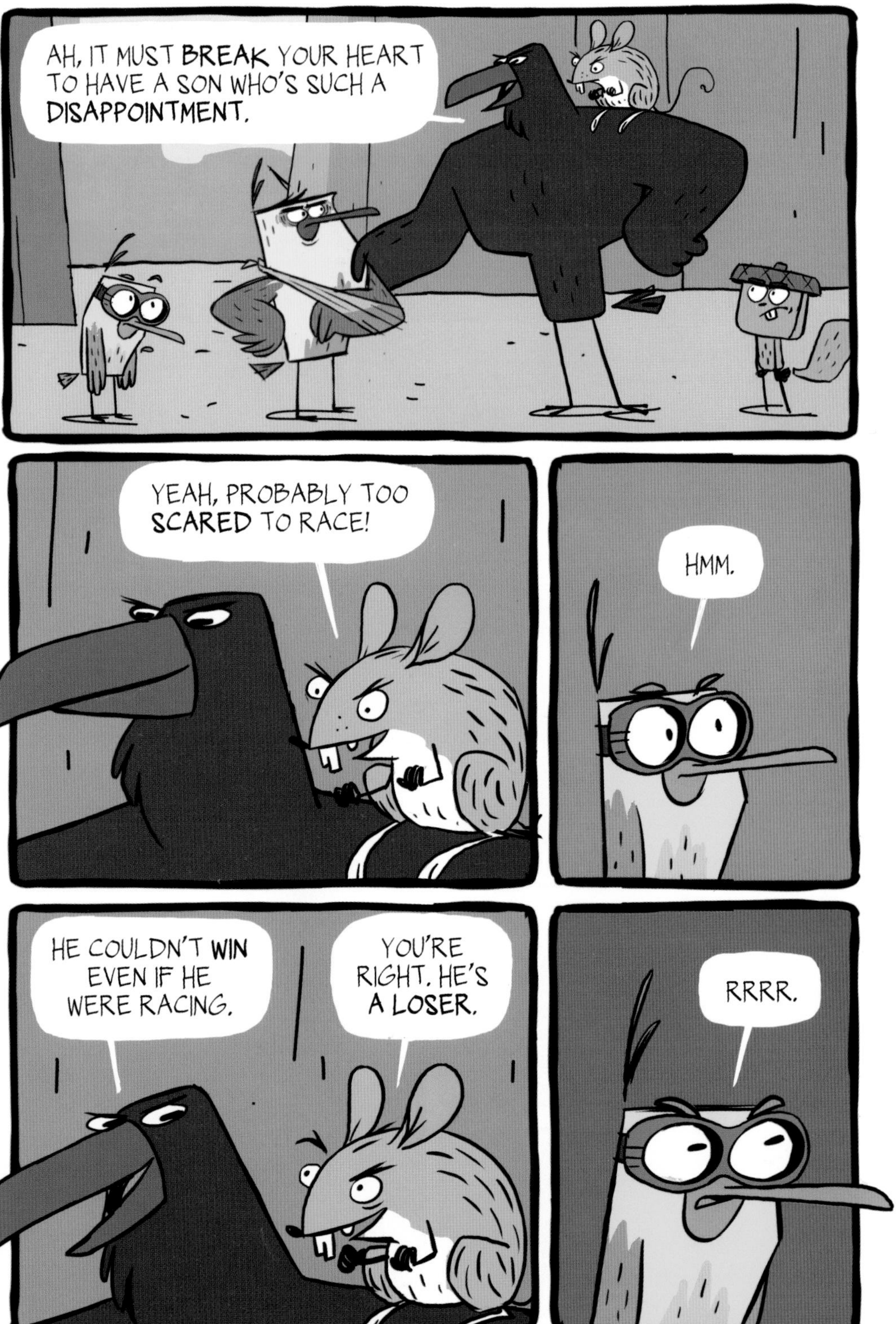
AH, IT MUST BREAK YOUR HEART TO HAVE A SON WHO'S SUCH A DISAPPOINTMENT.
YEAH, PROBABLY TOO SCARED TO RACE!
HMM.
HE COULDN'T WIN EVEN IF HE WERE RACING.
YOU'RE RIGHT. HE'S A LOSER.
RRRR.

HEY! BIRD CAN FLY **CIRCLES** AROUND YOU BOTH AND **WIN** THIS RACE IF—

W H O A!!

IF HE WEREN'T A **COWARD!**

SHOW 'EM WHAT WE DO TO **COWARDS,** CROW!

HEY!

PUT ME **DOWN!!**

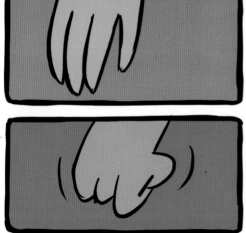

THAT'S IT!

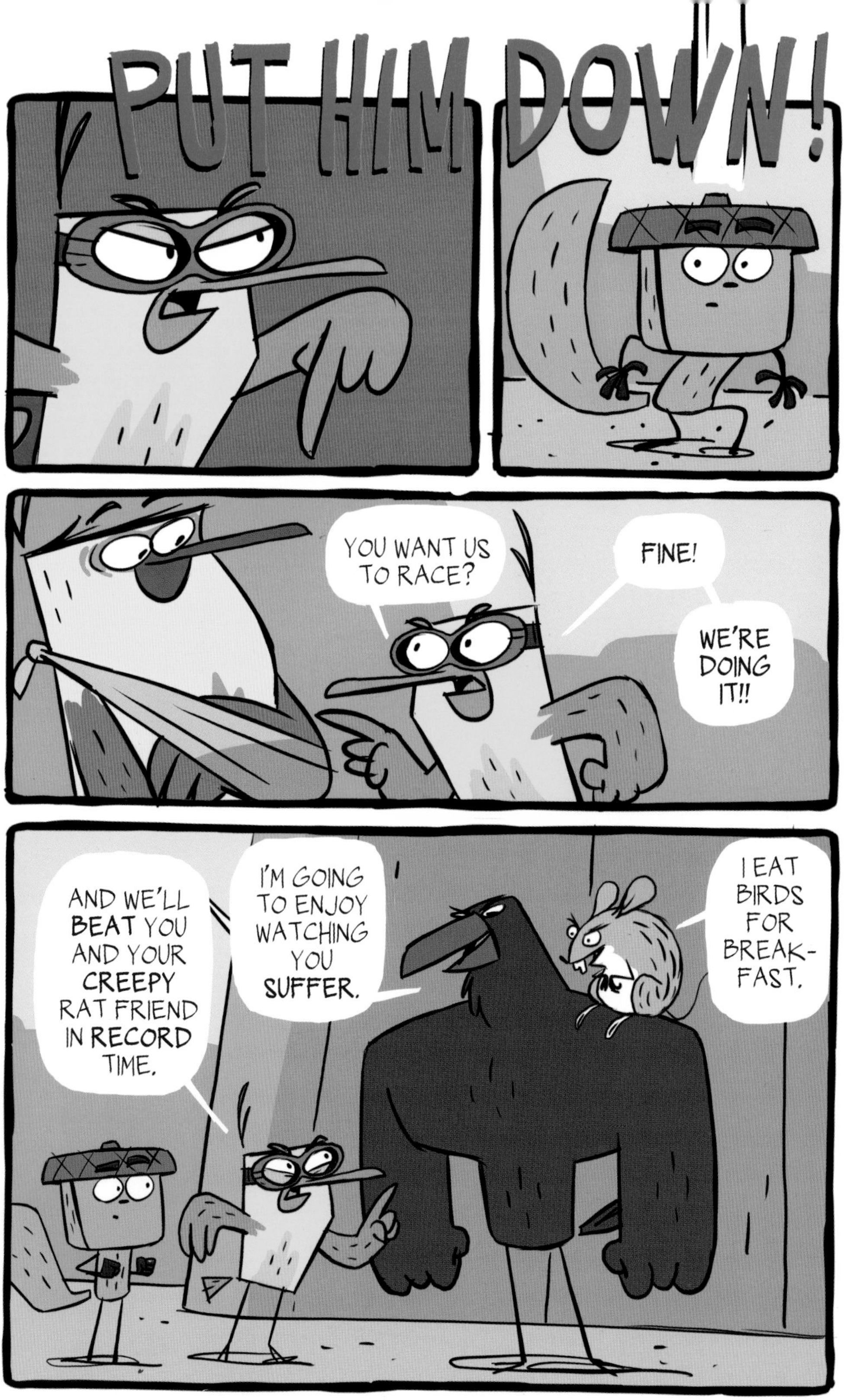
PUT HIM DOWN!
YOU WANT US TO RACE?
FINE!
WE'RE DOING IT!!
AND WE'LL BEAT YOU AND YOUR CREEPY RAT FRIEND IN RECORD TIME.
I'M GOING TO ENJOY WATCHING YOU SUFFER.
I EAT BIRDS FOR BREAK-FAST.

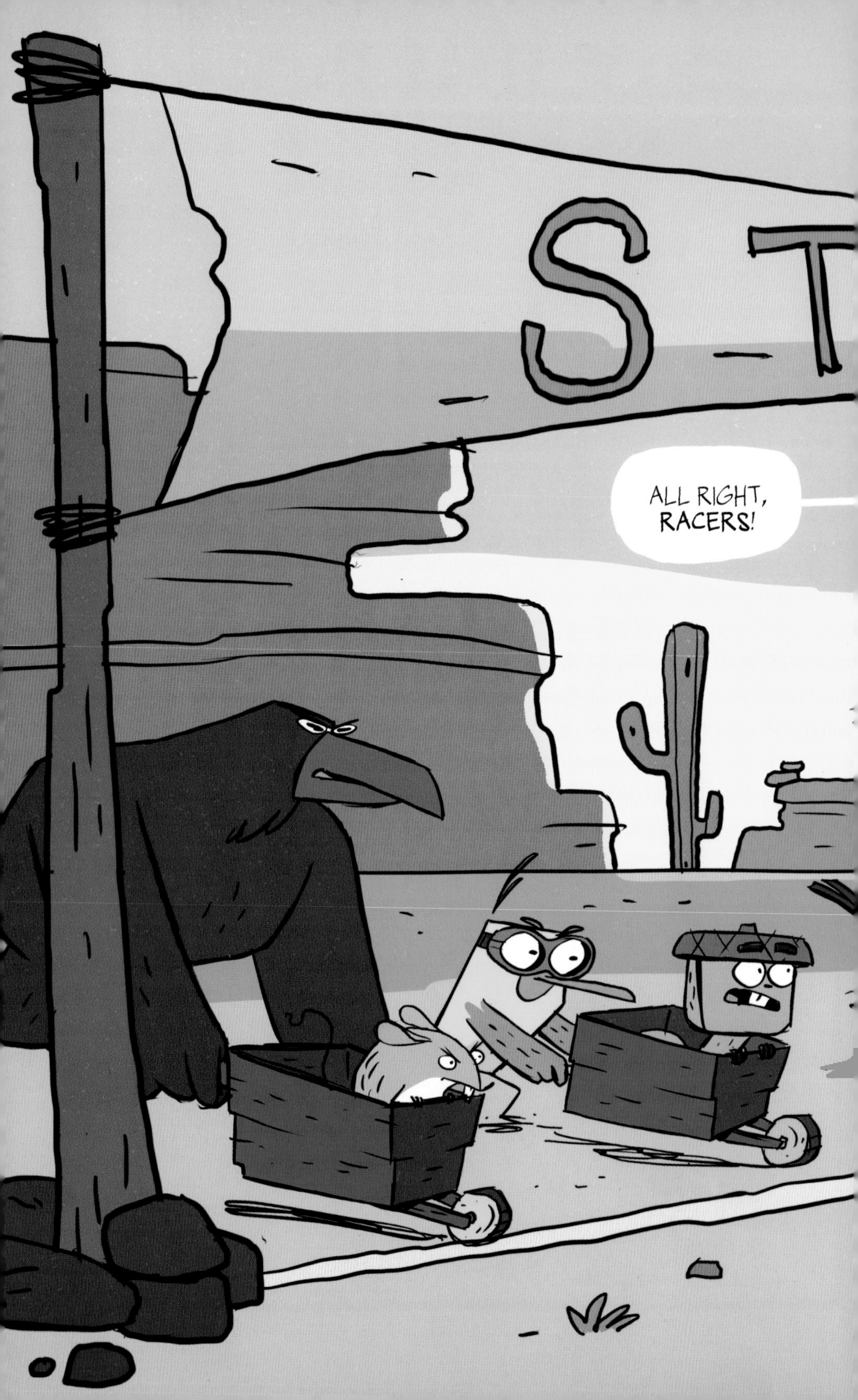
ST
ALL RIGHT, RACERS!

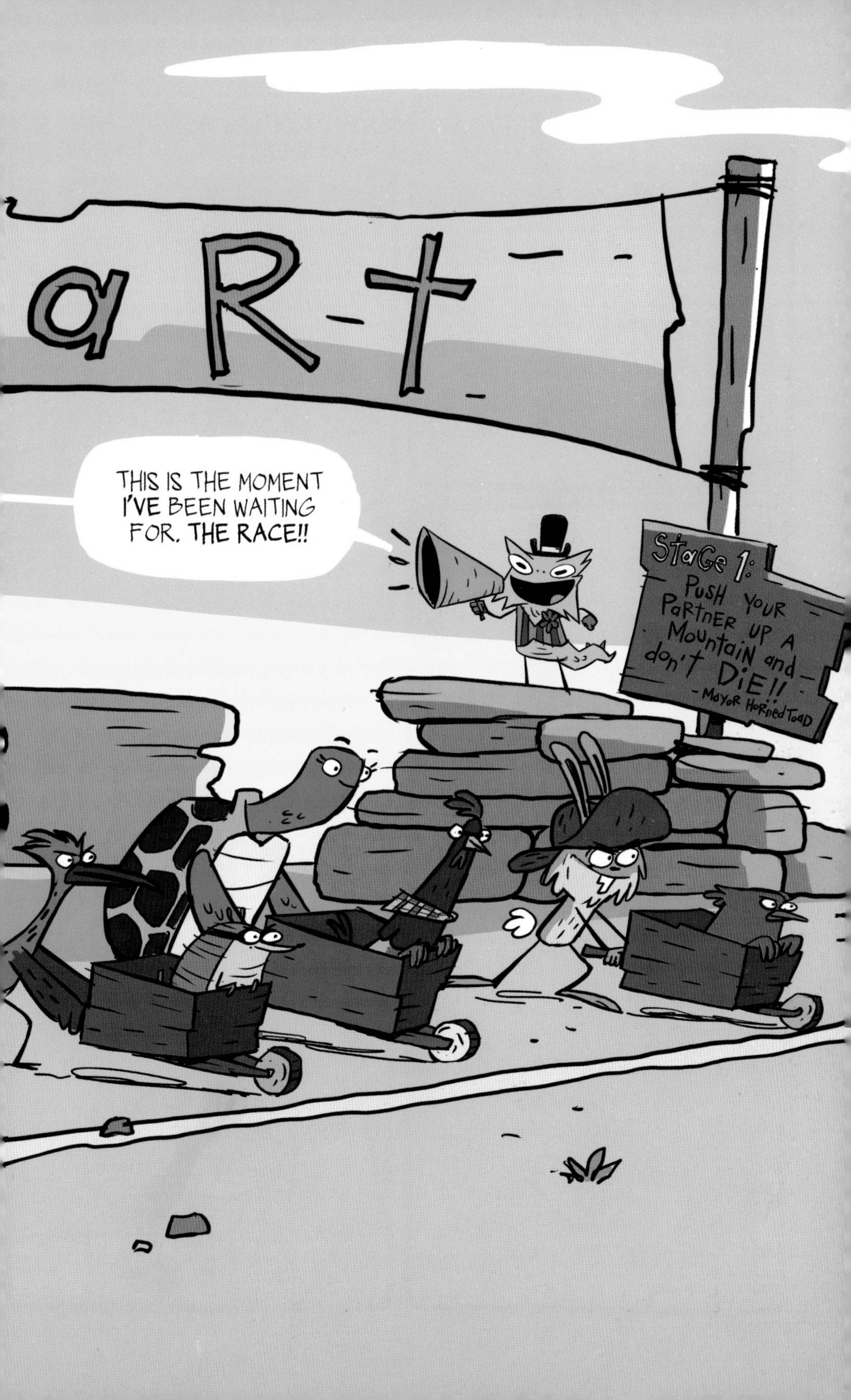
aRt
THIS IS THE MOMENT I'VE BEEN WAITING FOR. THE RACE!!
Stage 1: PUSH YOUR PaRtNER UP A Mountain and don't DiE!!
-MaYoR HoRned Toad

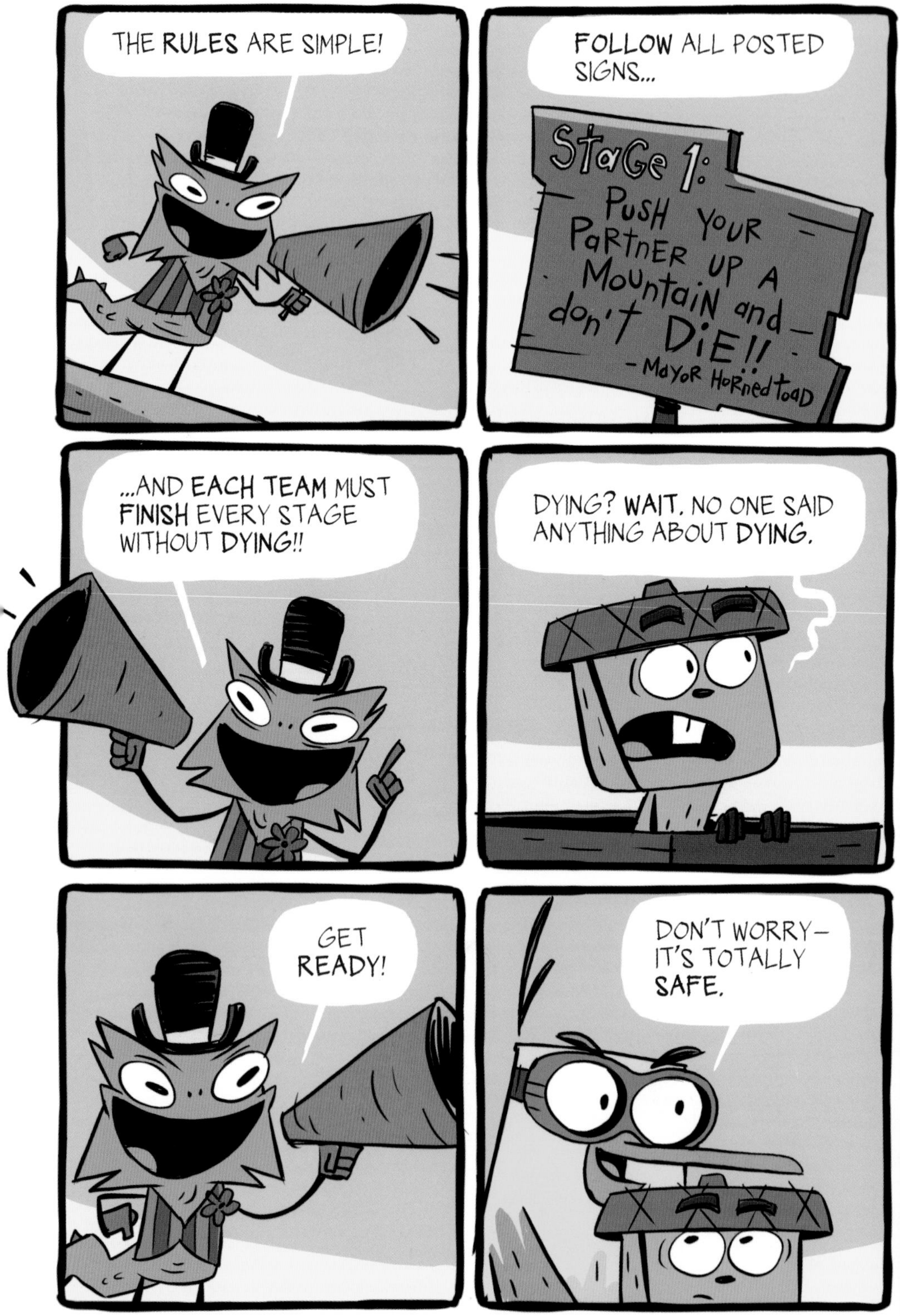
THE RULES ARE SIMPLE!
FOLLOW ALL POSTED SIGNS...
Stage 1: Push your Partner up a Mountain and don't DiE!! -Mayor Horned toad
...AND EACH TEAM MUST FINISH EVERY STAGE WITHOUT DYING!!
DYING? WAIT. NO ONE SAID ANYTHING ABOUT DYING.
GET READY!
DON'T WORRY— IT'S TOTALLY SAFE.

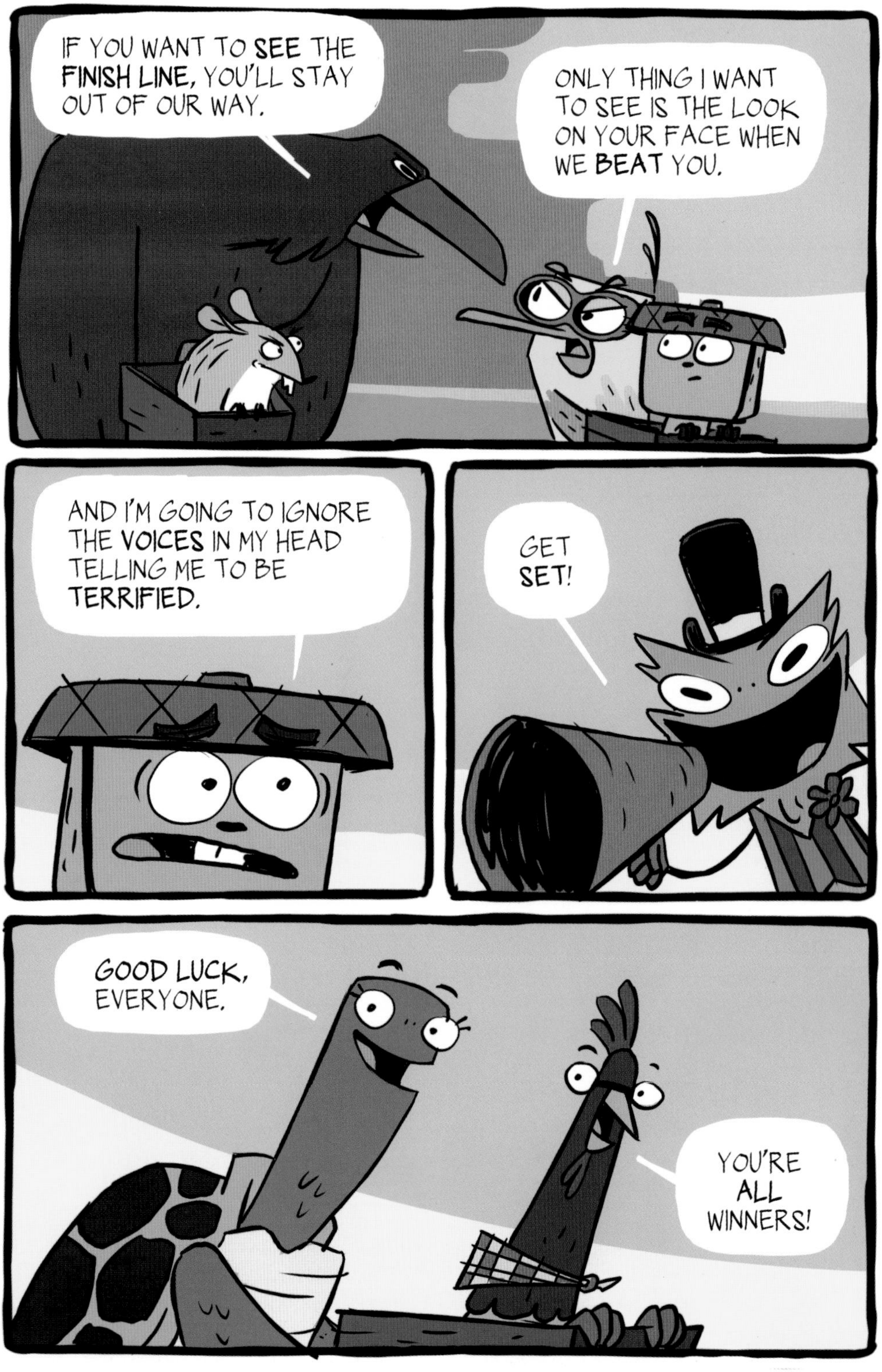
IF YOU WANT TO SEE THE FINISH LINE, YOU'LL STAY OUT OF OUR WAY.
ONLY THING I WANT TO SEE IS THE LOOK ON YOUR FACE WHEN WE BEAT YOU.
AND I'M GOING TO IGNORE THE VOICES IN MY HEAD TELLING ME TO BE TERRIFIED.
GET SET!
GOOD LUCK, EVERYONE.
YOU'RE ALL WINNERS!

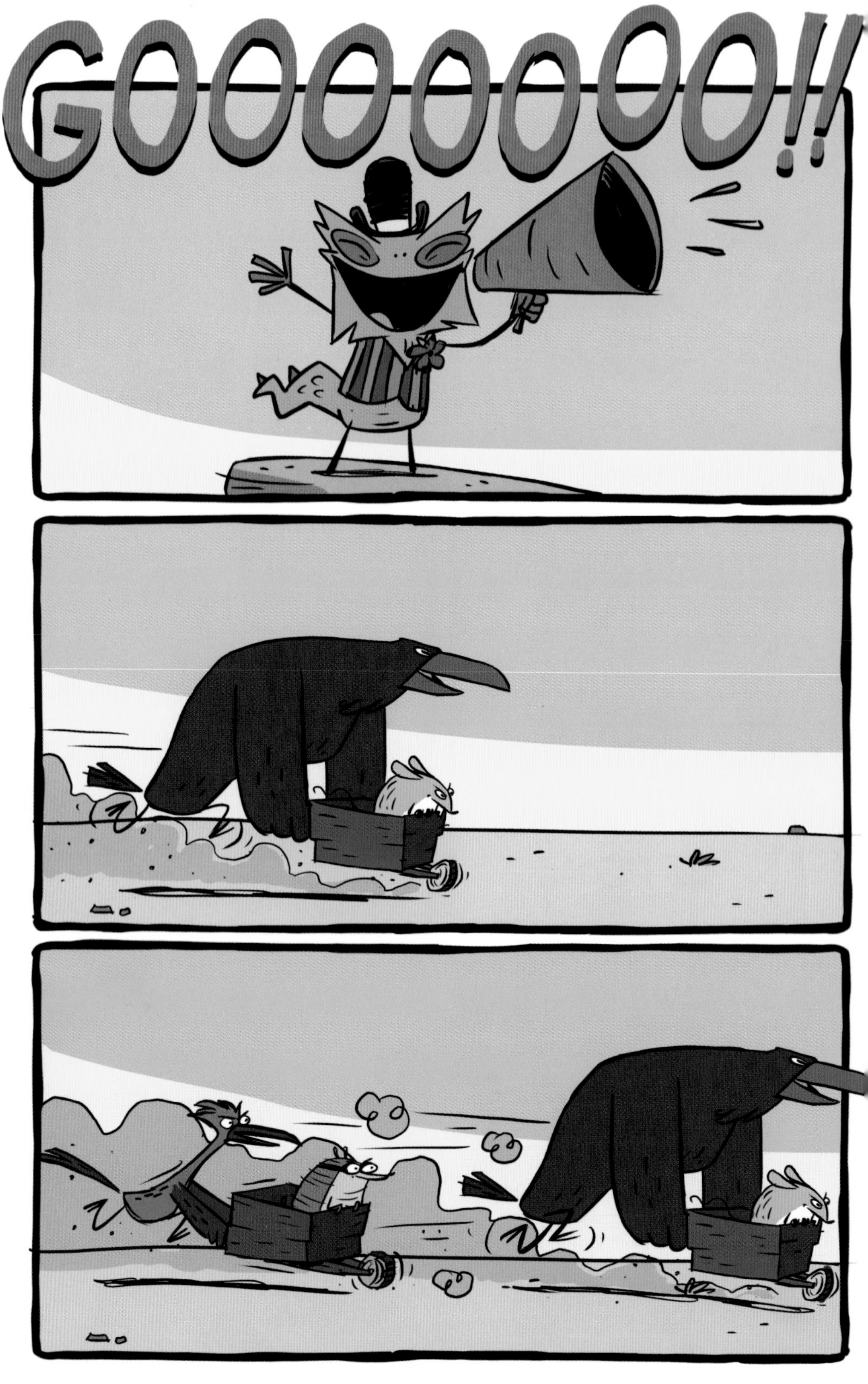
GOOOOOOOO!!

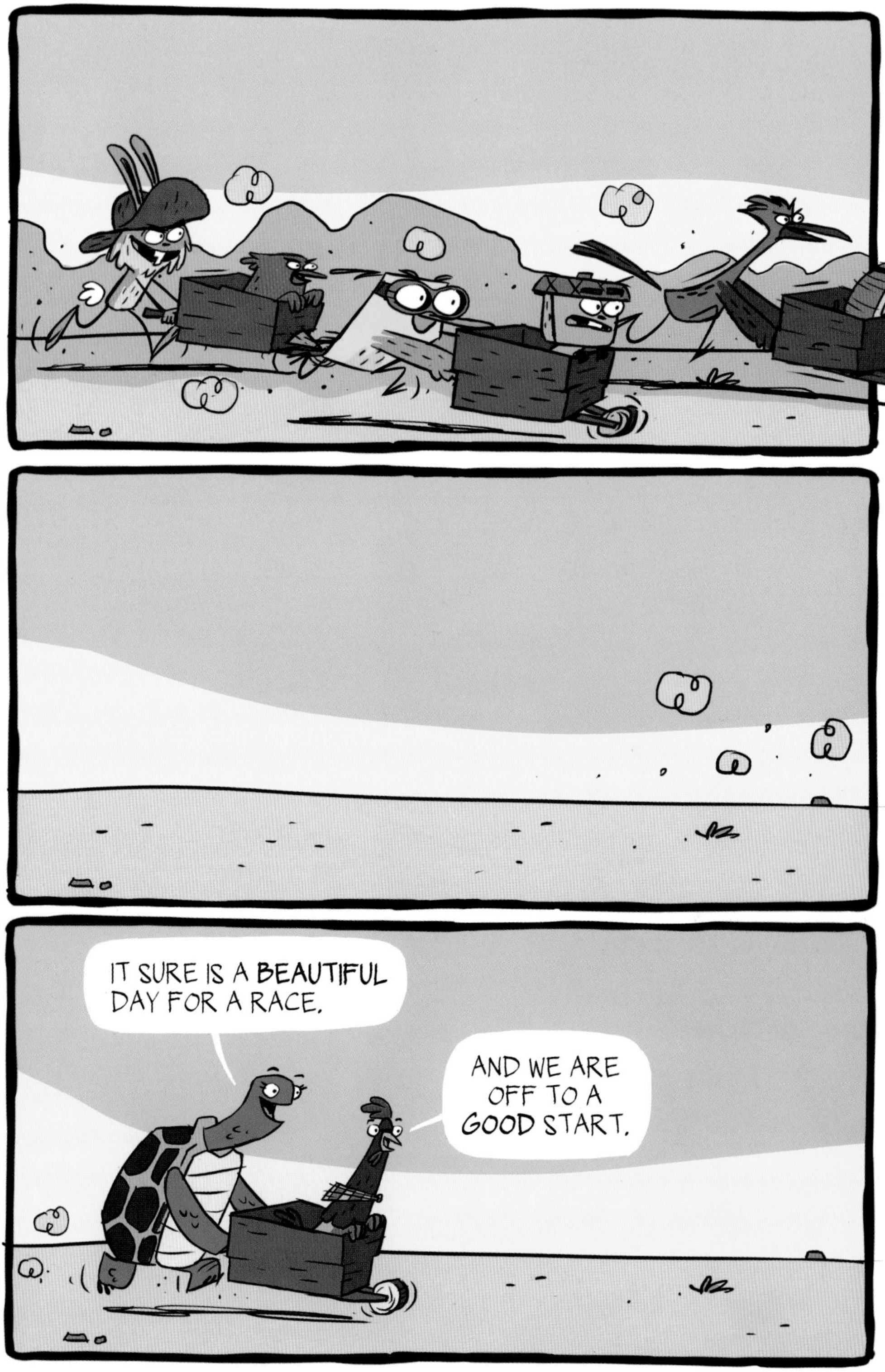
IT SURE IS A BEAUTIFUL DAY FOR A RACE.
AND WE ARE OFF TO A GOOD START.

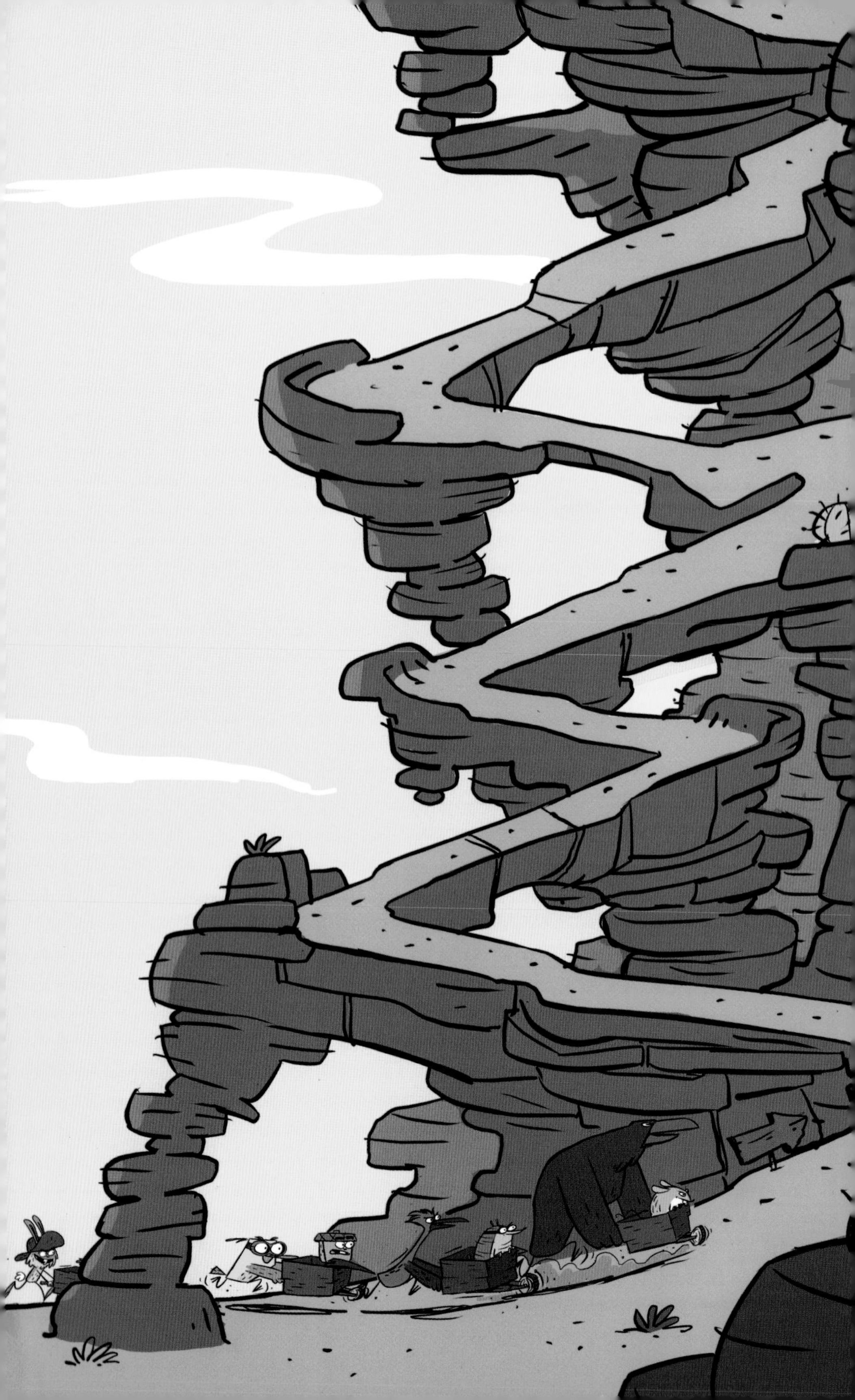

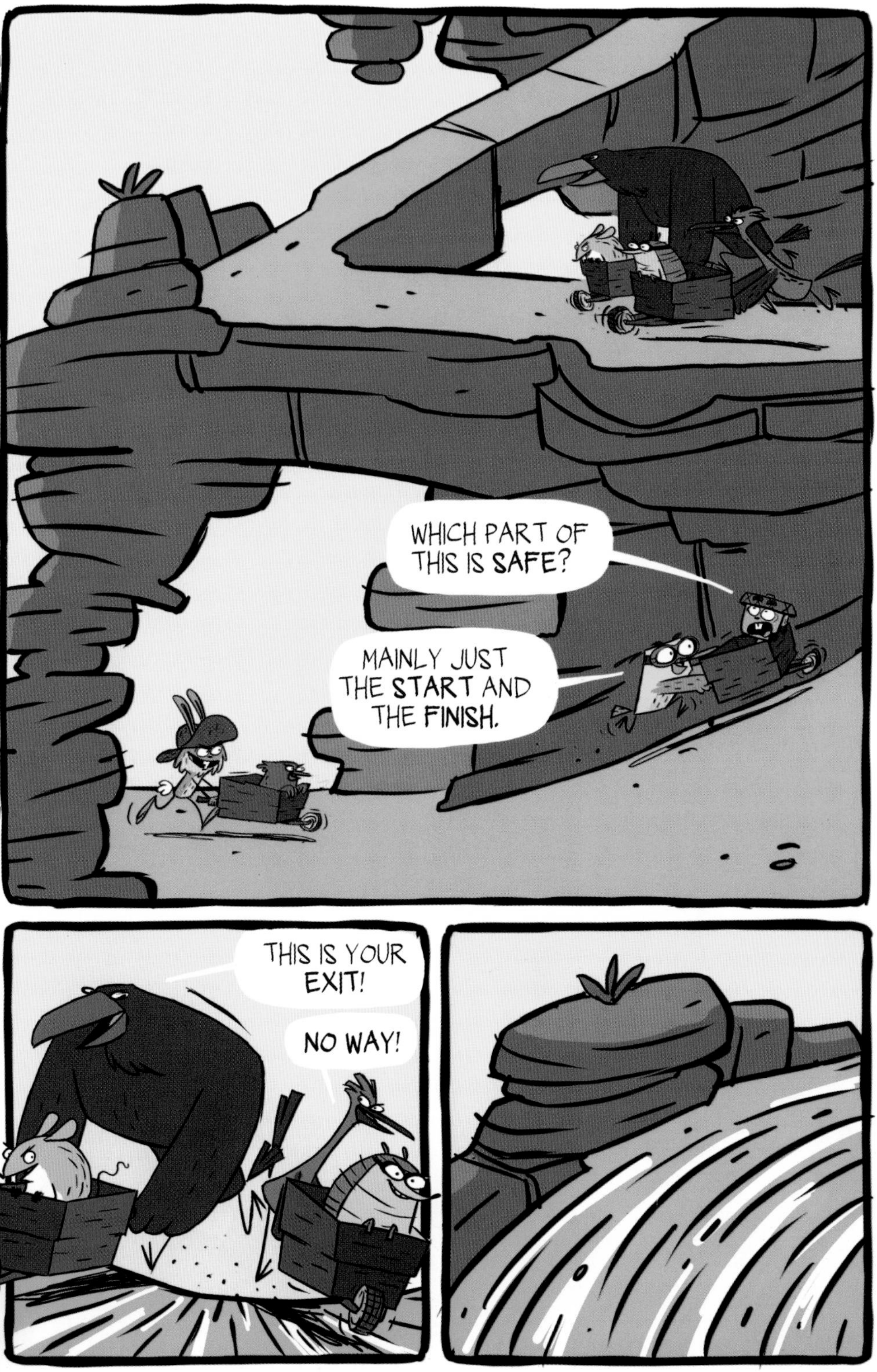
WHICH PART OF THIS IS SAFE?
MAINLY JUST THE START AND THE FINISH.
THIS IS YOUR EXIT!
NO WAY!

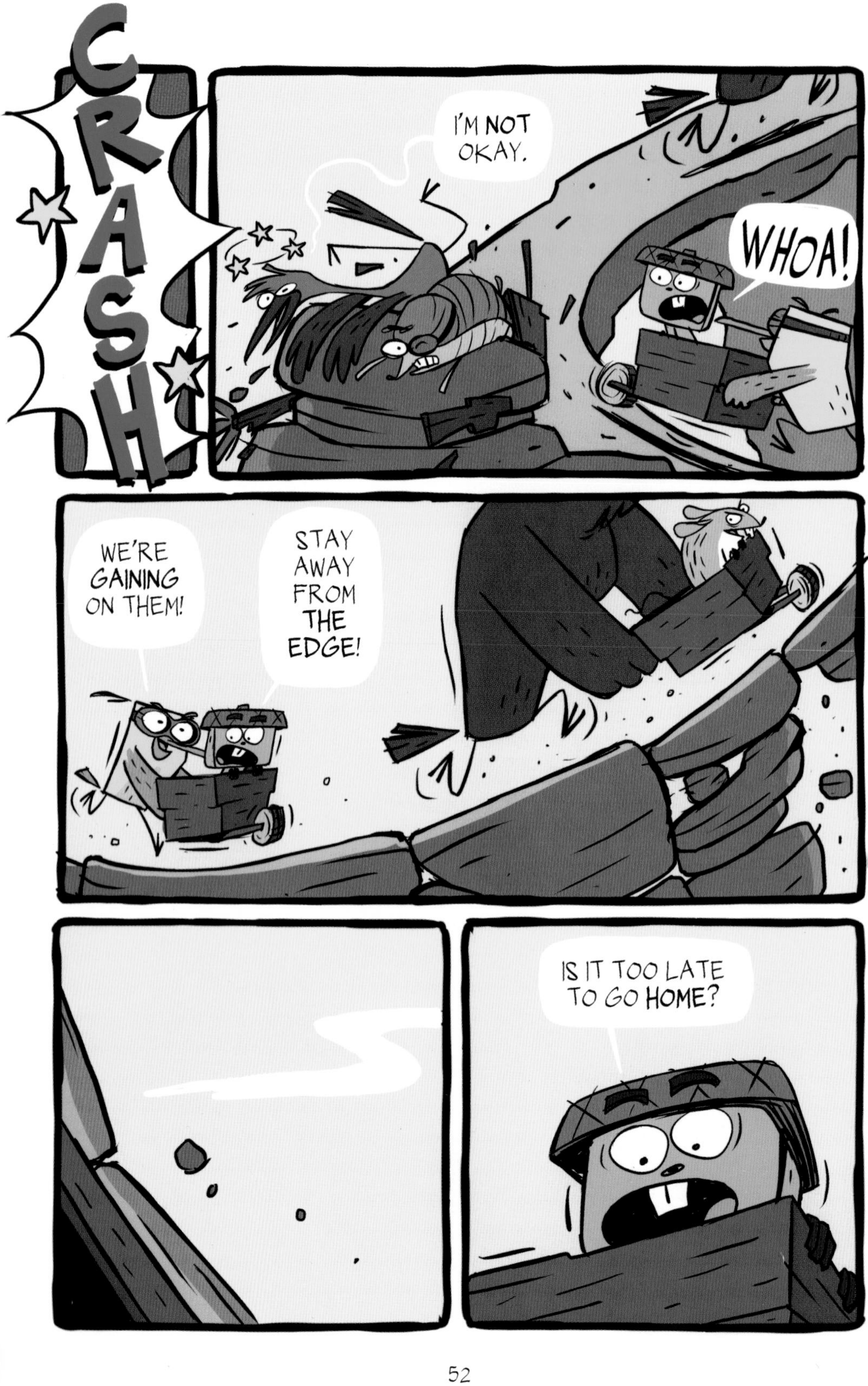
CRASH
I'M NOT OKAY.
WHOA!
WE'RE GAINING ON THEM!
STAY AWAY FROM THE EDGE!
IS IT TOO LATE TO GO HOME?

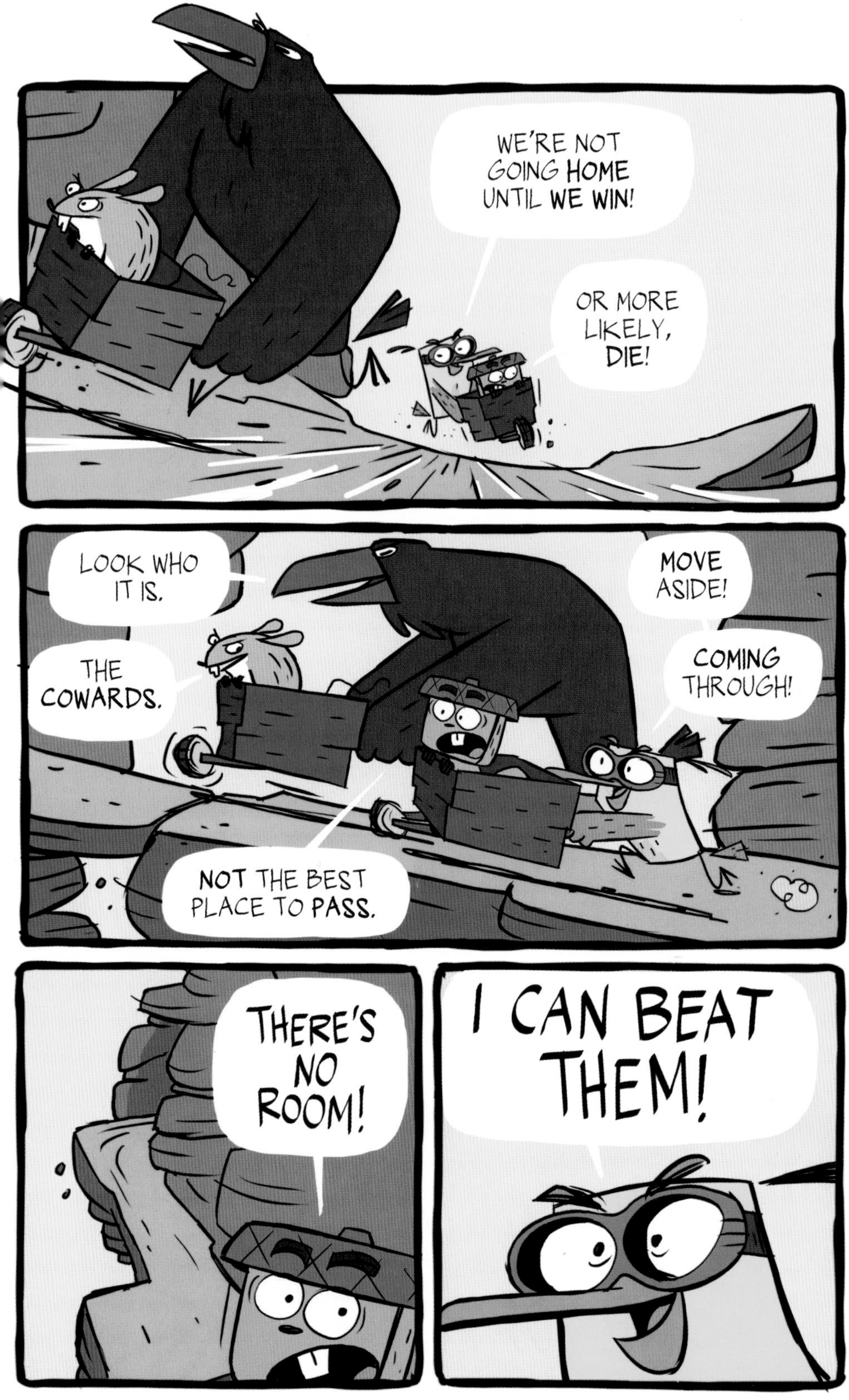
WE'RE NOT GOING HOME UNTIL WE WIN!
OR MORE LIKELY, DIE!
LOOK WHO IT IS.
THE COWARDS.
MOVE ASIDE!
COMING THROUGH!
NOT THE BEST PLACE TO PASS.
THERE'S NO ROOM!
I CAN BEAT THEM!

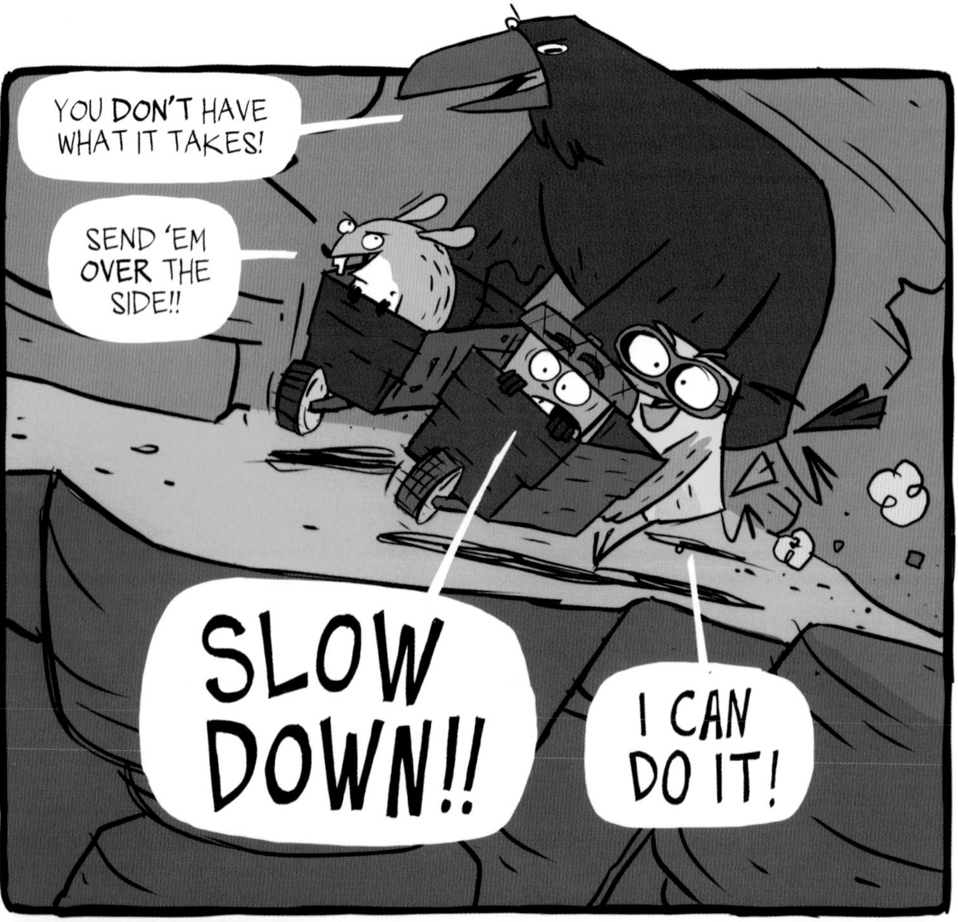
YOU DON'T HAVE WHAT IT TAKES!
SEND 'EM OVER THE SIDE!!
SLOW DOWN!!
I CAN DO IT!

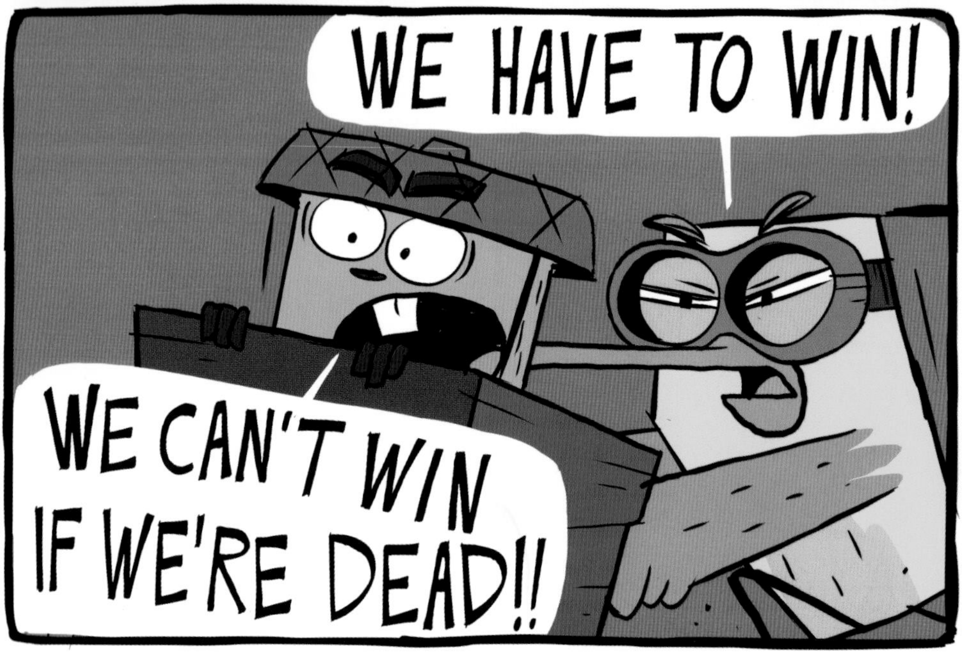
WE HAVE TO WIN!
WE CAN'T WIN IF WE'RE DEAD!!

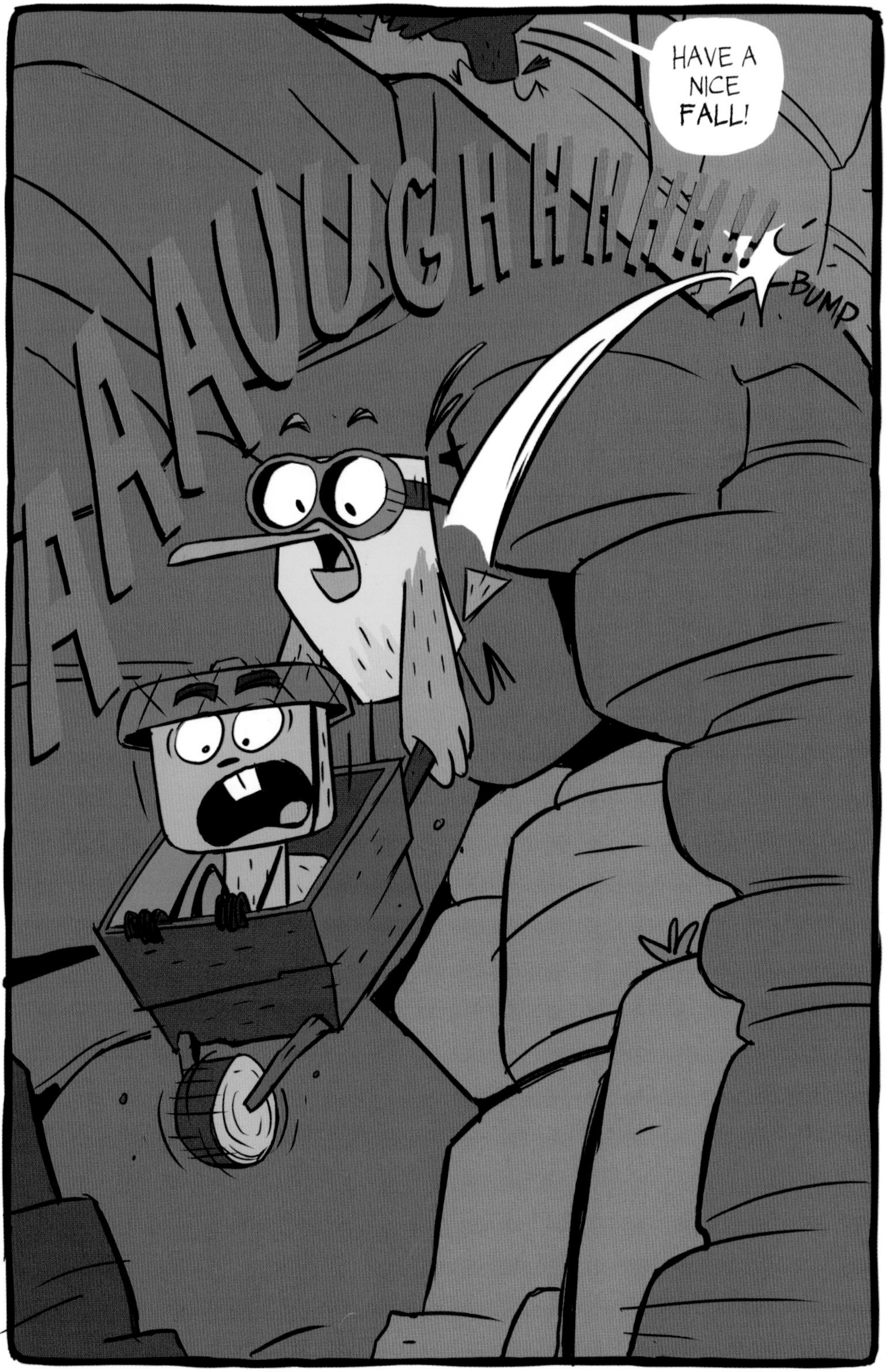
HAVE A NICE FALL!
AAAUUGHHHHH!!
BUMP

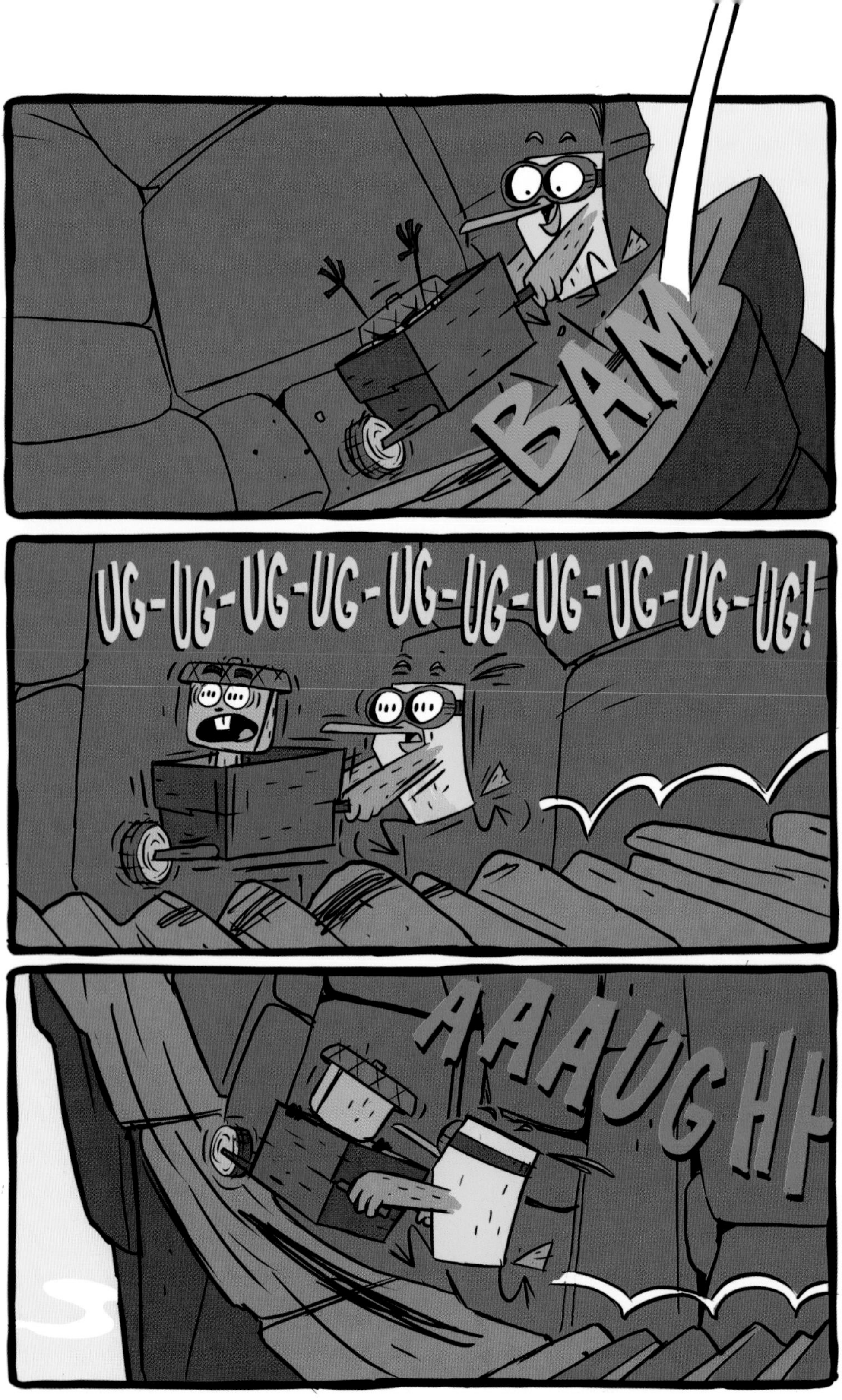
BAM
UG-UG-UG-UG-UG-UG-UG-UG-UG-UG!
AAAUGHH

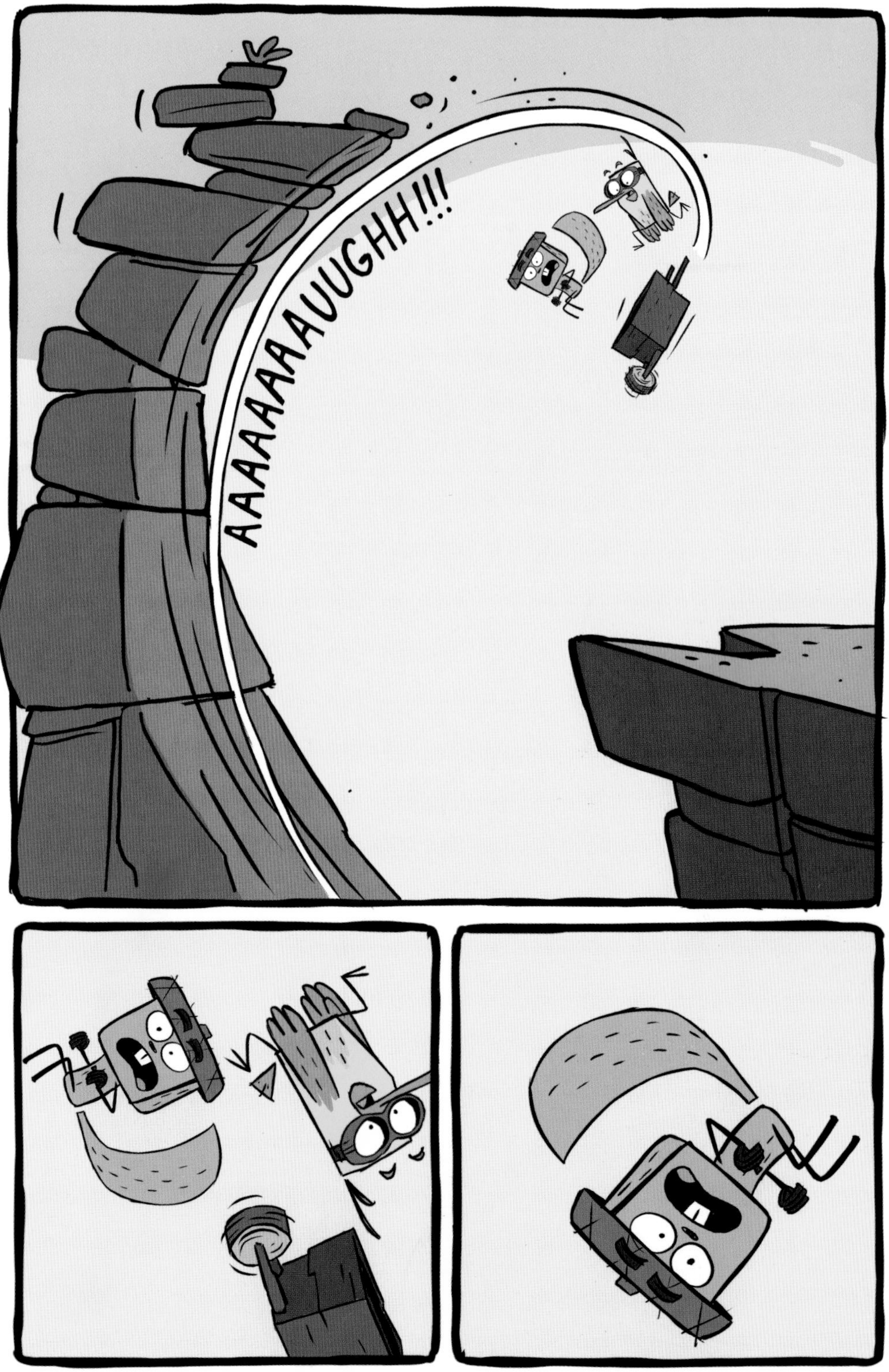
AAAAAAAUUGHH!!!

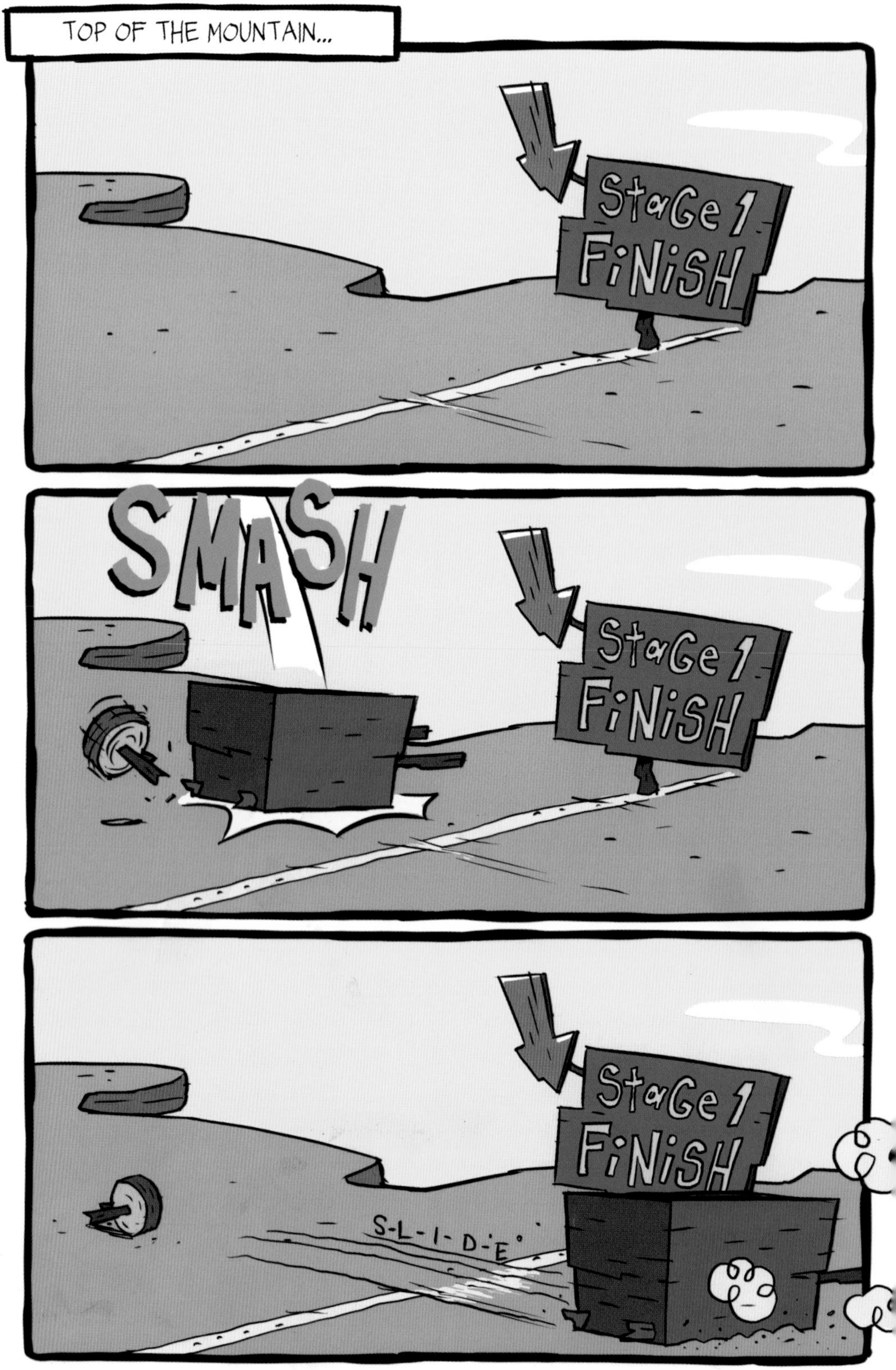
TOP OF THE MOUNTAIN...
Stage 1
FiNiSH
SMASH
Stage 1
FiNiSH
Stage 1
FiNiSH
S-L-I-D-E

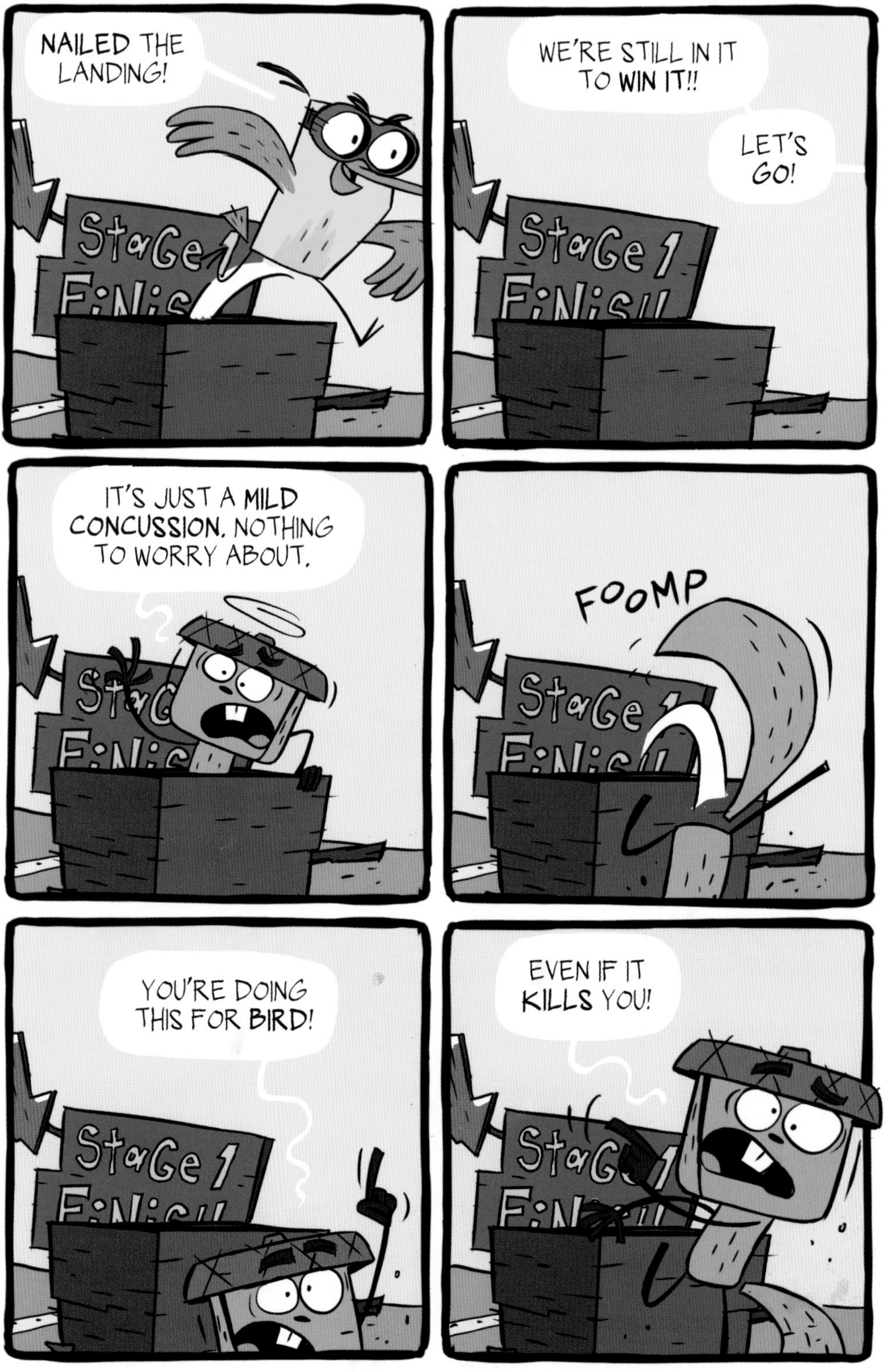
NAILED THE LANDING!
Stage 1 Finish
WE'RE STILL IN IT TO WIN IT!!
LET'S GO!
IT'S JUST A MILD CONCUSSION. NOTHING TO WORRY ABOUT.
FOOMP
YOU'RE DOING THIS FOR BIRD!
EVEN IF IT KILLS YOU!

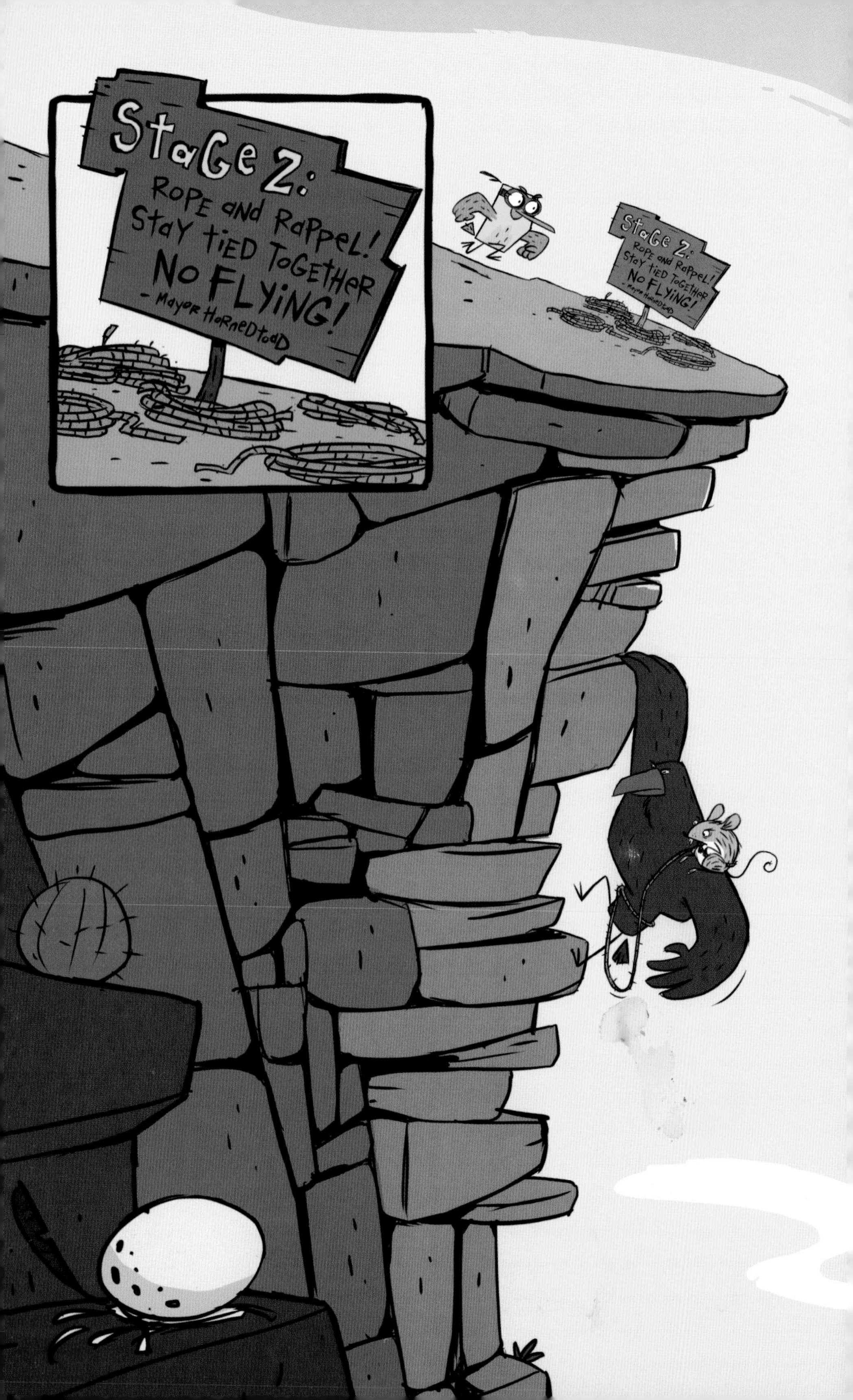
Stage 2:
Rope and Rappel!
Stay tied together
No FLYING!
- Mayor Hornedtoad
Stage 2:
Rope and Rappel!
Stay tied together
No FLYING!
- Mayor Hornedtoad

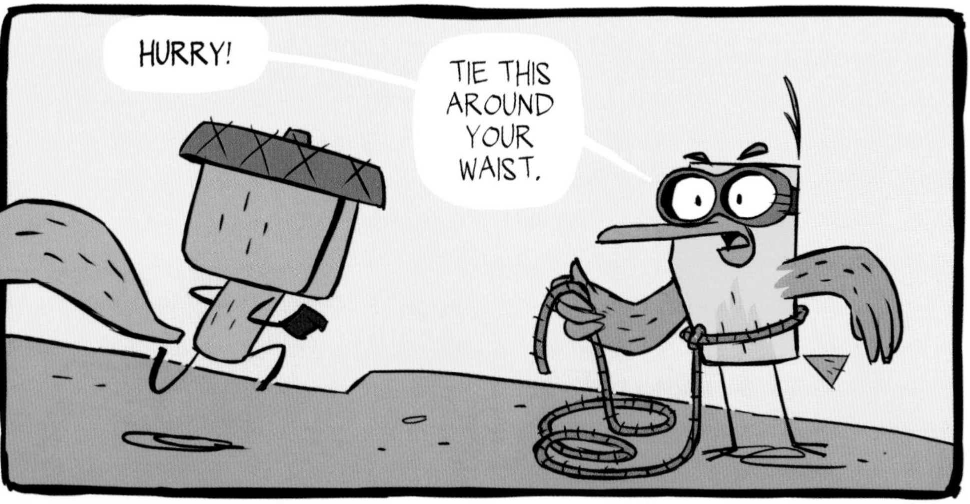
HURRY!
TIE THIS AROUND YOUR WAIST.

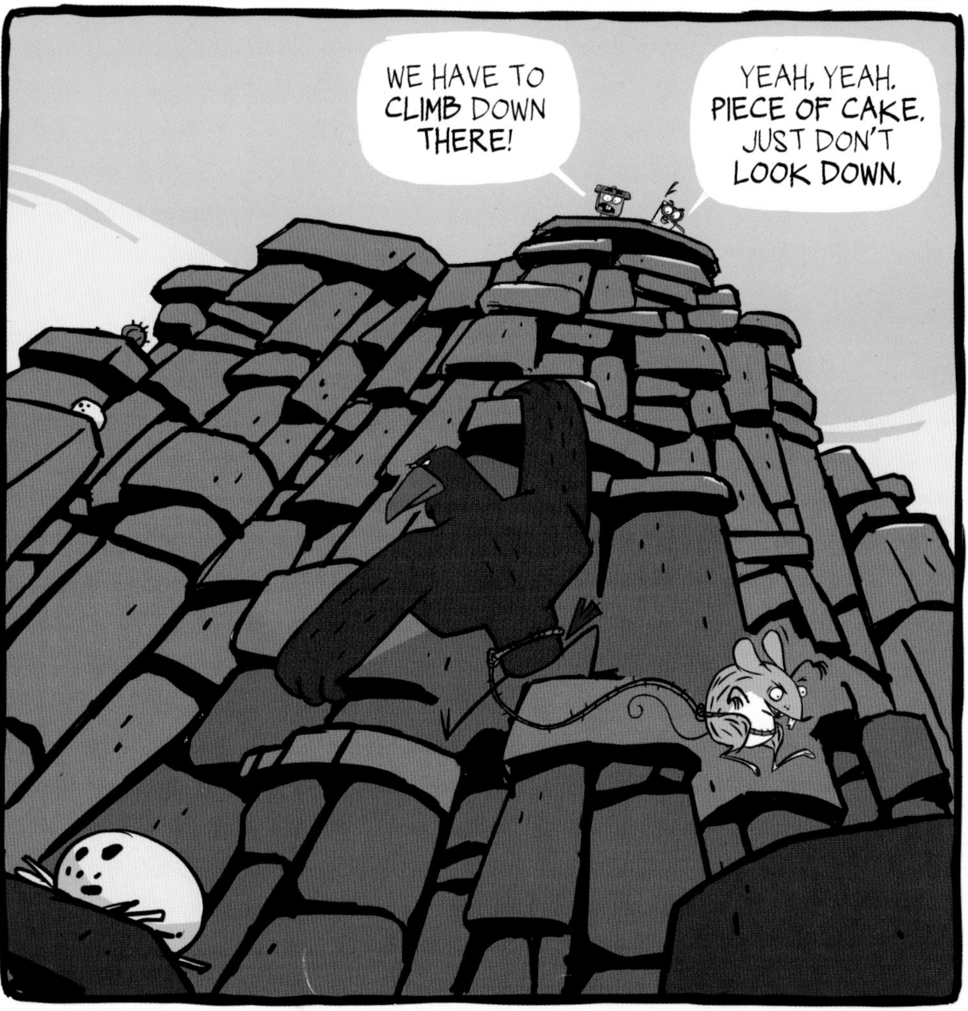
WE HAVE TO CLIMB DOWN THERE!
YEAH, YEAH. PIECE OF CAKE. JUST DON'T LOOK DOWN.

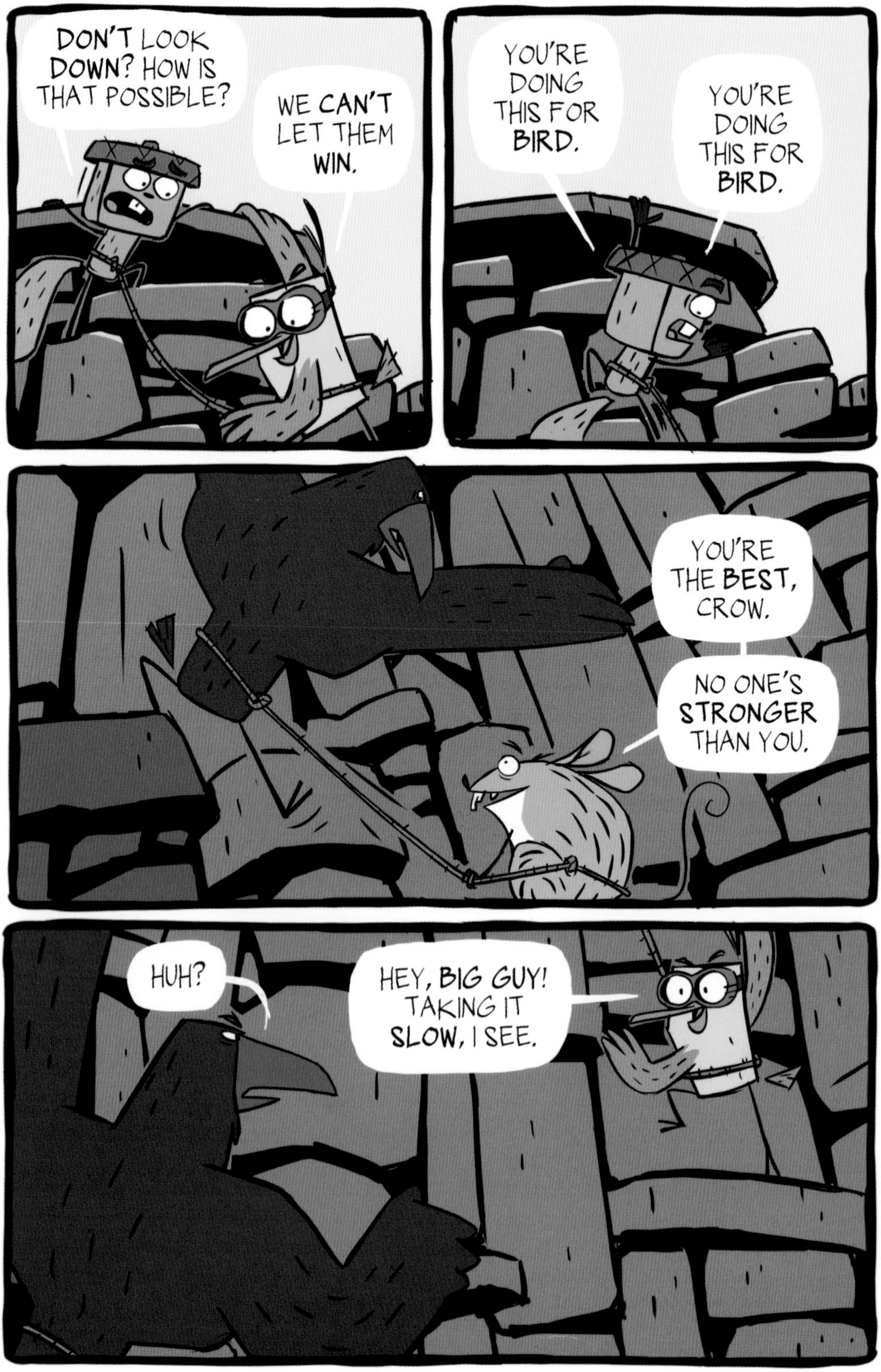
DON'T LOOK DOWN? HOW IS THAT POSSIBLE?
WE CAN'T LET THEM WIN.
YOU'RE DOING THIS FOR BIRD.
YOU'RE DOING THIS FOR BIRD.
YOU'RE THE BEST, CROW.
NO ONE'S STRONGER THAN YOU.
HUH?
HEY, BIG GUY! TAKING IT SLOW, I SEE.

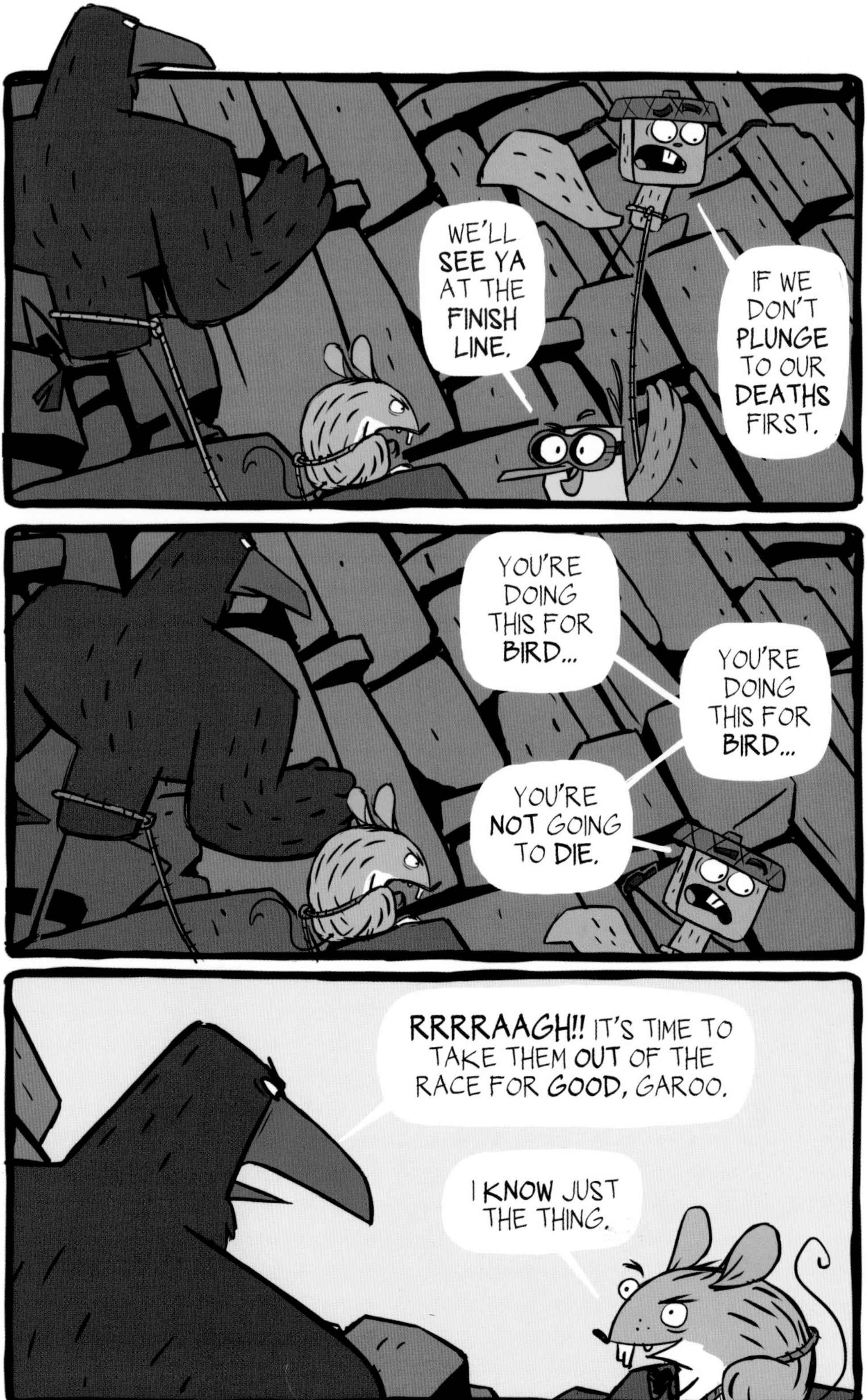
WE'LL SEE YA AT THE FINISH LINE.
IF WE DON'T PLUNGE TO OUR DEATHS FIRST.
YOU'RE DOING THIS FOR BIRD...
YOU'RE DOING THIS FOR BIRD...
YOU'RE NOT GOING TO DIE.
RRRRAAGH!! IT'S TIME TO TAKE THEM OUT OF THE RACE FOR GOOD, GAROO.
I KNOW JUST THE THING.

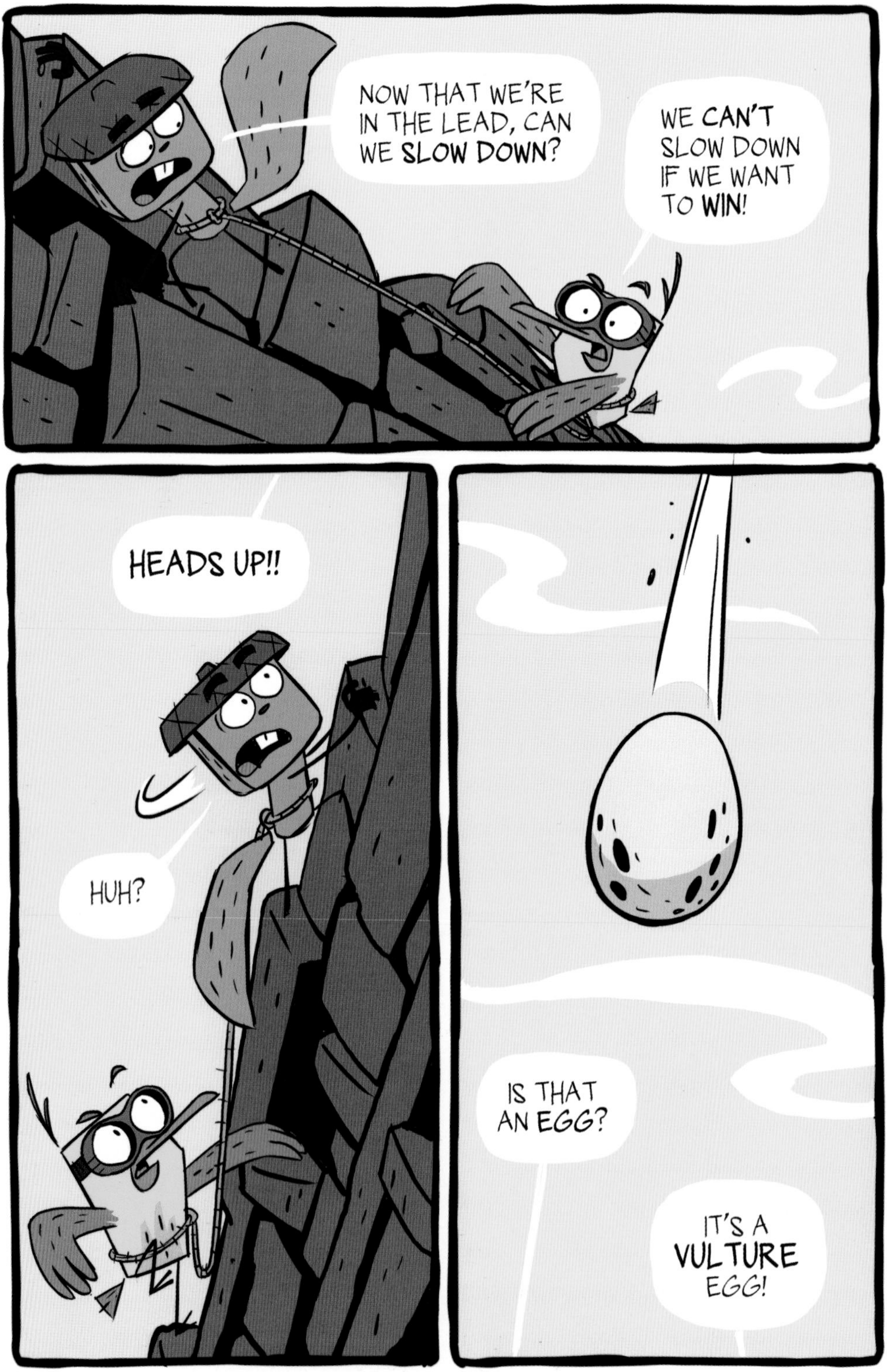
NOW THAT WE'RE IN THE LEAD, CAN WE SLOW DOWN?
WE CAN'T SLOW DOWN IF WE WANT TO WIN!
HEADS UP!!
HUH?
IS THAT AN EGG?
IT'S A VULTURE EGG!

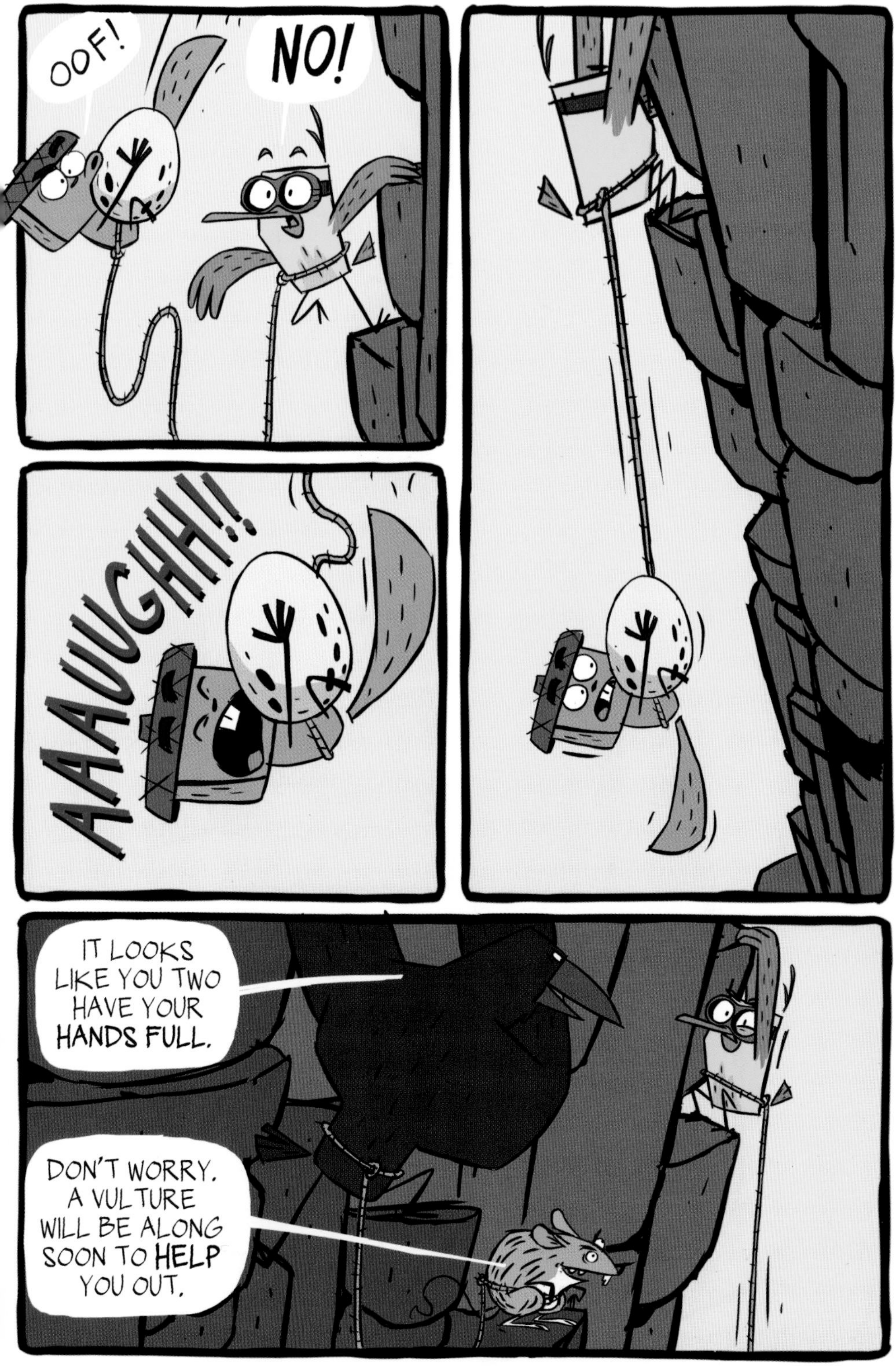
OOF!
NO!
AAAUUGHH!!
IT LOOKS LIKE YOU TWO HAVE YOUR **HANDS FULL**.
DON'T WORRY. A VULTURE WILL BE ALONG SOON TO **HELP** YOU OUT.

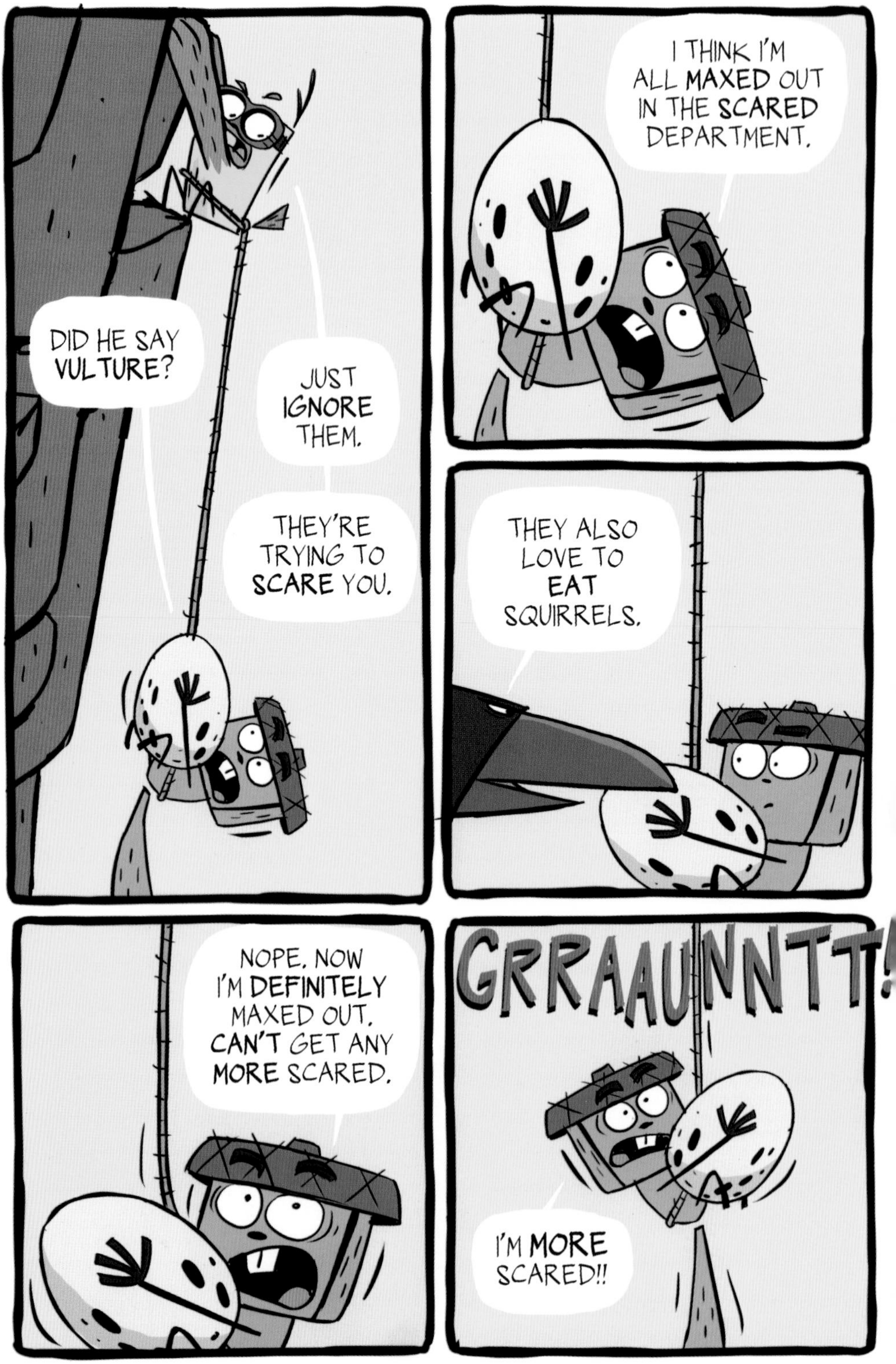
DID HE SAY VULTURE?
JUST IGNORE THEM.
THEY'RE TRYING TO SCARE YOU.
I THINK I'M ALL MAXED OUT IN THE SCARED DEPARTMENT.
THEY ALSO LOVE TO EAT SQUIRRELS.
NOPE. NOW I'M DEFINITELY MAXED OUT. CAN'T GET ANY MORE SCARED.
GRRAAUNNTT!
I'M MORE SCARED!!

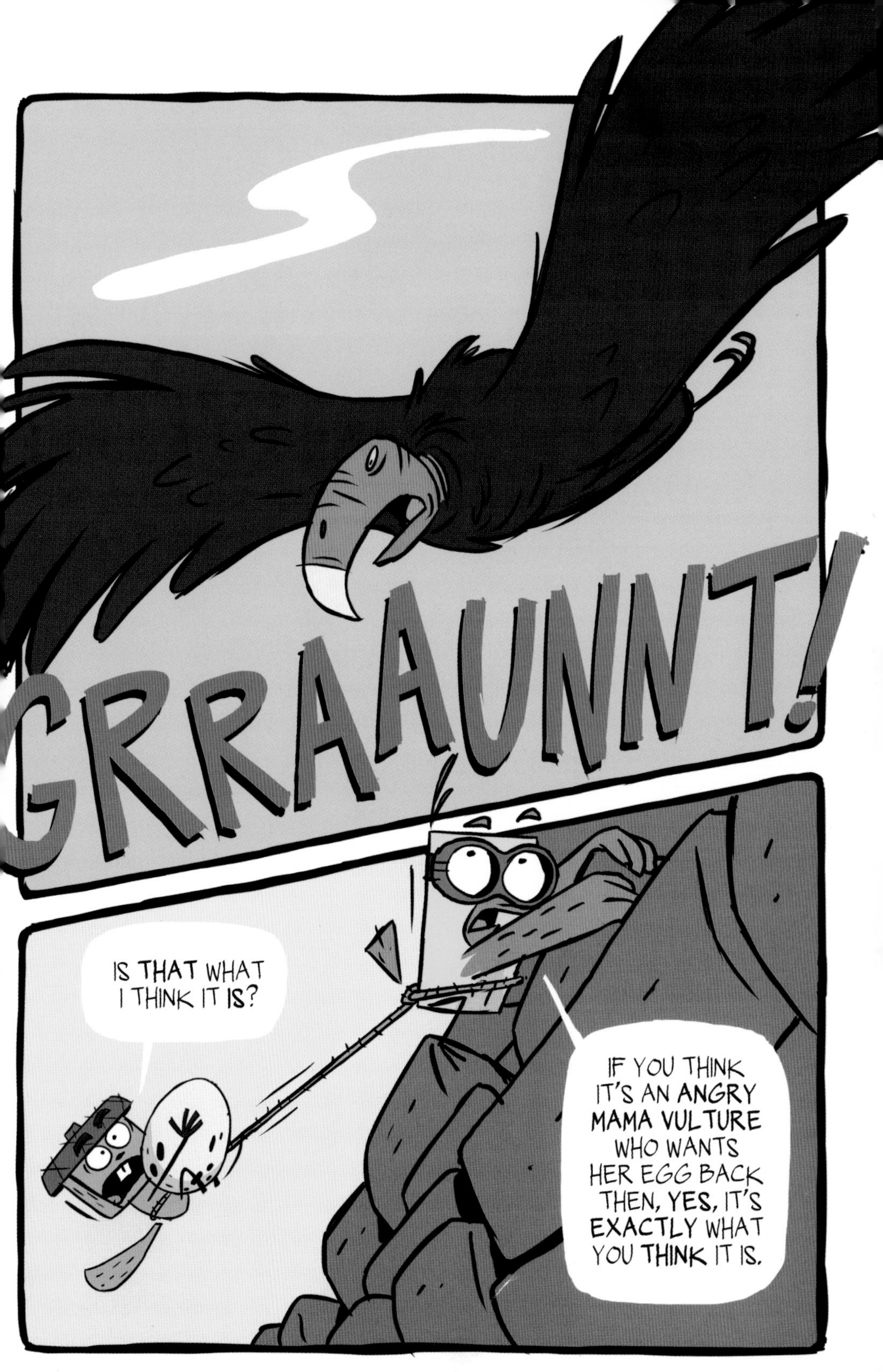

GRRAAUNNT!
IS THAT WHAT I THINK IT IS?
IF YOU THINK IT'S AN ANGRY MAMA VULTURE WHO WANTS HER EGG BACK THEN, YES, IT'S EXACTLY WHAT YOU THINK IT IS.

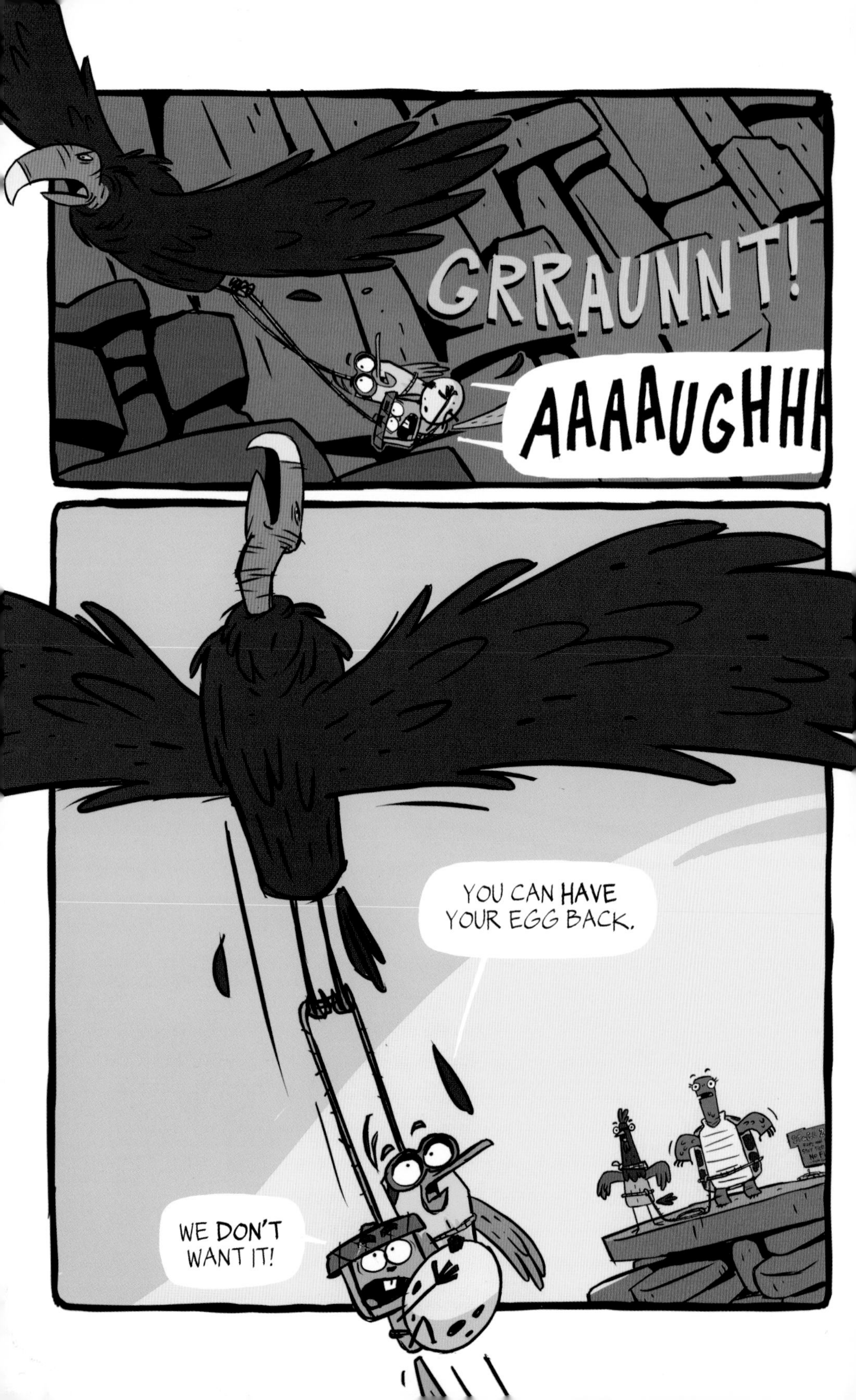
GRRAUNNT!
AAAAUGHH
YOU CAN HAVE YOUR EGG BACK.
WE DON'T WANT IT!

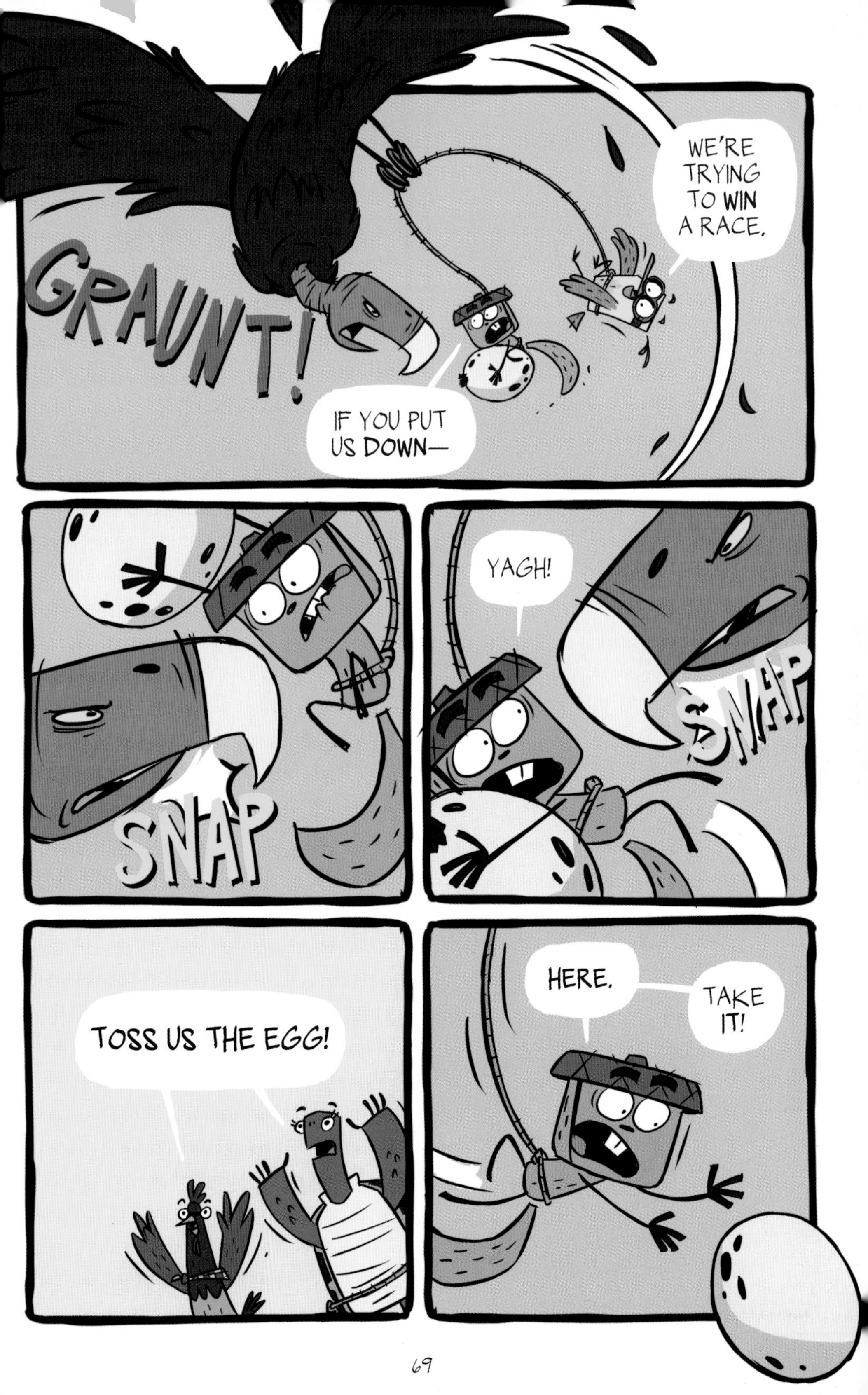
GRAUNT!
WE'RE TRYING TO WIN A RACE.
IF YOU PUT US DOWN—
SNAP
YAGH!
SNAP
TOSS US THE EGG!
HERE.
TAKE IT!

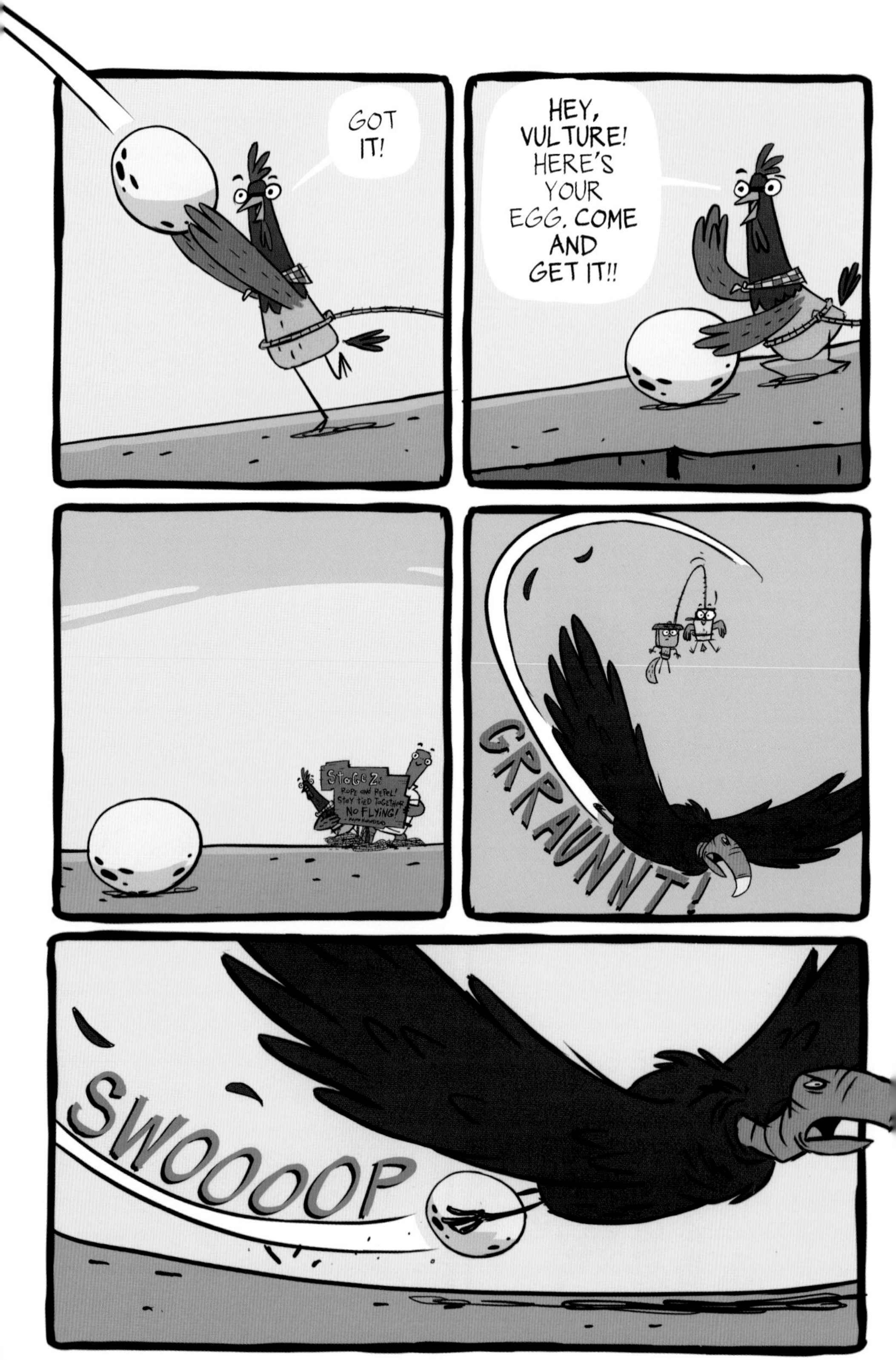
GOT IT!
HEY, VULTURE! HERE'S YOUR EGG. COME AND GET IT!!
Stage 2:
ROPE and REPEL!
STAY TIED TOGETHER
NO FLYING!
GRAUNNT!
SWOOOOP

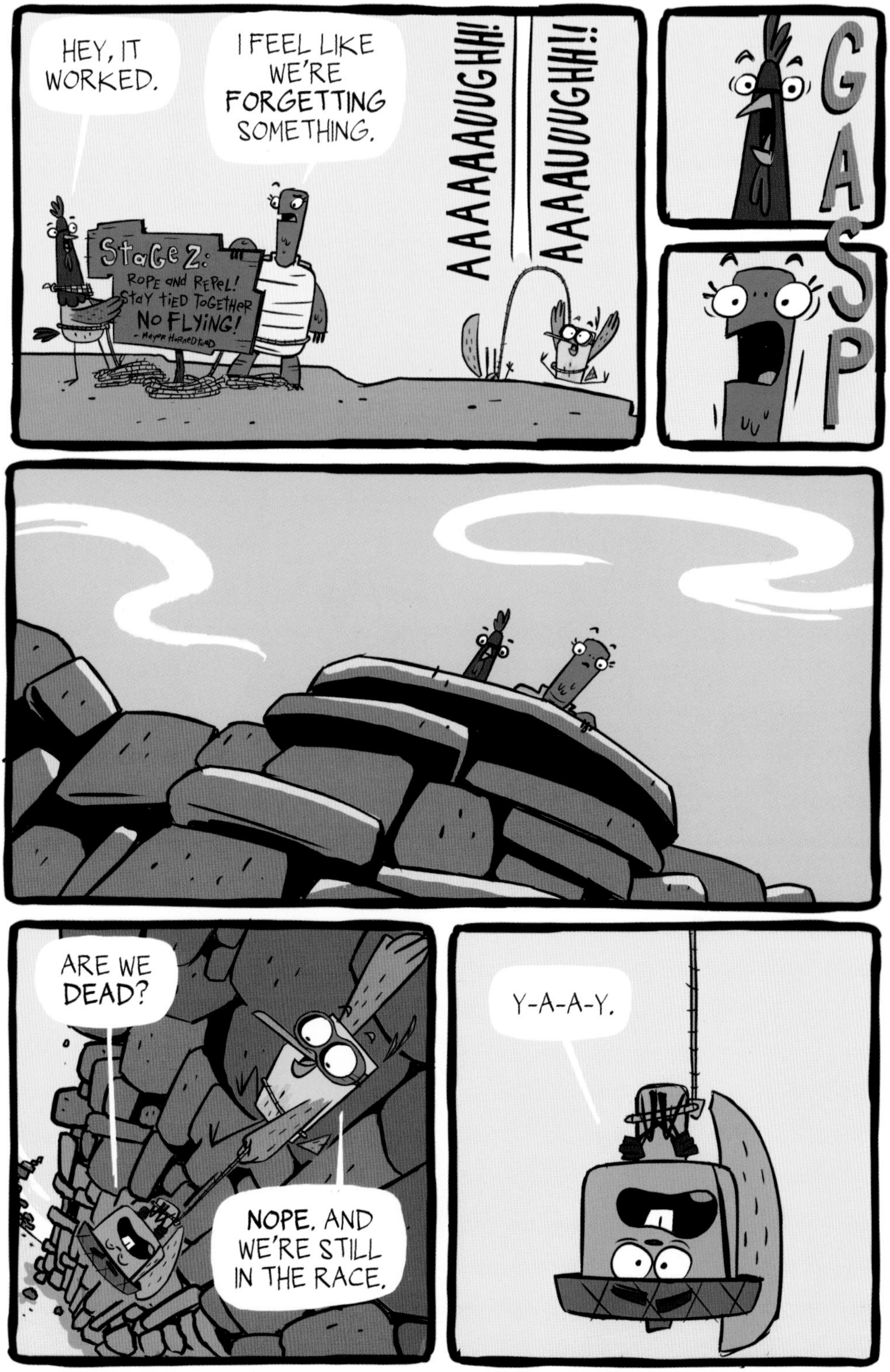
HEY, IT WORKED.
I FEEL LIKE WE'RE FORGETTING SOMETHING.
StaGe 2: ROPE and RePeL! Stay tied ToGether NO FLYiNG!
AAAAAAUUGHH!
AAAAAUUUGHH!!
GASP
ARE WE DEAD?
NOPE. AND WE'RE STILL IN THE RACE.
Y-A-A-Y.

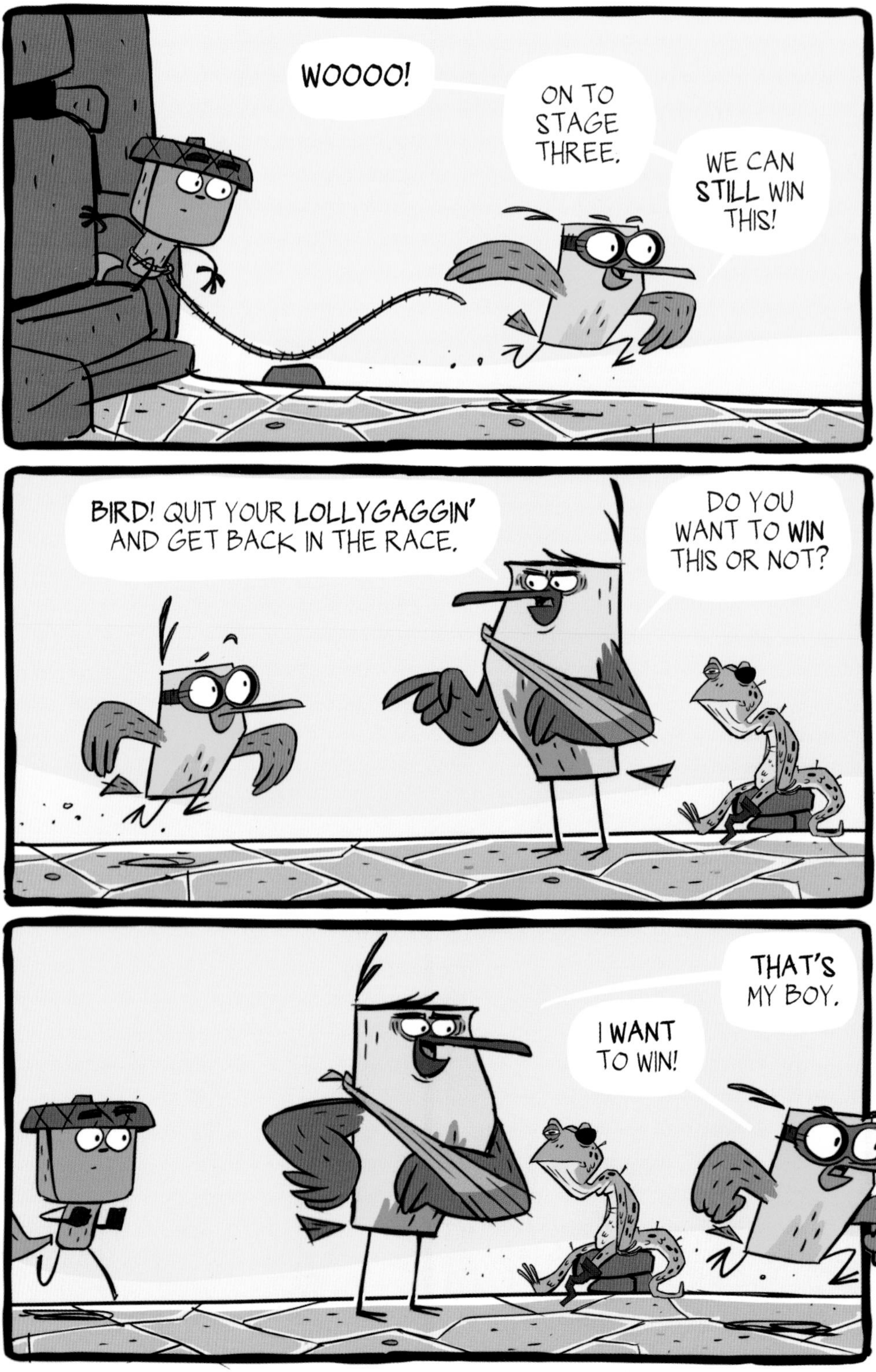
WOOOO!
ON TO STAGE THREE.
WE CAN STILL WIN THIS!
BIRD! QUIT YOUR LOLLYGAGGIN' AND GET BACK IN THE RACE.
DO YOU WANT TO WIN THIS OR NOT?
I WANT TO WIN!
THAT'S MY BOY.

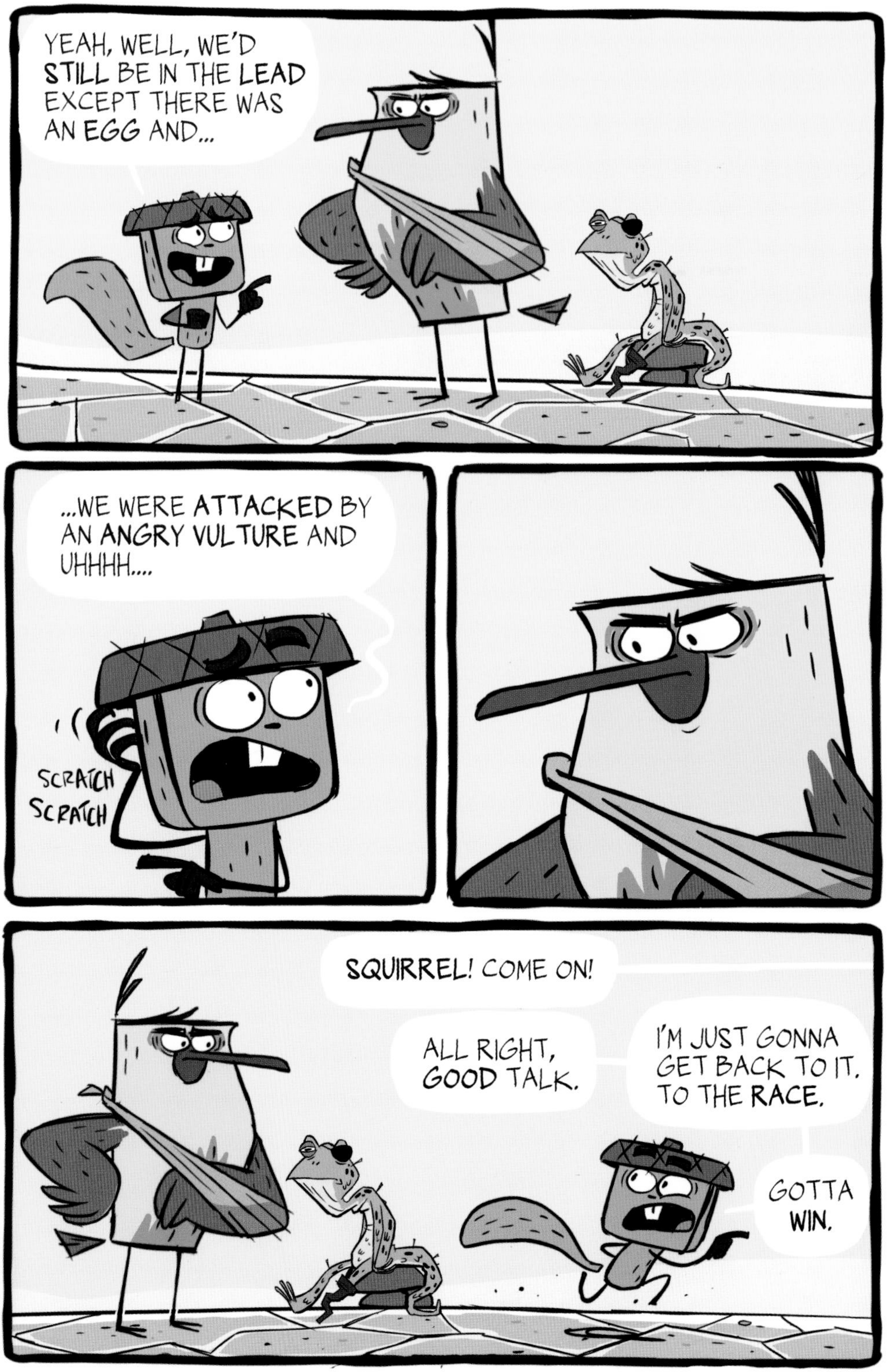
YEAH, WELL, WE'D STILL BE IN THE LEAD EXCEPT THERE WAS AN EGG AND...
...WE WERE ATTACKED BY AN ANGRY VULTURE AND UHHHH....
SCRATCH SCRATCH
SQUIRREL! COME ON!
ALL RIGHT, GOOD TALK.
I'M JUST GONNA GET BACK TO IT. TO THE RACE.
GOTTA WIN.

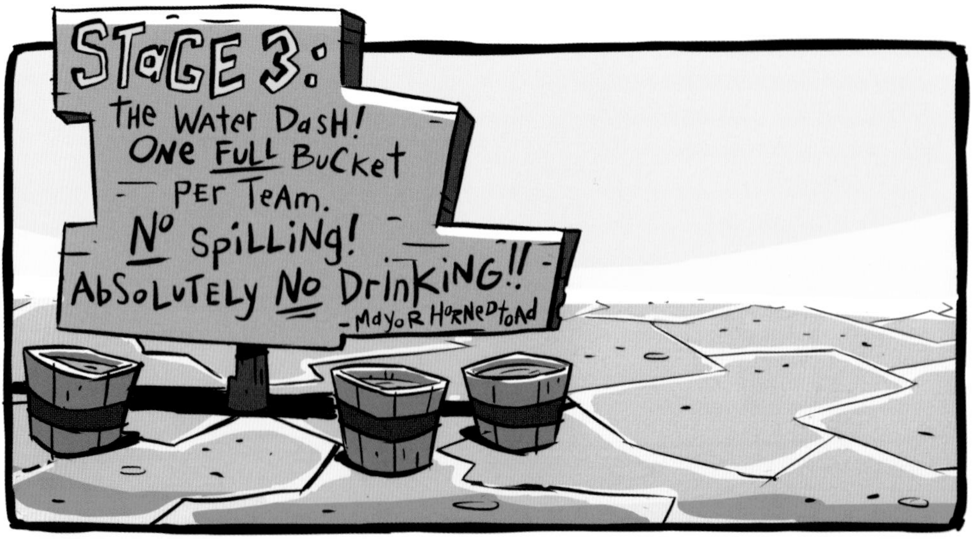
STAGE 3:
THE WATER DASH!
ONE FULL BUCKET
PER TEAM.
NO SPILLING!
ABSOLUTELY NO DRINKING!!
-MAYOR HORNEDTOAD

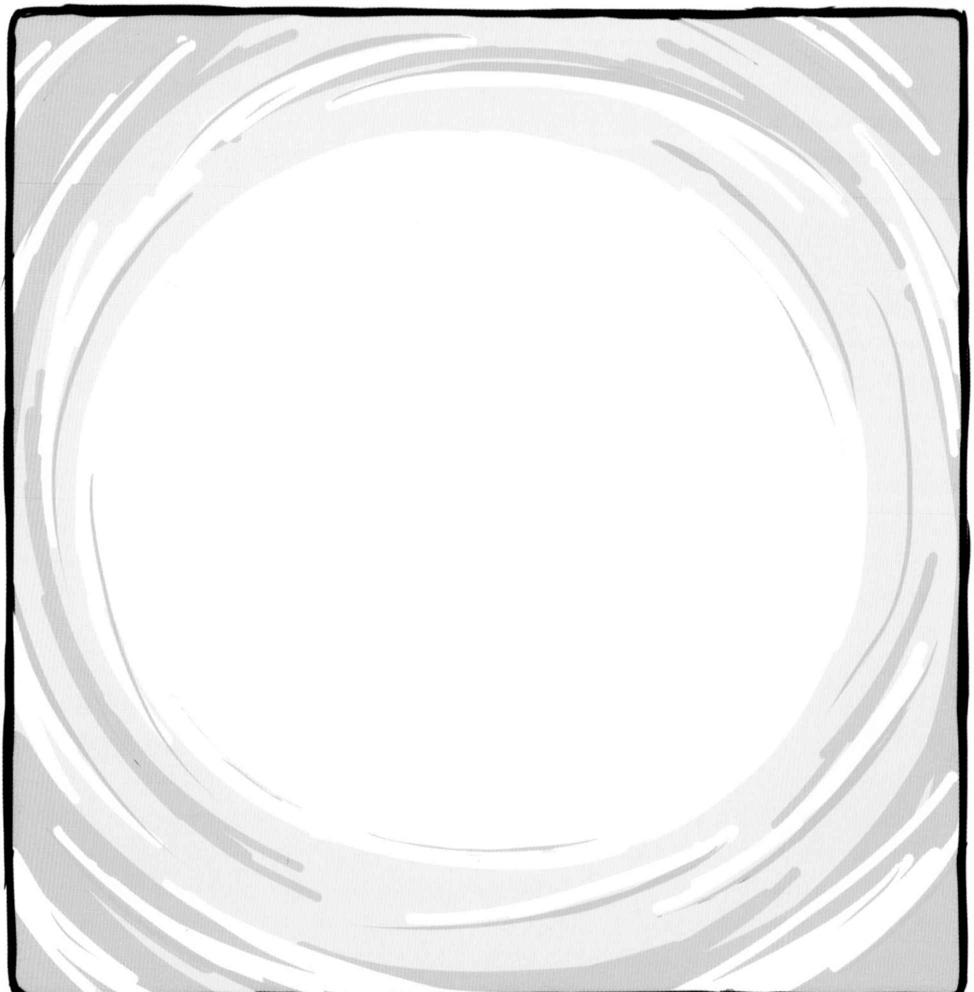

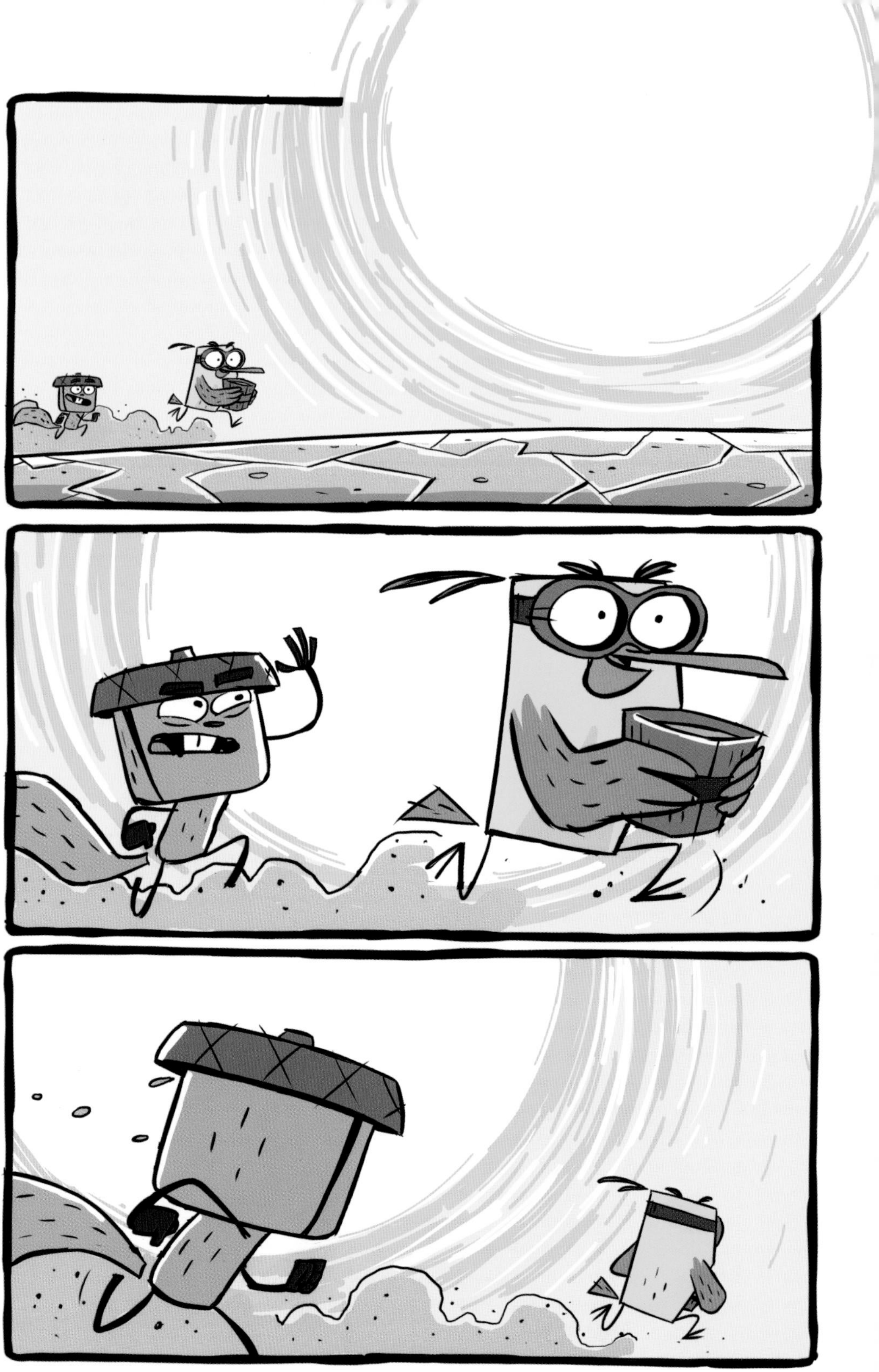

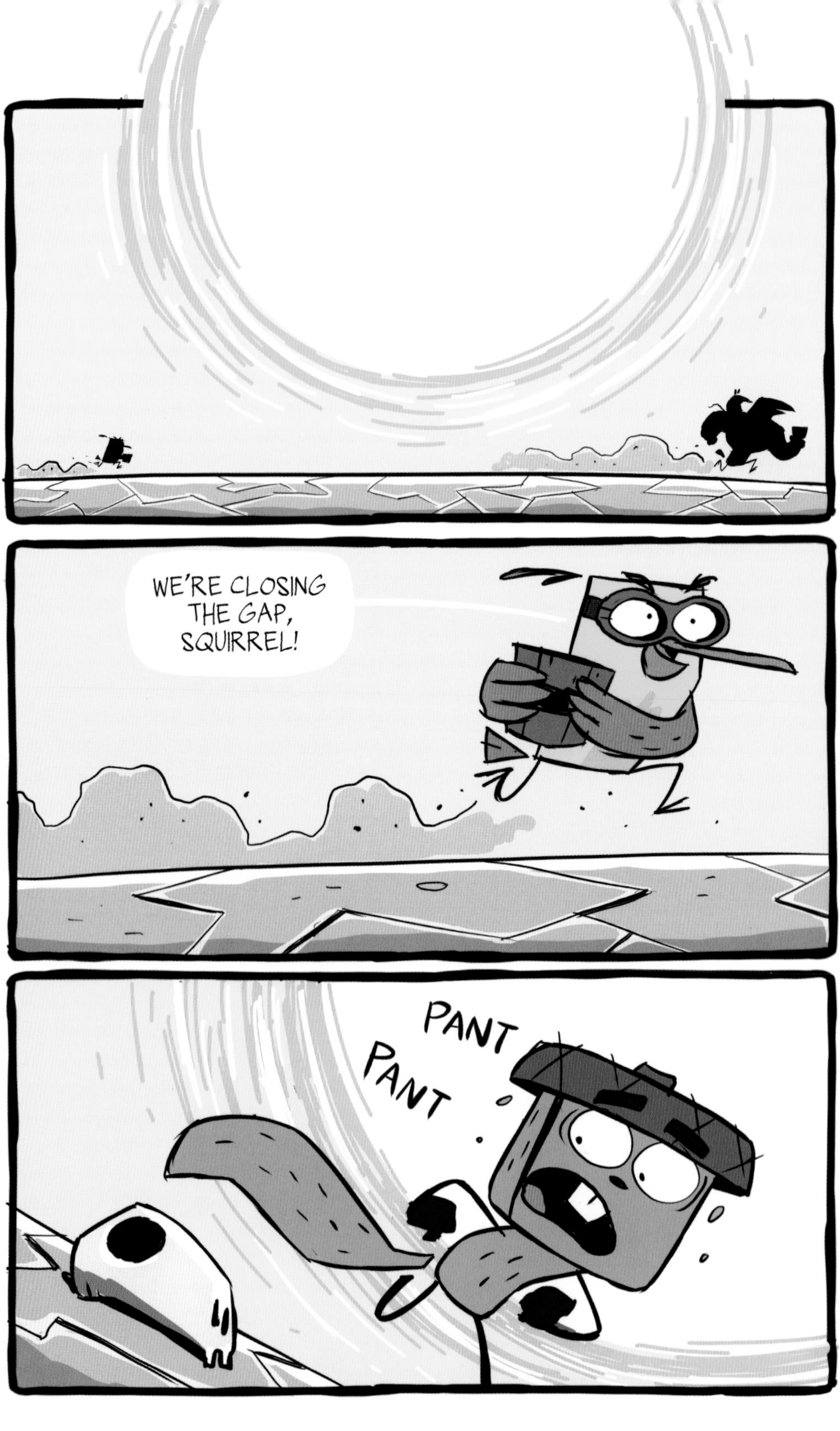
WE'RE CLOSING THE GAP, SQUIRREL!
PANT
PANT

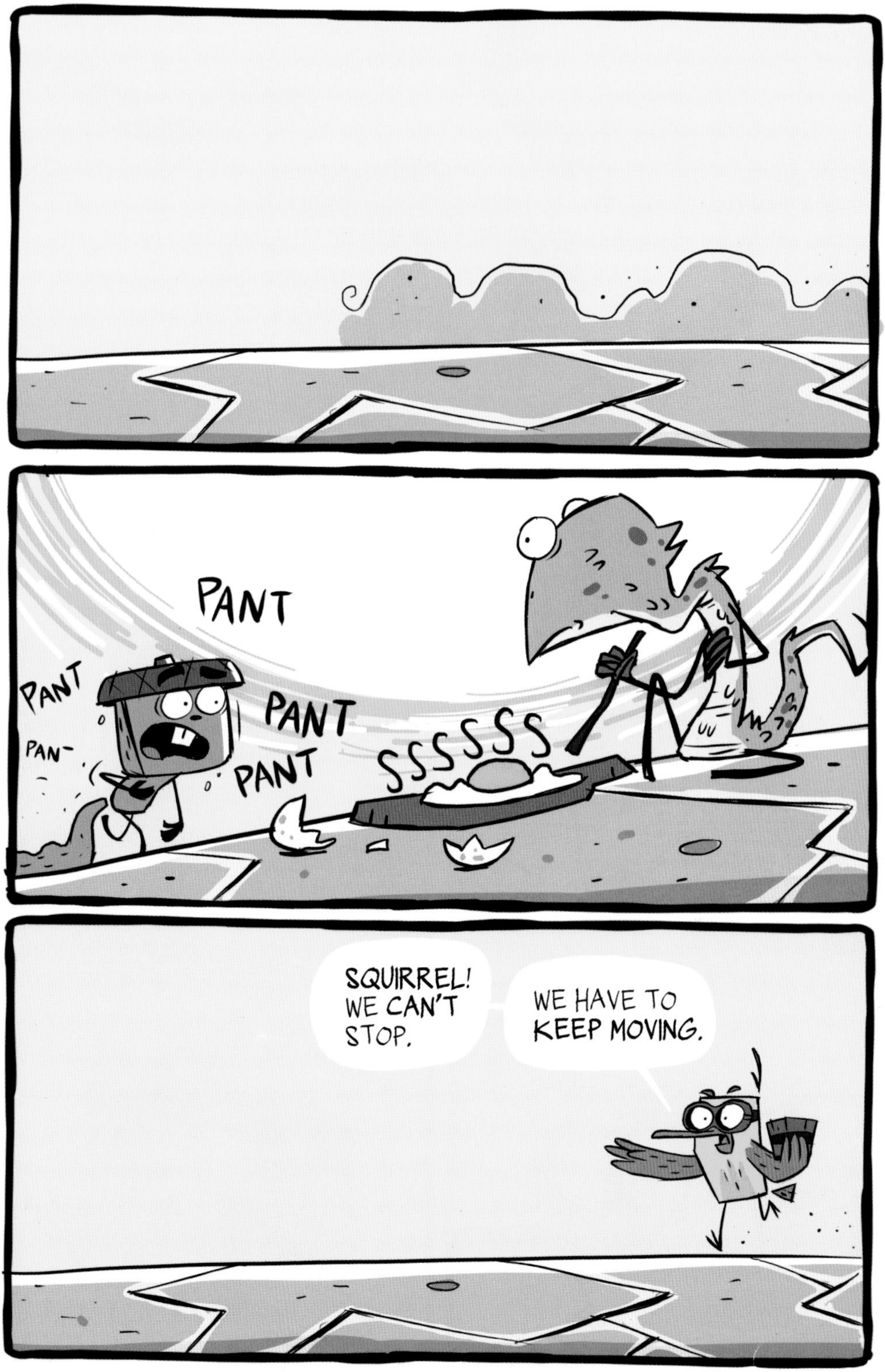
PANT
PANT
PAN-
PANT
PANT
SSSSSS
SQUIRREL! WE CAN'T STOP.
WE HAVE TO KEEP MOVING.

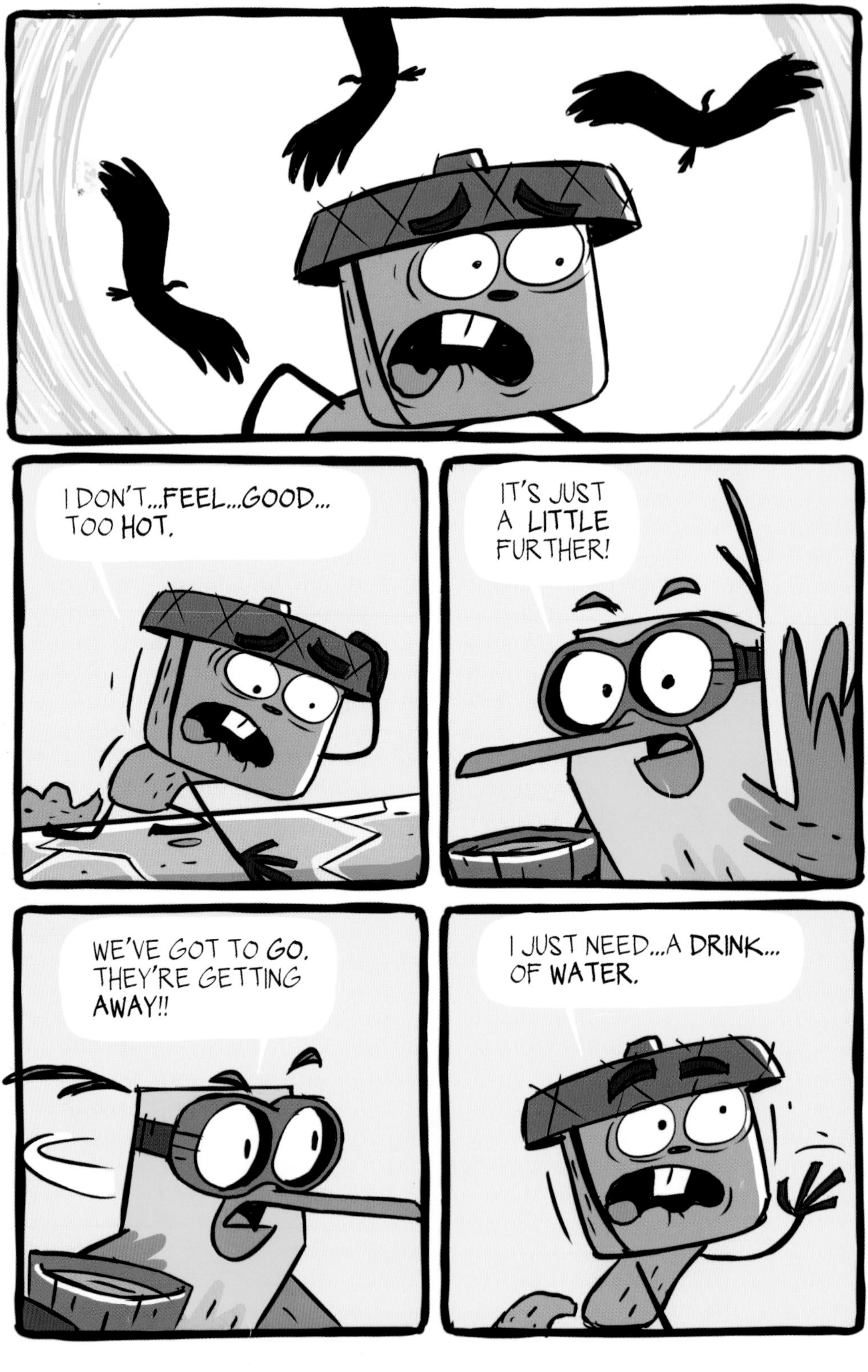
I DON'T...FEEL...GOOD... TOO HOT.
IT'S JUST A LITTLE FURTHER!
WE'VE GOT TO GO. THEY'RE GETTING AWAY!!
I JUST NEED...A DRINK... OF WATER.

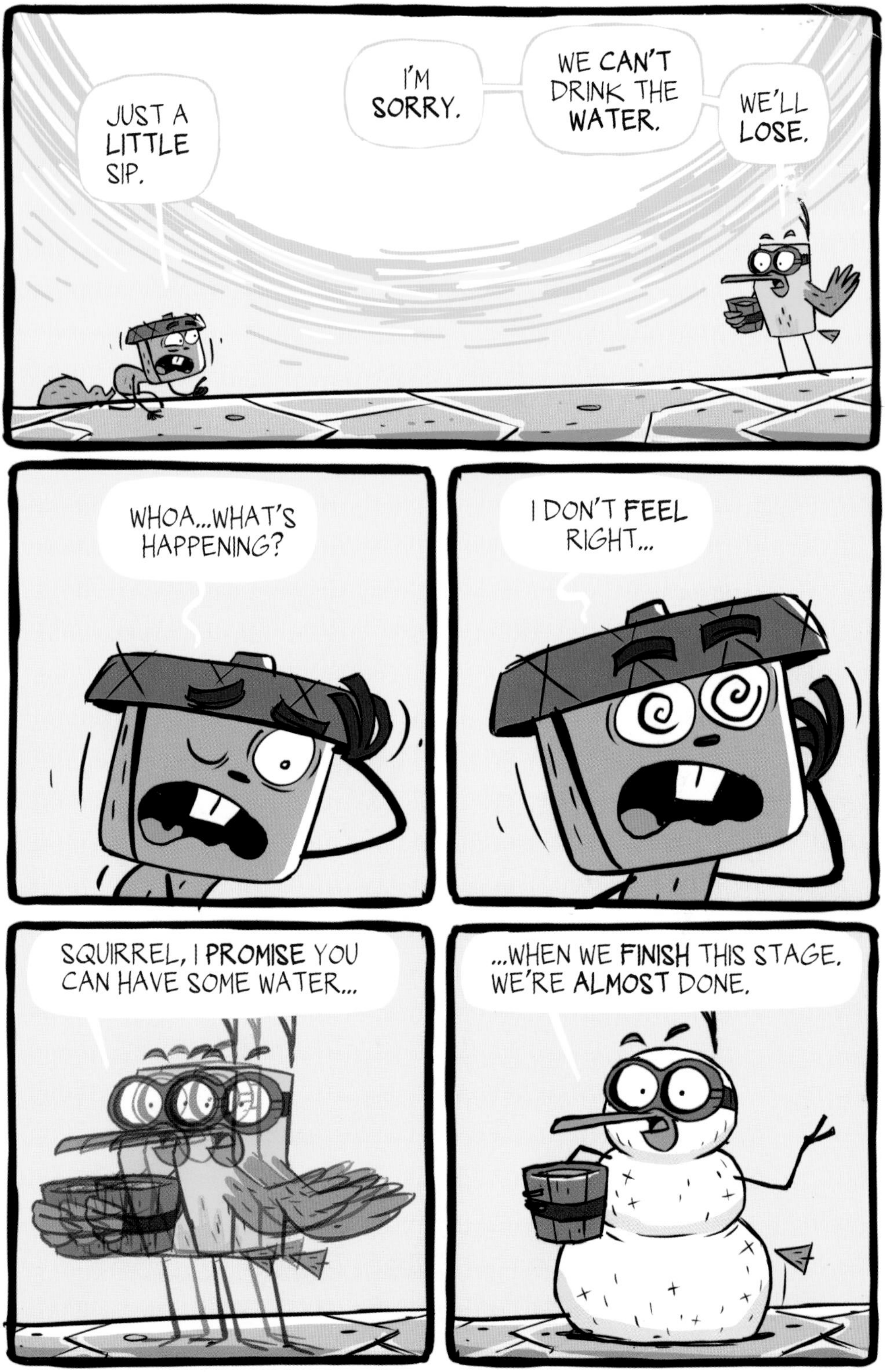
JUST A LITTLE SIP.
I'M SORRY.
WE CAN'T DRINK THE WATER.
WE'LL LOSE.
WHOA...WHAT'S HAPPENING?
I DON'T FEEL RIGHT...
SQUIRREL, I PROMISE YOU CAN HAVE SOME WATER...
...WHEN WE FINISH THIS STAGE. WE'RE ALMOST DONE.

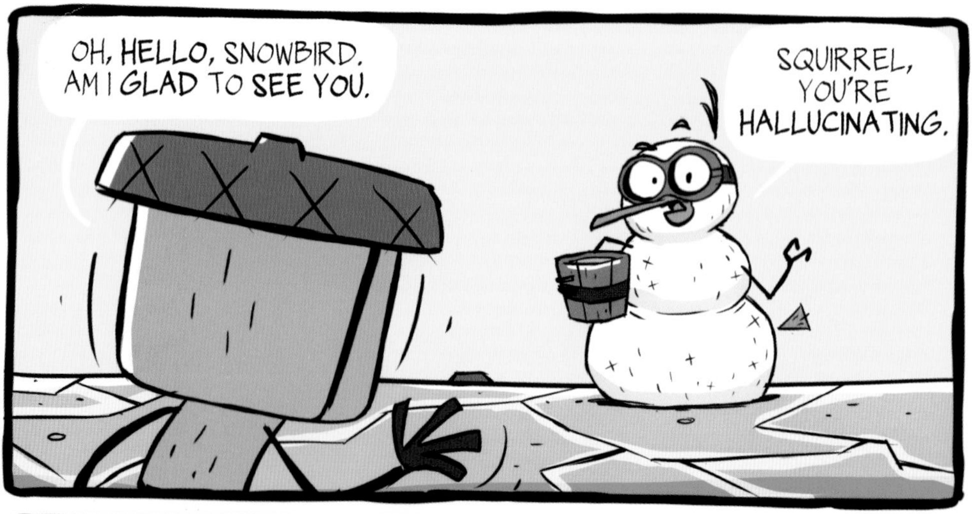
OH, HELLO, SNOWBIRD. AM I GLAD TO SEE YOU.
SQUIRREL, YOU'RE HALLUCINATING.

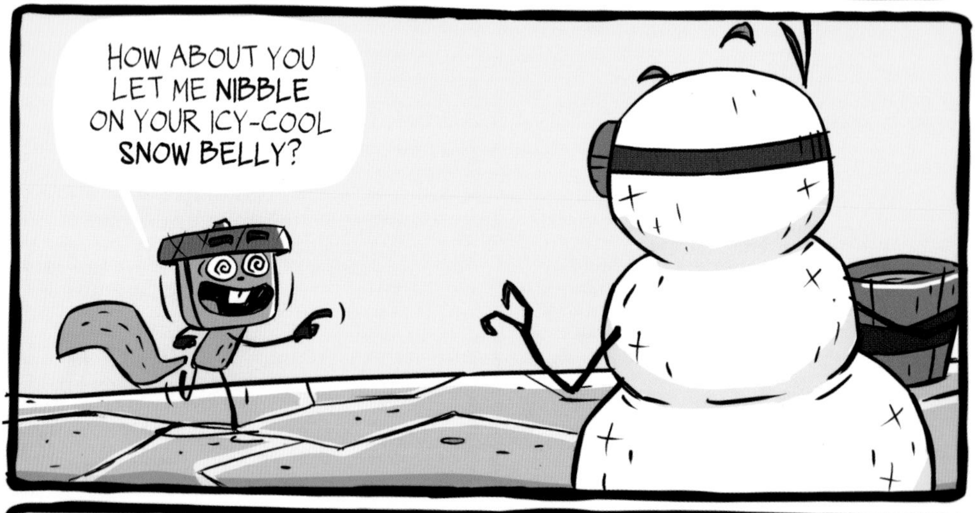
HOW ABOUT YOU LET ME NIBBLE ON YOUR ICY-COOL SNOW BELLY?

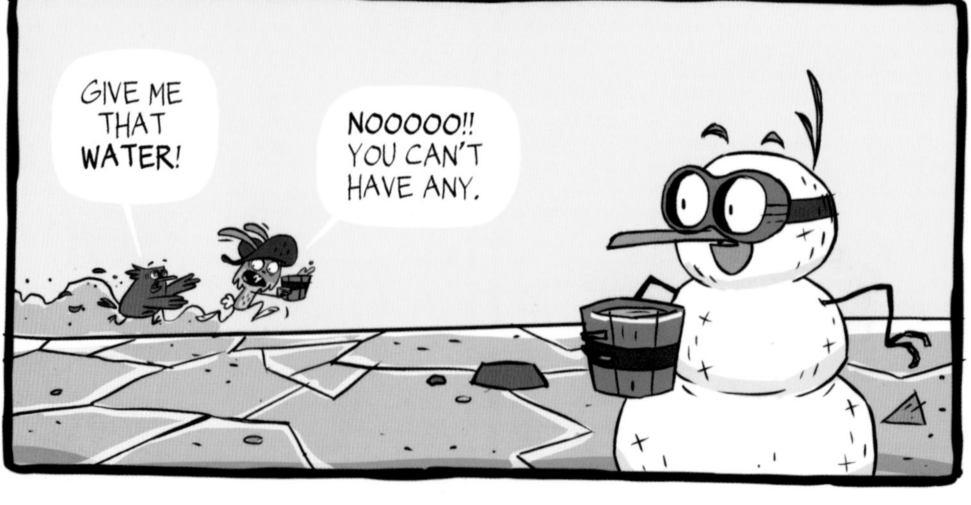
GIVE ME THAT WATER!
NOOOOO!! YOU CAN'T HAVE ANY.

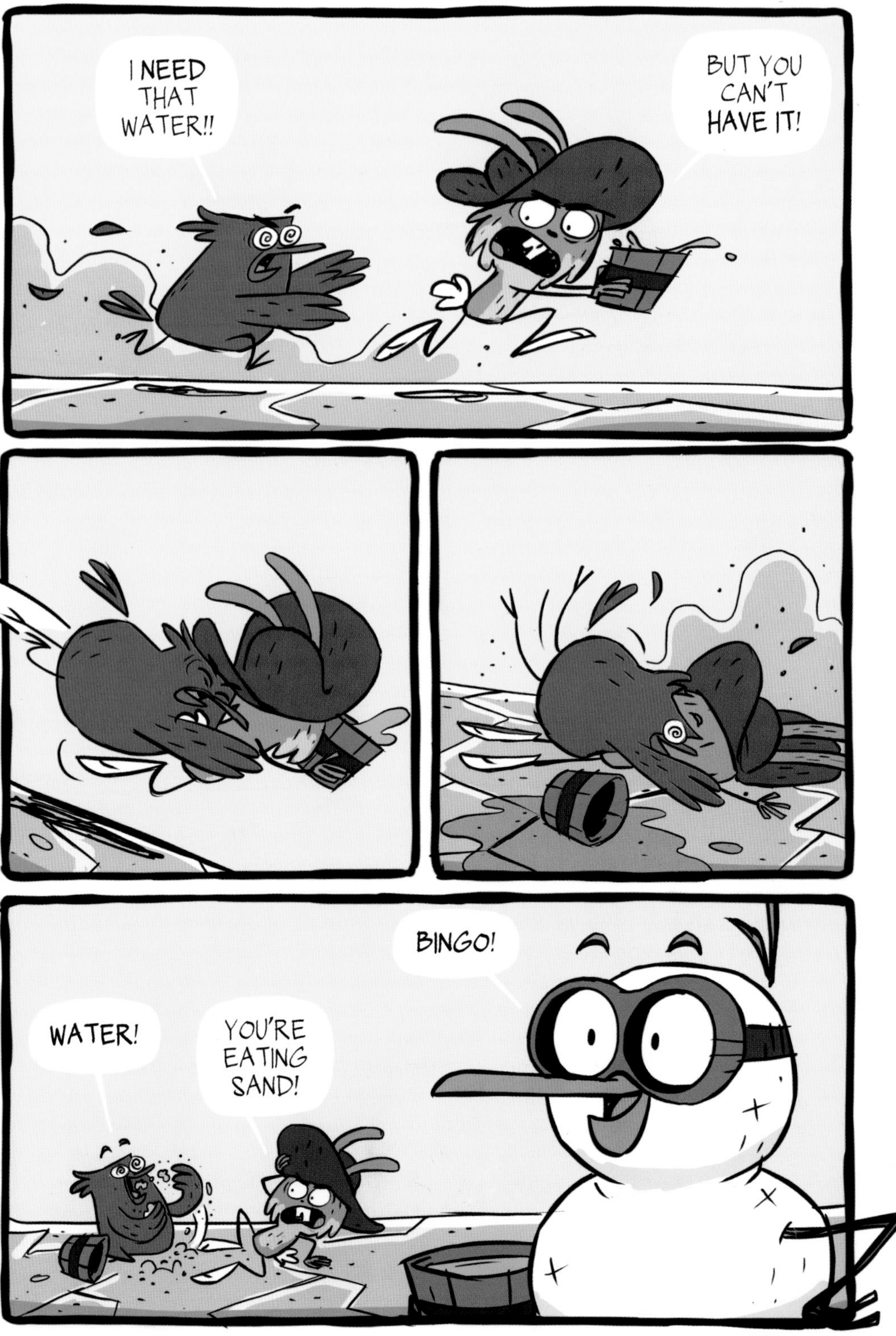
I NEED THAT WATER!!
BUT YOU CAN'T HAVE IT!
BINGO!
WATER!
YOU'RE EATING SAND!

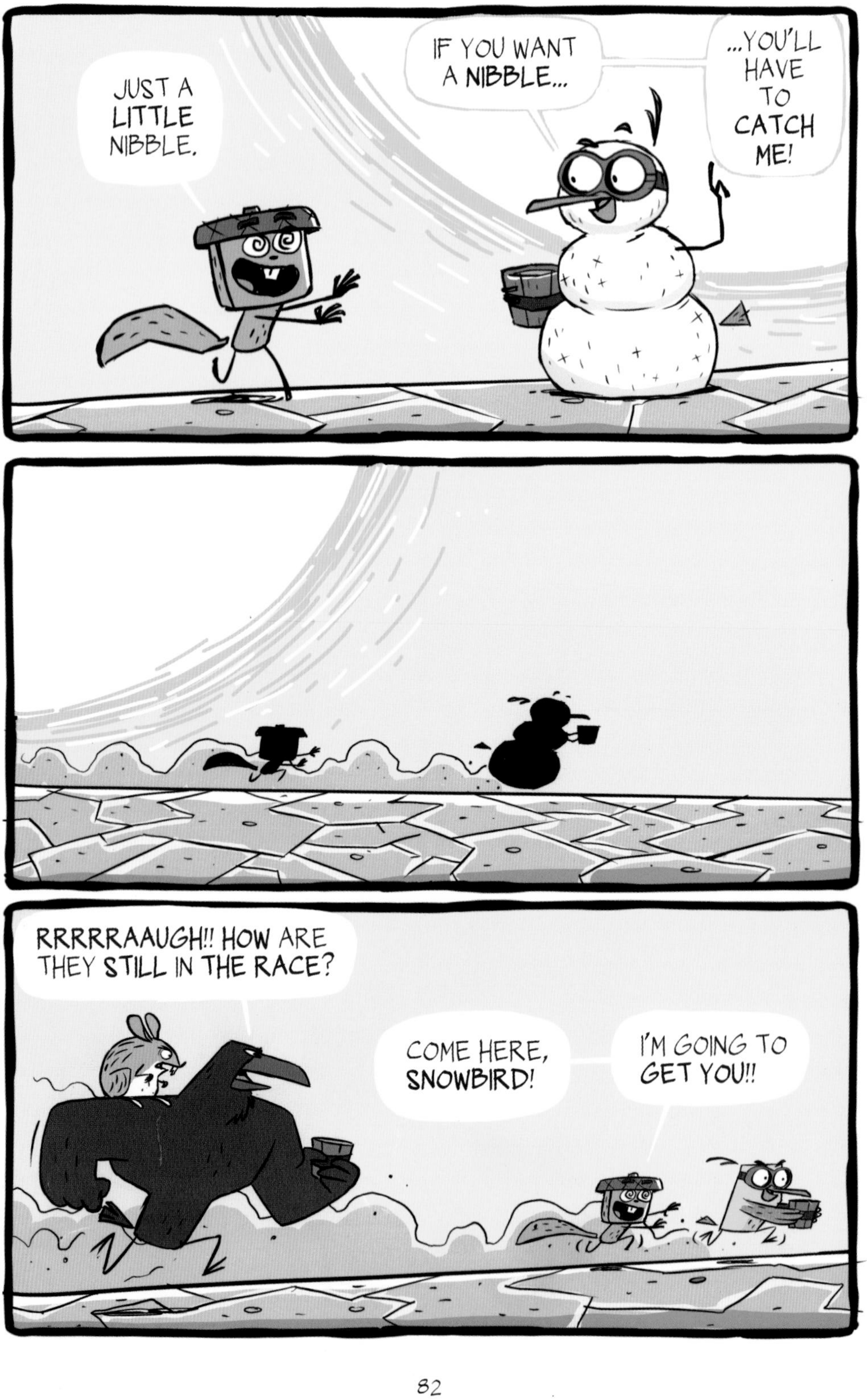
JUST A LITTLE NIBBLE.
IF YOU WANT A NIBBLE...
...YOU'LL HAVE TO CATCH ME!
RRRRRAAUGH!! HOW ARE THEY STILL IN THE RACE?
COME HERE, SNOWBIRD!
I'M GOING TO GET YOU!!

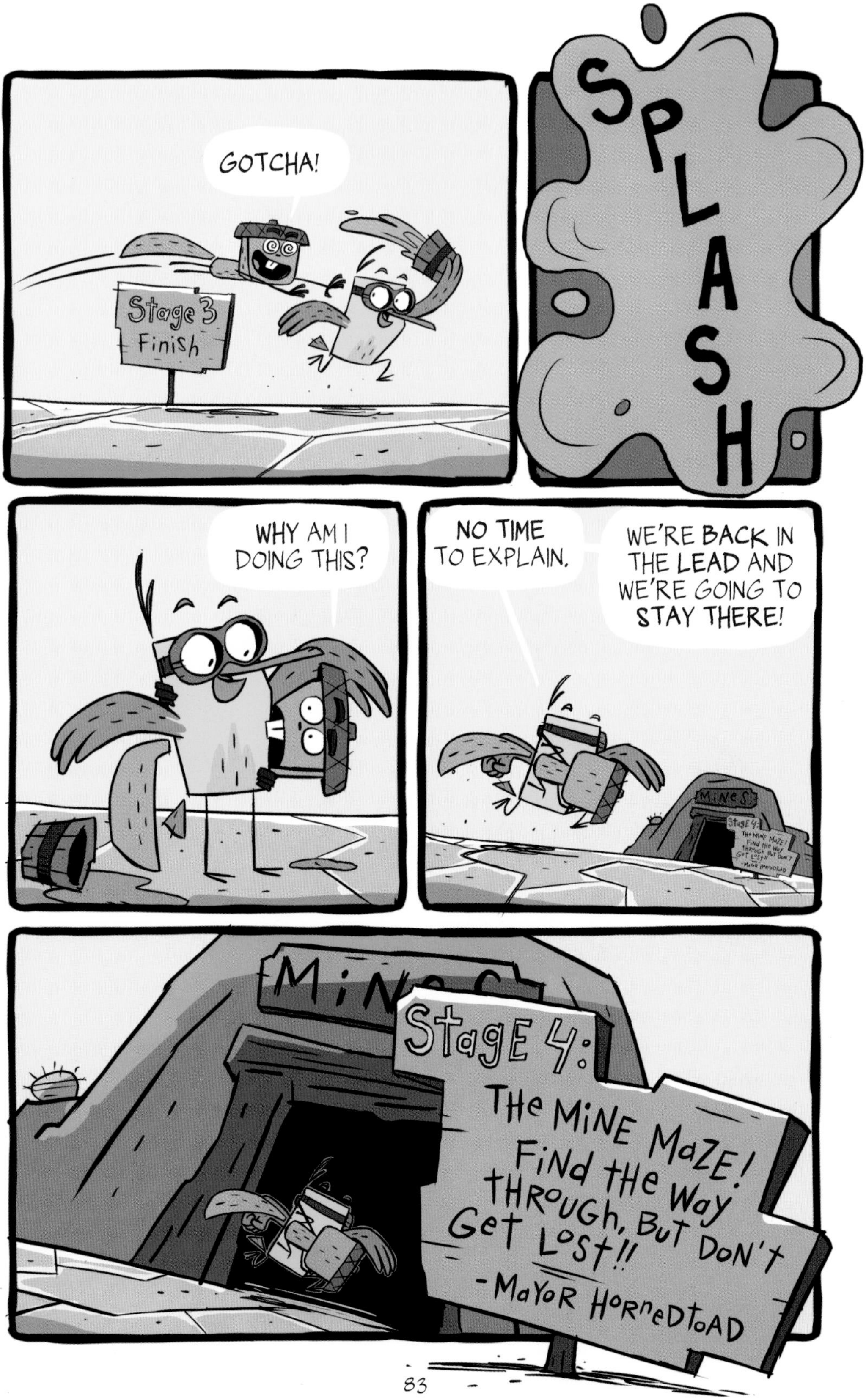

GOTCHA!
Stage 3 Finish
SPLASH
WHY AM I DOING THIS?
NO TIME TO EXPLAIN.
WE'RE BACK IN THE LEAD AND WE'RE GOING TO STAY THERE!
MINES
Stage 4: The Mine Maze! Find the way through, but don't get lost!! -Mayor Hornedtoad

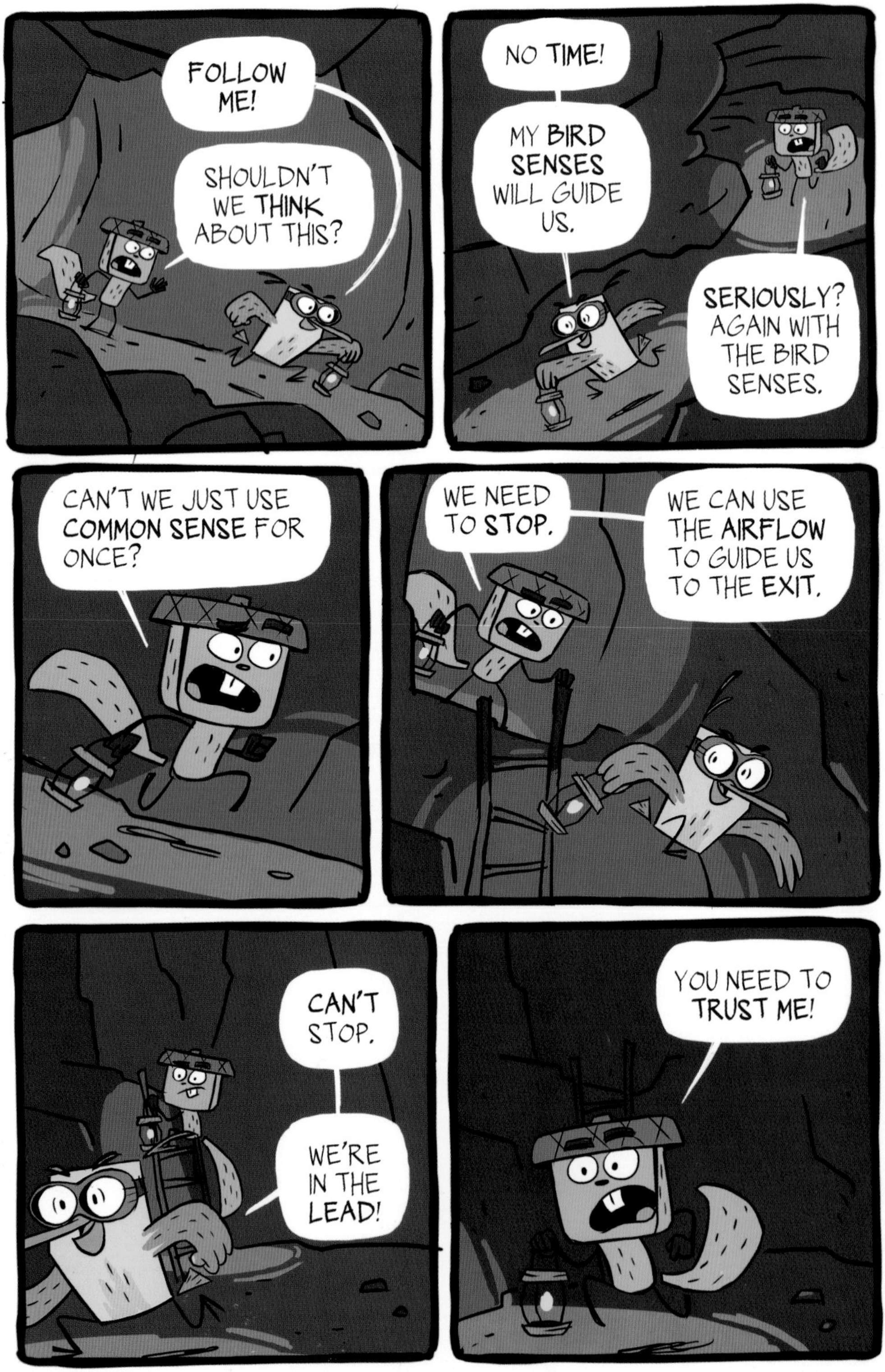
FOLLOW ME!
SHOULDN'T WE THINK ABOUT THIS?
NO TIME!
MY BIRD SENSES WILL GUIDE US.
SERIOUSLY? AGAIN WITH THE BIRD SENSES.
CAN'T WE JUST USE COMMON SENSE FOR ONCE?
WE NEED TO STOP.
WE CAN USE THE AIRFLOW TO GUIDE US TO THE EXIT.
CAN'T STOP.
WE'RE IN THE LEAD!
YOU NEED TO TRUST ME!

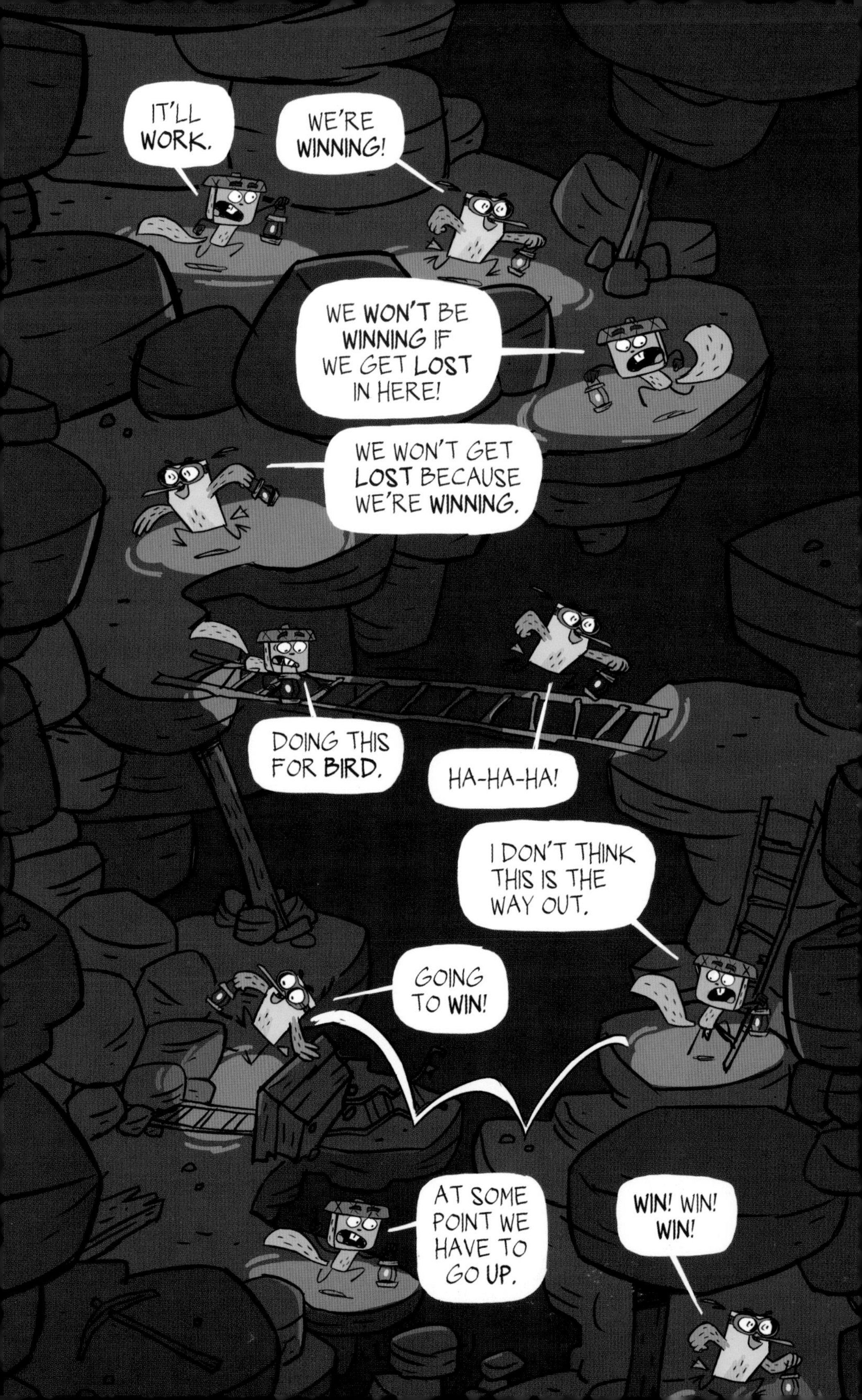
IT'LL WORK.
WE'RE WINNING!
WE WON'T BE WINNING IF WE GET LOST IN HERE!
WE WON'T GET LOST BECAUSE WE'RE WINNING.
DOING THIS FOR BIRD.
HA-HA-HA!
I DON'T THINK THIS IS THE WAY OUT.
GOING TO WIN!
AT SOME POINT WE HAVE TO GO UP.
WIN! WIN! WIN!

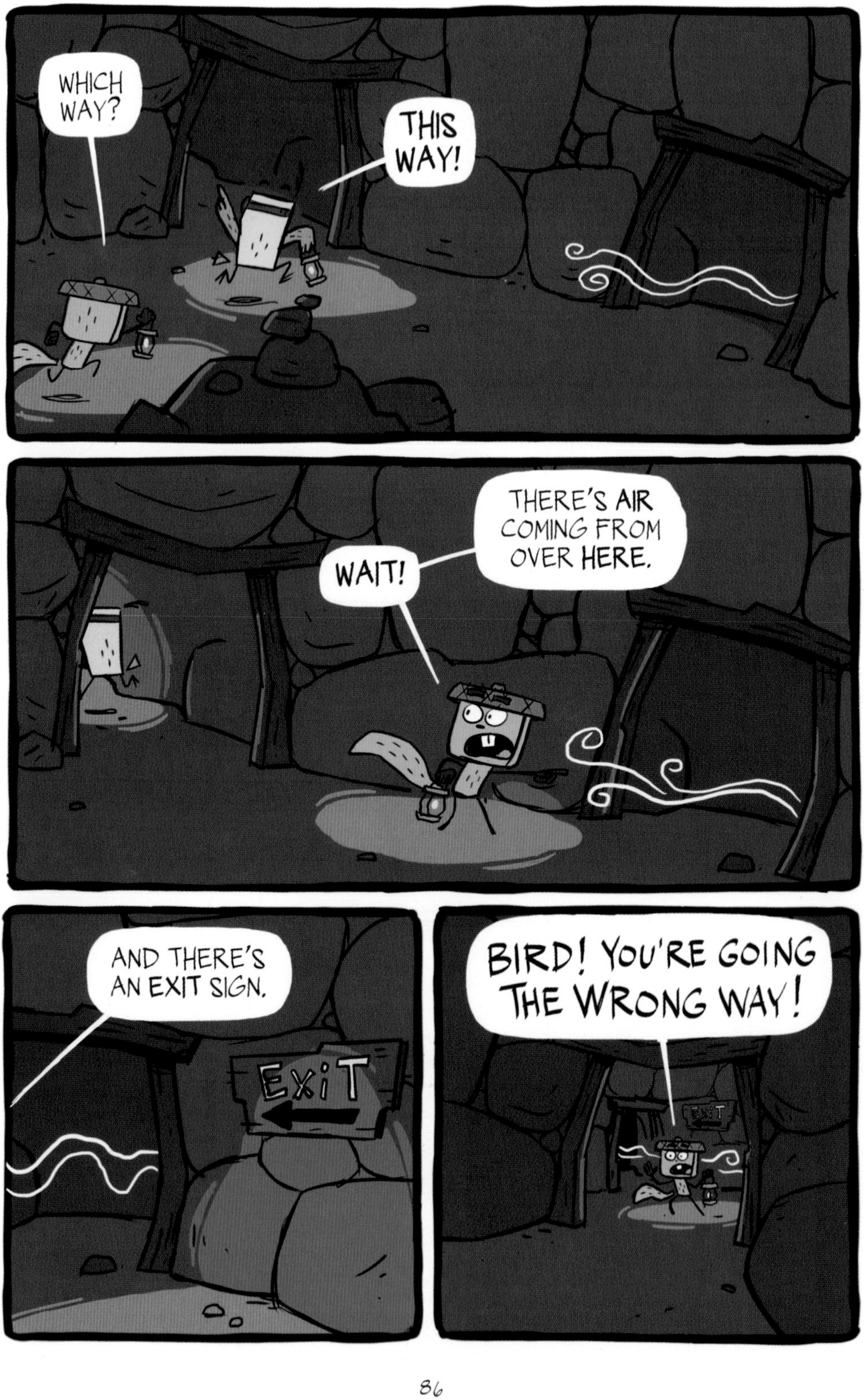
WHICH WAY?
THIS WAY!
WAIT!
THERE'S AIR COMING FROM OVER HERE.
AND THERE'S AN EXIT SIGN.
EXIT
BIRD! YOU'RE GOING THE WRONG WAY!

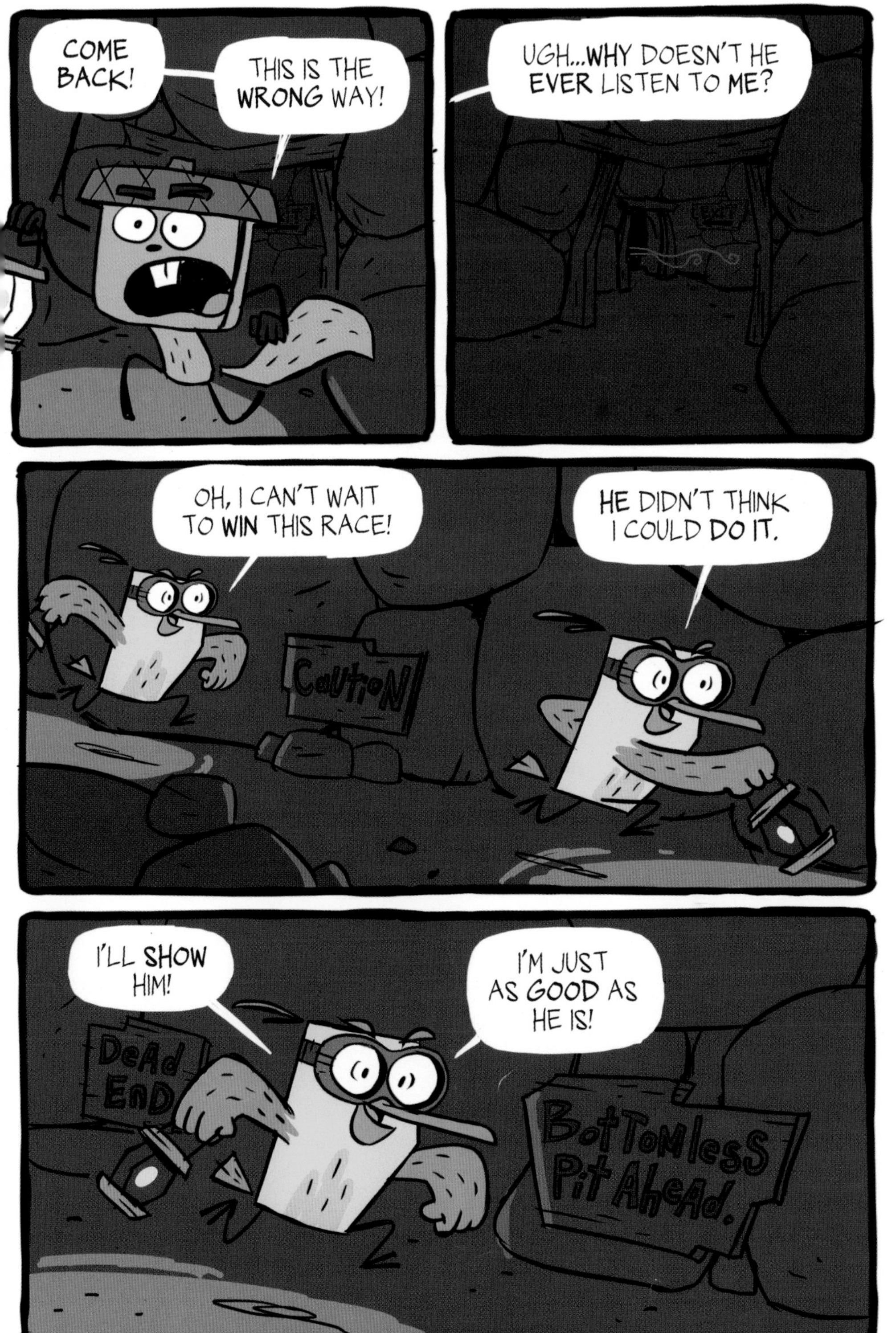
COME BACK!
THIS IS THE WRONG WAY!
EXIT
UGH...WHY DOESN'T HE EVER LISTEN TO ME?
EXIT
OH, I CAN'T WAIT TO WIN THIS RACE!
CAUTION
HE DIDN'T THINK I COULD DO IT.
I'LL SHOW HIM!
I'M JUST AS GOOD AS HE IS!
DEAD END
BOTTOMLESS PIT AHEAD.

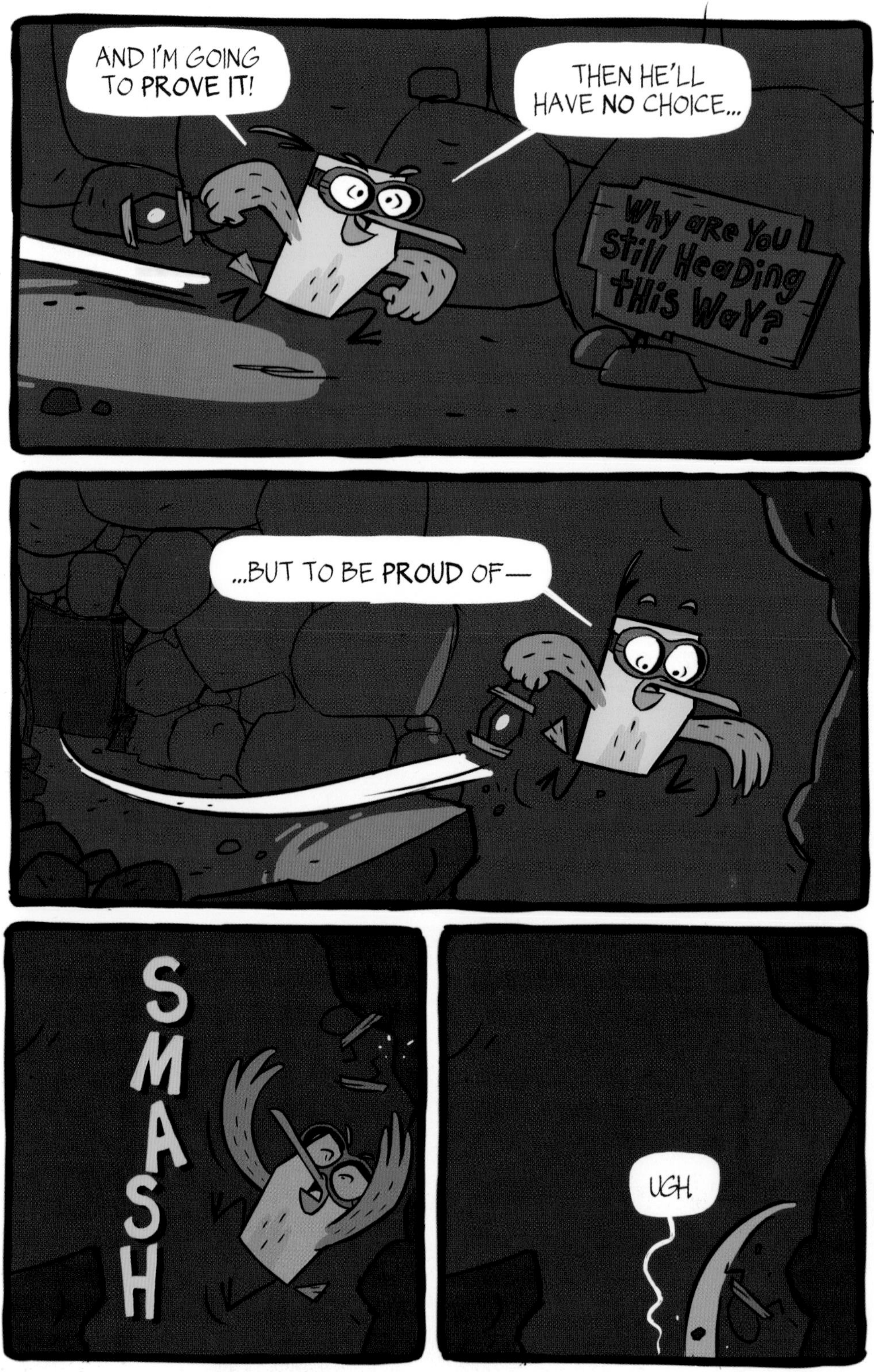
AND I'M GOING TO PROVE IT!
THEN HE'LL HAVE NO CHOICE...
Why are You still Heading tHis WaY?
...BUT TO BE PROUD OF—
SMASH
UGH.

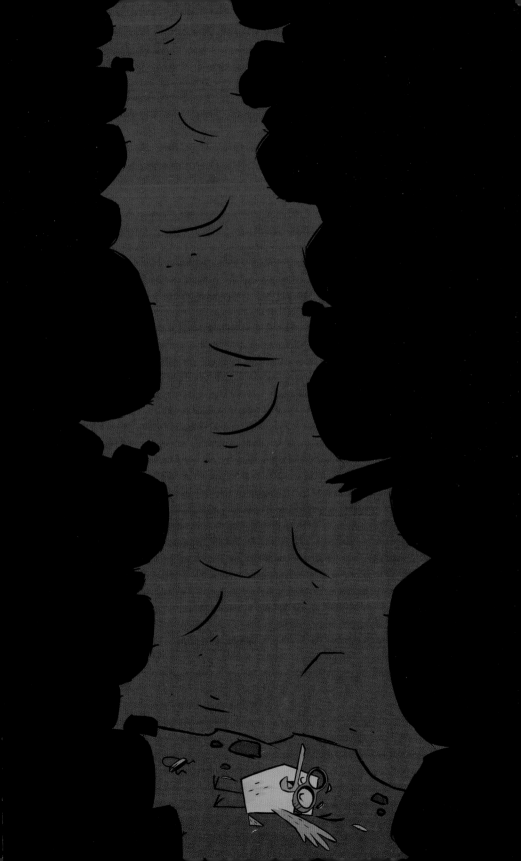

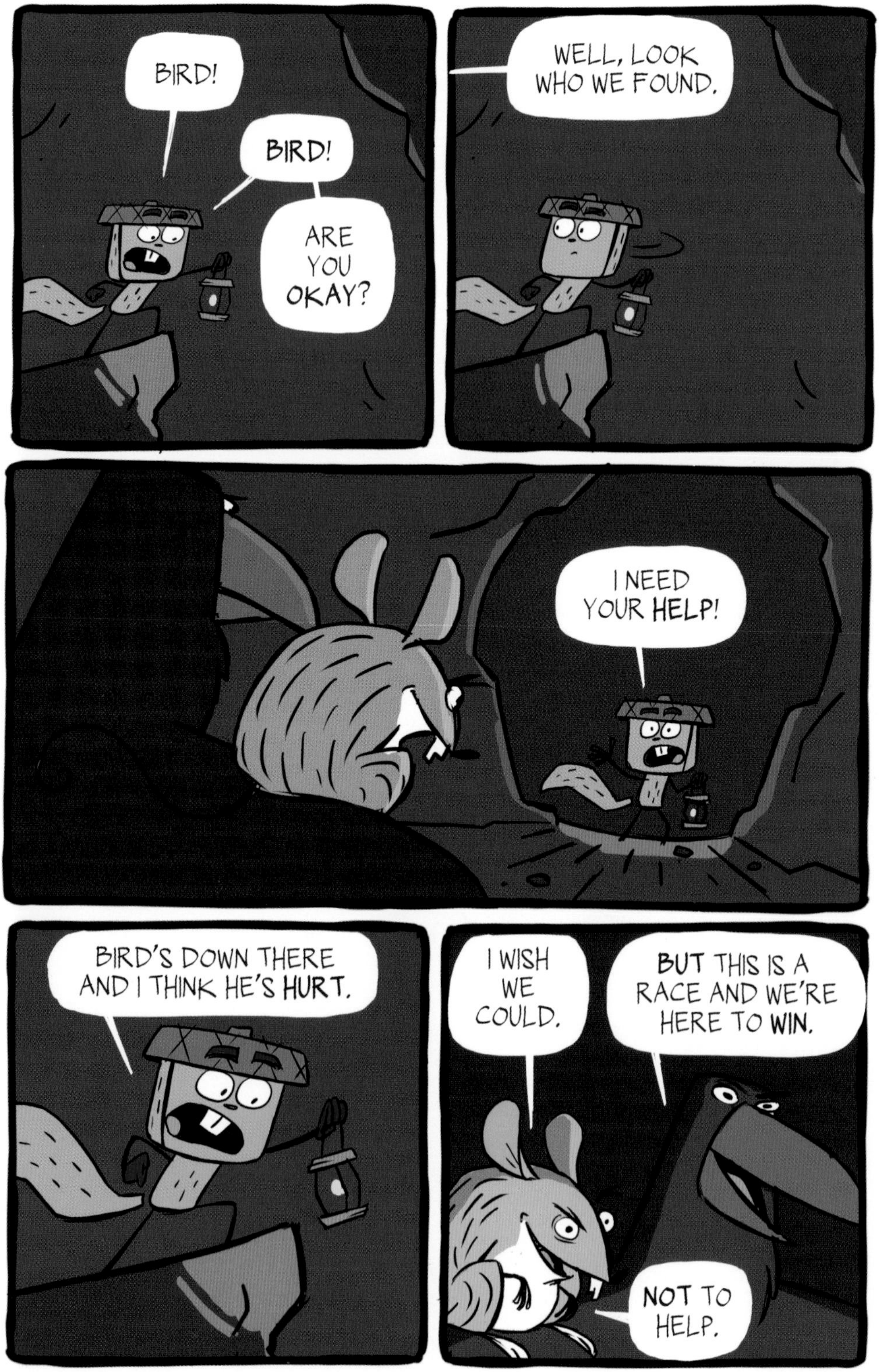
BIRD!
BIRD!
ARE YOU OKAY?
WELL, LOOK WHO WE FOUND.
I NEED YOUR HELP!
BIRD'S DOWN THERE AND I THINK HE'S HURT.
I WISH WE COULD.
BUT THIS IS A RACE AND WE'RE HERE TO WIN.
NOT TO HELP.

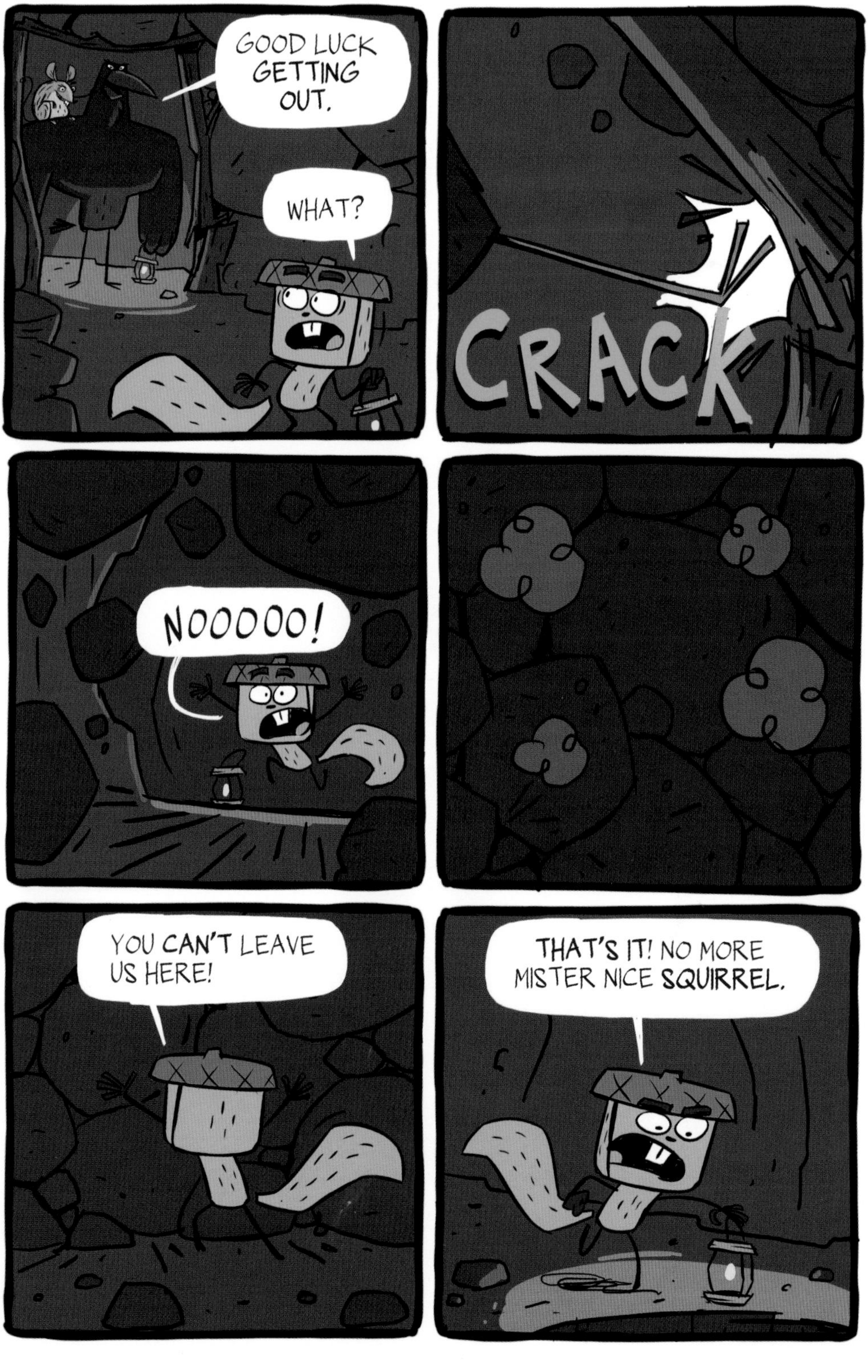
GOOD LUCK GETTING OUT.
WHAT?
CRACK
NOOOOO!
YOU CAN'T LEAVE US HERE!
THAT'S IT! NO MORE MISTER NICE SQUIRREL.

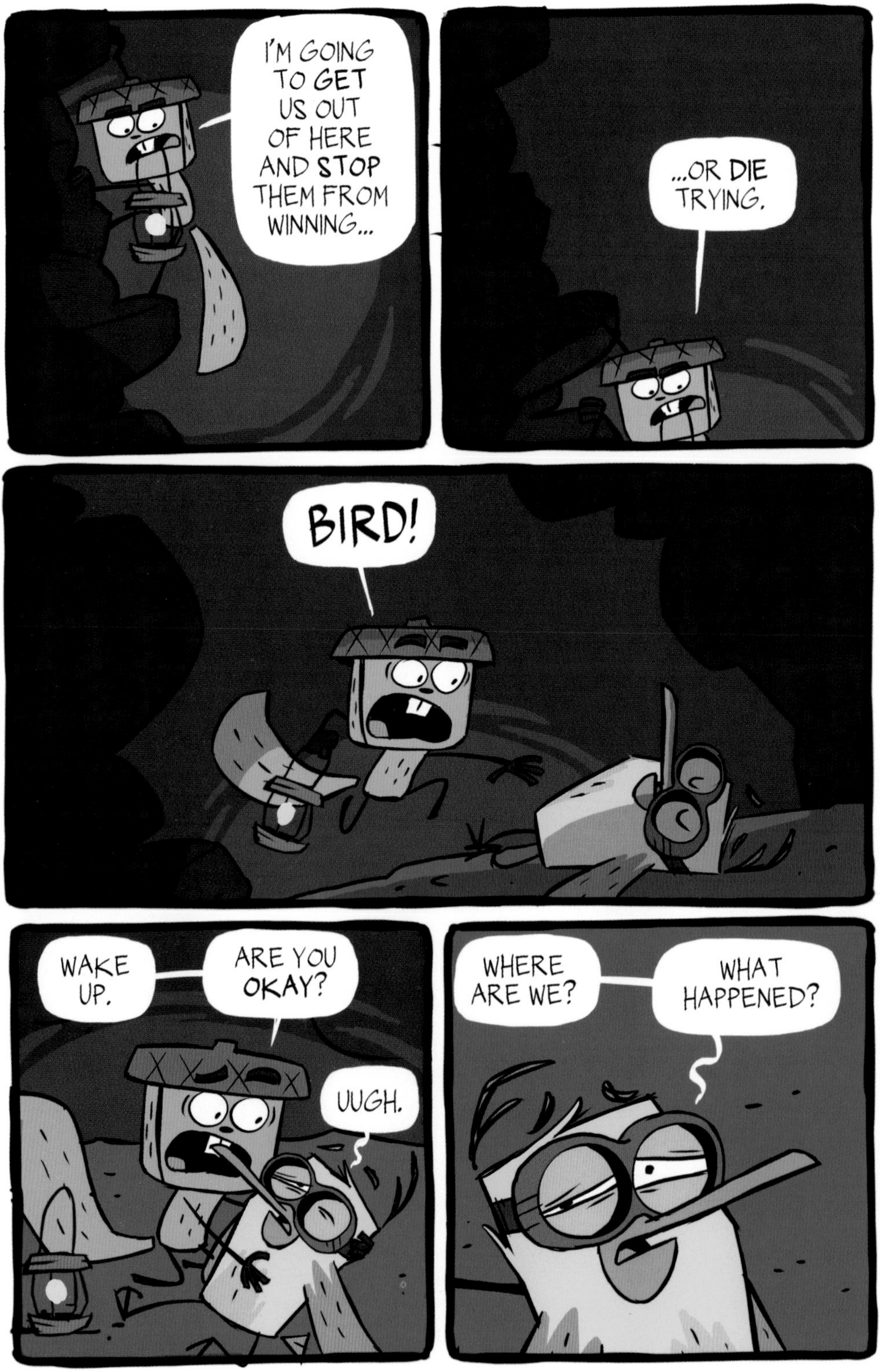
I'M GOING TO GET US OUT OF HERE AND STOP THEM FROM WINNING...
...OR DIE TRYING.
BIRD!
WAKE UP.
ARE YOU OKAY?
UUGH.
WHERE ARE WE?
WHAT HAPPENED?

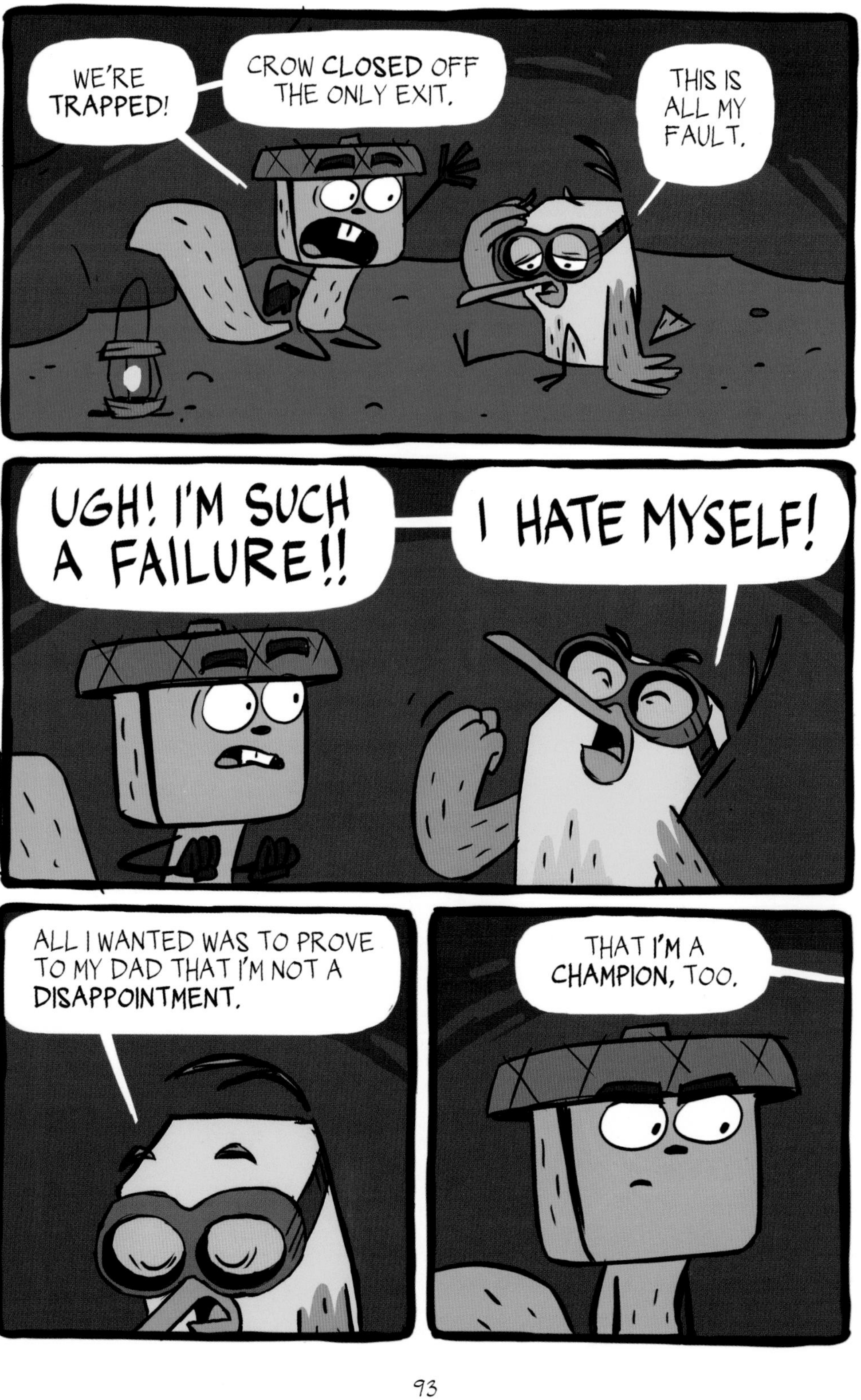
WE'RE TRAPPED!
CROW CLOSED OFF THE ONLY EXIT.
THIS IS ALL MY FAULT.
UGH! I'M SUCH A FAILURE!!
I HATE MYSELF!
ALL I WANTED WAS TO PROVE TO MY DAD THAT I'M NOT A DISAPPOINTMENT.
THAT I'M A CHAMPION, TOO.

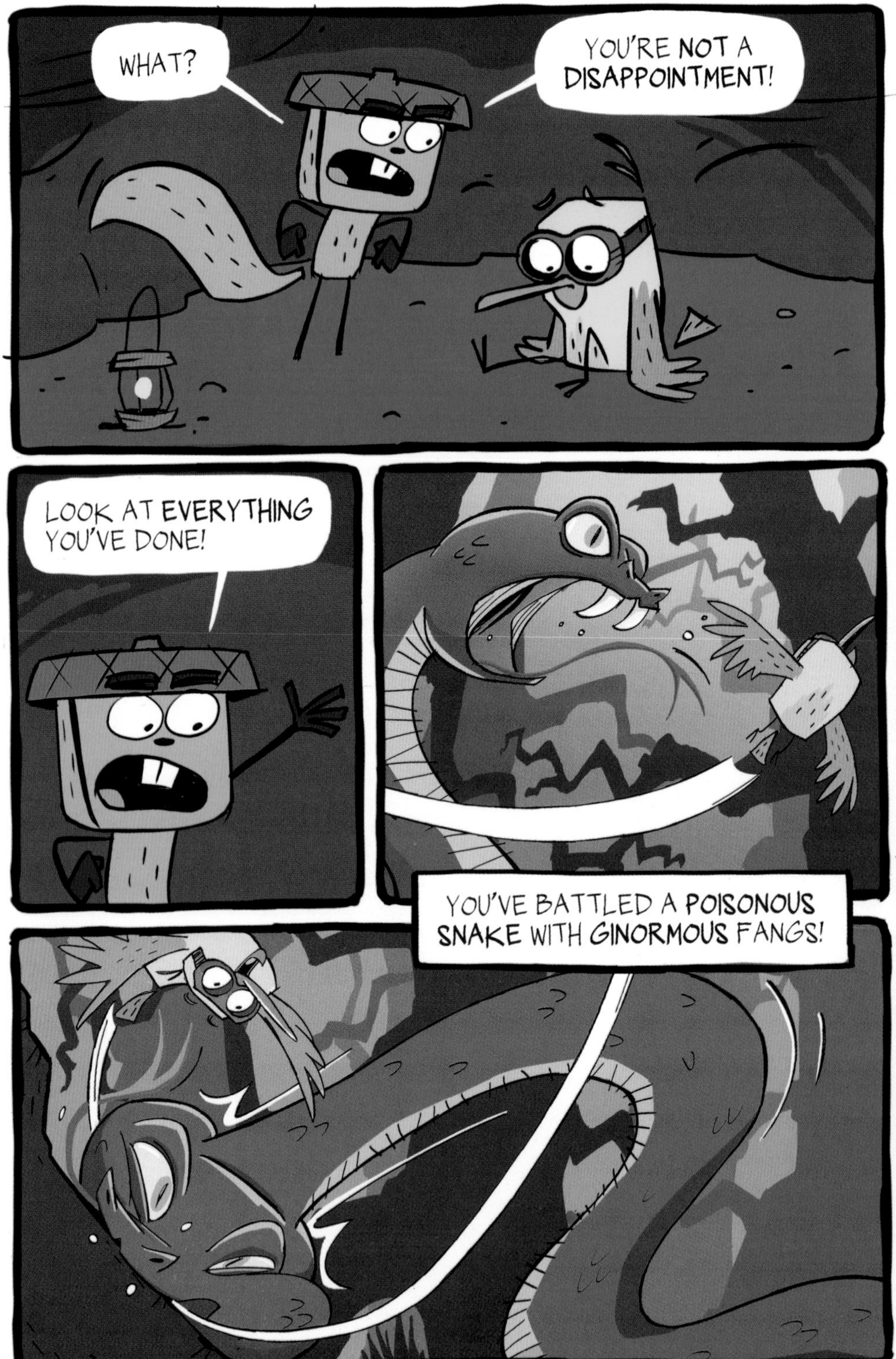
WHAT?
YOU'RE NOT A DISAPPOINTMENT!
LOOK AT EVERYTHING YOU'VE DONE!
YOU'VE BATTLED A POISONOUS SNAKE WITH GINORMOUS FANGS!

SURVIVED AN AVALANCHE!

SAVED A BEAR CUB
FROM HUNGRY WOLVES!

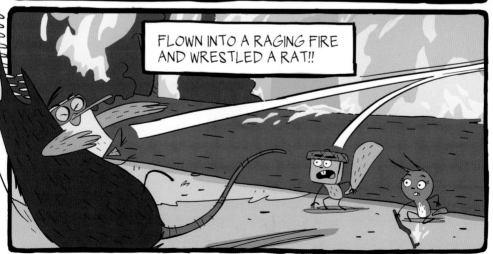

FLOWN INTO A RAGING FIRE
AND WRESTLED A RAT!!

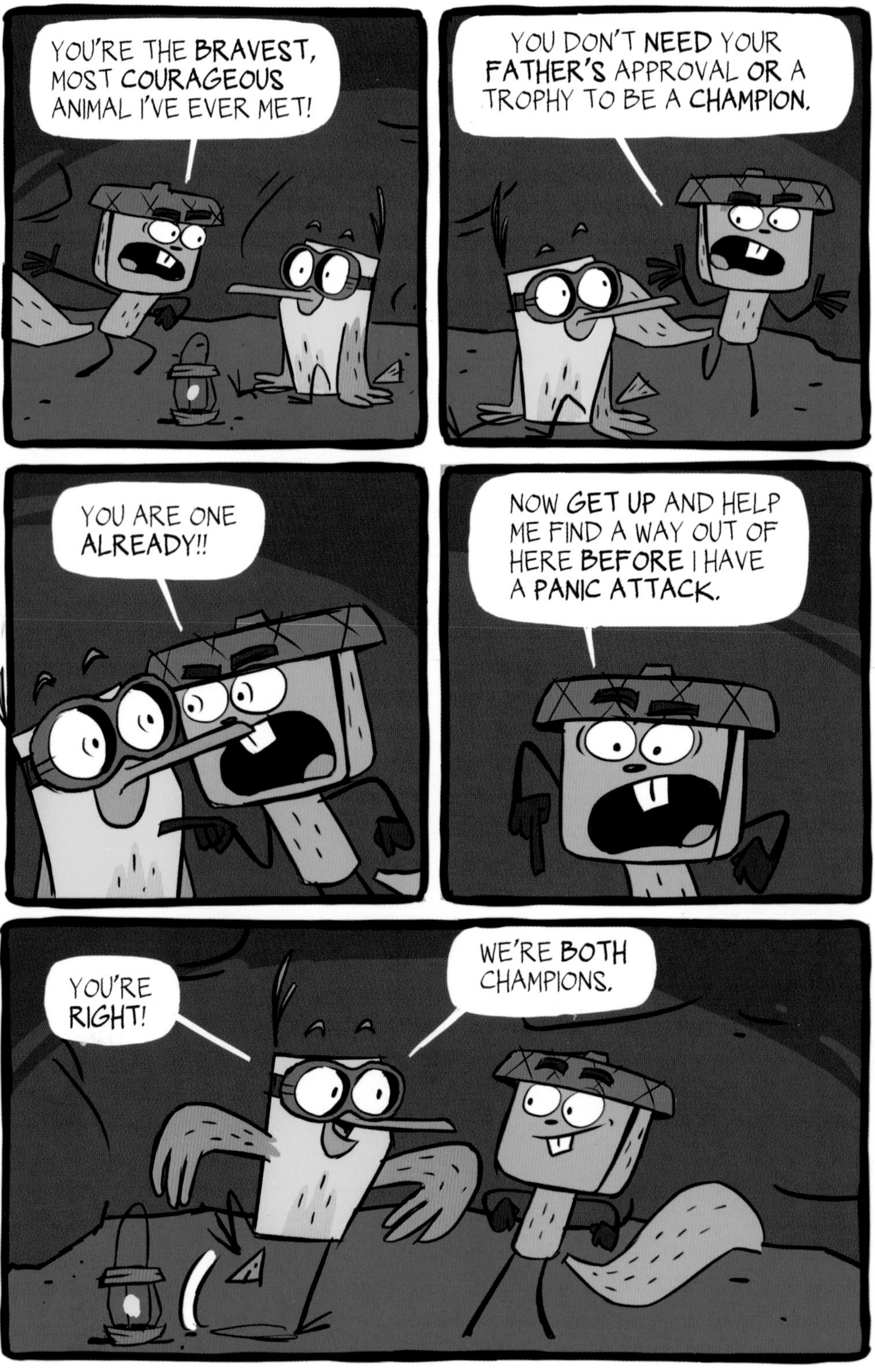
YOU'RE THE BRAVEST, MOST COURAGEOUS ANIMAL I'VE EVER MET!
YOU DON'T NEED YOUR FATHER'S APPROVAL OR A TROPHY TO BE A CHAMPION.
YOU ARE ONE ALREADY!!
NOW GET UP AND HELP ME FIND A WAY OUT OF HERE BEFORE I HAVE A PANIC ATTACK.
YOU'RE RIGHT!
WE'RE BOTH CHAMPIONS.

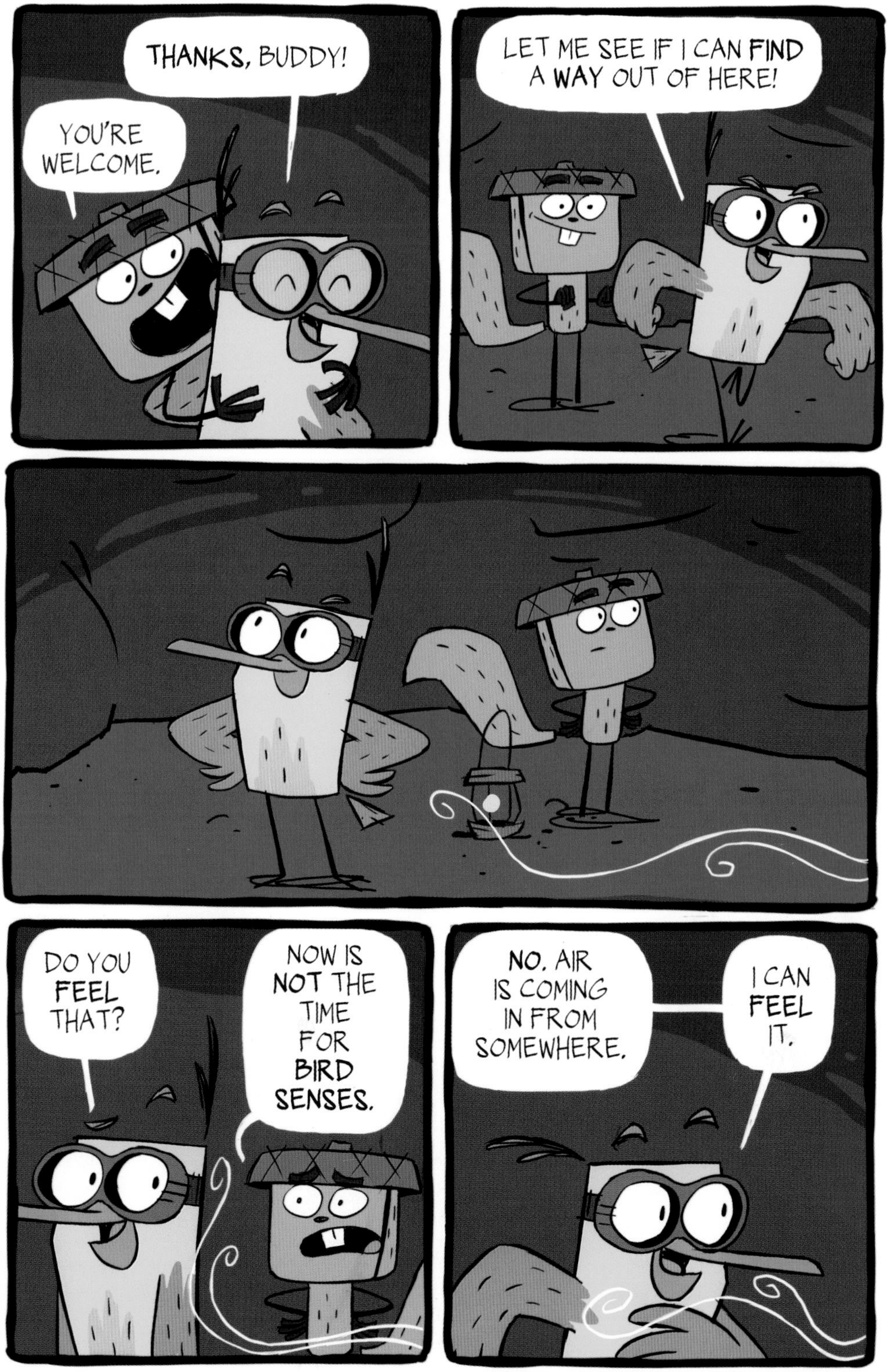
THANKS, BUDDY!
YOU'RE WELCOME.
LET ME SEE IF I CAN FIND A WAY OUT OF HERE!
DO YOU FEEL THAT?
NOW IS NOT THE TIME FOR BIRD SENSES.
NO. AIR IS COMING IN FROM SOMEWHERE.
I CAN FEEL IT.

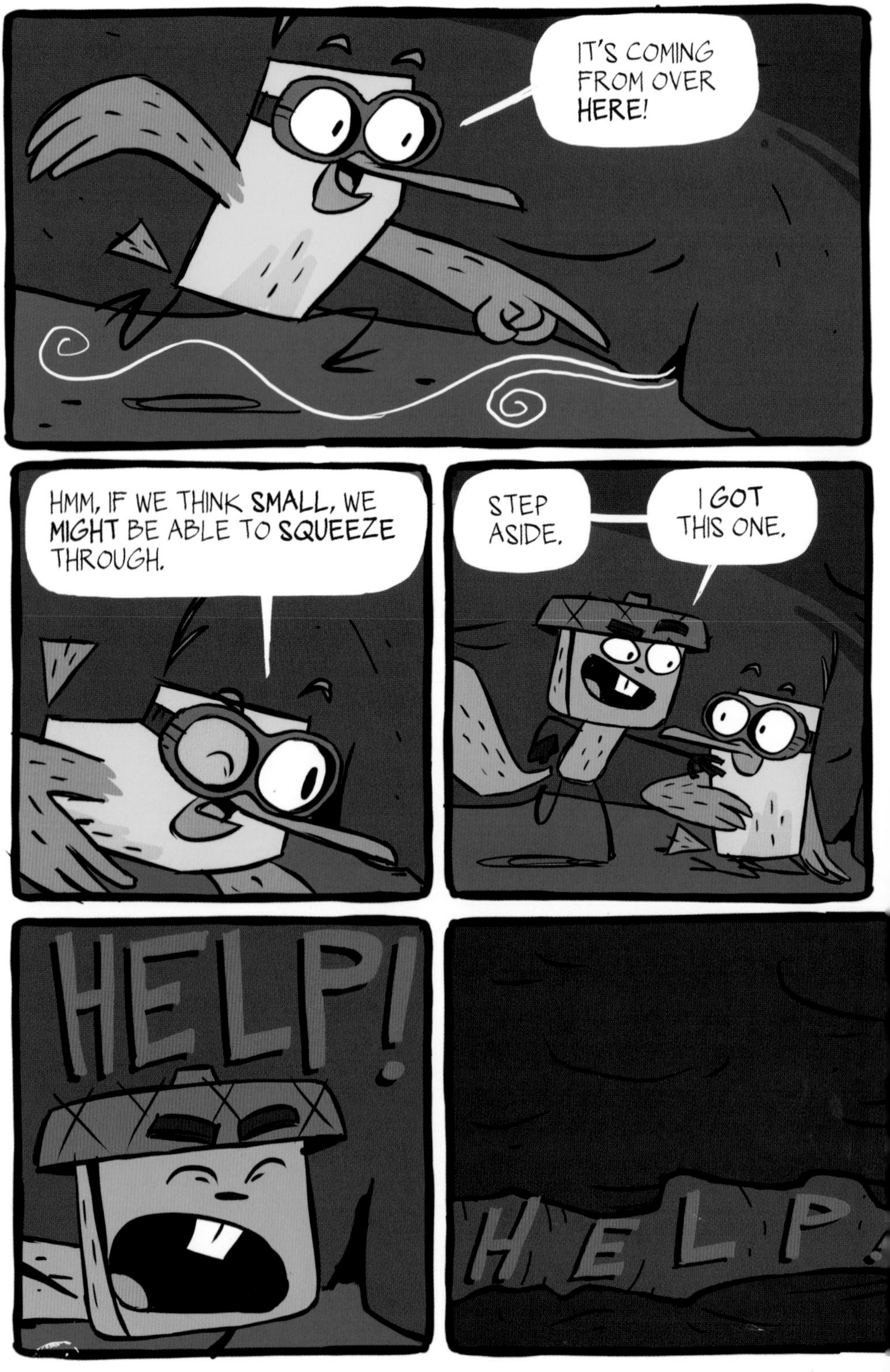
IT'S COMING FROM OVER HERE!
HMM, IF WE THINK SMALL, WE MIGHT BE ABLE TO SQUEEZE THROUGH.
STEP ASIDE.
I GOT THIS ONE.
HELP!
HELP.

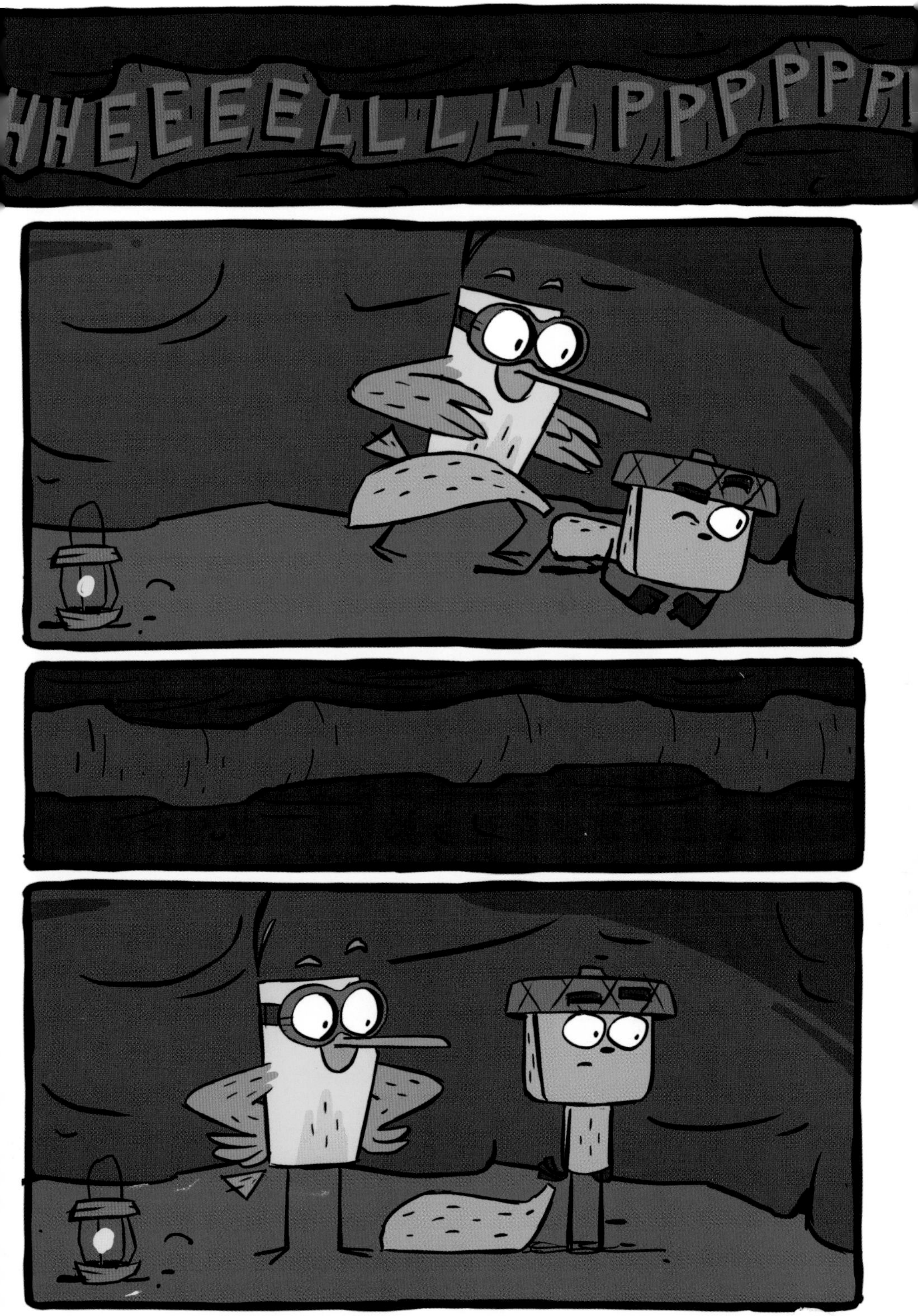
HEEEELLLLLPPPPPP

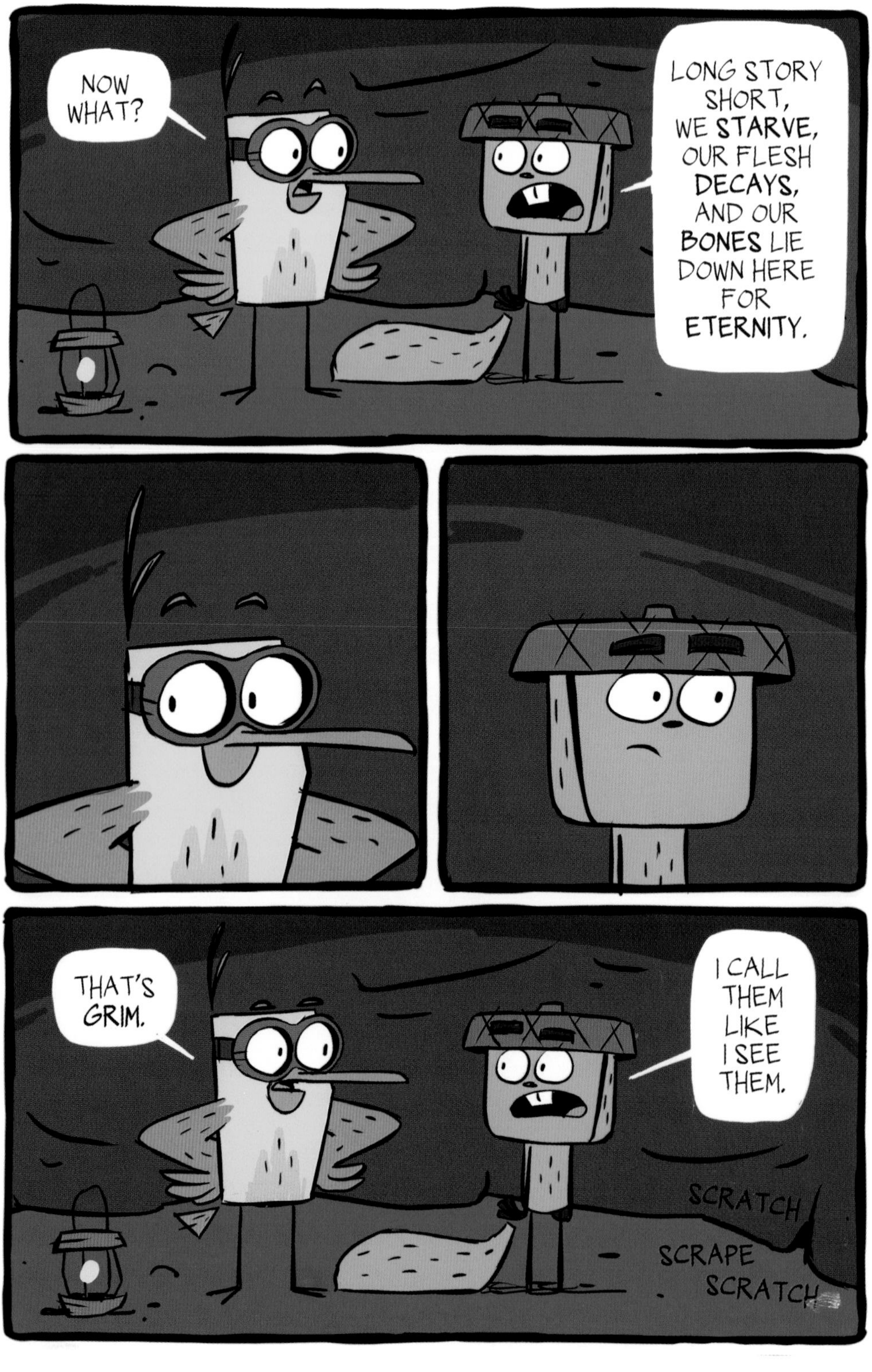
NOW WHAT?
LONG STORY SHORT, WE STARVE, OUR FLESH DECAYS, AND OUR BONES LIE DOWN HERE FOR ETERNITY.
THAT'S GRIM.
I CALL THEM LIKE I SEE THEM.
SCRATCH
SCRAPE
SCRATCH

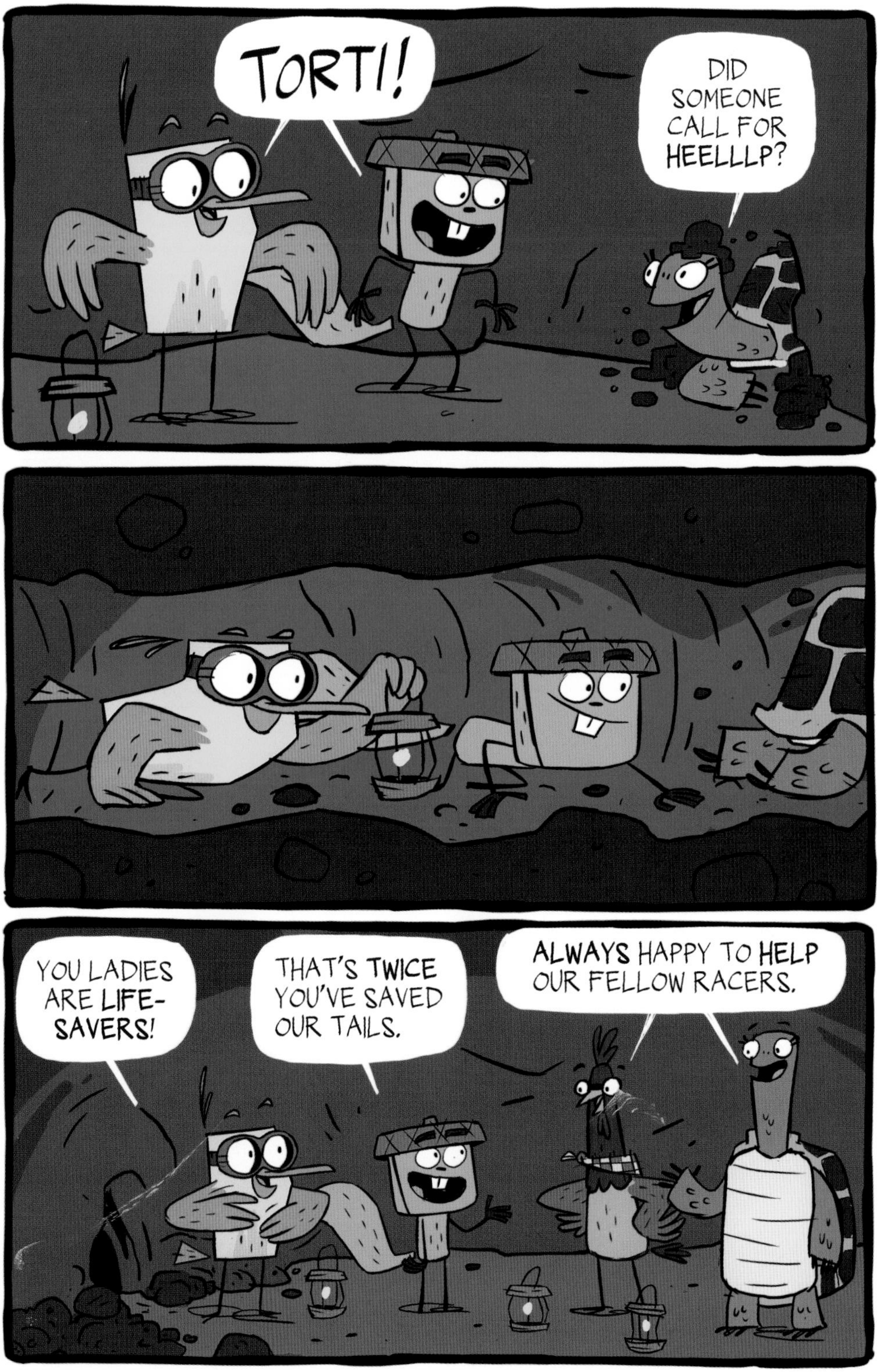
TORTI!
DID SOMEONE CALL FOR HEELLLP?
YOU LADIES ARE LIFE-SAVERS!
THAT'S TWICE YOU'VE SAVED OUR TAILS.
ALWAYS HAPPY TO HELP OUR FELLOW RACERS.

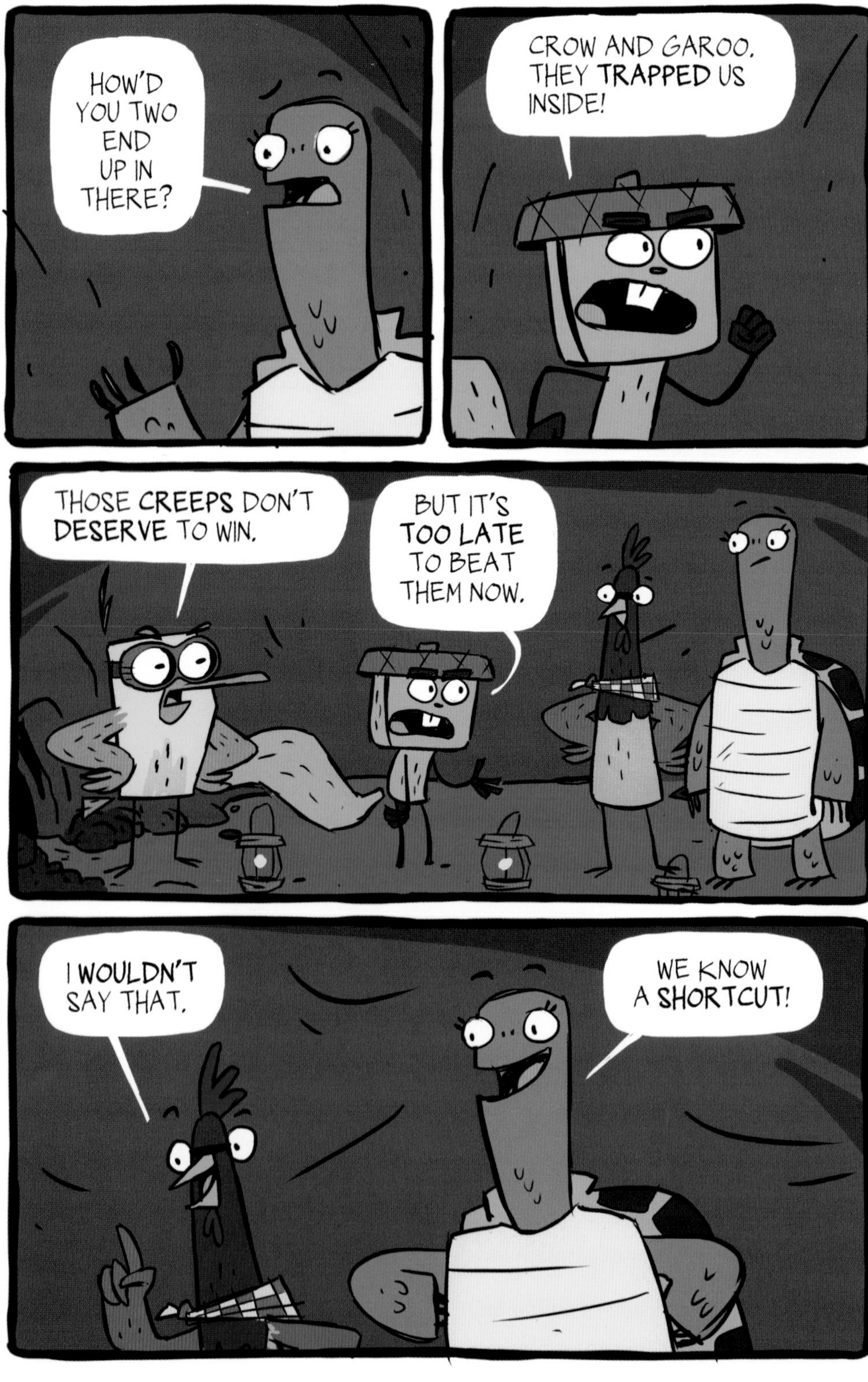
HOW'D YOU TWO END UP IN THERE?
CROW AND GAROO. THEY TRAPPED US INSIDE!
THOSE CREEPS DON'T DESERVE TO WIN.
BUT IT'S TOO LATE TO BEAT THEM NOW.
I WOULDN'T SAY THAT.
WE KNOW A SHORTCUT!

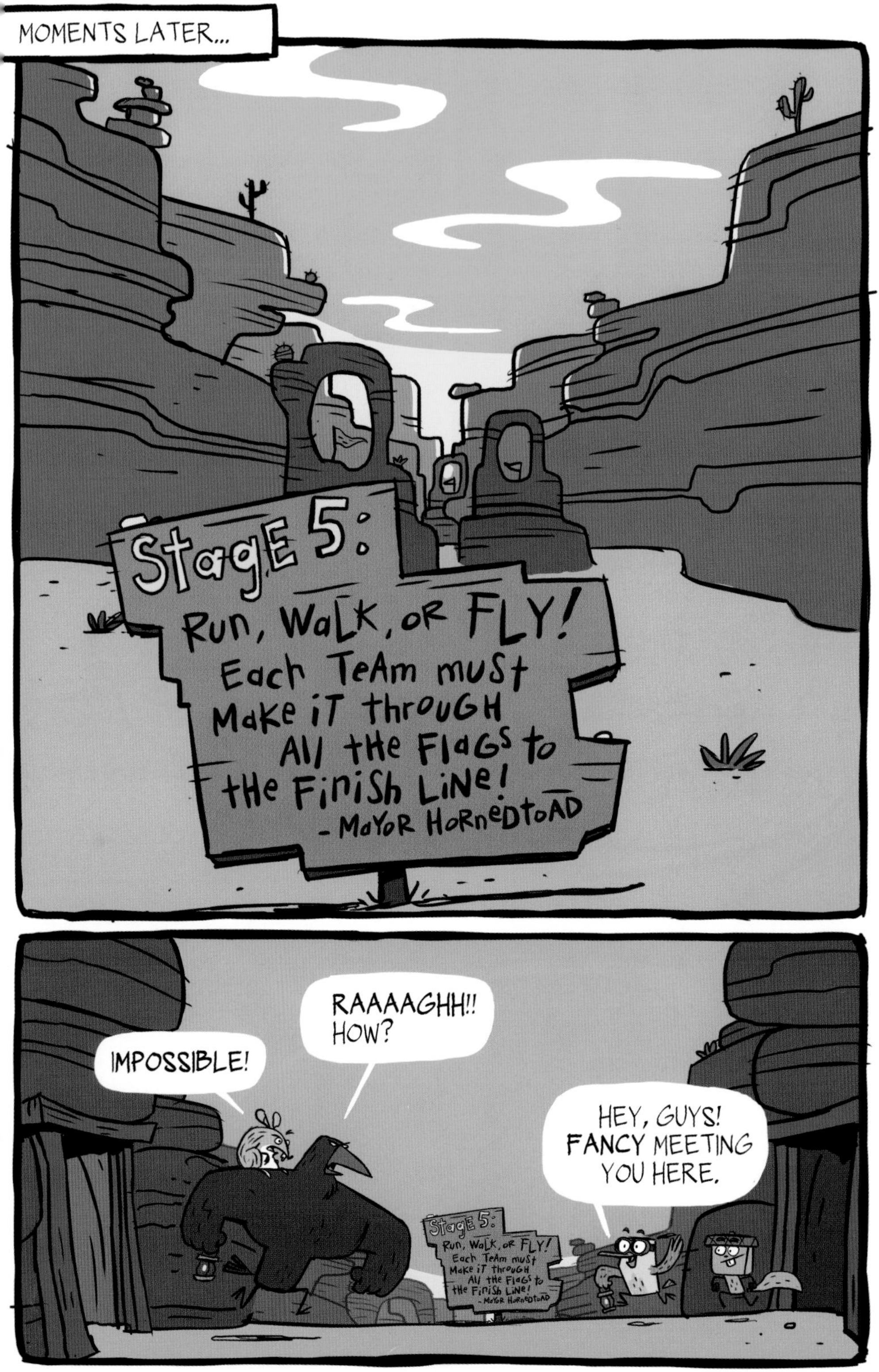
MOMENTS LATER...
Stage 5:
Run, WaLK, oR FLY!
Each TeAm must Make iT throuGH All the Flags to the Finish Line!
- MaYoR HoRnedtoAD
IMPOSSIBLE!
RAAAAGHH!! HOW?
HEY, GUYS! FANCY MEETING YOU HERE.

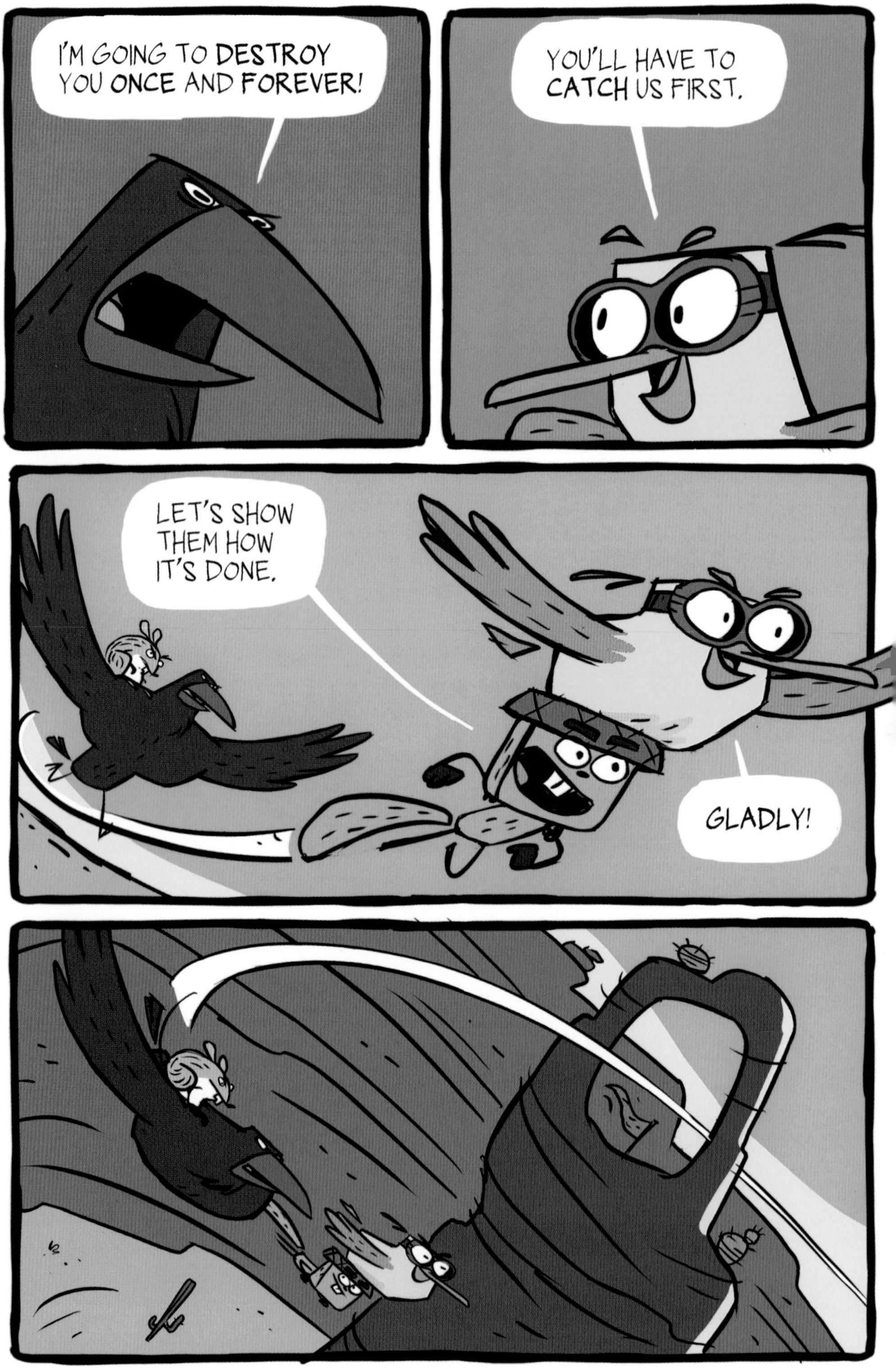
I'M GOING TO DESTROY YOU ONCE AND FOREVER!
YOU'LL HAVE TO CATCH US FIRST.
LET'S SHOW THEM HOW IT'S DONE.
GLADLY!

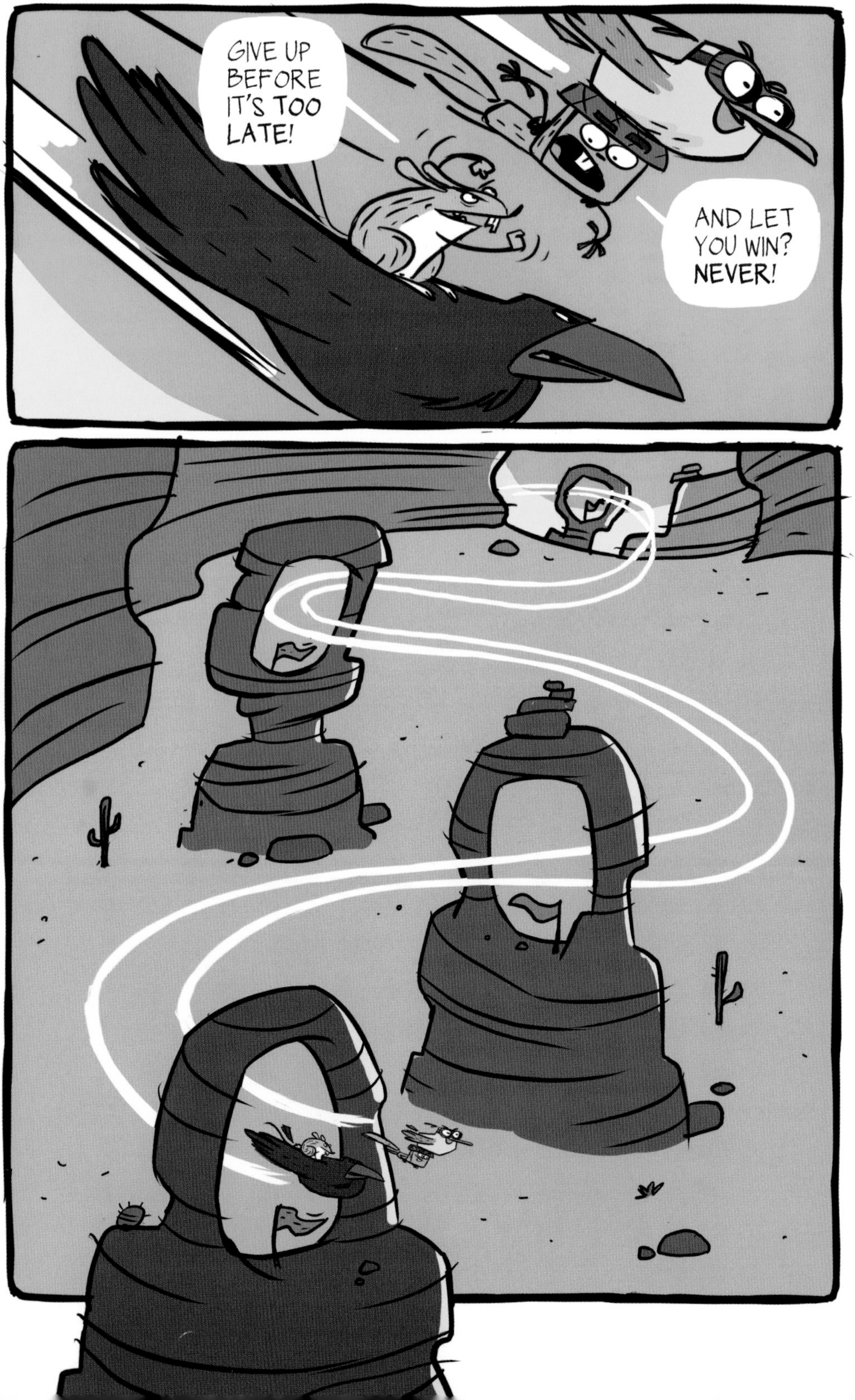
GIVE UP BEFORE IT'S TOO LATE!
AND LET YOU WIN? NEVER!

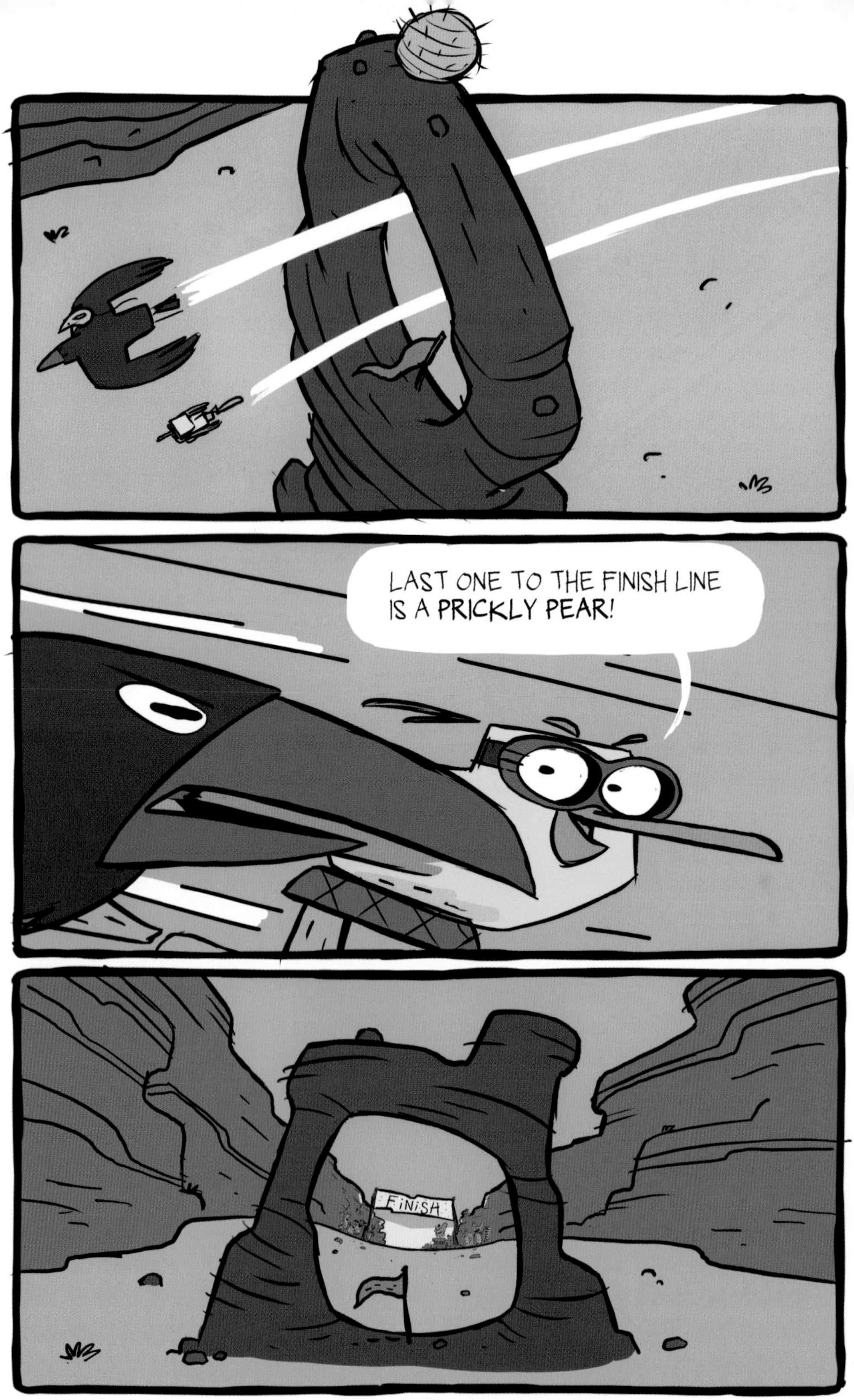
LAST ONE TO THE FINISH LINE IS A PRICKLY PEAR!
FINISH

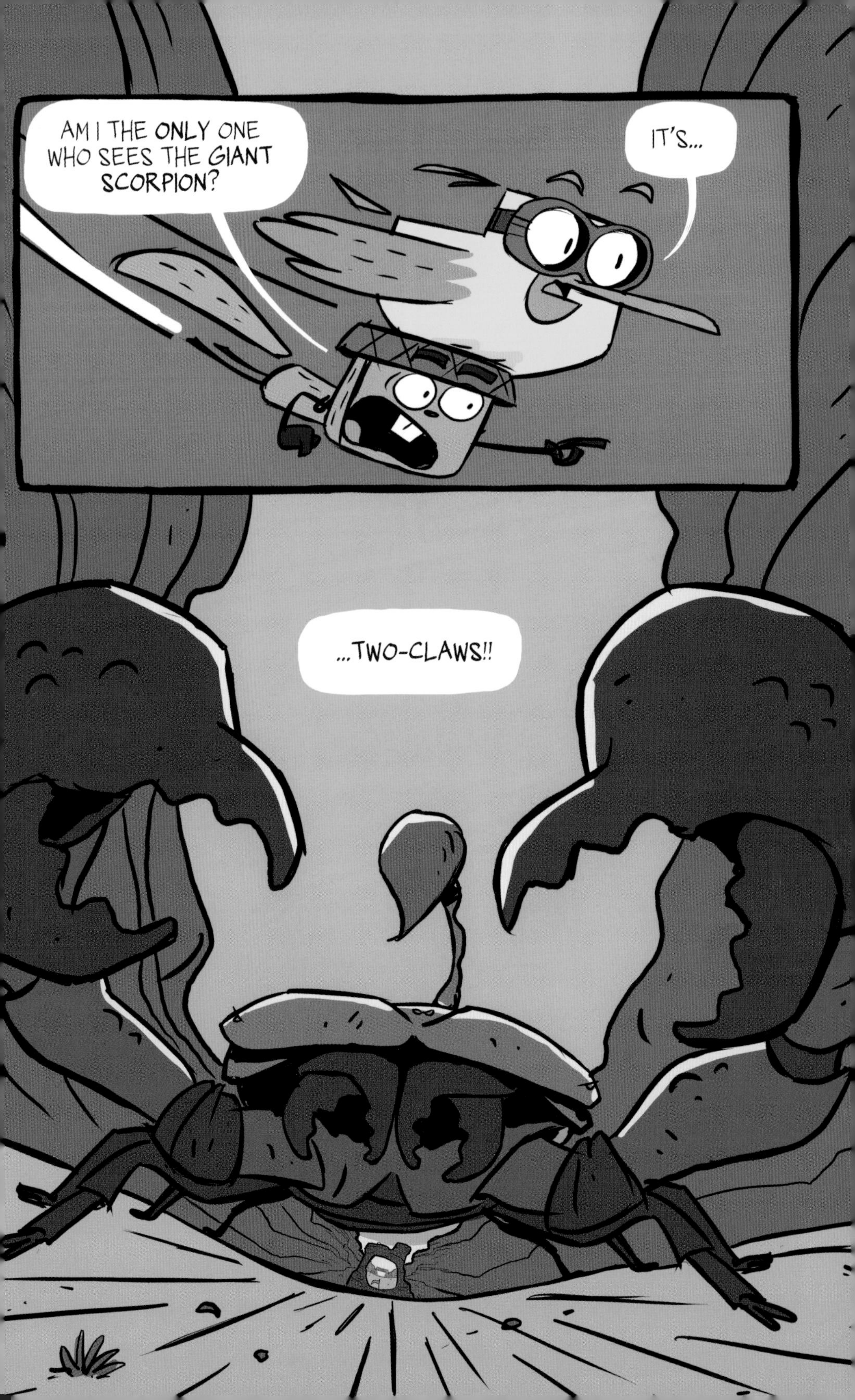
AM I THE ONLY ONE WHO SEES THE GIANT SCORPION?
IT'S...
...TWO-CLAWS!!

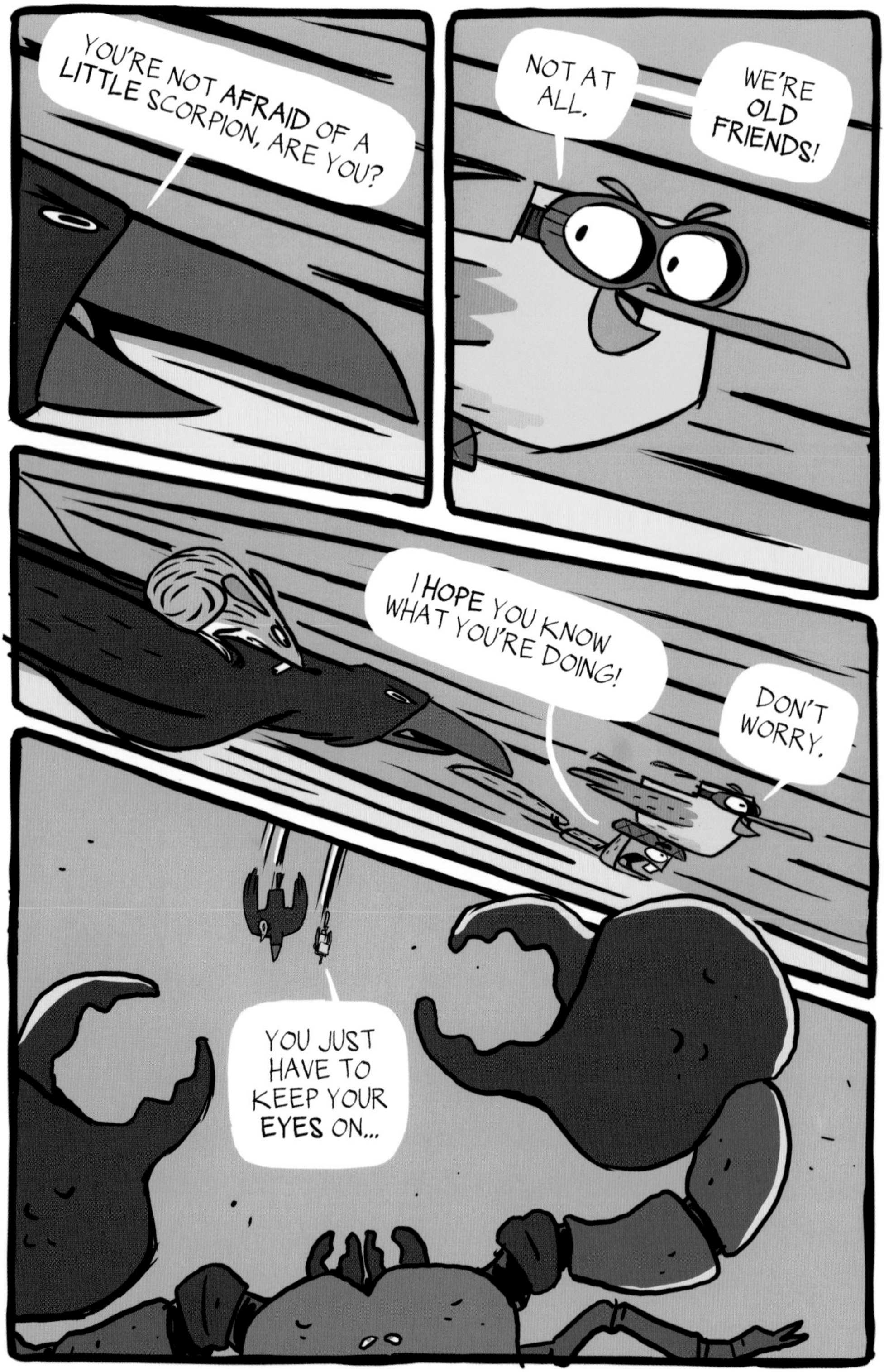

YOU'RE NOT AFRAID OF A LITTLE SCORPION, ARE YOU?
NOT AT ALL.
WE'RE OLD FRIENDS!
I HOPE YOU KNOW WHAT YOU'RE DOING!
DON'T WORRY.
YOU JUST HAVE TO KEEP YOUR EYES ON...

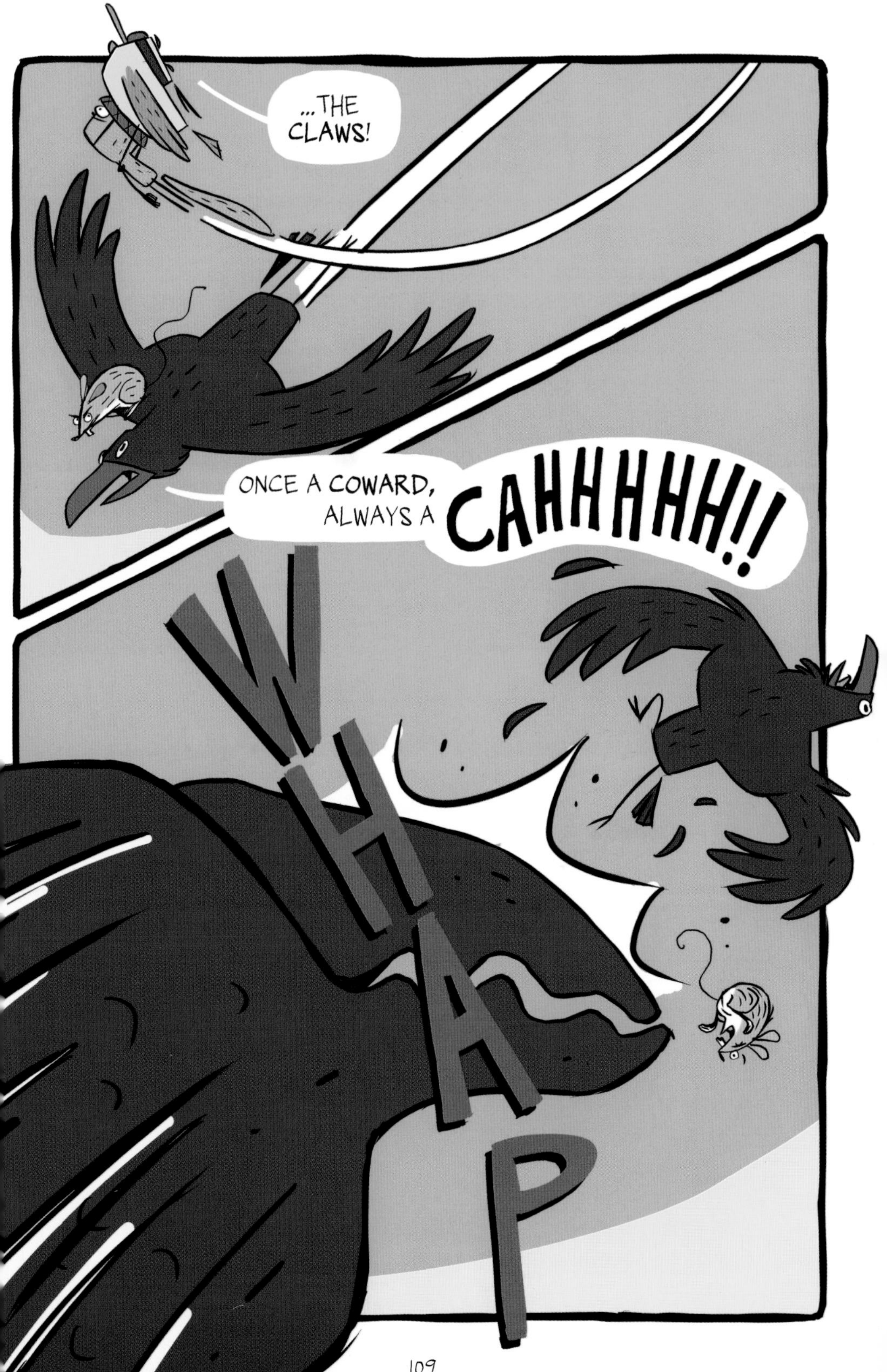
...THE CLAWS!
ONCE A COWARD, ALWAYS A CAHHHHH!!
WHAP

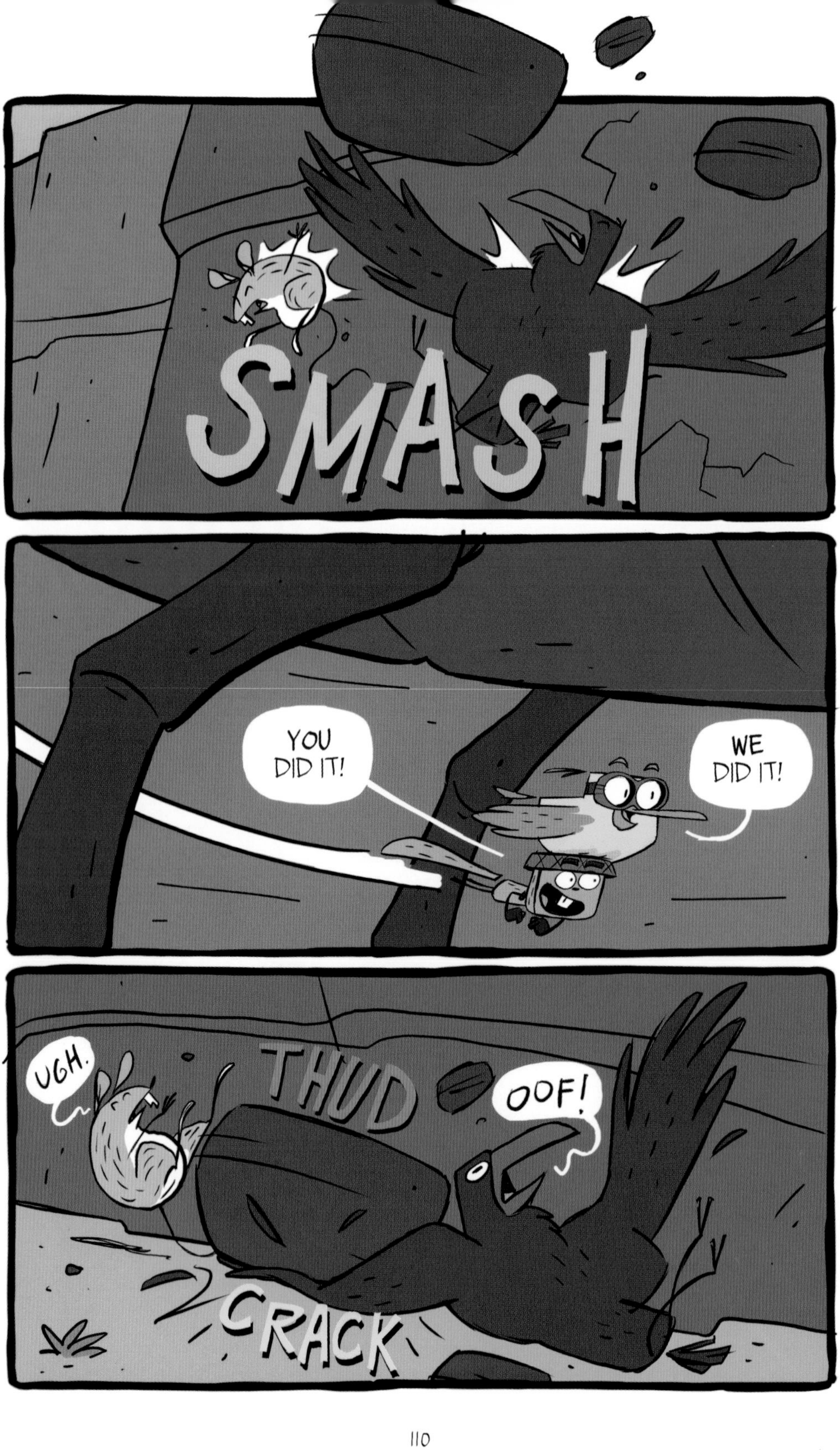
SMASH
YOU DID IT!
WE DID IT!
UGH.
THUD
OOF!
CRACK

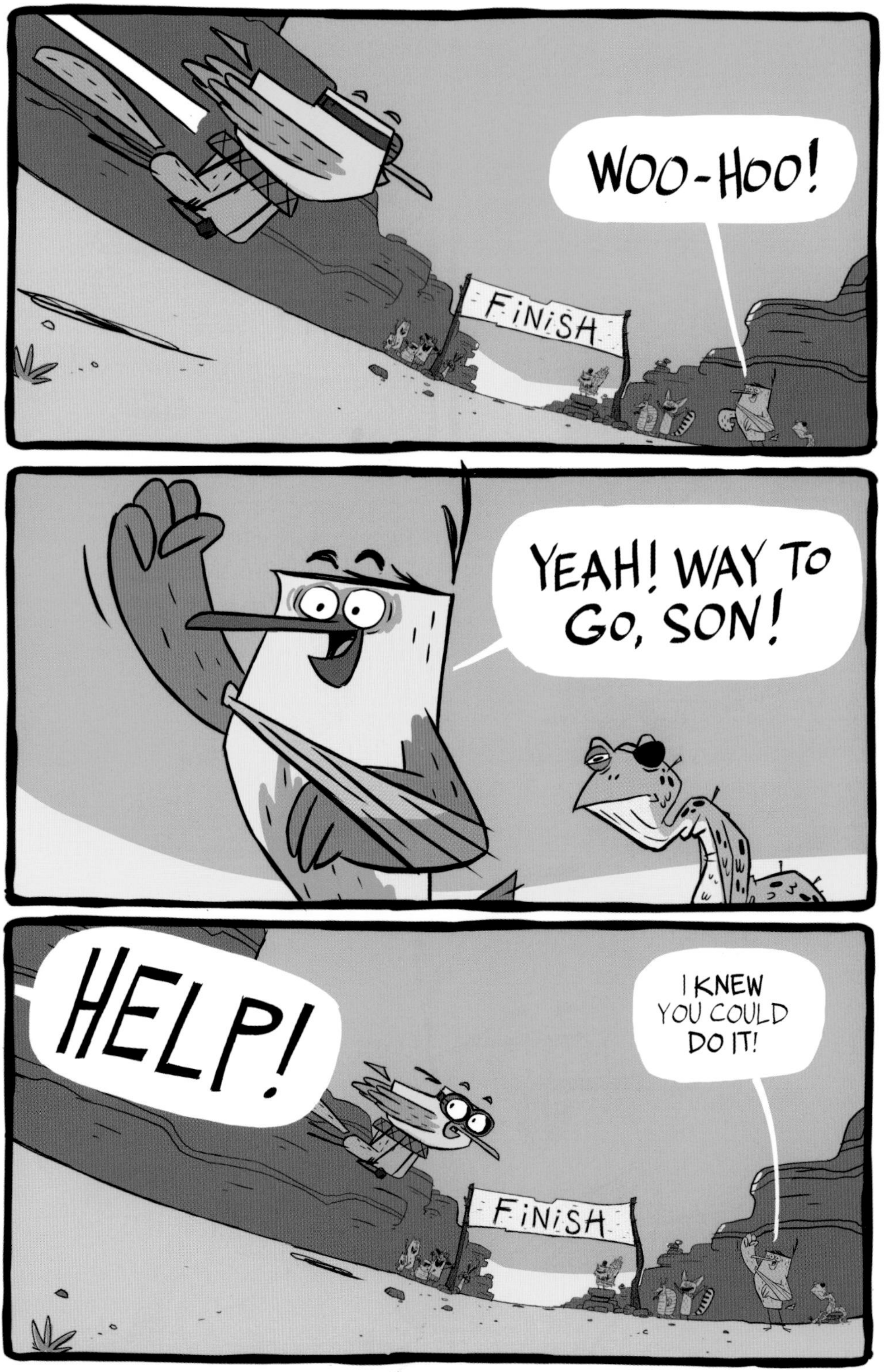
WOO-HOO!
FINISH
YEAH! WAY TO GO, SON!
HELP!
I KNEW YOU COULD DO IT!
FINISH

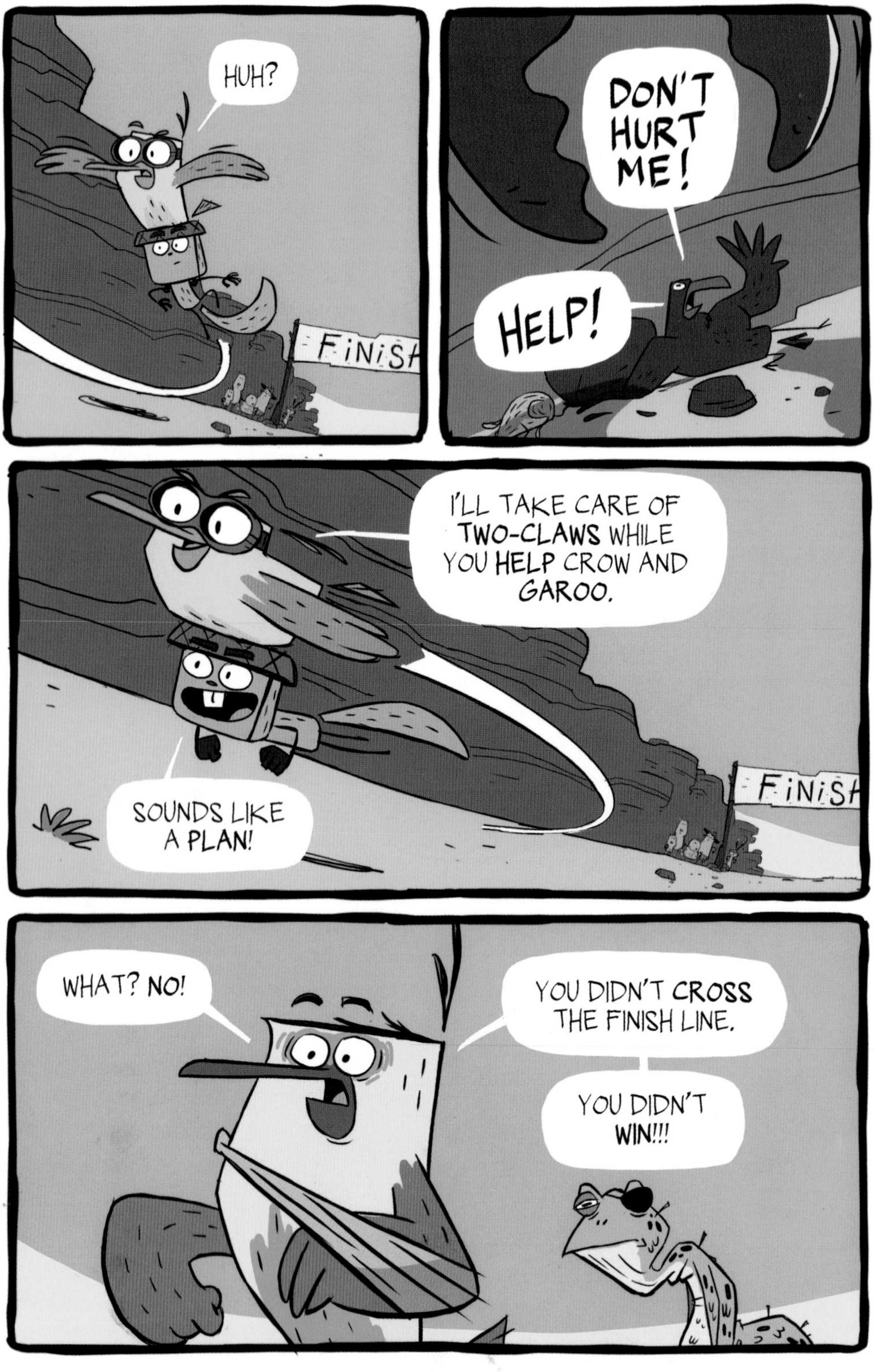
HUH?
FINISH
DON'T HURT ME!
HELP!
I'LL TAKE CARE OF TWO-CLAWS WHILE YOU HELP CROW AND GAROO.
SOUNDS LIKE A PLAN!
FINISH
WHAT? NO!
YOU DIDN'T CROSS THE FINISH LINE.
YOU DIDN'T WIN!!!

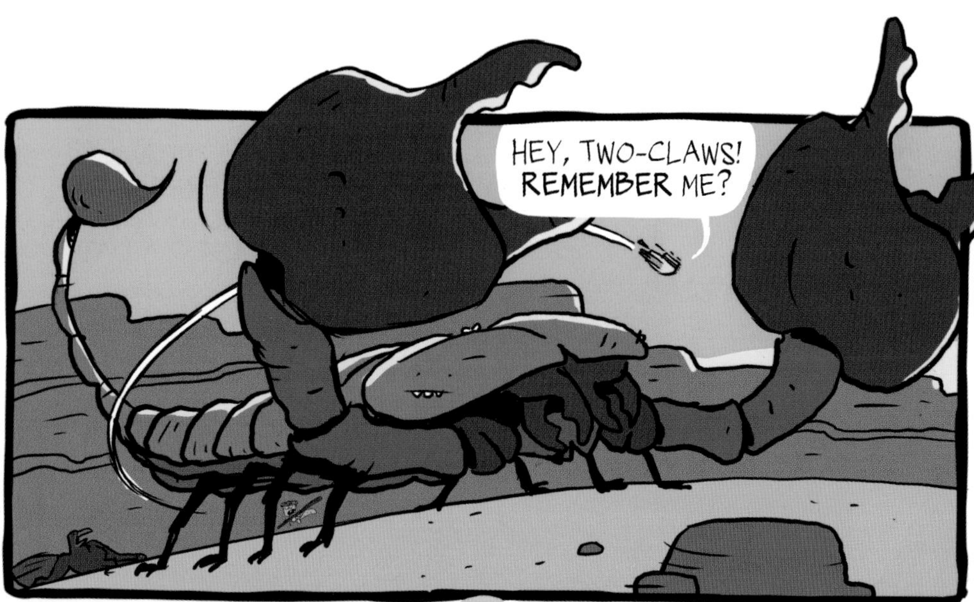
HEY, TWO-CLAWS! REMEMBER ME?

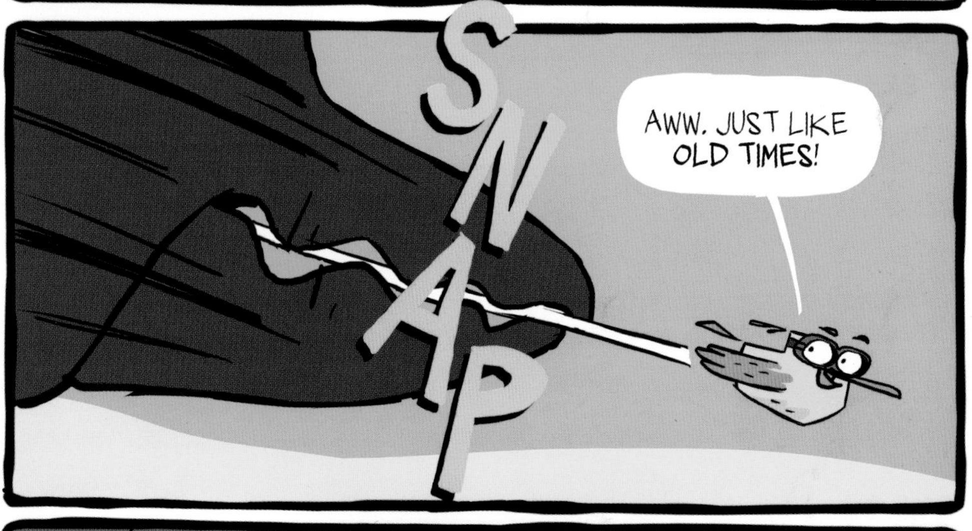
SNAP
AWW. JUST LIKE OLD TIMES!

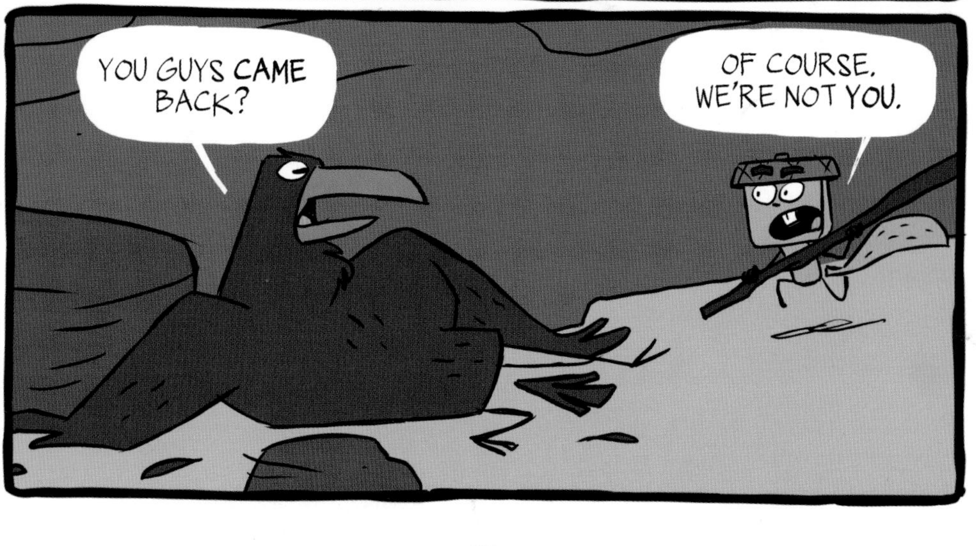
YOU GUYS CAME BACK?
OF COURSE. WE'RE NOT YOU.

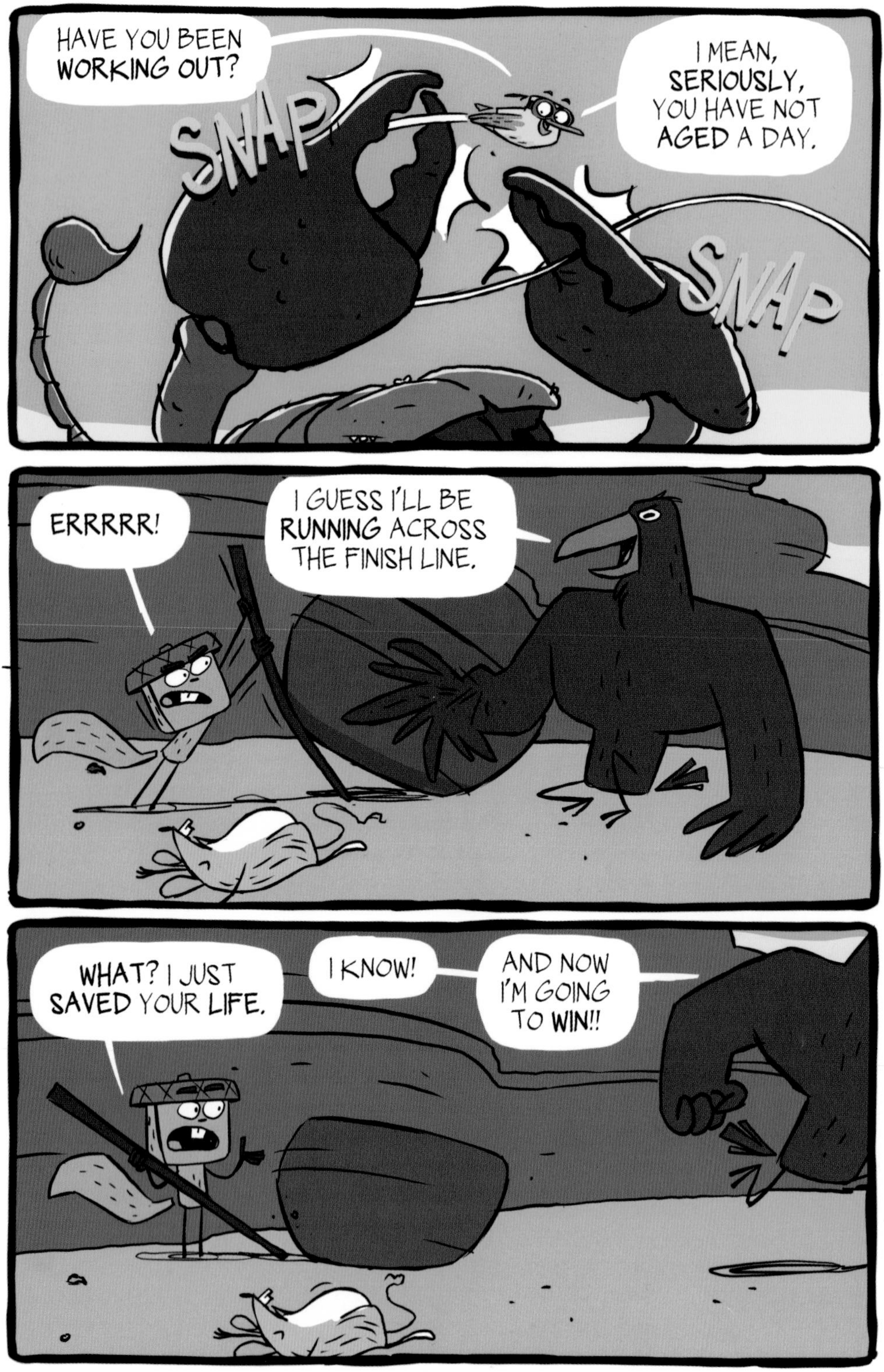
HAVE YOU BEEN WORKING OUT?
SNAP
I MEAN, SERIOUSLY, YOU HAVE NOT AGED A DAY.
SNAP
ERRRRR!
I GUESS I'LL BE RUNNING ACROSS THE FINISH LINE.
WHAT? I JUST SAVED YOUR LIFE.
I KNOW!
AND NOW I'M GOING TO WIN!!

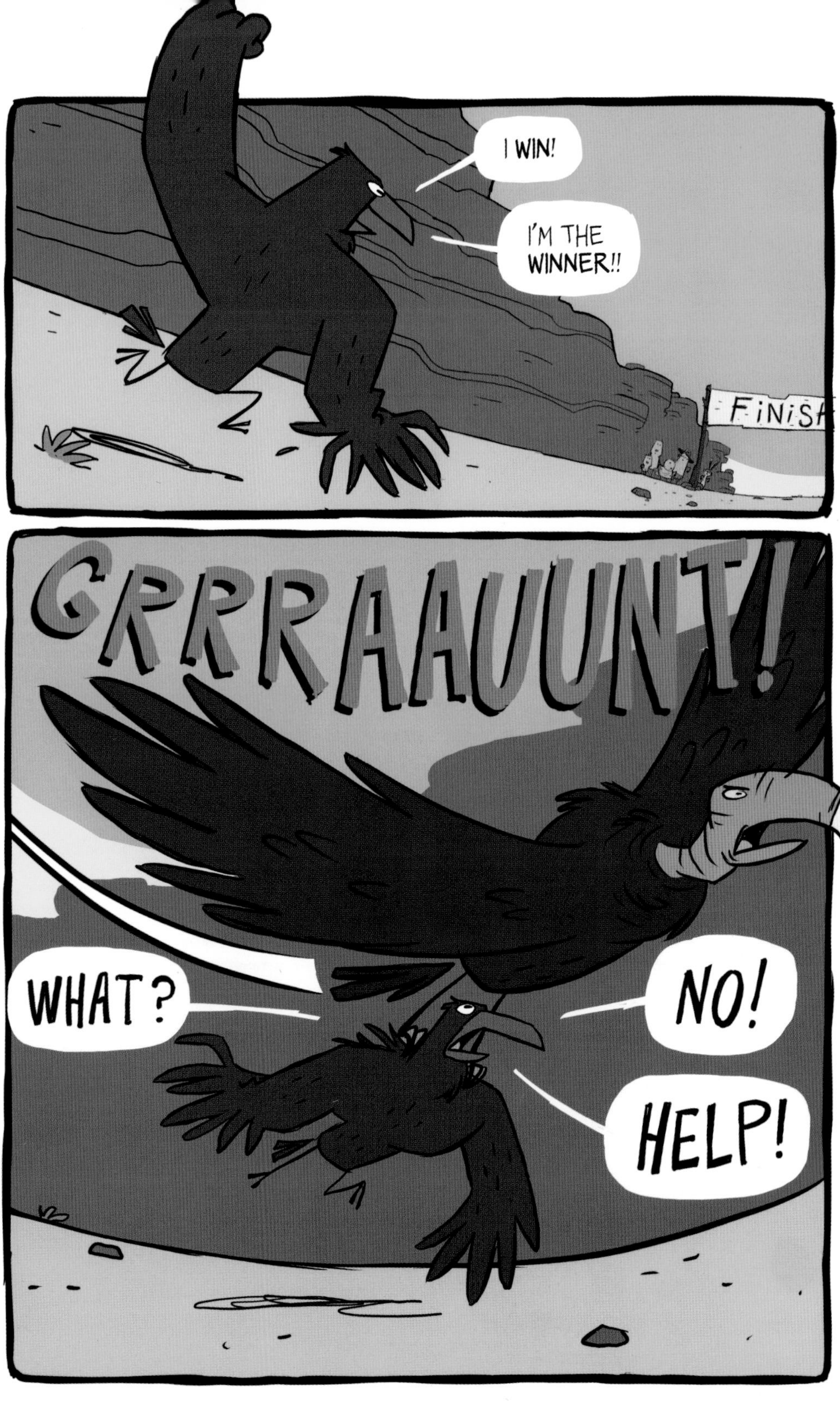
I WIN!
I'M THE WINNER!!
FINIS
GRRRAAUUNT!
WHAT?
NO!
HELP!

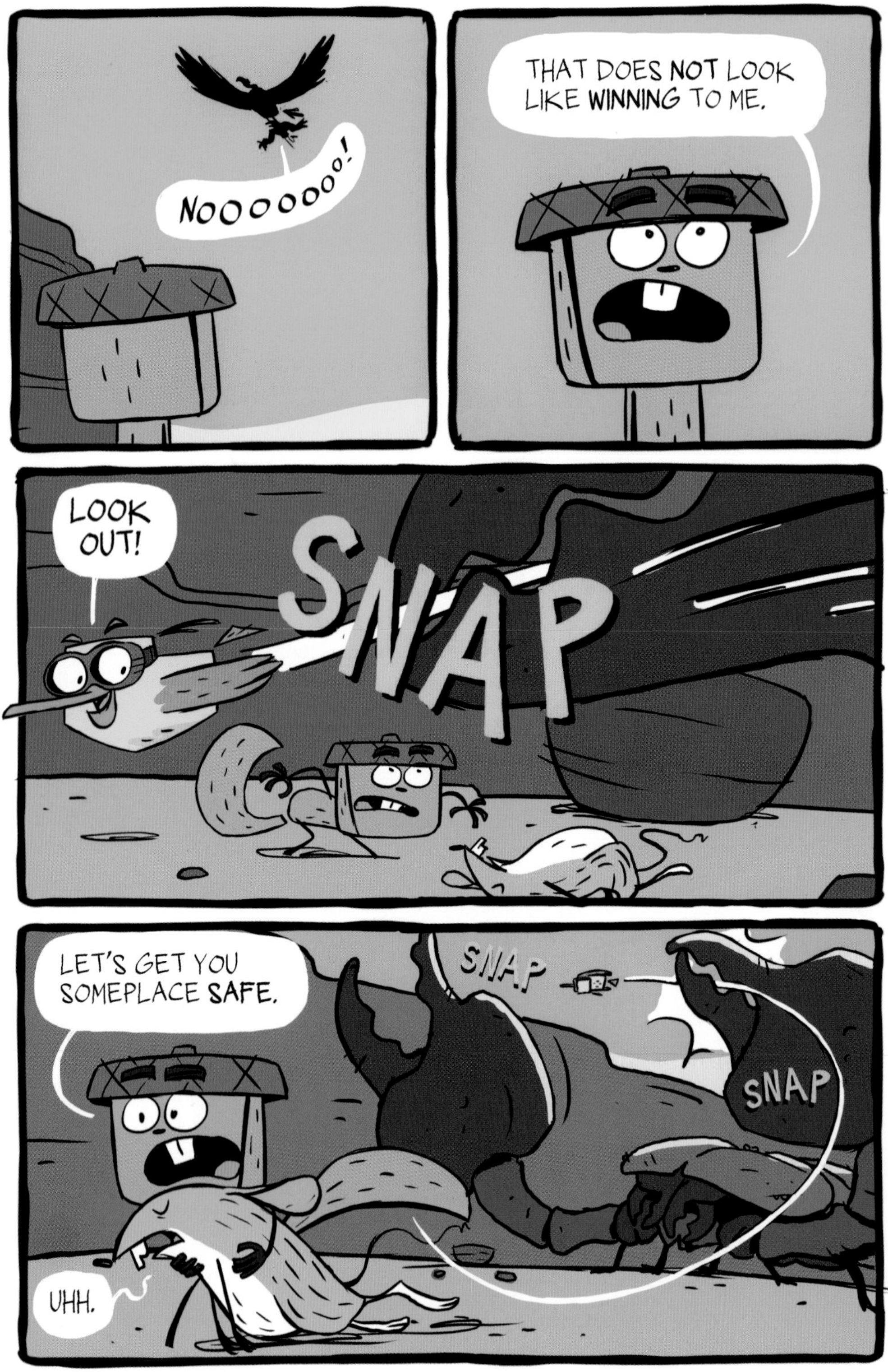
NOOOOOOO!
THAT DOES NOT LOOK LIKE WINNING TO ME.
LOOK OUT!
SNAP
LET'S GET YOU SOMEPLACE SAFE.
SNAP
SNAP
UHH.

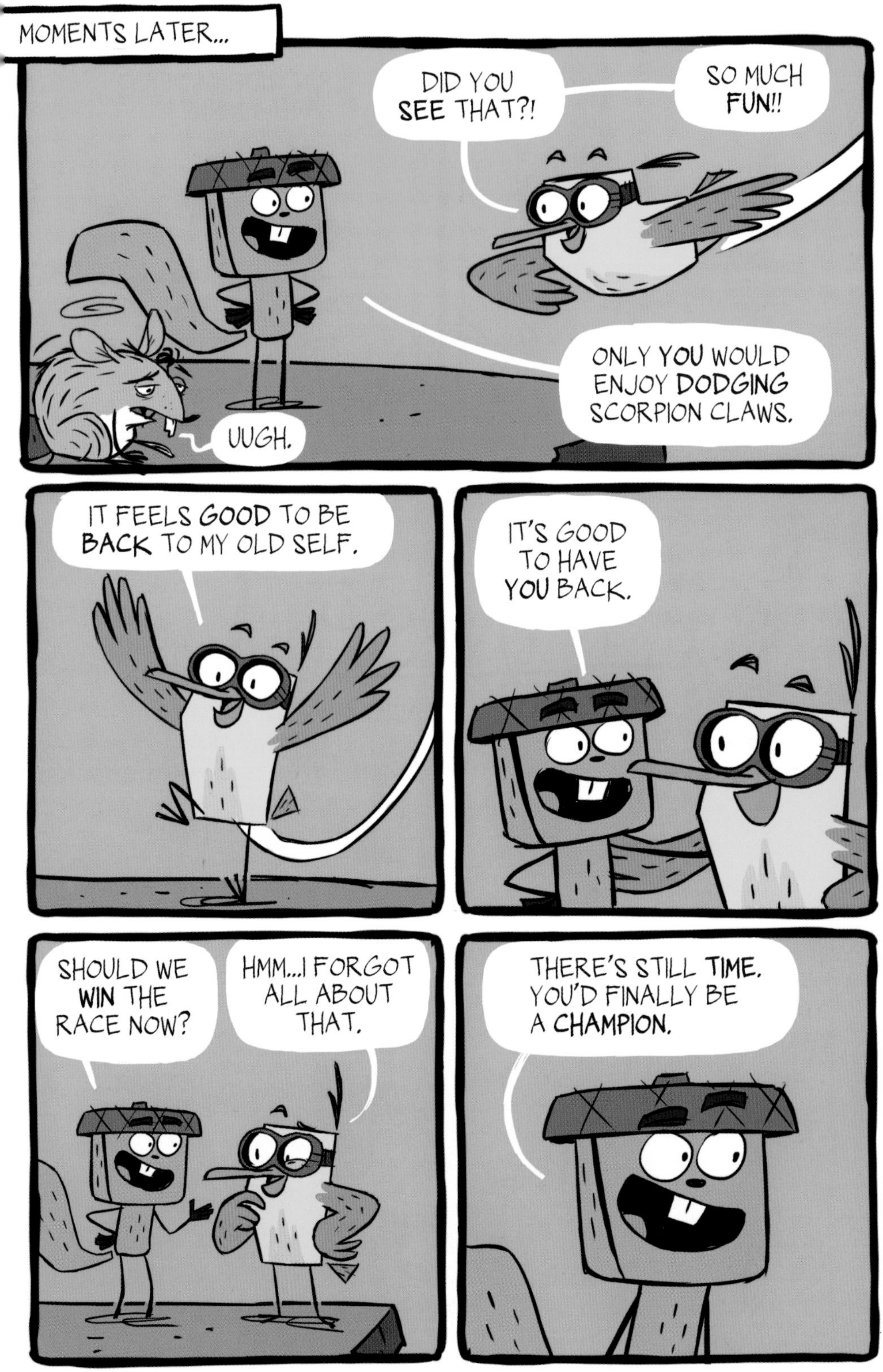
MOMENTS LATER...
DID YOU SEE THAT?!
SO MUCH FUN!!
ONLY YOU WOULD ENJOY DODGING SCORPION CLAWS.
UUGH.
IT FEELS GOOD TO BE BACK TO MY OLD SELF.
IT'S GOOD TO HAVE YOU BACK.
SHOULD WE WIN THE RACE NOW?
HMM...I FORGOT ALL ABOUT THAT.
THERE'S STILL TIME. YOU'D FINALLY BE A CHAMPION.

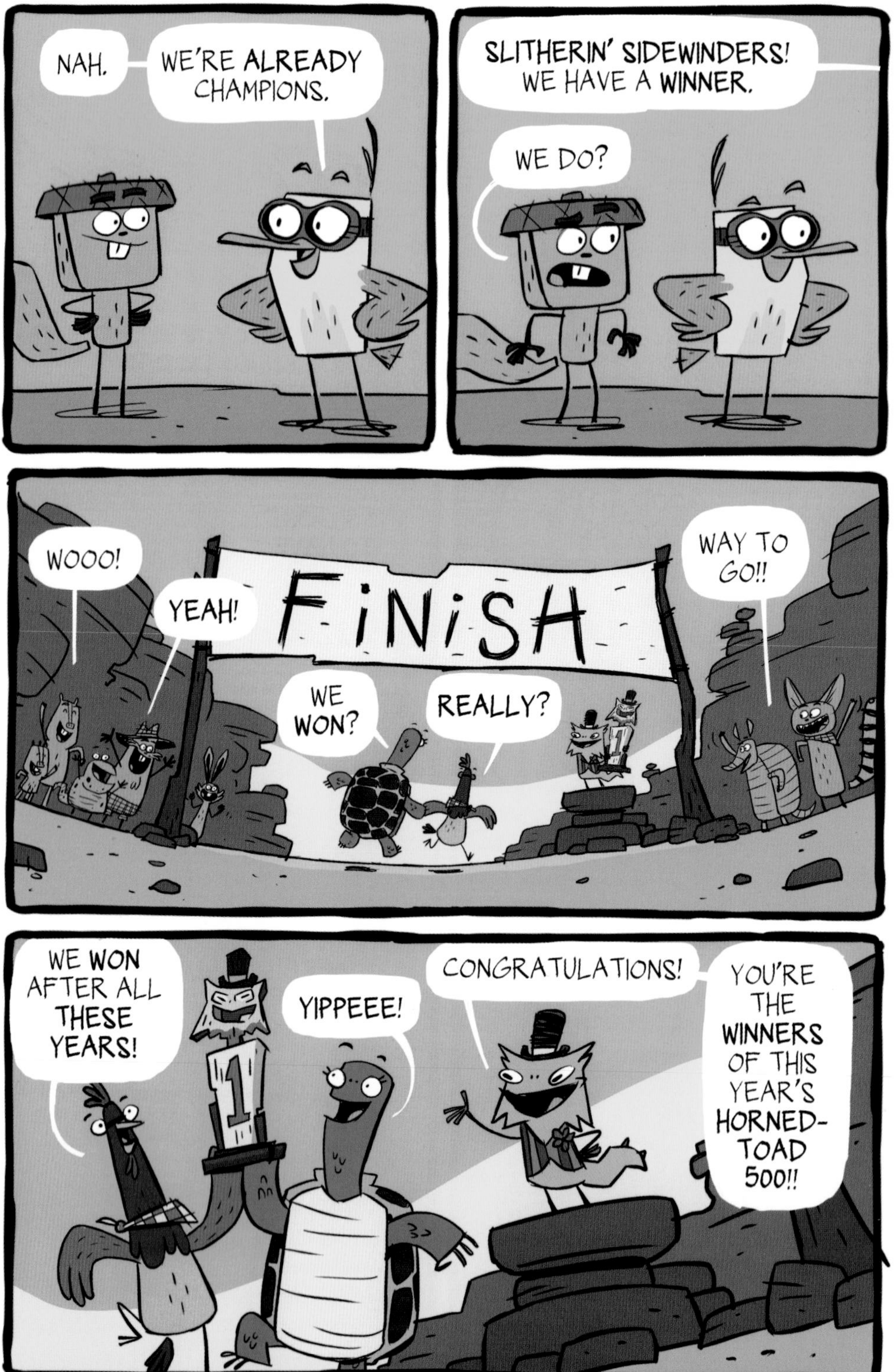
NAH.
WE'RE **ALREADY** CHAMPIONS.
SLITHERIN' SIDEWINDERS! WE HAVE A **WINNER**.
WE DO?
WOOO!
YEAH!
FINISH
WAY TO GO!!
WE WON?
REALLY?
WE **WON** AFTER ALL **THESE** **YEARS**!
YIPPEEE!
CONGRATULATIONS!
YOU'RE THE **WINNERS** OF THIS YEAR'S **HORNED-TOAD 500!!**

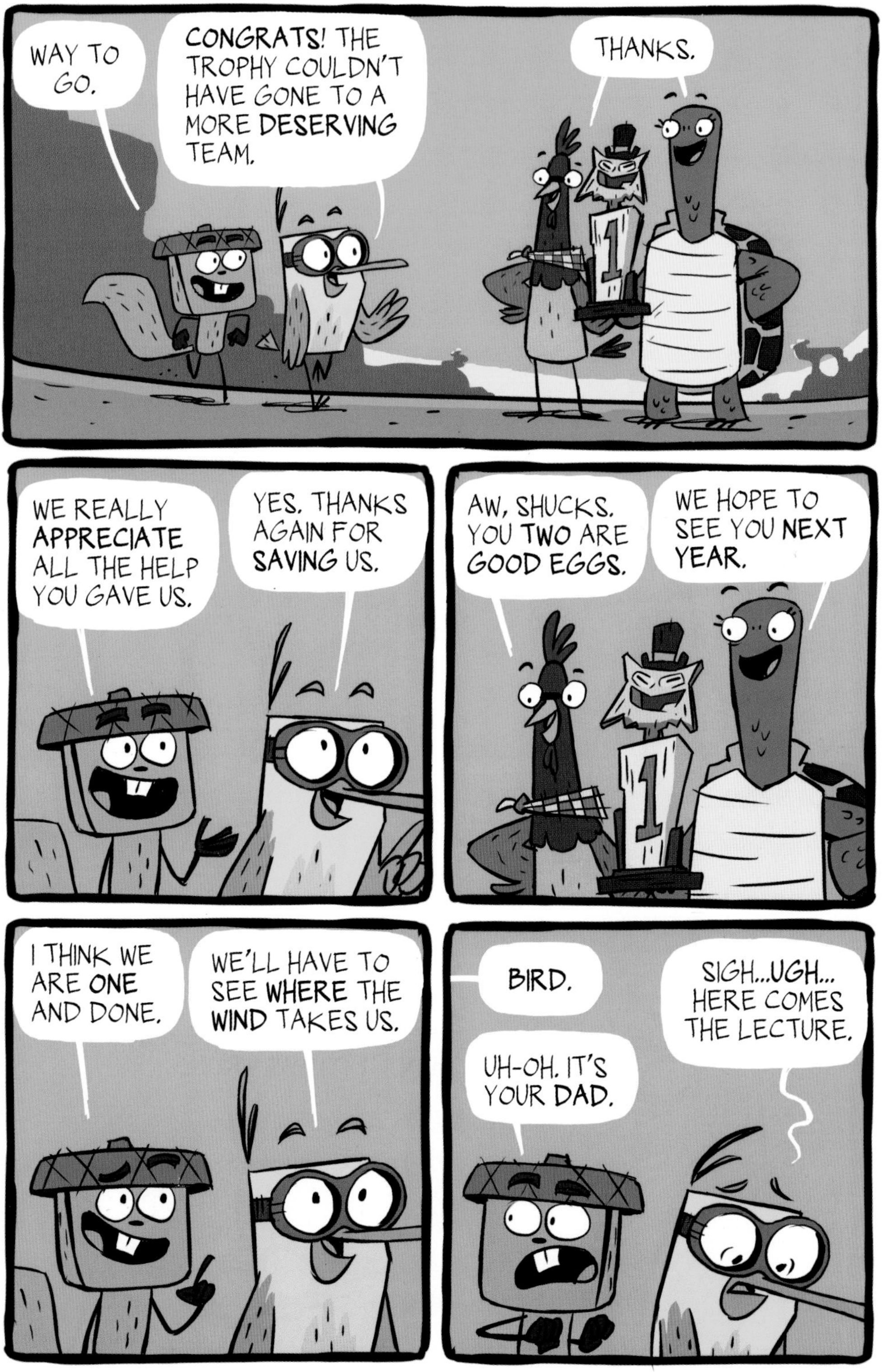
WAY TO GO.
CONGRATS! THE TROPHY COULDN'T HAVE GONE TO A MORE DESERVING TEAM.
THANKS.
WE REALLY APPRECIATE ALL THE HELP YOU GAVE US.
YES. THANKS AGAIN FOR SAVING US.
AW, SHUCKS. YOU TWO ARE GOOD EGGS.
WE HOPE TO SEE YOU NEXT YEAR.
I THINK WE ARE ONE AND DONE.
WE'LL HAVE TO SEE WHERE THE WIND TAKES US.
BIRD.
UH-OH. IT'S YOUR DAD.
SIGH...UGH... HERE COMES THE LECTURE.

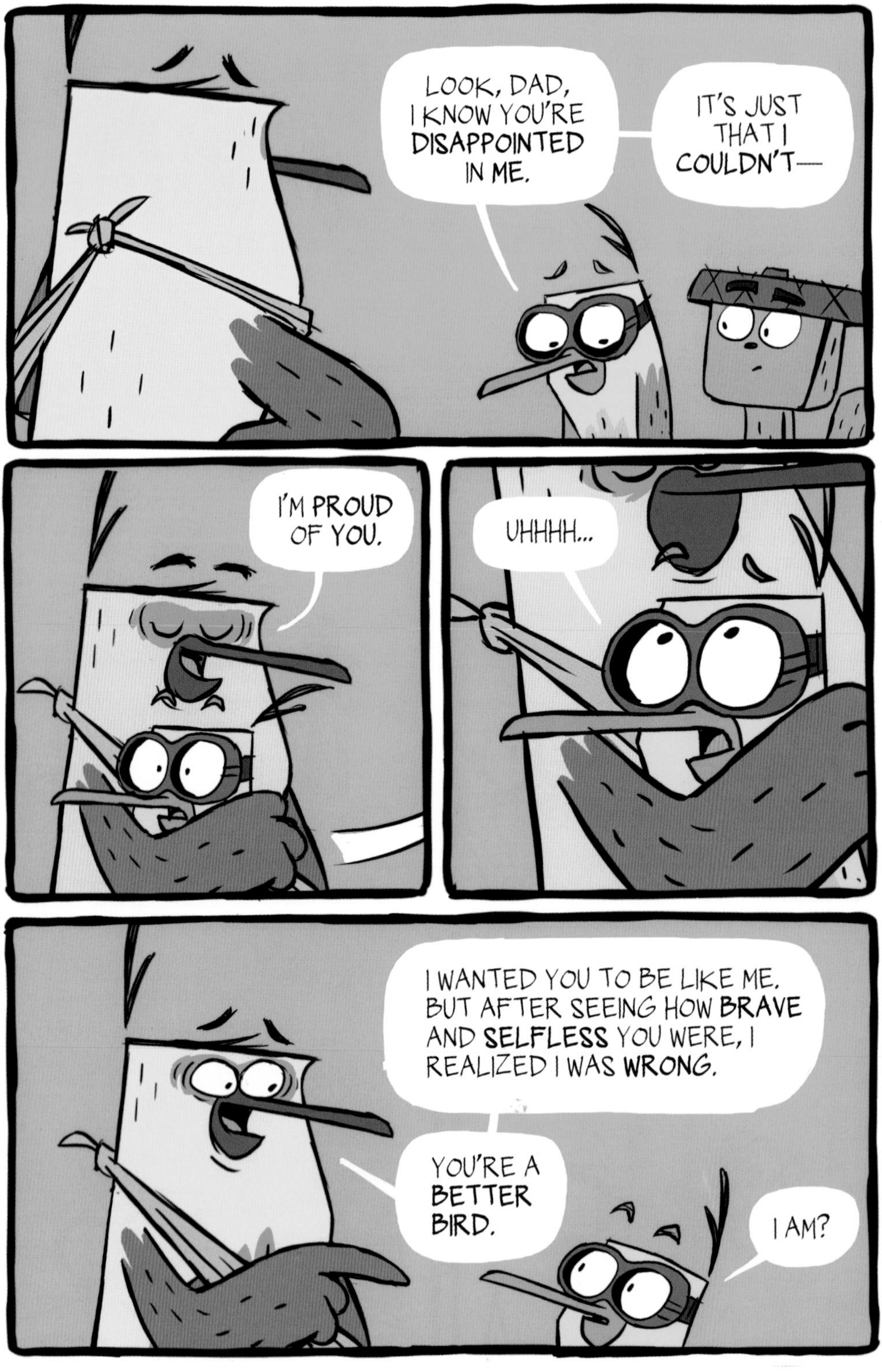
LOOK, DAD, I KNOW YOU'RE DISAPPOINTED IN ME.
IT'S JUST THAT I COULDN'T—
I'M PROUD OF YOU.
UHHHH...
I WANTED YOU TO BE LIKE ME. BUT AFTER SEEING HOW BRAVE AND SELFLESS YOU WERE, I REALIZED I WAS WRONG.
YOU'RE A BETTER BIRD.
I AM?

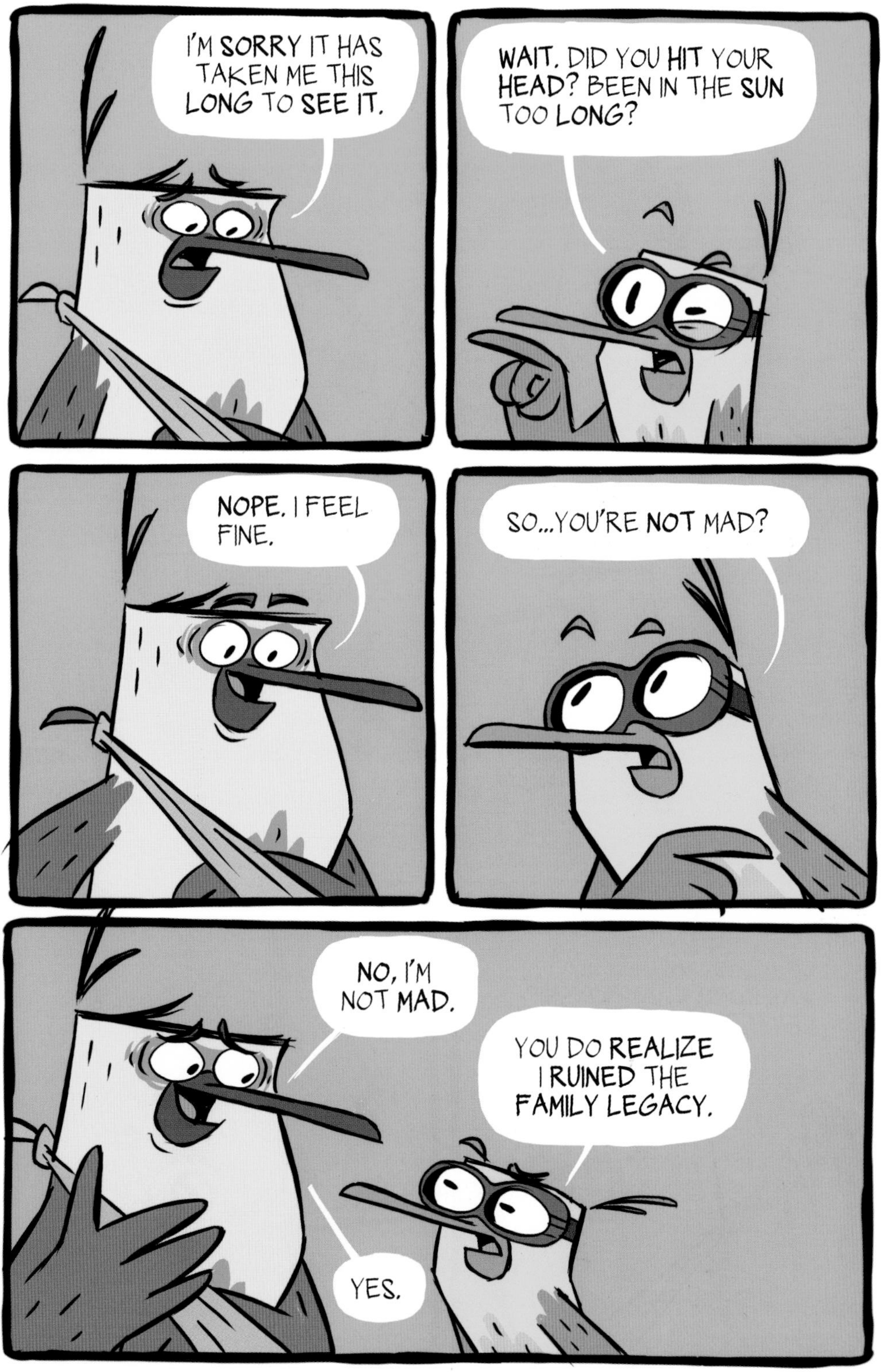
I'M SORRY IT HAS TAKEN ME THIS LONG TO SEE IT.
WAIT. DID YOU HIT YOUR HEAD? BEEN IN THE SUN TOO LONG?
NOPE. I FEEL FINE.
SO...YOU'RE NOT MAD?
NO, I'M NOT MAD.
YOU DO REALIZE I RUINED THE FAMILY LEGACY.
YES.

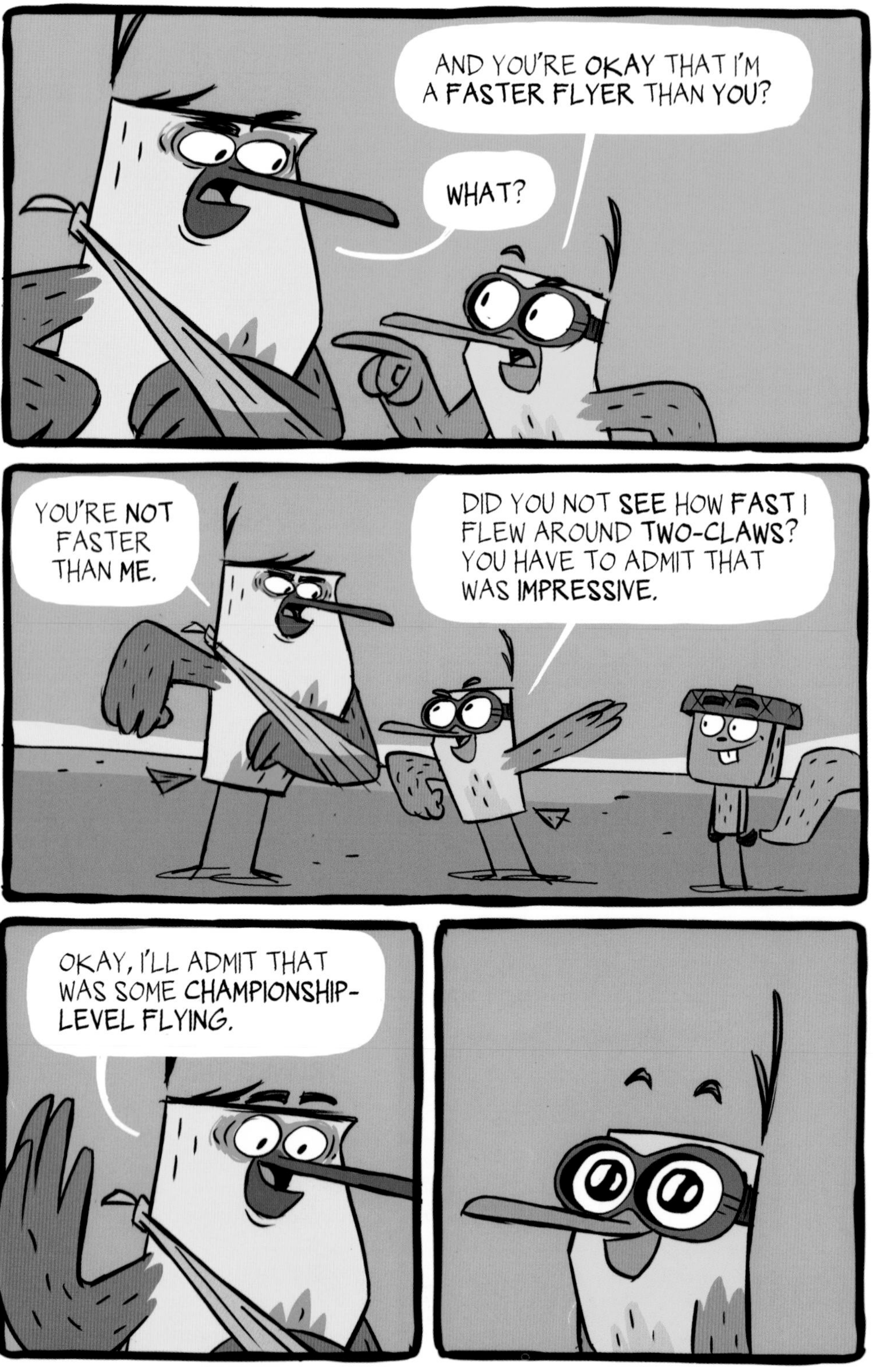
AND YOU'RE OKAY THAT I'M A FASTER FLYER THAN YOU?
WHAT?
YOU'RE NOT FASTER THAN ME.
DID YOU NOT SEE HOW FAST I FLEW AROUND TWO-CLAWS? YOU HAVE TO ADMIT THAT WAS IMPRESSIVE.
OKAY, I'LL ADMIT THAT WAS SOME CHAMPIONSHIP-LEVEL FLYING.

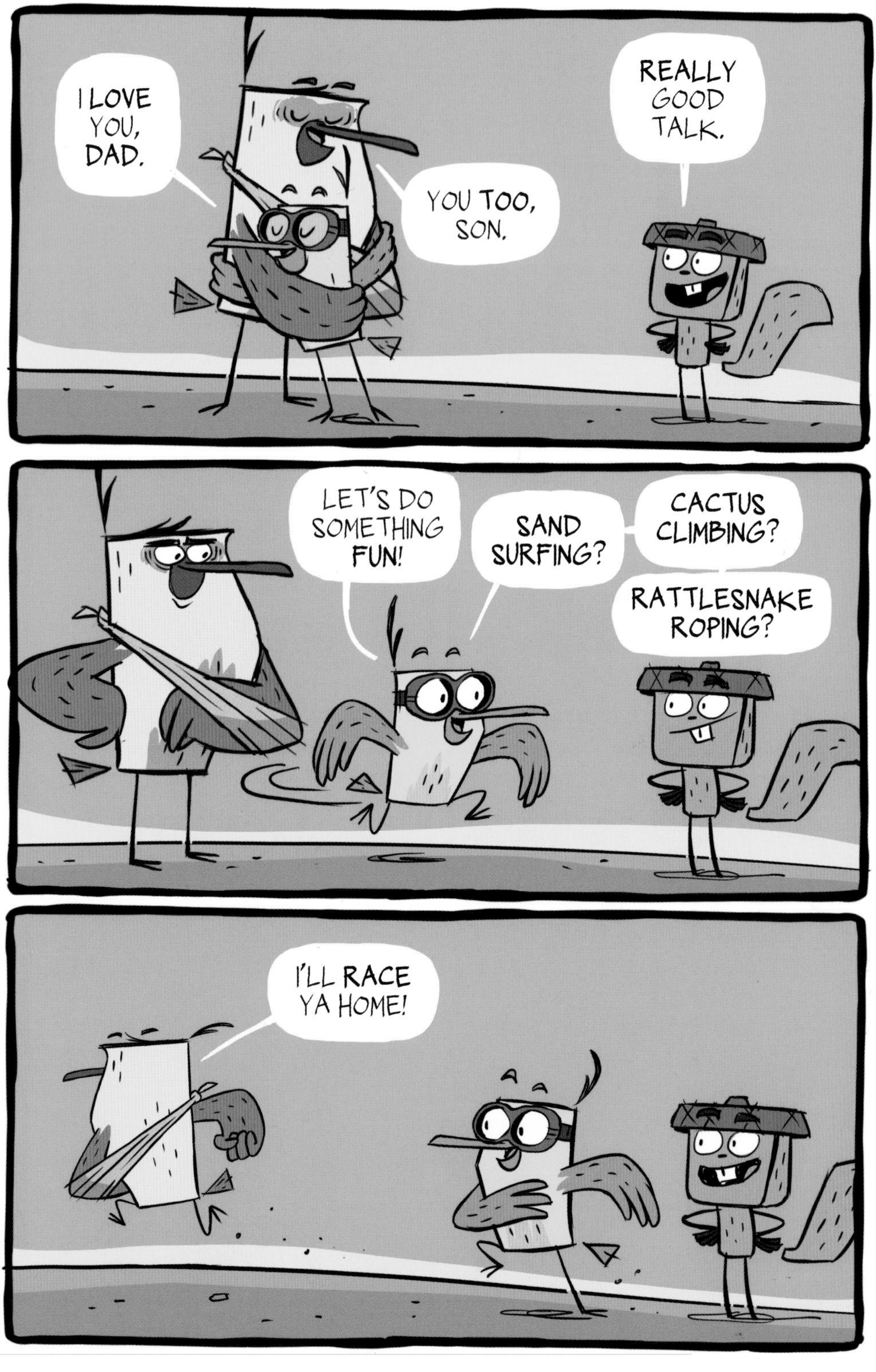
I LOVE YOU, DAD.
YOU TOO, SON.
REALLY GOOD TALK.
LET'S DO SOMETHING FUN!
SAND SURFING?
CACTUS CLIMBING?
RATTLESNAKE ROPING?
I'LL RACE YA HOME!

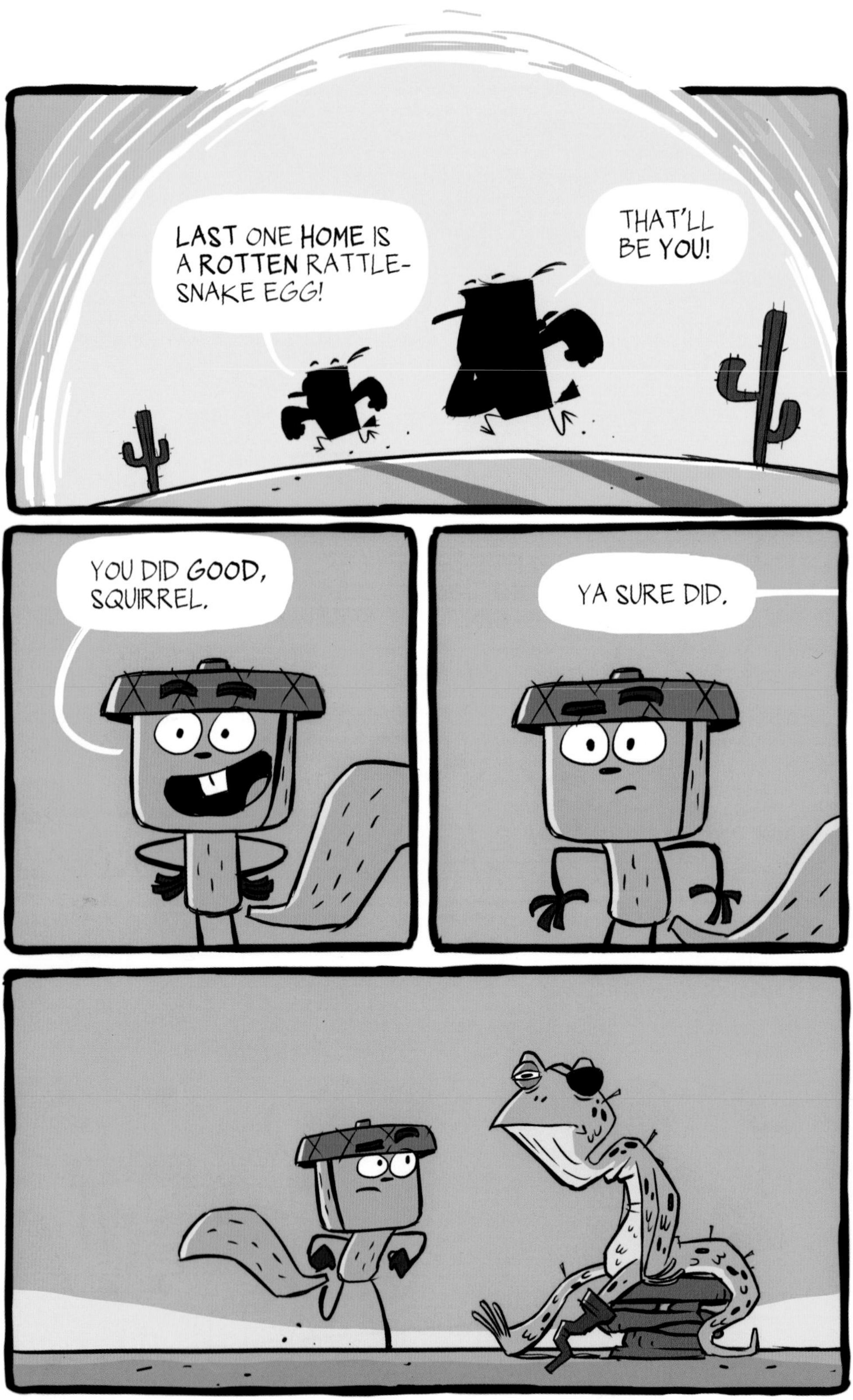
LAST ONE HOME IS A ROTTEN RATTLE-SNAKE EGG!
THAT'LL BE YOU!
YOU DID GOOD, SQUIRREL.
YA SURE DID.

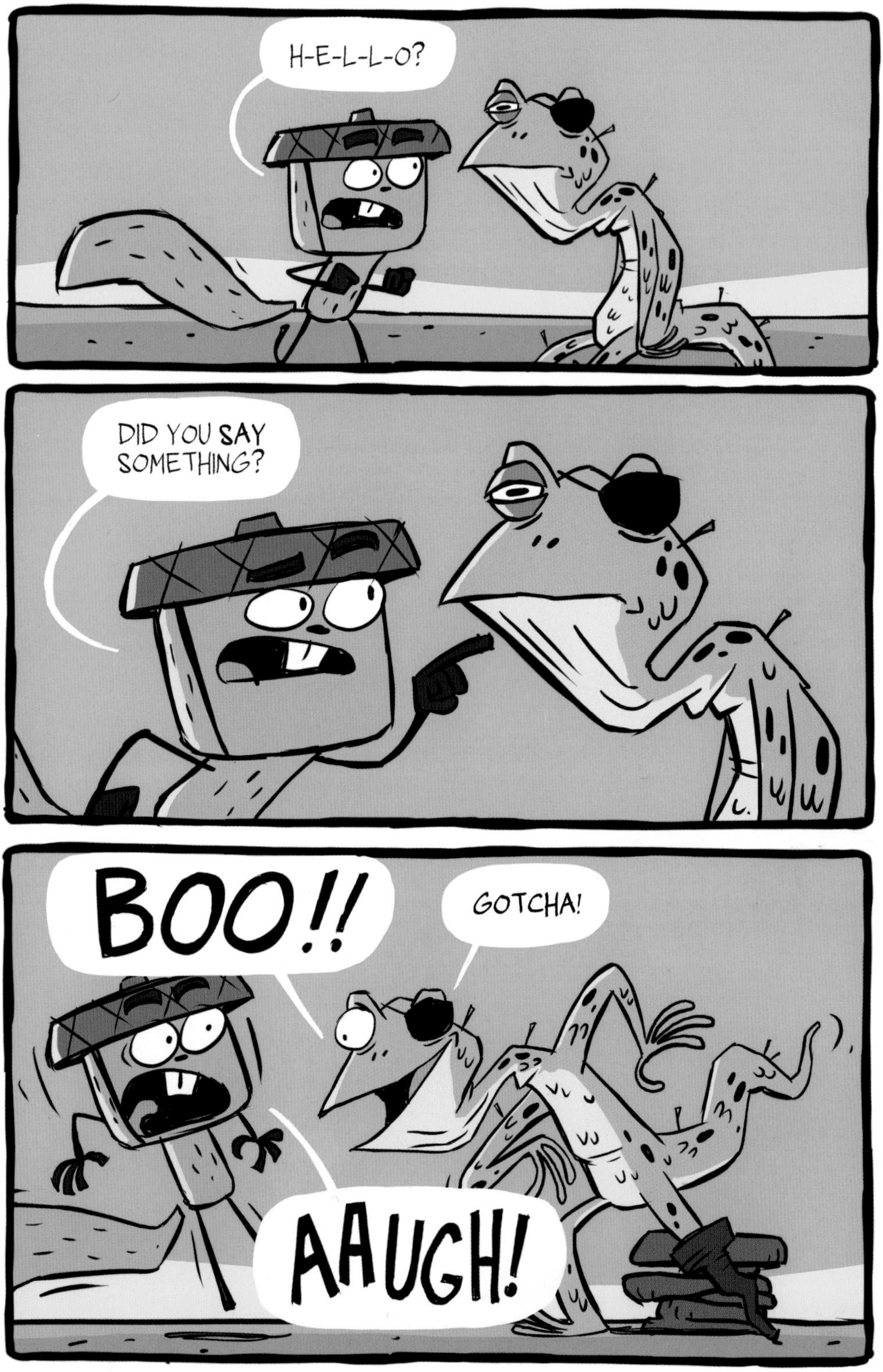
H-E-L-L-O?
DID YOU SAY SOMETHING?
BOO!!
GOTCHA!
AAUGH!

THE END

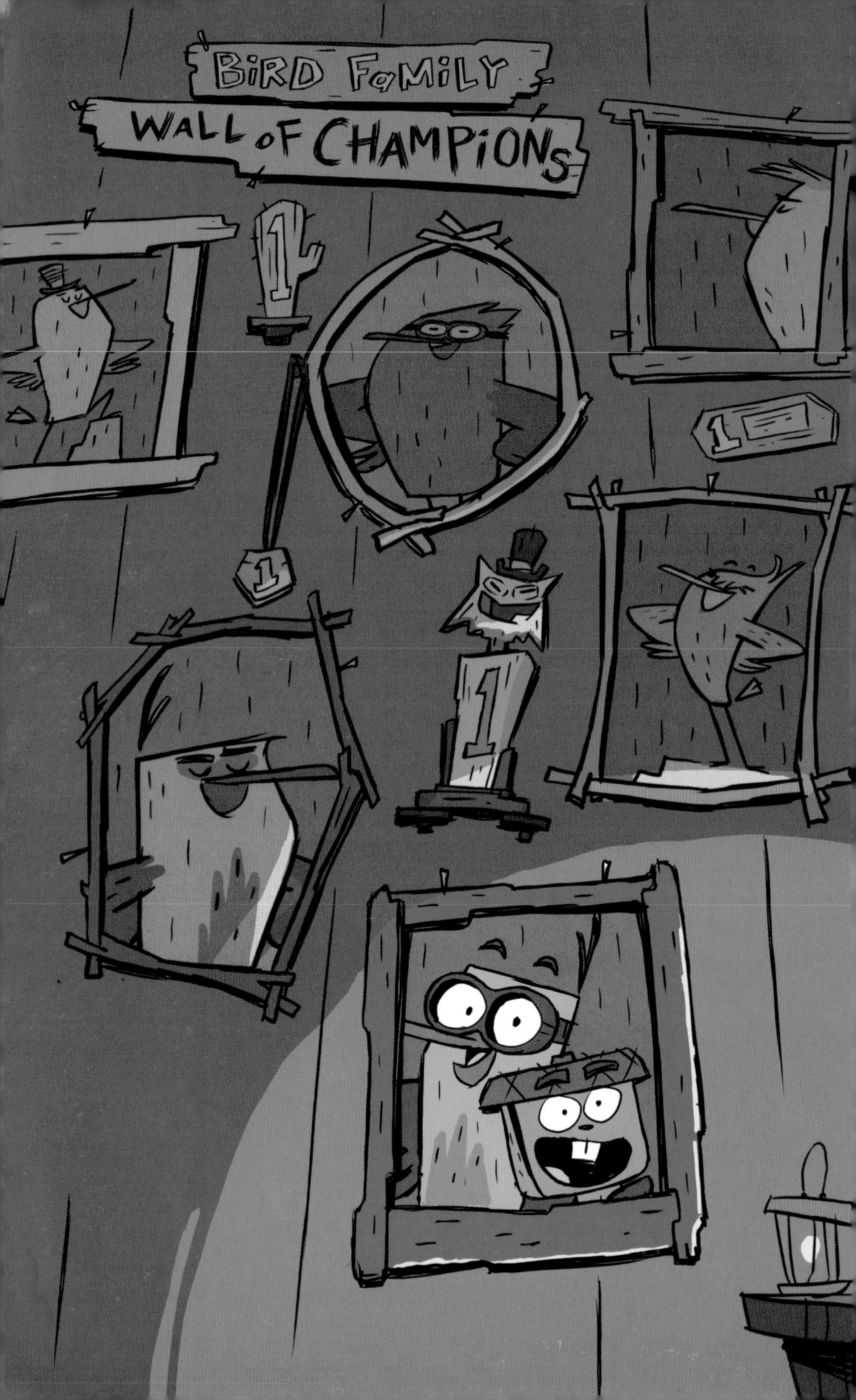
BIRD FAMILY
WALL OF CHAMPIONS